KT-132-385

Ian Flitcroft studied medicine at Oxford University, and then went on to complete a D.Phil in Neurophysiology. During these six years, he started developing a fascination with all things culinary and on finishing his doctorate, gained dining rights at Pembroke College as a John Lockett Memorial Scholar.

Ian has travelled around the world twice (once in each direction) and sampled many of the world's strangest foods en route from snakes and scorpions, to a soup in Thailand that required all his anatomical knowledge to deduce its contents. Ian is a long-term member of the Slow Food Movement in Ireland, a collector of old culinary-related books, an avid cook and wine collector. Ian now works as a consultant eye surgeon in Dublin, where he has lived for over ten years.

The Reluctant Cannibals was one of the winning entries for the 2012 Irish Writer's Centre Novel Fair competition, and was also shortlisted for the 2013 Amazon Breakthrough Novel Award.

The Reluctant Cannibals is Ian's first novel.

Acknowledgements

I would like to thank the team at Legend Press, especially my editor Lauren, for giving this curious story a life in print.

I like to think that its publication will put a smile on the lips of Arthur Plantagenet, wherever he may be - in Hades or, by some strange fluke of fortune, Heaven.

I would also like to thank Carrie and everyone at the Irish Writers' Centre for their Novel Fair competition which spurred me on to complete this final version of *Reluctant Cannibals* and, of course, for selecting this book as one of the winners in 2012. A small group of those winners continues to meet in the Library Bar in Dublin and I feel honoured to be among them.

This book has been helped on its way by many people who have commented upon (and I might add rejected) earlier versions. I would like to thank them for their comments, which in hindsight were extremely insightful. But beyond all others my wife and fellow-author Jean has been my greatest guide, critic and support. This book would certainly not exist without her. The dedication 'to my beloved Jean' is to her not Brillat-Savarin!

To my beloved Jean

Constitution of the Shadow Faculty of Gastronomic Science

Herein lie the immutable rules of the Shadow Faculty of Gastronomic Science:

Rule One
All members must be fellows of St Jerome's College, Oxford.

Rule Two
All members must ascribe to the gastronomic principles pronounced by Jean Anthelme Brillat-Savarin[1].

Rule Three
The Faculty must hold a dinner of gastronomic significance in the eighth week of each term.

Rule Four
Each member must invite one guest per dinner and ensure that their guest presents a new dish to the Faculty.

Rule Five
The Faculty must ensure that no dish is served more than once with the exception of a truffled turkey, which is to be served each year at the Michaelmas dinner.

Rule Six
A member of the Faculty is elected for life unless they breach rules one, two or four.

Rule Seven
The Shadow Faculty will remain in existence until the

---

1 Author of *La Physiologie du Goût* (The Physiology of Taste), which was first published Christmas 1825 in Paris. This book set out Brillat-Savarin's vision for gastronomy as a true science.

University of Oxford inaugurates an official Faculty of Gastronomic Science.

Membership:

Augustus Bloom	Lecturer in Physiology and Tutor in Medicine
Arthur Plantagenet	Professor of Ancient History
George Le Strang	Professor of Modern History
Hamish McIntyre	Lecturer in Zoology
Charles Pinker	College Chaplain and Lecturer in Divinity
Theodore Flanagan	Tutor and Reader in Criminal Law

Former Members:[2]

Conrad Petersen	Resigned following a breach of rule four
Gordon Maxwell	Deceased
Stanley Lovell	Deceased

---

2 A brief history of the founding and early years of the Shadow Faculty of Gastronomic Science is provided in the appendix at the back of this volume.

Chapter I

Trinity Term 1969

It took two men to lift the dismembered carcass. The departure of its copper coffin was met with a brief but respectful silence. Respect that derived from the fact that it contained the mortal remains of what was undoubtedly the largest turbot ever to grace a dining table in Oxford. Once the moment had passed, the room began to fill again with the sound of conversation. Augustus Bloom discreetly turned his head towards the ear of his distinguished guest, Takeshi Tokoro.

'You're up next. Do you want me to introduce you?' Dr Bloom whispered.

Mr Tokoro declined the offer with an almost imperceptible shake of his head. He then rose to his feet and stood motionless, waiting for silence. The others around the table appeared not to notice him as he remained quietly erect, with a posture no European could ever match. He had an austere dignity, but his slim five-foot-four-inch frame lacked the physical presence of his fellow diners. Apart from Dr Bloom, the other guests continued their animated conversations, not through disrespect but culinary enthusiasm; egged on it must be said by a particularly fine wine, a 1959 Condrieu. The shadow faculty of gastronomic science and their guests were barely halfway through the dinner but it was already clear that this was a night to be remembered. The sea urchin and fennel en papillote with its sublime, caramelised vermouth sauce had proved a magnificent success as a first course, but even this great dish had been eclipsed by the turbot – a recipe taken straight from the pages of the great man himself, Jean Anthelme Brillat-Savarin. A turbot of implausible proportion had been cooked whole in a copper fish kettle of even greater scale; poached with vegetables in a white wine and cream stock. By the time the fish was cooked, the sauce had transformed itself into a perfect chowder. Fillets of the turbot were served on a bed of spinach with the chowder presented to each person in a small silver salver to universal acclaim.

Augustus glared across the table, trying to catch the eye of the chaplain, Charles Pinker, who was being uncharacteristically talkative. With each passing second, Augustus felt an increasing sense of frustration. Mr Tokoro, accustomed to immediate deference due to his status within the diplomatic service, showed no hint of any such emotion. Augustus nervously fiddled with his cutlery. Tapping a glass with a spoon, the traditional method of calling the table to order, would certainly have worked, but Augustus held back for fear that Mr Tokoro might not appreciate the gesture. After a few more agonising seconds, he caught the eye of Charles Pinker across the table who correctly interpreted the impassioned, almost gymnastic movements of Dr Bloom's eyebrows. A discreet cough and tap of the elbow to his neighbour sent a signal that slowly spread around the table until the last man still talking, Professor Arthur Plantagenet, finally realised he was holding forth amidst the silence.

Mr Tokoro gave a slow and solemn bow. In an instant he turned the tables on his audience who tried to cover the embarrassment of their discourtesy by variously nodding and leaning forward in stilted half-bows.

'Distinguished Gentlemen,' said Mr Tokoro. 'I have the honour of bringing to you a national treasure of Japanese cuisine: Fugu-chiri.' Then, with perfectly timed theatricality, he clapped his hands. This was a cue to Gerald, the senior common room steward, to open the doors for Mr Tokoro's Japanese chef who, in contrast to Mr Tokoro, had the dimensions of a sumo wrestler. He walked in carrying a large wooden chopping board on which twelve small fish had been laid out. A table was carried in behind him and placed in the recess of the large bay window. This was followed by a large copper pot and a spirit burner, which were placed at one end of the table.

The chef placed his chopping board down on the table and from his apron produced an impressive set of wood handled knives, whose metal blades bore the swirling pattern of a medieval Damascene sword. He then set to work removing the skin and filleting the fish with extraordinary speed and deftness. Mr Tokoro was the first to rise from his seat and walk over to inspect the process at closer quarters. The precedent having been set, the others quickly followed him. When it came to the last fish, Mr Tokoro said a few words in Japanese to the chef who, with a deferential bow, stood back from the table and handed the knife to him. Mr Tokoro was clearly skilled with the knife but not to the same level as his chef. He removed the fins and skin with great speed but was more hesitant on the internal organs. He neatly excised the liver and intestines in a manner that appeared to meet the chef's approval, but in removing the ovaries he sliced through the edge of one of them and left it attached to the flesh. The only person who noticed his mistake could not remark on this dangerous oversight. The social rules that have defined Japan's society for centuries prevented the chef from passing comment, or taking any action that might have shown up a failure on the part of Mr Tokoro. The chef stepped forward, keenly aware Mr Tokoro was still closely observing him, and knowing there was no escape from his master's mistake. Without any flicker of emotion on his face, he placed all the fish fillets into the copper pan along with the light vegetable stock that had been brought back to the boil.

There was great excitement in the anticipation and discussion of these little fish when they were finally served. Sadly the actual consumption created less impact. The light broth was subtle and delighted Mr Tokoro, but seemed lost on Western palates used to richer food. The flesh of the fish itself was almost too delicate and the flavour an ephemeral mist that barely registered on the taste buds compared to what had come before. It was Mr Tokoro who raised the last piece to his mouth, with the mixture of triumph and sadness that greets the end of a fine dish. It was the very last fillet he had prepared. He washed it down with the fine white Burgundy that had been picked to accompany this course. He normally preferred sake but had to acknowledge the superior subtlety of the Nuits St Georges.

It was not until the seaweed ice cream that Mr Tokoro felt the first erratic beat in his chest. The perspiration that appeared on his brow was initially merely an imperceptible moistening. His lips felt peculiar but he put that down to the coldness of the ice cream. After a reassuring sequence of regular beats, Mr Tokoro's heart fell into a syncopated rhythm that made him draw a deep breath, or at least try to. He raised his chin to take in air but his diaphragm sat motionless on top of his distended stomach. There were no outward signs of any problem until his fork fell onto the table, his fingers losing their power of grip.

Mr Tokoro went to rise from his chair. He started the movement easily enough but after he had elevated barely an inch, his body rebelled and refused to move further. He held this position for a second until gravity conquered his failing muscles. He slid to the floor, his weight dragging the tablecloth as he fell, bringing with him an array of cutlery and wine glasses. Indeed, if it hadn't been for Arthur Plantagenet's fast reactions, an almost half-full glass of Nuits St Georges would have been lost too. Mr Tokoro, his mouth opening and closing in a silent and ironic parody of the creature he had just eaten, looked up at the equally stricken face of his host,

Augustus Bloom. It is true that Dr Augustus Bloom was in possession of a medical degree, but it was obtained with little in the way of practical experience and his years in academia had dulled whatever limited resuscitation skills he had ever possessed. Augustus Bloom, his own heart racing from panic, fell to his knees and, for want of anything better to do, cradled Mr Tokoro's head in his hands.

'For Christ's sake will someone call an ambulance,' Augustus shouted.

Gerald, the senior common room steward, who might have been expected to be the first to respond, stood rooted to the spot with a look of complete terror on his face. Mr Tokoro's mouth continued to open and close silently for another few seconds and then stopped.

'Gerald, you heard the man. Go and get Potts to call an ambulance,' said Dr McIntyre.

Arthur Plantagenet was the only person in the room to remain quite calm. He emptied his wine glass and murmured to no-one in particular,

'What a bloody marvellous way to die.'

Chapter 2

Michaelmas Term 1969

The new academic year of 1969 started in October with the reassuring inevitability of the rising sun. On that first morning its weak rays were valiantly trying to warm the chilled, golden stone walls of St Jerome's. The last geranium blooms of the year graced the window boxes of the quadrangle, though their tired foliage showed that the exuberance of summer was long gone. It would be hard to imagine a scene of greater calm or serenity. Certainly there were no hints of the drama that had occurred at the end of the previous term; in fact it had barely been mentioned outside the confines of the college walls. Death was no stranger to the shadow faculty of gastronomic science. Two of their members had died in previous years, though under less dramatic circumstances and certainly not during one of their dinners. These two deaths had given rise to the shadow faculty's alternative title: the declining dining society. At least on this occasion it was a guest who had died so their numbers had not suffered a further depletion. Of course it had devastated Mr Tokoro's family and caused a degree of consternation within diplomatic circles, but, beyond that, the death of Mr Tokoro had created barely a ripple within the college or the world outside.

The day was Monday of noughth week, so named because

it came a week before the official start of term, which is, reasonably enough, called first week. For Mr Potts, the head porter, these were the last precious moments of peace before the college was re-invaded by the noisy legion of students. During the quiet summer months, Mr Percival Potts had been practising his peculiar art of sleeping upright, a skill part innate and part honed during his years on guard duty in the army. In this finely poised state he could ignore all ordinary sounds and background voices, but if a question were put to him he could in an instant wake up and, without otherwise moving a muscle, feign an excusable touch of deafness with the words 'Sorry, sir, didn't quite catch that.' This remarkable ability was concealed by his black bowler hat, which was perpetually tilted down at an angle that was finely judged to hide his eyes from anyone presenting themselves to the porter's lodge. It is true that a dwarf or small child might have been able to rumble Potts' secret, but dwarves and children were rarely, if ever, seen in the lodge of St Jerome's College.

On this particular day an unexpected and unwelcome noise entered the head porter's ears, insinuating itself into his dreams. The sound was certainly not human, so there was no imperative to wake, but neither was it an everyday noise. The scuttling noise grew louder and, in the increasingly distressed imagination of Potts' dream, more rat-like. Salvation burst through the door of the porter's lodge in the substantial form of Dr Hamish McIntyre.

'Morning Potts. Now where are these squills?'

Potts, still troubled by dissolving images of rats, found that his normally poised response on waking was shortened to something rather less coherent.

'Er, wha, sir?'

'Squills, Potts. The *canocchie del mare* you so skilfully procured.'

Guided by the increasingly frenetic scratching noise, McIntyre's eyes alighted on his precious delivery. He grasped the package and within seconds was gazing admiringly at the curious crustaceans.

'Oh, them.' It was with some relief that Potts identified the source of the strange sounds from his dreams.

'Glorious little creatures, aren't they?' said McIntyre proudly.

Even allowing for the typical English sentimentality when it came to animals, Potts felt that Dr McIntyre's description of these creatures was generous in the extreme. If Potts had been a more educated man he might have described these creatures as ugly trilobites. In the absence of all but the most basic education, he offered a description that was as simple as it was accurate.

'Look like ugly great earwigs to me, sir.'

'Well, we're all God's creatures, Potts, and while they're not the prettiest, I dare say they're tastier than you or I.'

Hamish McIntyre slipped out of the porter's lodge with remarkable grace for a man of his girth and disappeared around the corner into Old Quad, chattering to his reluctantly captive audience of crustaceans.

Just as McIntyre and his squills stepped into Old Quad, Augustus Bloom disappeared from it; a small door off a narrow passageway clicked shut to mark his departure from the crisp morning light. He descended into a gloom alleviated only by a rather sad and dim bulb overhead. This was nevertheless a great improvement over the hand-held paraffin lamp that Bloom had experienced on his first trip into this subterranean universe many years ago. It was not that Bloom was exceptionally ancient (he had barely turned forty), but rather that St Jerome's was proud of the fact that it was the last college in Oxford to electrify its wine cellars. On reaching the bottom of the stairs, in keeping with college tradition, he nodded in thankful acknowledgement to a small bronze bust of the first bursar of the college for his foresight in planning a college that had cellars twice the size of the buildings above.

In addition to the size of the wine cellars at St Jerome's,

the college also boasted the oldest wine cellar ghost. In years gone by every college seemed to have ghosts in their cellars. Many a ghost has been born from the lack of light and a nervous but imaginative disposition. With sufficient illumination even the most creative mind is less prone to such flights of fancy. The arrival of the electric bulb had accordingly banished most of Oxford's cellar ghosts. St Jerome's ghost, the Reverend Hieronymus Bloch, proved to be much more tenacious. Reverend Bloch was the college's first chaplain who had, according to college lore, gone to the cellars during a dinner in search of a particularly fine port sometime towards the end of 1752 and had never been seen again in the flesh. Shortly after this he started appearing at regular intervals within the confines of the cellars, apparently still searching for the elusive bottle.

Over the years Bloch became bolder, with more frequent apparitions. He was considered as no more than an entertaining diversion, until one particularly disreputable cellar steward in the 1930's had incurred Bloch's wrath by stealing some of the finest bottles of wine and selling them on through a well-established, if equally disreputable, wine merchant in London. Justice came not from the Oxford constabulary but mysteriously one night when the unfortunate man's skull was broken with a bottle of Château d'Yquem 1921. No-one in St Jerome's doubted Bloch's involvement in this crime. Nor were they surprised that with Bloch's assistance, this bottle of precious nectar had miraculously proved to be stronger than the steward's skull. The bottle was found alongside the corpse, the label heavily bloodstained but the wine otherwise intact.

There are those who condemn wine decanters as an affectation but this event admirably proved their worth, allowing the same bottle to be the splendid finale of a Master's Dinner in 1955. The '21 vintage d'Yquem had turned out to be a jewel of the century. All the more rare because of a late spring frost that year. It was served without a murmur of disquiet from a fine crystal decanter. A beautiful golden colour with an orange blossom nose and a symphonic blend of flavours to follow – walnut, banana, grapefruit – unified by a thread of lavender running through it all. Meanwhile the bloodstained murder weapon lay safely out of sight in the college kitchen.

Despite such stories the cellars were Augustus Bloom's favourite place. Hieronymus Bloch's murderous reputation ensured that Bloom was unlikely to be disturbed during his visits and he felt sure that his devotion to oenology would protect him from the Reverend's wrath. Augustus came here to think, be inspired and to escape. Add to that the beneficial physiological effects of a fine Claret and one can easily see the appeal of the cellars for Augustus. They were also an important part of his research. Dr Augustus Bloom, in his role as medical tutor, was a leading figure in the investigation of the French Paradox. This is the curious injustice that allows the French to eat, drink and smoke more than the rest of Europe and yet have healthier hearts and longer lives.

Augustus Bloom pottered along the dusty racks, occasionally stopping to examine a bottle in more detail before finally selecting one. At this time of day a good Beaujolais would go down well and the temperature straight from the racks would be just about perfect; Augustus often railed against the tendency in recent times to serve red wine half-cooked. After an enjoyable hour searching, he had finally chosen a bottle of Morgon, the 1964 Château Bellevue, and was approaching his preferred resting spot. At the end of a particularly long tunnel lay a chamber. This was directly underneath the chapel and Augustus felt doubly blessed when his thoughts and wine appreciation were joined by the low rumble of the organ pipes above. The experience was made particularly resonant by the fact that only the deepest, most visceral notes could permeate the stones and earth to reach the cellars below.

When Augustus entered the gloomy chamber in a state of almost meditative peace, he was brought up short by the sight ahead. In the old wooden chair that had been in the cellars for as long as anyone could remember sat a dark, slumped figure. It took a second to gather himself and to be able to observe the figure rationally. His thoughts raced ahead to the vastly improbable possibility that this might be his first encounter with the ghostly Reverend Bloch. He inched forward, excited rather than fearful, but these fanciful notions were cut short by an explosive awakening of the slumbering figure.

'Whoaaaaa. Wazgo, who, er.'

'Arthur? Is that you?'

'Who? Oh, Bloom, thank God. I thought I'd died, having an awful dream. Gates of hell, earthquakes.'

'Just Charles Pinker upstairs doing a bit of early morning practice on the organ; either that or we're both dead, but it's too cold to be hell and too dark to be heaven,' said Augustus Bloom smiling at his old friend and colleague. In reply Professor Arthur Plantagenet shook his head in the manner of a wet dog before surfacing back into full consciousness, still wearing the gown and clothes he had worn last night at dinner.

'Have you been here all night Arthur?' asked Augustus.

'I couldn't sleep, kept wandering and suddenly I'm down here being woken by a shrieking maniac.'

Augustus desperately wanted to say that Arthur had cried out first, but he graciously allowed the Professor of Ancient History the privilege of rewriting history on this occasion.

'Don't suppose you fancy a glass of Château Bellevue?' asked Augustus.

'What year?'

'The '64.'

'Hmm, not a bad year. Anyway it won't last much longer, so pour away.'

Augustus pulled his prized scrimshaw-handled corkscrew from his jacket, deftly plucked the cork from the bottle with a sound that raced off into the darkest reaches of the cellars only to return in a shower of faint echoes. He gave the cork to the professor for the requisite sniff. After finding approval, he offered the bottle.

'A little liquid history, Arthur?'

'Good God man, do you expect me to swig from the bottle like an inebriated townie?'

'Heavens forbid no, just hold onto the bottle for a moment. I'll get something to drink from.'

Augustus rummaged in a small alcove just to the left and emerged with two silver goblets carrying the college crest.

'Will these do?'

'Perfectly.'

After polishing them with his tie, one of few practical uses for such a garment, Bloom filled both goblets and raised his for a toast.

'To the new academic year, Arthur.'

'Indeed. Eat, drink and be merry, for tomorrow we may die.' The mention of death caught Augustus Bloom off guard and, while Arthur Plantagenet drained his glass, Augustus was thrown back to the moment three months ago where Mr Tokoro's head lay cradled in his hands.

An hour later, Augustus Bloom surfaced thoroughly recharged by a fascinating discussion on the battle capabilities of ancient Greek fighting ships, diets of gladiators and the wicked sins committed by ancient physicians on their trusting patients. Arthur Plantagenet had finally nodded off again while Augustus was holding forth on the medicinal value of wine, and Augustus had left him as he had found him, deeply asleep. Heading into the porter's lodge he was faced with a wall of trunks. The invasion of the undergraduates had begun. Augustus dived for the door to check his mail, dodging the trunks and avoiding all eyes as he went in case he met a pair that he might be forced to talk to.

Potts was absent from his chair, corralling the gathering masses somewhere outside, so Augustus flicked through the envelopes in his pigeonhole looking for letters more interesting than the usual start of term memoranda.

What he was hoping to find was an envelope with an American postmark written in a familiar flowing hand. His search stopped temporarily at a fine ivory envelope with the university crest and the ominous printed message indicating its source: from the office of the vice-chancellor. This letter was not totally unexpected, but was definitely unwelcome. He stuck the letter between his teeth and kept searching for better news from across the Atlantic, but like the day before and most likely the day after, no such letter had arrived. He put the rest of the letters back unopened. Taking the letter from his mouth and placing it in his jacket pocket, he turned to leave and locked eyes with the returning Potts.

'Good day, Dr Bloom.'

'No, not really Potts.'

Chapter 3

Augustus Bloom started the day with a fine breakfast at the King Edward Hotel. Perfectly poached eggs with smoked salmon, capers, Earl Grey tea and toast lavishly adorned with salty butter. As in college, the scrambled eggs at the King Edward Hotel were an affront to a delicate palate, yellow rubber robbed of flavour by the misguided use of milk and excessive heat. Poached eggs were a safer bet when eating out, not that poaching eggs isn't an art in itself. For all the mystique and bizarrely complicated methods, it is hard to ruin a poached egg except by overcooking. Bloom had experimented methodically with all the described methods for poaching. He found the use of vinegar unnecessary and ruinous in terms of flavour. As for the challenging task of rapidly whisking water into a whirlpool while dropping an egg into the centre, he had dismissed this long ago as no more than French culinary theatre. The result of his endeavours was this: simply lower a truly fresh egg into a shallow pan of water heated just enough to coat the bottom with fine bubbles. Turn down the heat and in five minutes the resulting egg would invariably meet his exacting standards, though if the egg weren't fresh or the water were actively boiling the result could, all too easily, become a chaotic mass of white strands and an inedible yellow ball. At a temperature well below boiling, Augustus had discovered that the egg white would cook perfectly while leaving the yolk, as it should be, gloriously runny.

The treat of breakfast at the King Edward cast the day into a much better light than it had started; the first thing Augustus remembered on opening his eyes at dawn was his meeting with the vice-chancellor. The letter had merely stated:

'In light of recent events, the vice-chancellor requests that you attend his offices at 10 a.m. Monday next.'

The letter may have been gently worded, but Augustus was under no illusion that this was to be a friendly encounter. His only hope was that the vice-chancellor was feeling in a mellow mood this morning although, under the circumstances, that seemed unlikely.

*

Professor Arthur Plantagenet had started the day with a less enlightening culinary experience at the hands of St Jerome's kitchen staff. The college chef Monsieur Roger never supervised breakfast. As a result, this meal fell far short of what St Jerome's kitchens could offer. In a triumph of hope over experience, Arthur Plantagenet had opted for kippers. Shocked by their inedibility, he consoled himself with copious quantities of the one reliable breakfast offering: tea. He too was venturing into town summoned by a letter. On this occasion it was from his physician who had rooms on St John's Street. Doctor Reginald Pierce was an eminent man who, for all his eminence, had spectacularly failed in his attempts to curtail Plantagenet's gargantuan appetite.

Shortly before 10 o'clock in the morning, Professor Plantagenet walked into the waiting room of Dr Pierce. *Vanity Fair* prints of famous doctors adorned the walls that themselves wore elegant striped wallpaper. He had barely settled into the burgundy leather Chesterfield sofa before he was ushered in.

'Good day, Arthur.'

'Reginald.' Arthur nodded.

Arthur Plantagenet settled down and Reginald Pierce pulled up a chair and sat beside him rather than at his usual position on the other side of his large partner's desk. He took Plantagenet's wrist without saying another word and felt his pulse while looking intently down in deep concentration. Dr Pierce finally looked up and gave his verdict.

'Arthur, those tests I did last week on your heart. I've gone over the results and I'm afraid it doesn't look good.'

'Good God man, I'm as fit as a fiddle; never felt better. I must say you're looking a little peaky yourself these days. You could do with a little more flesh on your bones.'

'Quality not quantity is what counts in health, Arthur. With your unfortunate family history you must know that your current eating habits are putting you in significant danger.'

'Danger of what?'

'The grave, if I must be so stark.'

'We're all dying, so we might as well enjoy ourselves during the process. I'd rather die now than starve myself for the sake of a long but miserable and hungry life.'

'A rather bizarre philosophy, don't you think, Arthur?'

'Not at all Reginald, an ancient and entirely logical stance. I take my cue from Apicius.'

The lack of reply and slightly baffled look on Dr Pierce's face told Arthur he was on winning ground and he took great delight in pushing forward his advantage.

'Marcus Gavius Apicius. Greatest food writer of the Roman Empire. Nobly decided to poison himself in the prime of life rather than face the prospect of poverty and starvation in old age.'

'Noble indeed, Arthur, but I think your risk of starvation would be slight and imagine how many meals you'd miss by an early death.'

Uncharacteristically Arthur didn't have an immediate retort, so Dr Pierce cut straight to the point he had been circling around for the last few minutes.

'I'm afraid that your situation is rather serious, Arthur. Your heart has become very enlarged and developed a dangerous rhythm.'

'Surely there's nothing wrong with a big heart, Reginald?'

'It's a sick heart, Arthur. Dilated cardiomyopathy. I'm not sure there is much I can do at this stage to reverse the process.'

'Excellent. So I can keep on just as I am.'

'An unusually optimistic interpretation. In terms of eating, my only advice is that if there is anything you haven't yet tasted I'd suggest you try it soon. I don't know how much longer this heart of yours will keep ticking.'

'Oh now, Reginald. It can't be that bad.'

'I'm afraid it is.'

'Oh… '

'Indeed.'

'Not much time then?'

'If the gods are smiling you may have a few months. If not it might be a matter of days. Shall I waste my breath by telling you that losing weight could take a lot of the strain off your heart? That might help it to keep beating a little longer.'

'With the greatest respect, I wouldn't bother. I preferred your earlier advice about eating everything I haven't tried yet.'

*

Another member of the shadow faculty of gastronomic science was in town that morning too, on a mission of great gastronomic importance. Professor George Le Strang wasn't a man for breakfast, so a brief cup of tea in the covered market on his way to the Bodleian Library amply serviced his morning requirements. Today the covered market was itself his principal destination. Furlong and Furrow were Oxford's best game butchers. They were also reasonably game when it came to meeting Le Strang's sometimes curious requests for meats. These requests inevitably involved some beast or fowl that rarely graced English dining tables. They were usually tricky to locate but the founder's great grandson, Philip Furrow, took pride in meeting any challenge. All the more so as George Le Strang was generous in his thanks, which was often expressed in the form of extraordinarily good Claret from the college cellars.

Le Strang worked his way through the intricate maze of the covered market and stopped short of Furlong and Furrow's threshold to take in the glorious sight that greeted his eyes. Pheasants, rabbits, ducks and venison all arranged with the casual, compositional beauty of a Caravaggio painting. He stepped inside and was a little put out to find the shop populated with customers. After waving a greeting from the back of the queue to Mr Furlong, Le Strang duly waited in turn. On reaching the counter he was troubled by the shoppers that stood politely behind him waiting their turn, ears alert, all apparently waiting for him to speak.

'Professor, always a delight. What can we do for you today? We've some excellent rabbit just in.'

'Marvellous Philip, but this is more of a special order for later in term,' Le Strang half-whispered.

'We'd be delighted to help. So what's on the menu this time?'

Looking over his shoulder before looking back to Furrow, he muttered quietly, 'Something a little out of the ordinary.'

'You know us, Professor, the extraordinary takes a while, but it's always worth waiting for.'

'Any chance we could pop out back to chat about it?'

'Of course, of course.' Furlong called a young man who was boning geese at the side table to take over at the counter. He then retired to the back of the shop with the professor who was greatly relieved not to have to discuss his specific requirements in a shop full of English animal lovers. Le Strang always felt the English had a curiously inconsistent and sentimental approach to eating animals, but he was sensible enough to know when discretion was worthwhile.

Even though it was only the first week of term, Le Strang was already thinking ahead to the shadow faculty of gastronomic science's Michaelmas dinner. This was by far his favourite dinner of the year and not only because of the unmatched pleasure of sharing a truffled turkey. With great Gallic pride he was planning a Napoleonic dish that would be impressive even by the high standards of the shadow faculty. It would require a particularly unusual cut of meat that might take a while to locate. With the time also needed for ageing the meat, it meant he had no time to lose.

*

Augustus sat in the room outside the vice-chancellor's office. It was a drab utilitarian attempt at modernity. The garish lamp that hung from the ceiling had made Bloom physically shudder when he entered the room. The vice-chancellor had declared himself to be a reformer who would bring the university into the twentieth century, 'straight from the 1860's to the 1960's' as he often said. Since it was already 1969 with little evidence of change, his chances of succeeding in this task looked bleak. The door opened and the vice-chancellor stood in the doorway. Dr Ridgeway was a rather short man and like many short men, made up for his lack of stature and indeed charisma with dogged determination.

'Dr Bloom, so good of you to come.'

'How could I resist such an eloquent invitation?'

Dr Ridgeway smiled, but a flash of irritation sped across his face.

'Indeed. Now I'm sure you appreciate why I asked you here today?'

'Your letter was a trifle brief, so perhaps you could enlighten me.'

The vice-chancellor prickled again at Bloom's politely disrespectful tone.

'Your little accident last term at dinner, Dr Bloom. You do remember that?'

'With Takeshi Tokoro? Yes, indeed. An unfortunate and indeed tragic accident.'

'Unfortunate? It was a major diplomatic incident. Good God, man, you can't go around killing the cultural attaché of a major international power without people noticing, Bloom.'

'It was an accident, vice-chancellor. I might also remind you that Mr Tokoro was proud of introducing a dish that is of great cultural importance in Japan. I believe it was the first time that Fugu had been served at Oxford.'

'And the bloody last.' Ridgeway rose to his feet hoping to give these words greater impact. Bloom merely looked at him impassively. Ridgeway sank back into his chair.

'Bloom, it may be culturally important to the Japanese, but it is poisonous as you have amply proven. Do you know who in Japan is forbidden from eating this ugly little fish?'

'Yes, I believe the Japanese Emperor is forbidden from eating it, presumably to avoid this sort of… event.'

Ridgeway sat back in his chair and glared at his adversary. Seeing no signs of Bloom faltering, the vice-chancellor changed tack.

'What disturbs me most, Bloom, is that I've heard that this was part of some ludicrous secret dining society.'

He enjoyed the look of surprise in Bloom's eyes.

'He was indeed invited by our shadow faculty of gastronomic science, but as we have in the past petitioned the chancellor himself regarding the merits of gastronomic science it can hardly be described as secret.'

'Be that as it may, I have decided that this ridiculous boys' club has put the university in a bad light and therefore must be disbanded. Now, what do you have to say about that?'

A pall of silence fell on the room, each second passing slower than the last.

'With the greatest respect,' replied Augustus finally, 'I don't believe you have any jurisdiction over the private activities of the fellows of St Jerome's.'

'Don't try my patience, Bloom. If I hear of any more antics like this I shall take action and, trust me, the question of jurisdiction won't save you. If the coroner hadn't been so obliging – at my request I might add – you would be in gaol right now as an accessory to murder.'

Walking back down St John's Street, Augustus reflected on this conversation. It had gone much as he had expected apart from the bit about being an accessory to murder. Guilty as he felt over the whole incident, he did feel that was a bit much. Augustus had put on a good front with the vice-chancellor but, truth be told, he found himself a little shaken by the memories of Mr Tokoro's death. He was forced to stop abruptly to avoid colliding with a man who emerged unexpectedly from one of the doorways.

'Good God, Arthur, you look as if you've seen a ghost,' said Augustus, shocked at the appearance of Professor Plantagenet, whose normally ruddy complexion was showing distinct signs of pallor.

'No, just pondering the prospect of becoming one.'

'What in God's name does that mean?'

'According to my physician, I'm going to die rather soon.'

Chapter 4

Reverend Charles Pinker, the college chaplain, was a rather nervous creature most of the time. Within the confines of the chapel, he undoubtedly gained a modicum of confidence and could deliver a fine homily when the need arose. The most remarkable alteration came over Charles Pinker when it came to playing the organ, an instrument at which he truly excelled, particularly when he was playing the works of J.S. Bach. Today was a day when he had a particular need for that transformation. The Reverend Charles Pinker had taken news of the meeting with the vice-chancellor far harder than Augustus Bloom had imagined. In search of solace, Charles found himself early that morning sitting at the organ in the chapel. For reasons he couldn't fathom himself, this wasn't a Bach day. With the briefest of delays for air to breathe life into the ancient pipes, the chapel erupted with the opening chord of Olivier Messiaen's *Dieu parmi nous*, a piece a much younger Charles Pinker had once heard being performed by Messiaen himself in the church of La Sainte Trinité in Paris.

Playing the organ with its myriad of stops, pedals and multiple manuals is a prodigious feet of human coordination. This made Charles Pinker's ability to play so effortlessly while thinking about something entirely different all the more remarkable. Would the vice-chancellor drag them before Congregation, the parliament of Oxford dons, to be disgraced? It was hardly their fault if a Japanese expert poisoned himself at dinner. It wasn't as if any member of the university had died or even suffered, apart from the shock and the embarrassment, of course. The coroner had recorded a verdict of misadventure, so surely the vice-chancellor couldn't shut down a perfectly respectable academic society because of an accident? As the sounds of the last notes seeped away into the silence, he slowly lifted his fingers from the keys. While he had been playing, the world had continued to rotate on its axis without his intervention into a position that seemed that bit more balanced and manageable. The music did not have the same positive effect on everyone. In the wine cellars beneath the chapel a figure sat in a wooden chair. He cautiously lifted his hands from his ears, hoping the cacophonous noise had stopped. It certainly wasn't Bach and for the ethereal Reverend Hieronymus Bloch, it wasn't even music.

By the time Charles had reached his rooms in Old Quad, his anxiety and pessimism were seeping back. Now convinced that the vice-chancellor would act, he decided it was too dangerous to have all the records of the shadow faculty on open view in his rooms. It was surely an act of public folly to have the framed napkin on which their constitution had first been written hanging on his wall[3]. He was too committed to the cause of gastronomy to contemplate abandoning the faculty, but decided it would be prudent if they went to ground for a while. So he gathered his collection of menus from all the previous dinners and his carefully recorded notes of their equally important tasting meetings.

With arms full to the brim with the precious documents and constitution, Charles teetered down the narrow staircase. At the bottom of the stairs he paused to see if the coast was clear. He stood for a moment, framed in the stone archway, which was still adorned with faded chalk markings boasting the

---

3   The origins and significance of this napkin are fully explained in the appendix describing the early history of the faculty.

achievements of long-since graduated rowers. Old Quad was unusually deserted for this time of day, so Charles committed himself to the short dash to the chapel. As he emerged into the full light of the morning, the quadrangle was suddenly awash with people. The crows flying overhead had a wonderful view of nine people with armfuls of books and papers appearing almost simultaneously from the nine openings into Old Quad. The four staircases, the passage to the library, the junior common room, senior common room, porter's lodge and the passage through to the chapel all disgorged members of the college into what until a second before had been a totally deserted and peaceful quadrangle.

'Good morning, chaplain.'

'Morning, Mr Potts.'

'Could I help you with those, sir?'

'No, no Potts, that's fine; everything's under control, just a spot of tidying up.'

'Chaplain, could you pop in later? I need to talk to you about the chapel roof.'

'Indeed, Bursar, of course, of course, later. Yes, I'll see you later.'

Then disaster struck. A distracted young undergraduate walking backwards out of the junior common while shouting his last words towards the door, reversed straight into the overburdened chaplain. Books, papers and the framed napkin bearing the constitution of the shadow faculty of gastronomic science were scattered across the flagstones, accompanied by shards of glass from the broken frame.

Suddenly sixteen eyes were locked on the chaplain who was fervently wishing he were somewhere else and had his own eyes firmly shut. Apologies and more than a few curses were mumbled as the assembled pile of books and papers were collected together. In the confusion, a single menu had been gathered up by the very student who had caused the accident, and unwittingly filed away within the pages of the copy of Plato's *Republic* that he had just borrowed from the library.

Charles reached the chapel in a state of nervous exhaustion. He crossed the threshold and as the door clicked shut behind him, collapsed against the wall. His eyes closed again and he slowly slid down the cool stone until he was sitting on the floor. He waited in the silence until his heart's pounding had waned to a dull thud. He then opened his eyes. Reassured by the peaceful isolation, he struggled to his feet. Mr Potts, the head porter, had gathered up the constitution and broken frame, so the chaplain was left with just the menus and his notes. He re-balanced his load and made his way up to the organ loft. With great relief he placed his precious pile on the organ seat while he gathered them into some sense of order and then set off for his final destination.

Out of sight at the back of the organ was a concealed door in the wood panelling. Behind the door was a narrow and steep staircase cut into the stone fabric of the chapel. Charles slowly made his way up the staircase, leaning on the stone walls to keep his balance. At the top he stepped into a small room in the eaves of the western end of the chapel. The tallest organ pipes rose up through holes in the floor and light struggled in through a louvered opening high up on the gable wall. This room was a masterpiece of eighteenth-century architecture. Every feature was designed to ensure a steady flow of air to keep the organ at an even temperature come summer or winter. The plan had worked perfectly for over two hundred years and the original organ pipes were still in perfect condition. It was also one of the least-known corners of the college. Charles knew the papers would be safe up here from both prying eyes and the elements.

Chapter 5

'Enter,' shouted Augustus.

The door opened a few inches to reveal the timid looking features of a young man.

'Er, good morning, sir. Am I too early?'

'Not at all. Come in, come in.'

Speaking over his shoulder while huddled in a small alcove containing a small two-ring hob, Bloom was making a frantic clanking noise with a fork and a small bowl.

'Have a seat, Eccles. Do you prefer to be called Eccles or Patrick by the way?'

'Oh, either or whatever you prefer of course, sir.'

Bloom turned round, still beating his small bowl of eggs. The noise of this was now joined by the sputtering of salty Welsh butter in the pan behind him. He looked intently at the young man.

'As Eccles is a rather prestigious name in physiological circles these days, we'll just call you Eccles if that's all right.'

Not waiting for an answer, he continued his conversation facing back into the alcove. This was not how Eccles had visualised his first tutorial at Oxford.

'So, first time away from home?'

'No, well, I was off visiting... '

'Know how to scramble eggs?'

'Oh, you mix them up in a pan and cook them.'

'Milk?'

'No thank you, I'm fine.'

This at least caused Bloom to turn around and inspect his new student.

'I meant do you add milk to scrambled eggs?'

'Oh, I think you do, don't you?'

'First thing you've learnt at Oxford. Never put milk in scrambled eggs. Destroys them. Salted butter, preferably Welsh, fresh well-beaten eggs, gentle heat. Don't forget the fresher the eggs the more you have to scramble them first. Much thicker white in a fresh egg.'

Bloom returned to the alcove and his preparations.

'What's the next thing you'll learn at Oxford?'

'I couldn't begin to imagine, sir.'

Eccles was almost relaxing into the situation now, which was developing a charming Alice in Wonderland tea party feel.

'When to take them off the heat… Do you know that?'

'When they're cooked?'

'Logical enough, but wrong. Just *before* they are cooked: moist, shiny and mobile but not slimy. See?'

The pan was offered for inspection for the briefest fraction of a second before being swung back into the alcove for the last step.

'And my secret ingredient, which must go in at the very last moment. Too much heat can kill the flavour.'

Bloom uncorked a small bottle and with great care added a few drops of the precious liquid. Then stirring vigorously placed the pan right up to Eccles' face.

'Now what's that smell?'

An extraordinary aroma started to permeate the room, and Bloom involuntarily closed his eyes and breathed deeply while waiting for the reply.

'It's wonderful, but I couldn't place it I'm afraid.'

'White truffle, *Tuber magnatum pico*, young man. One of God's great gifts to mankind. Now, time to taste it.'

A fork was produced and Eccles took a taste. These were

truly the finest scrambled eggs he had ever had. While he pondered on their taste and this bizarre tutorial, Bloom finished off the remains of his creation, making curious noises as he wandered around his seated student. Despite what you might be thinking, Patrick Eccles had in fact been accepted into the college to read medicine and while he knew his first few years would be mostly physiology and what is delightfully called morbid anatomy – the anatomy in question being that of dead volunteers – this really wasn't what he expected.

'Now, a quick cup of tea and we can get going,' said Augustus, returning to the alcove.

Eccles hadn't quite understood the concept of 'going' on a tutorial until Bloom marched him out of the door and down the staircase. They then headed off together towards Christchurch Meadow. Bloom didn't slow his pace until he reached the wide arcade of trees called Dodgson's Walk that leads down to the river. Named, of course, after Charles Lutwidge Dodgson, mathematician and fellow of Christchurch College and better known as Lewis Carroll, who had shared Bloom's belief in the power of walking to stimulate the brain during tutorials. Finally, matters physiological were brought into the conversation.

'I don't suppose you are related?'

'To whom, sir?'

'Jack Eccles, the synapse man. Worked here in Oxford for a while before going back to the colonies.'

'I'm afraid not.'

'Pity that. He won the Nobel Prize for medicine six years ago with those Hodgkin and Huxley chaps from Cambridge, but I guess you were a little young to notice back then. Anyway I thought I'd start with the three of them. Brilliant scientists and between them they got to the very heart of how a nervous system works. The brain is the most fantastic and awe-inspiring organ, don't you think?'

'Oh, indeed.'

'So for next week I want you to know all about squid

giant axons and the action potential. I'll drop a list of the references into your pigeonhole. Track down their Nobel Prize acceptance speech too. It'll be in the Bodleian Library somewhere.'

'Of course, giant squid axons, yes, sir.'

Eccles walked on in uncomfortable silence with Dr Bloom for a few minutes, confused about whether or not he'd been dismissed. Eccles rehearsed some lines of conversation in his head. He even moved his lips to form some such words but none of them could quite escape from his mouth. So on they walked, accompanied only by the incoherent splashing sounds created by novice boats on their first outings and the bellowed orders of their coaches. Finally, as they headed up beside the Cherwell River, the silence was broken by the substantial bounding form of Professor Arthur Plantagenet, coming from the other direction.

'Good morning, Arthur. You're looking in remarkably good form. How are things?' asked Augustus.

'Have you forgotten already, Augustus? I've been told I'm going to die.'

'I know that. I'm just wondering why you're looking so happy now. Has your doctor changed his mind or has he found a cure?'

'Bah, not at all. I'm on a mission, Augustus. That damned quack has given me orders I can follow with relish.'

'Orders?'

'He told me that if there is anything I had always wanted to eat then I should eat it now. So I've been drawing up a list at the Bodleian, great fun. I've also been inspired by Mr Tokoro's wonderfully gastronomic death and I've thought up a particularly brilliant plan for this fine body when I'm gone. I shall go down in the annals of gastronomy forever.'

Professor Plantagenet gave as neat a pirouette as a man of twenty stone can muster.

'And how will gastronomy benefit from your death?' said Augustus, quite forgetting his student Patrick Eccles was still beside him. Fortunately, Arthur was more circumspect and replied while tapping his nose with his finger.

'It's still a bit hush-hush while I get the details ironed out. You'll be the first to know, Augustus, but trust me it will be the most extraordinary experiment in the history of gastronomy. Anyway, have a look at these.'

Professor Plantagenet held up a small bag of what looked like pears at first inspection. Augustus Bloom stooped to examine the contents of the bag while Eccles, feeling he was intruding in a private discussion, decided the best thing to do was continue walking.

'Quince. The golden apples of the ancient Greeks. Old Benson in the botanical gardens started growing them for me a few years back and this is the first decent harvest,' said Arthur.

'My goodness, haven't seen one of these for years.' Augustus slowly turned the quince he was holding, examining it from all angles.

'Must find a good quince dish for the faculty's dinner this term.'

'Speaking of which, did you hear we've all been summoned for a meeting with the Master?'

'Oh, yes. Flanagan was spreading the word this morning at breakfast. Do you know what it's about?' asked Arthur.

'I believe the vice-chancellor might have something to do with it. Well, I must be getting back. I'll see you later, Arthur, and please try to be there on time. The new Master is not a patient man.'

'Glad to hear it. I never trust patient men, Augustus. They are too good at hiding their feelings.'

With that, he turned and continued on down the path to the river, breaking out in song after a few yards.

Augustus walked on, struggling to make sense of Arthur Plantagenet's sudden good humour in the face of death and wondering about the mysterious experiment he seemed to be planning. Looking around he also wondered how he had managed to lose Eccles, hoping that the young man knew his way around Oxford well enough to get back on his own. He came through the large gates at the back of the meadows and pondered for a minute on which route to take. To cut back through the cobbled peace of Merton Street or walk along the bustle of the High Street? After a brief mental stocktake he convinced himself that his rooms were well enough supplied so he could avoid the physical and cultural shock of the world of commerce for another day. Merton Street it was.

Winding his way past innumerable bicycles, almost all black and practically indistinguishable from each other, Augustus finally reached the old wooden doors of the college. He silently nodded to the immobile Potts as he walked through to the back room of the gate lodge to gather his post from his pigeonhole. He didn't pause today to review the letters. Instead he just pocketed the small bundle and set off towards Charles' rooms. After a brief and unsettling conversation with the chaplain this morning, Bloom felt it prudent to tackle him again before the Master's meeting. Had he been less concerned about the mental well-being of Charles Pinker, Augustus Bloom would have discovered that the long-awaited letter from California had finally arrived.

Chapter 6

The sound of the old Bakelite phone shook the silence of the Master's lodgings at St Jerome's, resonating off the dark oak panelling that lined his study. Apart from this single intrusion of modernity, the rest of the room looked as it might a hundred years before. A small grate with a glowing coal fire, bookcases lined with leather-bound volumes nearly all published in the nineteenth century or earlier, a large mahogany desk whose green leather top was barely visible for the stacks of paper and a pair of high-backed green leather Queen Anne chairs. In this peaceful haven the accursed phone seemed to grow louder with each ring. It rang with a remarkable degree of persistence, which matched the personality of the short man at the other end of the phone, who was sitting in a brightly lit and tediously decorated office on the other side of Oxford. Finally, out of desperation, the Master was roused from his newspaper and forced to lift the hand piece.

'Faulkner.'

'Good morning, Lord Faulkner. Dr Ridgeway here.'

'Dr Ridgeway... Dr Ridgeway... Oh yes, I thought you might call.'

'Indeed, but as this is a rather delicate matter I was thinking it would be better to discuss it face to face.'

'Nonsense,' said Faulkner.

As the vice-chancellor had managed to disturb him in the

middle of completing the *Times* crossword, Lord Faulkner was in no mood to agree to any meeting and was equally determined to make this a brief conversation.

'Well, speaking plainly I think it's time we shut down this ridiculous gastronomy club before they cause any more harm to the university's reputation. I met your Dr Bloom yesterday and quite frankly was disappointed with his attitude to the whole affair.'

'Dr Ridgeway, I can assure you that senior members of this college are not known for their recklessness. As you are well aware, Mr Tokoro was bringing a unique cultural delicacy to Oxford. The fault in preparation of the dish was indeed his and we are lucky that he didn't manage to kill any members of St Jerome's, quite frankly. So I can't see what there is to discuss.'

In the slight pause that followed, Ridgeway's imagination raced ahead to the halcyon possibility that a few more mouthfuls of toxic fish might have ensured that Dr Bloom and the rest of his dining club would not still be around to vex him. Solely in the interests of diplomacy, he was forced to concur.

'Indeed Master, we are grateful for that, but you should understand that this event did cause very significant problems for the university. I was forced to call in favours at the highest – and I mean the very highest – levels to keep this out of the newspapers and to placate the Japanese ambassador.'

'I'm sure you handled things admirably, but then isn't that your job? And in relation to the newspapers I do believe a certain Neil Armstrong stepping onto the moon in July kept the journalists busy for most of the summer.'

'Indeed, indeed, but I don't want a repeat of this sort of incident. To that end I suggested to Dr Bloom that the activities of this frivolous dining club be drawn to a close. My problem is that Dr Bloom has refused to do so.'

'So there you have it. I don't believe you have authority over senior members of this college and I have the greatest faith that Dr Bloom will in future act with all due care and attention.'

'I'm sure he will, but I felt sure you could prevail upon Dr Bloom, and indeed the other members of this club, to do the honourable thing.'

'Well, Dr Ridgeway, you will be glad to know that I have already arranged a meeting with the entire shadow faculty of gastronomic science, as I believe they are called.'

'Oh, I see,' said the vice-chancellor, taken aback by this sudden turnaround. 'Well that is excellent. And what sort of message will you be conveying to these gentlemen?'

'I shall take heed of your comments, Dr Ridgeway, and decide later precisely what I shall be saying to them. Suffice to say that I am happy to ask them to act honourably, though I would not expect any of our fellows to do otherwise. Now I think that wraps up the matter for the time being, don't you think?'

Dr Ridgeway placed the receiver down on its rest and stared at it intently as he went over the call in his mind. He had made his way in the challenging world of university politics not by interpersonal skills, but by ceaseless analysis of each development and preparing for every eventuality. He took comfort that Faulkner didn't issue a straight rebuff. Ridgeway had personally briefed the foreign secretary on the events of last term and knew that Faulkner had been called up to the Foreign Office in London. On balance he felt that Faulkner would be minded to look after his own reputation in diplomatic circles rather than support the frankly bizarre culinary interests of the fellows of St Jerome's College.

Faulkner had indeed received an ear-bending from the foreign secretary on account of the incident. It had taken the offer of a case of 1927 Dow, one of the century's finest Ports, for both the foreign secretary and Japanese ambassador to calm the waters. Fortunately the College had amassed a large stockpile of this divinely complex transformation of mere grapes just before the Second World War. This was especially farsighted as most of the stocks of this fine vintage were destroyed by the Luftwaffe during the Blitz following a tragically direct hit on Dow's London warehouse. Unknown to most of the wine world, St Jerome's now had the world's largest stock of the '27 vintage, so this was in reality a small price to pay for international goodwill. Personally speaking, this was not the start to his tenure as master of St Jerome's that Faulkner had hoped for, and the incident had most certainly not endeared the members of the shadow faculty to him.

Faulkner returned to his favourite chair by the fire and sat back, pausing for a second until the annoying spectre of Dr Ridgeway faded in intensity. He took back up his folded newspaper and returned to the more important task of the *Times* crossword. He plucked a gold stopwatch from his waistcoat pocket. It was still running. He watched the ornate black hand glide around the dial for a few seconds before clicking the large furled top. He'd forgotten to stop the watch when he answered the phone. Today a potential personal best time was ruined and the vice-chancellor was of course entirely to blame for the failure of Lord Faulkner's right thumb to stop the clock before answering the phone.

*

That same morning, Augustus Bloom was reflecting on how he had singularly failed in his mission to placate Charles Pinker. On hearing that the entire faculty had been summoned by the Master, the chaplain had fallen into a state of inconsolable anxiety. Neither Bach, God nor Bloom could offer anything to improve matters. The only thing that would bring the Reverend Pinker peace was to hear his fate and that of the rest of the faculty. Lord Faulkner was new to the College, having been elected to the post barely six months ago. He had brought with him a formidable reputation and, most challenging of all, was his experience of the world outside Oxford. The world was a large, exotic and threatening place for the likes of Charles Pinker, and indeed many Oxford dons. To be called before Lord Faulkner for admonishment carried with it the prospect of having to face the judgement of the outside world, a world that Charles felt knew little of the ways of an Oxford college. The time and place were at least already settled: the Master's dining room at 6 p.m. Augustus set off from college on his bicycle, knowing he could do no more for his friend Charles.

Augustus turned away from the gothic brick edifice of Keble College and swept around the corner towards the University Laboratory of Physiology. As he approached the large tree in front of the main door, he stood up and slowly swung his right leg across the saddle and around the back wheel. Standing aloft on just the left pedal, his black policeman's bike tilted away from him to achieve a perfect balance, he glided to a halt. He pulled the two books from the wicker basket in front of the handlebars and walked through the double doors of the laboratory. He was met by the building's unique smell and the sound of his brogues on the polished floor echoing off the ceiling thirty feet over his head. The building was undeniably modern compared to collegiate Oxford, a 1930s temple to scientific progress. He picked up his departmental mail from the diminutive and equally modern porter's lodge, and stuffed the whole bundle into his jacket pocket that was already bulging with the unopened mail he'd collected in college.

On reaching his office on the first floor he gathered the letters and perused them all, taking his time in choosing which letter to open first. On some days it was a challenging task to find anything interesting on the envelope or postmark, but today there was only a single contender for the first letter. Augustus saw the California postmark and tore open the envelope.

My dearest Augustus,
I was delighted to get your letter. As ever a breath of fresh air to brighten dull Californian days. How I miss Europe and the delightful twists she shows us Americans at every turn. I know you English don't think of yourself as European. I'm forever intrigued by your love/hate

relationship with the 'Continent'. A word that is full of allure and promise yet mixed with a heady combination of distrust and danger. Although I have never set foot in Oxford, I feel I know her like a dear old friend.

I know I promised to visit this Christmas, but my publisher in New York has single-handedly dashed these plans. It seems that I have been rediscovered by those who thought I was dead and discovered for the first time by a generation that never knew I existed. Long-lost books are being reprinted and I am to rise from the grave of anonymity to do a tour of the East Coast. My dear editor John still looks down on the folk of the West Coast as barely literate sun-baked children not worthy of proper literature, indeed not even my frivolous literary morsels. So I don't even get the chance of fame in my own backyard.

I can sense as I write these words your disappointment, but trust me dear Augustus this is a deferral not a cancellation and I know you will be happy for my new-found popularity. I hope I can count on you to invite me again. I'm making firm plans to visit London in the summer and I do so wish to make history as the first woman to grace the table of the faculty of gastronomic science. I'm fascinated to see first-hand how all you men survive locked up in your famous ivory towers. Who knows, it may start a trend. I may become the Rosa Parks of Oxford and stimulate your dear St Jerome's to allow in students of the fairer and dare I say far brighter sex. I have fanciful visions of letting my long hair down from an ivory-towered window and letting my young sisters climb in.

Do please send me the menu for your next dinner and report on your latest discoveries in gastronomic science. They will brighten the long cold winter I'll have to endure from Boston to Philadelphia. In return I shall savor a martini at the Waldorf Astoria in memory

of our last delightful gin-soaked meeting.
So long, my dearest Augustus, and if another invitation
does not arrive soon I shall descend into a sulk of
transatlantic proportions. Be warned, a woman scorned
is a fearsome foe.
Sweetest regards,
Mary Frances

Augustus smiled and shook his head in wonder as he folded the letter back in its envelope. Totally outflanked. She breaks her promise and he is left feeling guilty about an invitation that has yet to be made.

*

By the time Augustus returned to college in the darkening gloom of an October night, the clouds and surviving members of the shadow faculty of gastronomic science were gathering. Passing through the heavy wooden gates of the porter's lodge, Augustus met Professor George Le Strang and Dr Theodore Flanagan. Le Strang, a man of strong opinions usually delivered with a strong dose of Gallic superiority, was holding forth. Bloom sensed Flanagan was in need of rescue.

'Good evening, Gentlemen. Any sign of the others?'

Flanagan spun round to see his saviour.

'Augustus, good evening. Apart from the professor here I haven't seen hide nor hair of the others all day.'

At that moment, Charles Pinker emerged from the passageway that led to Chapel Quad. They watched as the chaplain made his way towards them with all the enthusiasm of a man walking to the gallows. Flanagan tried valiantly to lift Pinker's spirits as he came within earshot.

'We'll be grand Charles, have a little faith.'

'Just a slap on the wrists over a glass of revolting sweet sherry,' added Le Strang.

As these weak attempts floundered, Augustus Bloom decided a change of topic was needed.

'So where will we find Arthur and Hamish?'

'Well they are both late and so wherever they are, they are likely to be together.'

'Very true, Theodore, but where?'

'At a guess finding courage hidden beneath the cork of a bottle or two of Claret.'

As if on cue, the cellar door swung open and the bear-like figures of Arthur Plantagenet and Hamish McIntyre emerged, just as the distant bells of Tom Tower began their ninety-nine chimes to mark the stroke of six o'clock. Augustus took the lead.

'Gentlemen, let's not be late.'

Chapter 7

They were fine rooms for a first-year undergraduate. The shared sitting room was magnificent in scale; the two large bay windows onto the quad provided an unparalleled view of the comings and goings below. On this particular evening, if anyone had been looking out of these windows, they would have witnessed the procession led by Augustus Bloom heading towards the Master's lodge. But the occupants of the room were otherwise engaged. The ceilings were plain, grandeur coming from their height at almost fourteen feet. The furnishings were completed with an elegantly faded oriental rug, two small desks and a three-piece leather chesterfield suite, which had seen better days but was maturing gracefully into shabbiness. In contrast the two bedrooms attached to this grand room were tiny and a little sad looking. In each, a small wooden locker accompanied a narrow single bed, the hair-filled mattresses sagging in the middle in memory of the horses from whence the hair came.

Such scale was, as a rule, strictly reserved for second or third-year undergraduates, but Patrick Eccles, Bloom's new charge, had benefited from the temporary absence of one of its intended occupants. An enthusiastic member of the high altitude club, the dashing Argentinean Felipe Banzarro, had come a cropper during the summer, descending an Andean glacier in a bathtub. He was moments away from the prestigious honour of being the first person to perform such a feat in the southern hemisphere, when he had dropped into the mouth of a glacial moulin at high speed. These ethereal blue caverns carved by meltwater are things of great beauty and the unfortunate Felipe had several hours to admire them until he was rescued. He emerged with his reputation amongst his peers elevated yet further but with a spectacularly fractured right arm, pelvis and left femur, that removed all prospects of returning to Oxford for the coming academic year.

It was in Banzarro's stead that the very young and decidedly unadventurous Patrick Eccles ended up sharing this magnificent room with one of St Jerome's leading socialites, Matthew Kingsley-Hampton. The honourable Kingsley-Hampton, educated at Eton and recently elevated to this title thanks to a life peerage his father had received for services to the Conservative Party, was less than impressed by this new roommate. Staircase five, room three was to have been the social epicentre of undergraduate college life in this coming year. Kingsley-Hampton wasn't one to be easily distracted from this goal, but it would be all the harder to achieve without the foil of his handsome Argentinean sidekick.

Stretched out on the chesterfield sofa, Kingsley-Hampton was flicking through the books on this term's reading list. His attention was diverted by the discovery of a menu tucked inside the pages of a book he had collected from the library that day. The menu, elegantly printed with an embossed college crest and bound with a black and purple ribbon, described a feast that challenged both credulity and imagination. As he read down the list of assorted gastronomic pleasures his fascination was marred by a growing sense of pique. This menu was clearly from a dining club from which he was not only excluded, but even worse, hadn't known existed. On both counts this was a novel and a thoroughly unwelcome experience for The Honourable Kingsley-Hampton.

***Shadow Faculty of Gastronomic Science
Trinity Term 1969***

Aperitif
French 75

Amuse-gueule
*A fresh oyster in dill-scented cream over Laphroaig
whiskey*

Hors d'oeuvres
*Courgette flowers lightly fried in a fennel and Courage's
Best Bitter batter with a fresh anchovy and pecorino
stuffing*

*Elvers in saffron oil
Served with 1929 Dom Perignon Champagne*

Entrées
*Giant sea urchin baked with fennel en papillote with
caramelised vermouth*

Grand turbot de Brillat-Savarin

*With a special presentation of the celebrated delicacy
Fugu - Prepared by Takeshi Tokoro
Served with Nuits St Georges Blanc 1962 and Condrieu
1964*

Dessert
*Seaweed ice cream
Served with Château D'Yquem 1947*

Fruit
Dragon fruit

Port
Dow 1927

Kingsley-Hampton paused after every dish, closing his eyes to imagine each flavour, and mentally sipped each wine. He had drunk plenty of Dom Perignon, but not of that vintage. He knew the other wines only by name or passing acquaintance. Kingsley-Hampton's education in oenology over the last year had at the very least equalled his education at Oxford in philosophy, politics and economics – the preferred course for gentlemen with political ambitions or indeed for gentlemen with sufficient means to need no ambition at all. Whenever the opportunity arose, The Honourable Kingsley-Hampton would head to London to attend wine auctions. Dressed in his finest suit and presenting his card, he would merely explain that he was tasting on behalf of his father who would be bidding by telephone. With this simple ruse, he and a select group of real bidders would be allowed to taste a bottle from select auction lots under the guidance of auction houses' finest experts.

Another item unknown to Kingsley-Hampton was the mysterious 'Fugu' prepared by the equally unknown Takeshi Tokoro. He rose to his feet and started pacing the threadbare carpet. On seeing the hunched figure of Patrick Eccles sitting at the desk on the far side of the room and driven more by his curiosity than his desire for social inclusion, he posed the question to his enforced roommate.

'Eccles. Any idea what Fugu is?'

Eccles turned in a state of surprise to look at his roommate with a look of incomprehension.

'Foogoo, F-U-G-U,' repeated Kingsley-Hampton slowly, as if talking to a deaf aunt or an imbecile. 'Something Japanese, I presume.'

'Oh, Fugu. It's a Japanese delicacy made from puffer fish.'

'How the hell do *you* know that?'

'I've just read about it for this essay I'm writing. You see it has a toxin that allowed scientists to work out the mechanics of the action potential.'

'If it's poisonous, why do they eat it?'

'Well the toxin is mostly in internal organs rather than the flesh, so the fish has to be specially prepared. Even so, there is apparently a rather unusual tingle on the tongue from the small amounts of toxin in the rest of the fish. I don't believe it tastes anything special, more a case of Russian roulette.'

'Russian roulette?'

'A little too much tingling and all the nerves in your body stop working and… well… you die.'

'How extraordinary. Well done, Eccles. Now your next task is to find out who this faculty of gastronomic science crowd are. Sounds like my sort of dining society.' He wandered over and dropped the menu on the desk.

Eccles cast his eyes over the menu, barely able to imagine the dishes and finding the names of the accompanying wines as unrecognisable as a foreign language.

'Where did this come from?'

'Seems to have been used as a bookmark. I found it tucked inside a copy of Plato's *Republic* I got from the library just before that clot of a chaplain tried to kill me with some picture he was lugging through Old Quad.'

'Well that's a start, there are only so many people who would have been reading Plato at the end of last term.'

'Excellent thinking. Now come on and let's see who's down in the college bar before dinner. It's time you met some people. You're taking this work thing far too seriously.'

*

The Master's lodge was located in the most ancient part of the college and was approached through a narrow and dark corridor. The six members of the shadow faculty of gastronomic science emerged from this gloom into a charming small courtyard with a yellowing but not yet leafless cherry tree. In spring, this tree was a source of great joy as its sheltered position made it one of the earliest trees to blossom in the whole of Oxford. Tonight, spring seemed a long way off as the assembled fellows approached the small iron nailed door of the lodge. Augustus knocked on the door, which opened without apparent human intervention until the diminutive figure of the Master's housekeeper came into view. They filed past her without any words being spoken or needed.

They were led into the panelled dining room, which was dramatically lit with a pair of silver candelabras. The heavy oak table was set with a plate of quartered figs on a silver platter and a decanter of a drink too pale for sherry surrounded by fine crystal glasses. As they silently admired the rich purple sheen of the figs and their blood-red flesh, Lord Faulkner made his entrance, already fully gowned in anticipation of dinner and carrying a silver tray adorned with food.

'Gentlemen. Many thanks for gathering here this evening. There are a few matters that need to be discussed but first, do please try some of these figs; they go very well with the white port. These duck and quince canapés are rather good too.'

Arthur Plantagenet's jaw dropped, adding yet another chin to his already impressive collection. The figs were passed around and though all were impressed by the Master's choice of white port as an accompaniment, the atmosphere remained decidedly chilly. Polite discussion ensued about the source of figs and whether they were best baked or, as here, eaten fresh. The smoked duck breast canapés with quince and juniper preserve were truly remarkable. Faulkner hadn't included juniper as part of the description, but it didn't take long for Arthur Plantagenet to identify this flavour along with the other herbs and spices. Arthur was truly impressed at such an unexpected use of quince from such a surprising source. The uneasy détente was finally broken by Lord Faulkner tapping an antique silver spoon on the table.

'Gentlemen, could you all take a seat.'

Everyone duly obliged and any sense of levity that had accompanied the food vanished in an instant. Even the eternally ebullient Hamish McIntyre looked crestfallen. Once everyone was seated and the final murmurs had subsided, Faulkner continued. He had a powerful natural presence, one that easily commanded respect. It was this one attribute, beyond all others, that had propelled him through life with such ease.

'Now I'm sure you all know why I've gathered you here.'

After a perfectly timed pause he continued.

'Is there anything any of you would like to say first?'

This elicited only an uneasy shifting of buttocks on seats and clearing of throats. Faulkner cast his eyes around the room looking for volunteers. The poor chaplain looked overwrought and an unsporting target, so his eyes moved on.

'Dr McIntyre?'

In a moment of uncharacteristic reticence, Hamish McIntyre demurred by casting his gaze to the remains of duck and figs on his plate. Faulkner moved on and looked towards Le Strang.

'Professor?' But the good professor offered nothing in reply.

'Dr Flanagan, your Irish eloquence seems lacking today, and Professor Plantagenet, it's unlike you to resist an invitation to hold forth.'

It was indeed quite unlike Arthur, who was dying to talk about how good the duck and quince combination had been.

'Well, Master, apart from congratulating you on this delightful combination of tastes, I am on this occasion happy to leave the floor to you.'

'So,' turning to the last of the assembled members, he addressed Augustus. 'Dr Bloom, I understand the gentleman who expired last term was your guest.'

'He was indeed, Master. If I may explain a little of the background, I think this may help to clarify the situation.'

A nodded cue from the Master left Augustus free to continue.

'Well, as you are aware, in our joint desires to develop gastronomic science, we each invite a guest for a dinner each term. This guest chooses, and on occasion creates, a particular dish. For Mr Tokoro it would have dishonoured him to refuse his suggestion.'

'Dishonoured, but perhaps a polite refusal might have saved his life?'

'Master, I still wake at night thinking of all the tiny twists and turns that could have altered the events of that night.'

'And this dish was prepared solely by Mr Tokoro and not the college kitchen staff?'

'Mr Tokoro had brought his own chef with him to prepare and cook the fish at the table, but he helped to prepare one or two of the fillets himself.'

'This was at the start or the end of the meal?'

'As the highlight of the dinner this was the last of our savoury courses.'

'So he had sampled the delights of the St Jerome's cellars by that stage. Don't you think that such a dangerous and delicate task as dissecting out the liver and ovaries of a puffer fish should be done with a steady hand and a clear head?'

The Master's detailed knowledge of which organs of the puffer fish are particularly toxic caught Bloom off guard.

'Well I imagine the aperitifs and the wine may have had... ' His voiced trailed off as Faulkner helpfully finished Bloom's sentence.

'... some contribution towards the making of this disaster? That is not an entirely unreasonable position and one that implicates you all in this affair.'

Theodore Flanagan, the law tutor, burst forth in their collective defence.

'But at the inquest the Coroner declared his death was misadventure. I assumed this matter was behind us.'

'Legally, yes, Dr Flanagan, but morally and diplomatically it is not so clear-cut. Gentlemen, secure within these walls you may not have been fully aware of the consequences of Mr Tokoro's death. It has caused problems for international relations with Japan, created an extremely bad odour with the university authorities and I have to consider the reputation of St Jerome's College.'

Turning to Augustus, the Master continued. 'I understand that you have been in discussions with the vice-chancellor's office, Dr Bloom.'

'Well I was summoned, but I felt this was a college matter rather than a university one.'

'And Dr Bloom, I hear that you told him as much... in no uncertain terms.'

Augustus tried to hide a smile under a mask of contrition and failed nobly.

'Master, I think I speak for us all when I say I'd rather answer to you than to Dr Ridgeway.'

'Thank you for your faith in my judgement, Dr Bloom. I cannot claim any great affection for Dr Ridgeway or for university interference, so I have indeed decided to handle this as an internal matter.'

Faulkner continued across the murmurings of relief that began to fill the room.

'So I have two requests to make of you all. Firstly, please don't serve anything that might possibly be poisonous, and secondly, keep your activities as secret or, at the very least, as discreet as possible. But don't underestimate the vice-chancellor. He is an irritatingly tenacious character by all accounts, and not without influence in the university. Try not to antagonise the man too much.'

Faulkner's words were met with a flurry of thanks and confusion as the faculty members rose to shake his hand. Once the hubbub had subsided, Faulkner motioned for quiet and for the fellows to take their seats again.

'That just leaves the international and diplomatic issues for me to address. Let's not forget that a foreign diplomat died on college grounds. I have had to use a lot of favours at the foreign office to keep relations with Japan on an even footing. Everything on that score seems to be back on track, but the Japanese ambassador does have one last request of you all which he has asked me to convey.'

Charles Pinker, eager for a sense of absolution from the Japanese ambassador, was a surprising leader in reply.

'Of course Master, we'll do whatever we can for the ambassador.'

'It is a simple if rather bizarre request. He is eager for your impressions of the experience of eating Fugu.'

This was met by a choking sound from Hamish McIntyre who broke into an enormous laugh once the small piece of fig had been dislodged from his gullet.

'My God, he just wants to know what it tasted like? Pass the phone there, I'll call him myself.'

'That won't be necessary Dr McIntyre. I understand he merely wants a brief written description from each of you. And as to his reasons, I understand that it was a promise to his wife who lost a brother to Fugu that has prevented him from trying it personally. Now all this talking of food is making me hungry. Shall we head across for dinner?'

Chapter 8

The next morning a thoroughly recharged and emboldened Augustus Bloom strode into the porter's lodge. Now that the immediate threat over their existence had been lifted, they had no time to lose in preparing for their next dinner at the end of term. In his hands were letters inviting his colleagues to this term's menu planning meeting. The shadow faculty of gastronomic science had, over recent years, fallen into a comfortable pattern of events during term time. They held a menu-planning meeting usually in the second week of term followed by one or more tasting meetings over subsequent weeks to refine the menu and recipes. In addition to suggestions for the menu, faculty members could also discuss their choice of guests for the forthcoming dinner at these meetings. Under rule four of their constitution each guest also had to provide a dish that was new to the faculty, so it was important to choose someone who could rise to this particular challenge. Of course the faculty chose the theme of each dinner and produced their own creations, but there had been many a dinner when the most spectacular dish had been devised by a guest. Such turns of events merely spurred on the members of the faculty to aspire to even greater heights in their pursuit of gastronomic perfection. The choice of wine was naturally important too, so this was always on the agenda. Arthur Plantagenet had in recent years taken this task to heart and made frequent forays within the wine cellars solely in the interest of gastronomic progress. The culmination of all this planning was the end-of-term dinner that was held on the Wednesday of eighth week – an otherwise dull day of the week – chosen for the sole reason that it didn't clash with other more official dinners held at the end of term.

Augustus had an additional letter to dispatch on this morning, an invitation to the dinner to be held next summer in Trinity Term. Although bizarrely early for such an invite, he was under orders from Mary Frances, a lady he had met just once but with whom a long correspondence had cemented a deep friendship. Augustus just hoped that on this occasion his invitation would bring the celebrated Mary Frances Kennedy Fisher, universally acclaimed as having produced the best translation of Jean Anthelme Brillat-Savarin's *The Physiology of Taste*, to Oxford.

Dear Mary Frances,

Thank you for your beautifully crafted missive. It is a deep disappointment for me that we won't have the pleasure of your company at our Christmas dinner this term, but you are right, I am delighted that your talents are being more fully recognised. In relation to your plans to storm our ivory towers, you may be disappointed to know that our college is only made of stone and we have no windows in high towers suitable for the casting down of long tresses of hair. I am nonetheless certain that these minor obstacles won't stop you being your usual radical, entertaining self when you do finally visit. To that end, and in great anticipation of the electrifying effect you may have on some of our more conservative members, I hereby invite you to the final dinner of the Shadow Faculty of Gastronomic Science for this academic year, which will be held on Wednesday of eighth week in Trinity Term. I shall be deeply offended by any rejection or deferral of

this most generous invitation.
With the very finest regards and deep admiration,
Augustus

*

Patrick Eccles was making his way up the ancient wooden stairs of staircase five. Centuries of use had darkened the steps to a deep, if dusty, patina and the centre of each step was worn into a slippery curve, which made the simple task of ascending them a significant challenge. On this occasion, Eccles was staggering up with such a large collection of books in his arms that it was a miracle he survived the three flights of stairs to his room. On reaching the door he tried knocking with his elbow and after a decent pause, calling to his roommate within for assistance. Cursing quietly, he unburdened his load and opened the unlocked door. He was irritated but not surprised to find Kingsley-Hampton sprawled on the sofa reading a book with a pot of tea resting on Eccles' second-hand trunk, which had been recruited into use as a table. The Honourable Kingsley-Hampton would never have used his own trunk, an elegant affair from the Maison Goyard *'malletier de luxe'* in Paris, for such a lowly purpose. Eccles deposited his books on one of the chairs and waited for some acknowledgement from Kingsley-Hampton, who leisurely finished his page before turning down the top corner and dropping his copy of *Zuleika Dobson* on the floor.

'Eccles. There you are. Any joy in our investigation?'

Finding his resentment suddenly vanish despite his best efforts to maintain at least a modicum of indignation, Eccles took a seat and delivered his report.

'Well, I've found a few things that might help. The Brillat-Savarin named in one of the dishes is most likely Jean Anthelme Brillat-Savarin, the author of the first real book of gastronomy, *The Physiology of Taste*. The clincher is that this book included a recipe for cooking a giant turbot.'

Eccles passed over an almost pristine copy of the new 1949 translation of *The Physiology of Taste*.

Kingsley-Hampton flipped through a few pages and glanced at the borrowing sheet inside the front cover. There were only two entries: one from 1951 and the second in October 1969 by a Mr P. Eccles.

'Does that really help us, Eccles?'

'Well it is one definite point of reference… '

'Anything more tangible?'

'I found out who Mr Tokoro is, or at least was. He was the cultural attaché to the Japanese embassy in London.'

'You say was. What is he now?'

'Dead.'

For the first time in this conversation, Eccles had the undivided attention of his conversant.

'Dead?'

'Most definitely, I found his obituary in *The Times*. Like most obituaries it rambled on about how great he was but didn't give much detail on how he died or even when. From the date it was published it must have been pretty close to the end of last term.'

'Splendid. Truly splendid.'

It wasn't at all clear to Eccles from this response whether his roommate was delighted Mr Tokoro had died or was impressed by his detective prowess. Kingsley-Hampton sat back on the sofa with his hands behind his head, a smile – or perhaps it could be better called a smirk – spreading across his face. Eccles watched and waited for the plan that was clearly crystallising in Kingsley-Hampton's head.

'I have to say, Eccles, an excellent bit of detective work.'

Though Eccles found Kingsley-Hampton more than a little patronising at times, he still felt an inordinate pride in the compliment. Unfortunately it was a short-lived glow. It didn't take long for Kingsley-Hampton to reaffirm his place in the social hierarchy.

'Looks like we have a real mystery on our hands now, Dr Watson. So why don't you go and start questioning the locals? Find anyone who's heard of Fugu or, even better, anyone who looks shifty when you ask the question. I've got a blasted essay to write and my usual scribe is in bed with the lame excuse of a kidney infection.'

Kingsley-Hampton rarely wrote essays as he had already mastered the art of delegation. With a small financial inducement, an impoverished PPE student from Hertford College would generally oblige with more speed and erudition than Kingsley-Hampton was able to offer, and this arrangement certainly required less effort than he was inclined to expend on such distractions.

Eccles had briefly settled into his chair, waiting for the offer of a cup of tea, but the slight elevation of a single eyebrow on Kingsley-Hampton's face was sufficient to indicate that he was expecting a prompt response to his instructions. Eccles wasn't sure exactly who he was meant to be asking. After all, he knew only a handful of his own year and anyone else he'd met had been through Kingsley-Hampton. Eccles reluctantly rose to his feet. He consoled himself with the thought of having his tea in the junior common room. As for Fugu, he had his next tutorial in less than an hour so he could always ask his tutor, Dr Bloom, about that.

*

After delivering his various invitations, Augustus turned to his second mission that morning: the challenging task of getting Professor Arthur Plantagenet to see sense. He had planned to tackle Arthur at dinner last night, but he had been far too engrossed in his conversation with the Master on quinces and every other variety of exotic fruit. For Plantagenet, who usually learnt of new and unusual fruits in the Bodleian library, the Master's first-hand experience as he had worked his way up the diplomatic ladder from the Turks and Caicos Islands to Peking was a gold mine. Later in the senior common room parlour after dinner when the Master had retired for the night, Augustus was forced to listen as Arthur waxed lyrical about Lord Faulkner and his virtues. The little matter of Arthur's dire medical situation seemed to pale into insignificance compared to the best way of determining the ripeness of a durian.

Augustus had first tried Arthur Plantagenet's rooms. Failing to find him he had checked the usual haunts, the parlour for breakfast and the informal morning crossword competition amongst the dons in the leather chairs of the senior common room. As it was still far too early for Arthur to be heading to the Bodleian to work, there was only one place left: Martha's. Augustus left St Jerome's and passed along the cobbled streets leading up to the High Street before turning towards the covered market. The market contained an eclectic combination of shops selling everything from goldfish to travel trunks, but it was above all a place for food. The very best butchers, fishmongers and grocers had their premises in the narrow alleys.

Arthur Plantagenet considered Oxford's covered market the best food market in the world. In truth, Arthur had seen very little of the world in person. He had never visited Venezia's Rialto or La Boquería in Barcelona for comparison. The lack of first-hand knowledge of the world's great food markets did not reduce the strength of Professor Plantagenet's opinion nor the frequency of its repetition. Augustus had once suggested they go on a tour together of the great food markets of the world. To Augustus' great disappointment, Arthur felt no need to see these places in person. As a professor of ancient history, Arthur's world survived only in books and manuscripts. They had visited Rome and Florence together many years ago, but Arthur was surprisingly unaffected by ruins and churches. Arthur was fascinated not by the stone but by what had happened inside these ancient buildings. He always began his first lecture for first students with the same words: 'If you are here because you have been beguiled by the splendour of Rome and its monuments then please leave now and look for a course in Architecture or Archaeology. This lecture is for students of history and history is made up of people and actions not buildings.' Many years ago, a student that had come up to read modern languages had found himself in Professor Plantagenet's lecture theatre at the start of term by mistake. Upon hearing these words he shuffled to his feet and apologetically squeezed along the row towards the exit. The audience responded with a murmur, followed by laughter and finally a roar as the red-faced young man struggled to escape the clamour, while being slapped on the back. Professor Plantagenet stood at the lectern beaming. Every year he hoped for a repeat of this theatrical triumph, in vain as it turned out, but for Arthur, the memory was sufficient to keep him repeating the same words year in and year out.

Today, Augustus was relying on Arthur's predictably habitual nature and peering over the top of the yellowed net curtains in the windows of Martha's café, he wasn't disappointed. The clientele were grouped in their usual tables. The far corner table was reserved at this time of day for Oxford's defenders of parking rectitude, its traffic wardens. The tables closest to the counter were always full of other market traders. This left tables along the windows free for students, shoppers and the occasional professor with a craving for greasy food. Augustus made his way towards Arthur's table, ordering a cup of tea as he went from the proprietor, Martha. He caught Arthur in the act of biting into a bacon sandwich with grease dribbling down his chin. Augustus saw signs of recognition on Arthur's face, with not the slightest hint of guilt.

'Good morning, Arthur. With the state of your heart I'm a little surprised to see you tucking into that. You have to start looking after yourself and that means being sensible about what you eat.'

'Good God, Bloom. You sound like my mother, God rest her soul.'

'And you are clearly on a mission to meet her as soon as possible.'

'Nonsense, she'll be in heaven and I'll be crossing the River Styx to Hades. Augustus, dear chap, do you honestly think that this bacon sandwich, which by the way tastes sensational, will make any difference to the outcome?'

'It won't help.'

'Or hinder. Augustus, you're going to die one day. I'm just dying a little faster, which means I have to eat faster to make up.'

As ever, when it came to being obtuse, Plantagenet's logic had a certain appeal. Augustus tried an ancient writer in response.

'Hippocrates said, "Let food be your medicine and medicine be your food" so at a time like this you should be eating things that are good for you.'

'Hippocrates was quite right but your interpretation is completely wrong. What a man dying from an incurable disease needs most of all is solace. Tell me what tablet ever discovered by science gives solace? Food for the soul, that's what I need, and this bacon sandwich is feeding my soul rather well.'

Arthur looked across at the crestfallen Bloom who was at a loss for a decent retort but reprieved by the arrival of his cup of tea.

'Now enjoy that cup of tea and if you stop badgering me I'll give you this last corner of my bacon sandwich.'

Augustus could only smile and, in response, the bacon sandwich was slid across the table. One bite and he knew he'd lost this argument. Arthur Plantagenet was right. It tasted bloody marvellous and despite the abject failure of Augustus' mission, it brought great solace to the well-intentioned doctor as well.

*

Eccles idled away the last few minutes before his tutorial, checking his pigeonhole in the lodge. The rest of the college E's – Eaton, El-Kabir, Edmonds, Ebury, Egerton, Eckhart and Easterby – seemed as popular as ever, and Eccles was starting to believe they simply left lots of mail in the pigeonhole for days to prove just how popular they were. There were two envelopes for Mr P. Eccles today: one an invitation to a prayer group from the college's Young Christian Society, the other a letter from his mother, which he pocketed for later. It wasn't the done thing to be caught reading a letter from one's mother in the lodge.

Eccles climbed the stairs to Dr Bloom's rooms and drew a deep breath before knocking on the door. To his relief, Dr Bloom was on this occasion seated, wearing a gown and looking reassuringly like an Oxford tutor rather than a cook. The stove in the alcove was bare.

'Ah Eccles, do take a seat. Now tell me what you have learnt about the mysteries of the action potential. I see you've brought your essay with you. Why don't you read that to me and we'll take things from there.'

Eccles settled back from the very front edge of the chair where he had initially perched and started into his essay on the nature of the action potential, the tiny electrical surges of current that drive our nerves and brains. Eccles' essay was a solid, if unimaginative, summary of the field. The original sources had been carefully sliced and paraphrased into something different but unoriginal. The one section in which Eccles had shown some sparkle was in relation to the use of toxins in isolating the electrical components. It was his reading around this topic that had unexpectedly brought him favour with The Honourable Kingsley-Hampton and it was the one part of his essay that he delivered with any conviction.

The observation that the neurotoxin tetrodotoxin blocked action potentials was the clue that Hodgkin and Huxley needed to unravel the mysterious generation of electricity in nerves that led to their classic 1952 paper. Tetrodotoxin gets its name from the Tetraodontidae, the scientific name for the various species of puffer fish, but is also found in other marine animals such as the blue-ringed octopus. The action of this toxin in blocking the activity of nerves makes it extremely dangerous. The first recorded case of death was noted in the voyage logs of Captain Cook. His crew ate some puffer fish and fed the leftovers and trimmings to the pigs they kept on board. The crew complained of a variety of symptoms including shortness of breath, but the following day the pigs were found dead. The Japanese also serve puffer fish as a delicacy called Fugu.

Eccles had hoped to catch Dr Bloom's expression as he delivered these words but before he could look up he was interrupted by a knock on the door. Bloom sprung to his feet, eternally grateful for the intrusion, and opened the door. Although he set this same essay every year for his first year students and tetrodotoxin inevitably came up, Fugu was rarely mentioned and hearing the word set his own nerves jangling. Dr Bloom's scout entered carrying a small tray covered with a linen napkin, which he deposited on a small table near Bloom's chair and then plucked the napkin neatly away.

'Your lunch as requested, sir.'

'Thank you, Peter, very kind of you to bring it over.'

'No trouble, sir, no trouble at all.'

The tray contained a tall glass of murky straw-coloured steaming liquid, a small bowl of finely chopped raw onions and another of finely grated Parmesan cheese. Eccles peered at this odd-looking lunch. Seeing his surprise, Bloom was more than happy to change the subject and explain.

'A few extra ingredients. Ever tasted a saffron risotto?'

Eccles merely shook his head and in response, Bloom leapt to his feet to recover a small jar of intensely deep orange-coloured powder from his cooking alcove.

'Saffron, the most expensive spice in the world. Made from the stamens of a type of crocus, *Crocus Sativus Linneaus*. Takes almost a quarter of a million hand-picked stamens to make a pound of this stuff. Now I think you were meandering a bit there on tetrodotoxin. Skip onto the Hodgkin and Huxley 1952 model, I presume you've covered that in detail.'

'Oh yes, sir. Of course and sorry… ' Eccles shuffled his

papers and continued on to the very much more technical and duller aspects of the topic, a little aggrieved that it was *he* that was being accused of meandering off the topic. He delivered the rest of his essay with few interruptions aside from a few probing questions from Bloom on the finer details of the sodium and potassium currents that drive the action potential, while his tutor continued preparing the risotto. When he'd finished, he sat back and waited for a verdict.

'Excellent, very good start, Eccles. I think you've got the grasp of that. Now for next week I'd like you to cover synapses, and don't forget to track down all the papers of your namesake, Jack Eccles.' He pulled a reading list from a folder by his chair and handed it to Eccles who took this as his cue to leave. He was almost at the door when he turned back.

'Dr Bloom, have you ever tasted Fugu?'

Augustus hid his surprise, though in truth the words had hit him as hard as a well-struck cricket ball to the temple. After a moment to gather his thoughts he answered truthfully, if somewhat disingenuously.

'There are lots of things that I haven't yet tried. Now if you excuse me I need to taste this rather fine-looking risotto.' And with that, he unceremoniously ushered Eccles out of the room.

Chapter 9

The last glimmers of a weak autumnal sun had just abandoned St Jerome's when the members of the shadow faculty of gastronomic science began to gather for their first menu-planning meeting. This was to be held in the kitchen cellars, an area that the kitchen staff had refused to enter after the cellar steward was killed in suspicious circumstances thirty or more years previously. As a result, this part of the cellars had fallen into disuse for many decades until Augustus Bloom suggested that they use them to create a tasting kitchen. It was an ideal location due to its privacy and proved easy to have basic kitchen equipment installed. A quiet word and a small envelope for Mr Potts was all that was needed for the required items to arrive unseen under the cover of darkness. A fine old mahogany door and a few wooden wine cases served as their table. It was a little crowded when their meetings first started, but with the loss of several members over the last five years, the surviving six now fitted quite comfortably.

Even the most observant soul in college would have been hard pressed to detect any such gathering. Through force of habit and natural inclination all the members tended to arrive by their own particular route. The most direct path was generally taken by the Reverend Charles Pinker, and today was no exception. After leaving his rooms, Charles ducked into the college chapel to collect his folder of past menus from their new hiding place. He was responsible for looking after rules four and five of the constitution of the shadow faculty; the rules that ensured their palates were always exposed to new and challenging tastes. With the passing of each term it became increasingly hard for the faculty members to remember every detail of their previous dinners. It was also a source of great pleasure when a question arose that required the Reverend Pinker to read out a particular menu. Proceedings would at this point always dissolve into a round of comments, grunts of approval and the occasional groan when a gastronomic experiment had failed to live up to expectations was revisited. With the folder safely tucked under his arm he set out across Chapel Quad for the most direct route to the kitchens.

Professor George Le Strang and Dr Hamish McIntyre converged on the tradesman's entrance of the kitchens, which was located on a quiet cobbled street at the back of the college. Both were laden with the supplies intended to inspire the faculty in today's deliberations.

'A good day hunting and gathering, George?'

'One of the finest. Bloxham's even had some girolles.'

He lifted the clutch of bags in his right hand in triumph. 'How about yourself, Hamish? Any new treasures from the animal kingdom?'

'Shiny, spikey and wriggly. Something for everyone.' McIntyre winked back at Le Strang who valiantly tried to hide his distaste for that particular quirk of English bonhomie.

Beneath the damp turf of Chapel Quad, Arthur Plantagenet was selecting the last bottle of wine. He gently wiped away the cobwebs on the label with the tenderness of a mother stroking the head of a sleeping child, then passed the bottle behind him.

'There you go, Theodore. That'll do.'

Poor Theodore Flanagan took the bottle and struggled to add this to his already heavy load. A bottle in each outside jacket pocket, two half bottles in each inside jacket pocket, three bottles under his left arm held against his chest and a bottle of port in his right hand, leaving just three fingers to grasp and carry the last precious bottle. Professor Plantagenet strode on, leaving poor Flanagan struggling to keep up in the gloom. Theodore took a few seconds to balance his extensive cargo of precious wines and, in that time, Arthur had disappeared entirely from view. While Arthur could walk from one end of the cellars to the other with his eyes shut, these were less well-known parts for Flanagan.

'Arthur?' called Theodore. He stood looking at the choice of two underground passages, entirely uncertain which path to take. Flanagan was well versed in the folklore of the cellars and the lurid stories concerning the spectral Reverend Bloch. He certainly had no desire to either meet him or follow him in becoming the second fellow of St Jerome's College to disappear in the cellars. Arthur did finally come to his rescue, not by wondering where his colleague had got to and coming to find him, but by a loud and prolonged laugh that solved the dilemma of which passage led to the kitchen cellars.

The meeting was already underway by the time Augustus reached the kitchen cellars. George Le Strang was at the stove holding forth on mushrooms and chopping parsley finer than seemed humanly possible. The girolles were being pan-fried in butter with finely sliced garlic and towards the end, needed only a light dusting of chopped parsley and lemon juice to bring them to their peak.

'Can I help?' asked Augustus.

'Only by trying some of these,' said George, tilting the pan to show the contents. Arthur was walking around the table, filling glasses with a white wine.

'Evening Augustus. A drop of Condrieu?'

Plates and glasses were filled and Le Strang had a forkful of mushrooms poised on his lips when Theodore Flanagan tried to bring order and decorum to the meeting. 'Gentlemen, Gentlemen. Aren't we forgetting something?'

They all looked around rather blankly with the exception of George Le Strang whose ire was rising with each cooling wisp of steam that left his girolles.

'Grace? Charles will you do us the honour?'

'Oh, yes, indeed. *Pro hoc cibo, quem ad alimonium corporis nostri sanctificatum es largitus, nos Tibi, Pater omnipotens, reverenter gratias agimus; simul obsecrantes ut cibum angelorum, panera verum coelestem, Dei Verbum aeternum Jesum Christum Dominum nostrum nobis impetiare, ut eo mens nostra pascatur, et per carnem et sanguinem Ejus alamur, foveamur, corroboremur. Amen.'*

The chaplain delivered grace with his eyes shut. This helped both to enhance the sense of solemnity and helped his often erratic memory. He was as a result, more than a little peeved to discover when he opened his eyes that the rest of the party, Flanagan included, were already tucking into the mushrooms and uttering collective grunts of delight akin to those of pigs routing out truffles.

George Le Strang was elated that his girolles were so well received. He was in full flow, recounting the exact time and place when he had first eaten these forest delights, a small restaurant in Les Halles, Paris, when Hamish McIntyre introduced a note of discord.

'Excellent George, but I think they could be improved a little.'

'Nonsense,' retorted Le Strang, emphasising the point by shoving a few more mushrooms into his mouth with an uncharacteristic lack of finesse.

'Taste great to me,' said Arthur, spraying a fine miasma of mushroom and parsley across the table. It fell to Augustus to arbitrate the matter.

'In the spirit of gastronomy we should hear Hamish's suggestion. So Hamish, how could George's marvellous girolles be improved?'

Le Strang's wounded Gallic pride was soothed by the compliment, which was of course its intention, and all their eyes turned on Hamish.

'These would be fantastic with black pudding. A little

spicy saltiness would be great.'

A cacophony of outrage and laughter filled the small vaulted room accompanied by a muttered torrent of French insults.

Augustus was forced to stand to get anyone's attention.

'Gentlemen, please. Why don't we settle this with our taste buds rather than our tongues? Theodore, do you still have any of that fabulous Irish black pudding your aunt sent you?'

'There should be some in the cold store, I'll go and check.' Theodore Flanagan headed off, ignoring Le Strang's bitter complaints that the girolles would be ruined by the time he returned. The mood was restored by Arthur Plantagenet who, after a noisy slurp of Condrieu, embarked on an exploration of the delightful fruit end-notes of the wine. He offered peach, apricot and honey, but couldn't place the final aroma as the wine slipped gracefully down the gullet. Flanagan had returned while this debate was still in full throe and had six slices of Patrick McSweeny's secret-recipe black pudding in the pan before anyone noticed his return. It was rare that he got the chance to promote Irish produce, so he was delighted for Hamish's suggestion. He felt sure that it was made primarily in the spirit of devilment, but was equally sure that Hamish was onto something. The delightful change in colour from a dark brick to shiny black, along with the sound and smell, took him back to his childhood in Cork. He was roused from his daydream by Hamish bellowing in his ears.

'Good God, man, what are doing, cooking it or cremating it?'

'I think it's just about done now.' Theodore circled the table sliding a piece of black pudding on each plate.

'Scoop the girolles on top, the pudding will heat them up.' After taking his seat, Theodore obligingly donated some mushrooms to Le Strang who had childishly tried to avoid the experiment by eating all of his. Hamish led the charge only to be rebuffed by the searing heat still coming off the black pudding, much to Le Strang's delight. After a soothing glass of wine and some frantic blowing, the experiment commenced.

'Mmm… '

'Bloody marvellous.'

'Well done, Hamish.'

'Excellent.'

'Another great leap for mankind.'

After the others had all passed judgement, it came to Le Strang. He slowly lifted his laden fork and, with a look of distaste, delivered its contents to his taste buds. He chewed slowly, trying to keep the rest of his features immobile. Then one of his exuberantly bushy eyebrows lifted. Hamish leapt to his feet and danced around the table.

'He likes it. I knew it. Come on, admit it, Le Strang, not everything has to be French.'

'I agree it tastes… agreeable, very good in fact, but don't forget black pudding was invented in France.'

'What?' Poor Flanagan was almost speechless with outrage.

'Of course, *boudin noir*. It was probably the Normans that brought it here and most likely Ireland too.'

'*Boudin noir* is just blood, so it's nothing like black pudding. It's all the other interesting bits of pig that makes black pudding so much better,' said Hamish.

Arthur Plantagenet broke up proceedings by banging his fork on the table.

'Complete twaddle, you're both wrong. The ancient world invented nearly everything that matters while the Celts and Gauls were still running around half-naked. I'm afraid to disappoint you, but Homer described blood sausages in *The Odyssey* around 2700 BC but I doubt he ever tasted this exquisite combination.'

Lifting his glass first to Hamish and then to George, Arthur continued.

'A toast to our new dish.'

They raised their glasses and in a motley chorus gave their toast in direct quotation from Jean Anthelme Brillat-Savarin.

'The discovery of a new dish does more for human happiness than the discovery of a new star.'

It would no doubt have been as galling to Brillat-Savarin as it was to the assembled faculty that almost one hundred and fifty years after the death of the man in whose memory the faculty was created, astronomy with one less letter was an accepted science and gastronomy still struggled to escape from the kitchen.

Hamish McIntyre then rose to his feet.

'Gentlemen, may I propose another delicacy?' Hamish lifted the large bucket he had brought along onto the table. 'Squills… '

The others all peered forward to see the creatures. They were in fine fettle having been nurtured back to health and happiness in one of the large saltwater aquariums that Hamish maintained in his rooms for scientific and culinary reasons. Squills are curious back-to-front looking creatures that look like a monstrous pre-Cambrian combination of shrimp and earwig. Arthur Plantagenet seemed particularly impressed.

'Excellent work, Hamish. Are these the same squills the Romans used to eat? They are definitely mentioned in *Apicius* but I had no idea what a squill actually was.'

'A fine delicate creature designed by our creator to be eaten.'

'Hamish, I'm sure God had some purpose for these creatures before he created your stomach,' said Charles Pinker.

'Wait until I show you their secret, then you might change your mind, Charles.'

Hamish turned to increase the heat under a large pan of water that had been simmering on the cooker behind them. Before he could launch the squills into the pan, Augustus Bloom interceded on their behalf.

'Hamish, could I offer you a little chloroform to ease their way into the afterlife?'

'Oh, for goodness sake, Augustus. They're crustaceans. There are probably more nerve fibres in my little finger than in these little critters' brains.'

'That may indeed be true, Hamish, but I doubt you would

volunteer to stick your little finger in boiling water for four minutes or have it cut off without an anaesthetic.'

'Well put, Augustus,' said the chaplain, who was not particularly attached to the ugly-looking creatures but felt obliged to join the moral high ground when it was presented to him.

'It will ruin the taste, Augustus old boy.'

'Nonsense, you know as well as I that chloroform is so volatile that within a minute or two there won't be a molecule left in the pan. Go on Hamish, humour my foibles.'

A look around the table showed Hamish that he was on his own. Even George Le Strang, who had no truck for this sort of English sentimentality, was in no mood to stand by Hamish after his black pudding stunt.

'All right, hand me over the bottle.'

Augustus pulled down the dusty dark brown bottle he kept for cooking lobster and put a few anaesthetising drops into the bucket. He covered the top with the discarded wooden lid of an empty wine box. By the time Arthur had opened the next bottle of wine, a fine white from the Loire valley, the bucket was silent and Hamish was allowed to continue with his demonstration.

After a few minutes he scooped them out of the boiling water into a colander. He picked up one of the steaming crustaceans and then started bouncing it between his hands, blowing hard to cool it to a manageable temperature.

'Now, Gentlemen. What's the only problem with crustaceans?'

'Too bloody hard to open. If God was kind he'd have designed lobsters with zippers down their backs.'

'Exactly, Theodore, I couldn't have said it better myself. Now watch this.'

Taking a pair of scissors, Hamish made two cuts along the edges of the body. Then, with a deft movement, he cracked the tail end and lifted the entire top half of the shell, revealing a wondrously presented morsel of crustacean flesh. He picked this up with a small fork and, pausing only to dip it into a bowl of hollandaise sauce kindly provided by the college chef, delivered it to his mouth.

'Charles, I rest my case. A crustacean designed for consumption.'

At that point, gastronomic imperative eclipsed theological debate and within minutes the table was awash with the exo-skeletal remains of the marvellously designed little creatures.

Arthur then rose to his feet.

'Gentlemen. To squills.'

After the toast, Arthur remained standing and waited until he had their undivided attention.

'Gentlemen, I have something important to share with you. My physician has informed me that I have but a little time left within this mortal coil. So I shall soon be leaving you all.'

Arthur raised his hands to quell the rising tide of outrage at this injustice.

'I have just one hope when I die; that I may be as appreciated in my passing as much as these exquisite creatures have been tonight. Then we both shall have died well. I also have one wish while I am still alive; to partake of as many of the culinary wonders in the world that I have so far missed. With this excellent start I'm sure this wish will be fulfilled at this term's dinner. A toast to you all.'

As each man rose and lifted their glasses, any sense of premature grief was washed away by the beaming visage of Professor Arthur Plantagenet and his extraordinary enthusiasm for life, or at least food, even in the face of death. If only he'd left it at that, Arthur Plantagenet could have saved his colleagues a considerable amount of strife and anguish over the coming months. But it had never come naturally to Arthur to say just a few words, so he remained on his feet and when his audience fell quiet again he continued.

'Sadly I have to recognise that if my doctor's morbid predictions are accurate, then this term's dinner with the shadow faculty of gastronomic science may be my last,' again he motioned to stifle protestations.

'I haven't yet seen gastronomy take its rightful place in the pantheon of the sciences, but I am convinced this noble society will see that momentous day even if I don't. To further this cause I have come to a decision. When I do pass on I have decided to donate my body not to medical science but to the science of gastronomy.' The others took this final announcement as a turn of levity after all the serious talk of death. They were cheering and clanging spoons and forks on plates, glasses and even the table. It was Augustus who was the first to broach the subject again once some semblance of order had returned, happy to humour Arthur in one of his typically outrageous diversions.

'Good man, Arthur. Now, what aspect of gastronomy will your body illuminate?'

'Ah, well I do have a few ideas of my own but what do you think would be of most gastronomic interest Augustus?'

'We could examine your brain to see if there is a part that is unusually enlarged. We may discover the gastronomy lobe. Like that Einstein chap, they looked at his brain.'

'I'd say his liver would be more revealing,' said Hamish, leaning over to affectionately pat the good professor's protuberant stomach.

'I had a rather different thought in mind,' replied Arthur. 'Sometimes, in the interest of gastronomic science and adventure, you have to eat things that at first thought seem grotesque or inedible. I propose to you that this road leads much further to the ultimate gastronomic question: what do humans taste like?'

The poor chaplain was unlucky enough to be the only person at the table to have his mouth full as this extraordinary pronouncement was made. The quite involuntary cough sent a small piece of squill across the room at a velocity it could never have experienced in life.

Chapter 10

'Good God, Augustus. Try and keep it straight.' Arthur bellowed into the battered brass megaphone. The pair of them cut a curious shape along the riverbank. Augustus was at the front of the tandem in charge of direction, and, in the interests of Arthur's heart, all the propulsion. Arthur, with his feet resting above the pedals, was at the back shouting instructions, encouragement and a few words of abuse to the rowers who were competing for places in St Jerome's first VIII for next term's bumps races or 'Torpids' as it is generally known. The curious reference to slowness supposedly reflects the fact that the very best oarsmen are prevented from rowing for their colleges in the Lent bumps as they are busy preparing for the Oxford and Cambridge boat race.

In Torpids, the racing boats of the various colleges line up at different positions along the bank. When the klaxon sounds for the start, each boat careers off under the partial control of the cox with the aim of hitting the boat in front to secure a bump and to move up one place in the rankings for the next day's races. In these winter races the unfortunate boat that is bumped must complete the course while the victors pull over to the side for celebrations. The ultimate indignity in Torpids is to be bumped a second time, an over-bump. This disastrous fate befell St Jerome's first VIII on the final day of racing last year when the cox came too close to a sunken willow tree while steering in pursuit of their own bump. They ended up limping home with only seven oars and the man in the bow entertaining the crowds on the banks with curses and expletives of extraordinary originality. The two crews following them had shown an ungentlemanly eagerness in taking advantage of their plight and bumped them.

Keeping in a straight line was the least of Augustus' worries as Arthur's large form shifted back and forth on the back saddle. The towpath was pockmarked with puddles and crowded with other coaches. At least Augustus could look ahead, most of the coaches on more conventional single-seated bicycles had to ride while spending nearly all their time watching their crews on the river. Collisions and inelegant headlong dives into the river were not uncommon. Taken together with the drizzle and excoriating north wind, this was not one of Augustus' most pleasurable afternoons. At the end of this last run down the towpath, cold, wet and exhausted, he found it hard to agree with Arthur's verdict.

'Well that was an excellent outing. Very enjoyable all together. Now let's get down to the Head of the River pub and buy some drinks for the lads.'

Augustus stood with one leg on either side, trying to balance the sturdy old tandem while the wind caught Arthur's full figure side on.

'Would you mind if we walked down, Arthur? I'm just about done-in with riding this contraption.'

'Oh come on, Augustus. Young fit man like you. The tandem was your idea after all. We'll leave it up at the pub so it'll be there for tomorrow's session.' Then Arthur pointed down the towpath and shouted into the megaphone, '*Lay on, Macduff, And damn'd be him that first cries, "Hold, enough!"*'

It was true that Augustus, in a moment of concern about Arthur's plans to take to the riverbank on a bicycle, had suggested a tandem as an alternative for the sake of Arthur's health. The cursed tandem felt three times heavier than it had a few minutes earlier. Augustus stood on the pedals to get some forward momentum and they trundled down the last part of the towpath with Arthur moving from Shakespeare into a quixotic rendition of Gilbert and Sullivan with the aid of the megaphone.

A British tar is a soaring soul
As free as a mountain bird
His energetic fist should be ready to resist
A dictatorial word

It was past ten o'clock at night when Augustus headed back to college, leaving Arthur and the members of St Jerome's boat club engaged in increasingly complicated drinking games. Patrick Eccles was still there in the thick of things. Augustus was delighted to see that this young man was finally finding his feet. Augustus stepped through the small door within the massive wooden gate. Wishing Mr Potts a good night, he headed back to his rooms. Thinking back on the evening, he had changed his mind. It had turned into a rather enjoyable outing.

*

It was two o'clock in the morning when Arthur awoke, gulping air as if emerging from a deep dive. Once he had filled his lungs with as much life-restoring oxygen as they could plausibly hold, he managed to rise from his bed and make his way to the window. His heart was leaping in his chest, beating out an erratic syncopated rhythm. He looked out to the quad, drinking in each familiar detail. A sudden peace and clarity of purpose came over Arthur, along with a premonition that he wouldn't see the dawn of this day and the thought that the memory of this view may have to serve him for a very long time. Then from deep within his abdomen came an odiferous, beery belch. The thought that he might leave this world with his body dominated by the uninspiring scent of hops filled him with a sudden terror.

He had spent the last few weeks in a discreet but determined campaign to soak his body in the best combination of flavours and spices. Salt is the other important component in preserving meat and so Arthur had committed himself to a diet that combined all three of these elements. To maximise his salt intake he had been consuming prodigious quantities of Fortnum and Mason's anchovy relish on hot buttered toast. Following his doctor's advice he had been dining on the finest and rarest food he could lay his hands on all term. This just left the herbal infusion as the last component of his plan. He had settled on a combination of chartreuse and sloe gin, the former for the secretive combination of one hundred and fifty herbs and the latter for taste.

Unfortunately, his night of excess with pints of bitter had put this great plan in significant peril. Convinced that dawn would rise on his inanimate corpse and wishing to pass on with some dignity, Arthur slowly pulled his gown over his striped pyjamas. He had no time to lose. To ensure that at the moment of his death he had the optimal combination of alcohol and flavours, there was only one reasonable plan of action. He decided at that moment to contract at least a week's worth of preparation into one last frenzy. He collected a few essential items into his shopping bag: his favourite silver goblet, a bottle of green chartreuse, a bottle of sloe gin and a corkscrew. These items were essential to Arthur's plans as the hour of his death approached.

He started by downing a whole jug of water in one continuous gulp. With all the other requirements he could muster from his room, he headed towards the college wine cellars by way of the toilets. Stage one was to get rid of as much of the common attributes of an evening's consumption of beer. When he reached the cellars he headed for the small chamber directly beneath the chapel. After a few spoonfuls of anchovy relish his thirst was beginning to return. He set out the bottles of chartreuse, sloe gin and the fine wines he had collected over the last few weeks as part of his grand plan; the best offerings of Château Lafite, Latour and Petrus.

If he had been mistaken in his premonition, the assembled volume of alcoholic beverages in front of him would surely mean that this prophecy would be fulfilled. In a strict cycle he drank, with indecent haste for such fine drinks, a goblet of each. Each glug was punctuated with the occasional spoonful of anchovy relish to maintain his thirst. Steadily he moved ever closer to the next realm of existence. It was almost half-past six in the morning by the time the silver goblet slipped from his fingers. Arthur's eyes closed but the beatific smile remained on his lips. Never has a man faced his final demise with such equanimity.

*

Augustus woke early on the back of the promise he had made in the pub the previous night to coach the novice VIII that contained his own student, Patrick Eccles, at the position of stroke. By quarter to seven he was in the lodge, with seven of the crew members, in the bitter cold of a dark and freezing November morning. One of their number was dispatched to pull the cox and the last rower from their beds. The cox finally appeared in an understandably dishevelled state along with the young man who rowed at number six position, Oscar Wainwright. While none of the crew looked athletic or indeed even sober from the night before, they were at least keen. The one exception was young Mr Wainwright who trailed at the back of the pack as they ran down St Aldgate's towards Folly Bridge. Augustus was slowly freewheeling down the hill behind them as Wainwright stopped to lean against a wall. He appeared to be examining his shoes in some detail but then vomited over them. Pulling up just behind him, Augustus silently watched as he wiped his mouth on the back of his sleeve. It was then Wainwright noticed Augustus watching him.

'Oh God, I'm sorry Dr Bloom. I'm not sure I'll make it as far as the river, let alone be able to row.'

Even under the dim illumination of the streetlights, Augustus could see the sweat almost freezing on the young man's forehead.

'You go back. I was thinking yesterday I'd like to get back in a boat sometime. So now seems like a good time.'

'Oh thank you so much, Dr Bloom, and tell the guys I'll be there tomorrow for sure.'

Augustus had rowed in St Jerome's first VIII when he had been a student, but that was more than a few years ago. As Augustus picked up the pace on his bicycle to catch the rest of the crew, he started to have doubts as to whether this was such a good idea.

At the boathouse, when he announced that he'd sent Wainwright back to college on doctor's orders, there was almost a riot with multiple threats of violence and not an iota of sympathy for their missing crewmate. As the first of them turned to head back to college, Augustus made his suggestion.

'I could fill in.' Seeing only puzzled looks, Augustus pressed on. 'I did row in the first VIII as a student so I could row with you today and coach at the same time… '

There was an uncomfortable moment as the suggestion sank in. It ran against the normal separation of students and fellows, but with Christchurch regatta drawing ever closer, a novice crew couldn't be choosy. To Augustus' great relief, Patrick Eccles was the first to break rank.

'Great, so let's get the boat out.'

The racing VIII is a curious craft. Implausibly long but barely two feet wide with a draft of a few inches and no keel. Its hull is so thin that if you stood on it your foot would go straight through. If the crew all got in without the oars in place, the boat's centre of gravity is so high and the stability so low that the whole lot would be upside down in the river within seconds. It is a challenging craft at any time, especially for a novice crew in a state of disrepair. Augustus wasn't dressed for the occasion, but the rest of crew were little better. Novice VIII's are typically drawn from those members of a college that don't usually partake of any other sport and so naturally have little or no sporting attire in their wardrobes.

Augustus locked his oar into the gate, and, holding each edge of the boat for balance, put his feet into straps before lowering his body onto the sliding seat. Although he was quite trim by the standards of the fellows, he was positively obese compared to the rangy students, most of whom, like Patrick Eccles, were freshmen. He cautiously slid the seat backwards and forwards, delighted that the extra padding that had gathered around his hips in the intervening years didn't catch the sides of the boat. Seeing the ineptitude of the rest of the crew in simply getting into the boat, Augustus relaxed. However rusty he was, he couldn't be worse than the rest of them.

The boat eventually teetered out into the stream, slopping from port to starboard with the boat looking as drunk as the crew. Augustus, growing in confidence, decided to put some structure on the morning's outing. After all, they were not on the river to entertain other crews and scare ducks, but to row. Starting at the bow pair, Augustus had them balancing the boat in pairs while the others had the novel experience of rowing the boat in a balanced state. Just as Augustus was beginning to enjoy the sensation of the boat skating along the surface of the water, the stroke caught a crab with the oar being trapped under water at the end of the stroke. After he had recovered his oar, they slowly took off up the river to the Iffley locks, rowing through the narrow curved part of the river affectionately referred to as the gut as the sun started to rise over the water meadows.

By the end of the outing the whole crew, Augustus included, were convinced that the only thing now between them and racing glory was the intervening days. Even the wet and exhausting process of lugging the boat out of the water didn't noticeably dent their spirits. Augustus hadn't felt this good for years and happily lagged behind pushing his bike as the animated and babbling group headed back up Dodgson's Walk in Christchurch Meadows. Just as they reached the road, Patrick Eccles trotted back towards him.

'We're all heading for breakfast in hall, sir, would you like to join us?'

'Thanks, I'd be delighted, but I might need a bath first.'

'Not at all, we'll stink together... Not that I mean you stink, sir, well... '

Augustus smiled as he gallantly saved his student from himself.

'Patrick, I'm sure I stink more than the lot of you put together, but I'm starving so hygiene can wait.'

*

After breakfast Augustus retired to his rooms and a bath that was urgently needed not for hygiene but to relax his aching muscles, which had started seizing up when he raised himself from the benches in hall after breakfast. He was relaxing in the bath with a cup of Lapsang Souchong tea when the door was rattled on its hinges by an insistent knock that could only be Mr Potts.

'Potts, is that you?'

'Sorry to bother you, sir, it's Professor Plantagenet. 'E's 'ad one of his turns again.' Potts shouted through the closed door.

Potts was still waiting at the door when Augustus yanked it open, dressed but still steaming from the bath as he hit the cold air on the staircase.

'Gerard found 'im down in the cellars sir. 'Ad bit of a session. Testin' lots of bottles, it seems.'

'Is he all right?'

'Well I can't imagine 'e could be any worse, to tell the truth.'

The pair launched themselves down the stairs of the wine cellars, Augustus barely needing to be told where he'd find Arthur. As they approached the old wooden chair with the crumpled form of Professor Plantagenet, Augustus could tell even in the gloom that this was no simple alcoholic stupor. Arthur's grey form was surrounded by a graveyard of bottles. Augustus knelt down and felt for a pulse.

Chapter II

Augustus slowly walked around the fountain of Triton that stood in the front courtyard of the Radcliffe Infirmary and was glazed with the first frost of winter. Modelled on Gian Lorenzo Bernini's statue of Triton that stood in Rome's Piazza Barberini, Oxford's version was at the cold epicentre of the city, and during winter the fountain could be frozen for weeks on end. He paused for reflection, thinking of the last time he was in the real Piazza Barberini. It had been a summer evening with Arthur on their tour of the ancient sites of Rome. He remembered a meal they had taken in a small trattoria near the Piazza, a fine Barolo with a simple but sublime pasta puttanesca, but it seemed to be a memory from a different lifetime. Now even five days seemed a long time ago. It had only been that long since Potts had hammered on his door with the news of Arthur. It was natural enough for Mr Potts to have come to find Augustus on that fateful morning. Augustus was, after all, the medical tutor, but it was a long time since he had been at what might be called the 'coal face'.

Augustus had never quite come to grips with hospitals and the three years he'd spent as a medical student on the wards had not been the high point of his life. His obvious discomfiture around sick people had led to the advice of a career in pathology or perhaps radiology from his medical mentors. Though neither involved much contact with sick people, they would still have involved Augustus spending most of his working and hence waking hours in a hospital. When the option of the alternative life in research and working as a college tutor had arisen he had leapt at the chance. As he entered the entrance of the hospital for the first time in over ten years, the air trickled up his nostrils and within seconds the unique aroma of the building had brought back a torrent of memories. He paused at the porter's desk to ask for directions to the office of Dr Reginald Pierce.

Compared to the more sumptuous accommodations on St John's Street where Dr Pierce catered for his private clientele, his office just off St Aloysius' ward was a small, cramped affair with an oak war-issue desk whose surface was invisible under a shanty town created from high-rise piles of papers and medical charts. Augustus knocked on the door, which in response rattled perilously on its hinges. As his hand reached the knob, the door was suddenly pulled from his grasp and he was standing face to face with the incongruously dapper Dr Pierce in a green Donegal tweed three-piece suit, polka dot bow tie and stethoscope wrapped over his shoulders like a fox wrap.

'Can I help you?'

'Augustus Bloom, we spoke on the phone.' Augustus' hand was still suspended in the air at the point at which the door handle had been pulled away and Dr Pierce now grasped it in a vice-like shake.

'Augustus, of course, delighted, delighted. Just going on rounds, tag along, we can have a chat en route.'

The pair headed down the corridor to the sound of Dr Pierce's shoes click-clacking on the polished floor. White-coated students appeared from corners and doorways to coalesce into a line that straggled behind.

'He's done remarkably well, all things considered. Have to say I didn't think he'd make it past the first couple of days,' said Dr Pierce.

'I didn't think he'd made it at all at the start, but he's a strong character.'

'Strong? I think stubborn is closer to the truth and he's a bloody fool to boot. As soon as he could talk he was refusing the treatment that saved his life and complaining about the food.'

Augustus smiled in sudden realisation that his friend was most certainly on the road to recovery. Pierce struck on down the corridor towards the bed of his most ungrateful patient. On entering the ward, the straggling parade led by Dr Pierce was joined by the ward sister. Pierce took his place at the foot of the bed and busied himself with the observation charts of his patient's blood pressure and fluid balance. The ward sister tutted volubly as she bustled aside the one eager medical student who was standing in her appointed position. The rest of the students jostled for position, most trying to be as far away as possible without looking as if they were trying to dodge questions, which of course all but the swottiest were. On this occasion the unusual element of this ritual dance was the patient who was certainly feistier than normal.

'So Professor, how are you feeling this morning?' said Dr Pierce, once he had satisfied himself that all was in order with the charts.

'Hungry and thirsty, as you bloody well know, Pierce.'

In the interests of their future careers the students all fought to suppress any reaction to Arthur Plantagenet's comments.

'Well, clearly our patient is improving. Now anyone like to offer a suggestion as to why this gentleman who was admitted with complete heart block and cardiac failure is on a fluid restriction and low salt diet?' Dr Pierce looked around amongst the gaggle of students for a willing volunteer or, better still, an unwilling victim. Just as he was about to take aim on the particularly bored-looking medical student trying to hide his six-foot frame behind the short but wide ward sister, Arthur took charge of proceedings.

'Augustus! Good God, man, have you changed sides and started roving the wards again?' Before Augustus could speak, Arthur was starting to move his legs around to get out of bed, but Dr Pierce was quick to intervene.

'Now Arthur, that's fine just as you are. Let's loosen that top and listen to this heart of yours.' Dr Pierce had Arthur's pyjama top opened in a second. With a firm hand on his shoulder and the cold metal bell of the stethoscope on his chest, Arthur was pinned back to the bed. When he tried to speak he was sharply shushed by his physician. As no-one had done that to Arthur for at least forty years, he was stunned into silence. The stethoscope was lifted only to be replaced by Dr Pierce's broad spread-out hand over the left side of Arthur's ribcage. A deferential silence fell on the proceedings until the verdict was passed.

'Seems to be back in sinus rhythm, a little blowing mitral regurgitation but the apex is still displaced due to his dilated cardiomyopathy and heart failure.' Dr Pierce's house office nodded sagely at these words. The nodding motion spread through the assembled gaggle of medical students like a congregation rising to stand in church.

'Is that good?' asked Arthur.

'Well it's better than it was. Sister, did you get an ECG done today?'

The heart recording was delivered up for inspection. Dr Pierce ran his finger between the various small squiggles on different parts of the page.

'Still in heart block but only first degree.'

'Nothing but the best for me, Pierce,' said Arthur proudly.

'Yes, well you came in almost dead in third-degree heart block, which isn't so impressive.' Dr Pierce turned to Augustus.

'Well done for getting him here so quickly Augustus. You almost certainly saved his life. Having done it once, you might be able to do it again. Do you think you can talk our dear professor into taking my advice?'

Augustus found himself smiling and shaking his head at the same time.

'Arthur isn't one to take advice, he prefers giving it. You may have noticed that.'

'Well, it all hinges on him losing weight. That will reduce the strain on his heart enormously. But he also needs a pacemaker as the next turn like this could be his last. Of course he has refused so I'll leave you the job of talking some sense into him. Come to my office later and let me know how you got on.'

With that, Dr Pierce turned on his heels and led his entourage off down the ward to the next patient, who he hoped would be closer to the grateful reticent type he preferred. Augustus looked at his friend and lifted his eyebrows to silently ask the question that had been asked of him.

'Well, what do you expect Augustus? All you medical types are the same, you don't know when to stop meddling.'

'That meddling saved your life, Arthur.'

'Yes, but having got a second chance I don't want to ruin it by being miserable until I die, which of course I will as sure as eggs.'

'Quality not quantity, Augustus. I'd rather live my life than merely endure it. Now if you really want to help me, start by bringing in some food. The stuff in here is slop and there's so little of it a hummingbird would starve. As for this no salt thing, God that really is purgatory.'

'Okay, I know we won't change your diet. But the pacemaker, that's a sensible option.'

'Not for me it isn't. Having some machine stuck inside my chest? No, this ticker only has so many ticks left and I'll enjoy each one as it comes, no more, no less. Anyway it was a wonderful experience.'

'What was wonderful?'

'Almost dying. Take the most extreme nightmare, but change the fear into peace and you are not even halfway there. I was floating above my body at the start. I saw all the commotion with Gerard, Potts and then you. What was all that pounding on my chest about?'

'Trying to get some blood pumping, that's probably why you remember it. It got some blood circulating to your brain.

You were in some semi-conscious state.'

'Don't be so damn… physiological, Augustus. I've been unconscious every night of my life. Drunk myself semi-unconscious on an occasion, or two. Even been knocked unconscious when I fell off a horse on that fox hunt with Theodore in Ireland. But this was completely different. After that I left the room and floated through a tunnel and ended up in this glowing white mist. Do you know who was there? Gordon Maxwell[4], as alive as you are and asking if I'd brought any books with me, would you believe. Then I was surrounded by images from my life: the whole shooting match flew past in seconds, but I could remember every day. Imagine being able to relive every moment, remember every book, every conversation, every mouthful. It was beyond comparison. I felt more alive being dead than I do now lying here. Then I was being pulled back through a crowd as they called to me. I can tell you now, Augustus, at that moment I'd have rather stayed where I was.'

'Aren't you glad to be alive?'

'Oh, yes. I realise now there are a few things I need to sort out and plan. But when the day comes again, I'll be happy to die.'

Augustus sat stunned, looking at the smiling visage of Arthur Plantagenet, who despite lying in a hospital bed with possibly only months to live, was clearly happier than Augustus, wanting for nothing more than a decent meal.

*

That night at dinner in the senior common room parlour, Augustus announced Arthur's remarkable recovery and tried to do credit to his description of dying, though he couldn't come close to matching Arthur's extraordinary enthusiasm for this usually unpopular activity. This naturally led to a long

---

4 Professor Gordon Maxwell, erstwhile Professor of Modern Languages at St Jerome's College, was a founding member of the shadow faculty of gastronomic science who died a fine Proustian death by choking on a Madeleine several years previously.

academic discussion on everything from religion to UFOs as the prodigious powers of random-thought association of Oxford dons surged into action. For his part, Augustus didn't know what to make of it. He hoped it might be true but he was, as Arthur had pointed out on more than one occasion, at times too physiological for his own good.

As the dinner drew to a close, the dons agreed to visit Arthur at regular intervals over the next few days. As the offer of a pacemaker had been rejected by his patient, Dr Pierce had no need to keep him in hospital for long and knew better than to try. Augustus suggested that they might all bring a book or two and something small, exotic and tasty to keep Arthur's spirits up. Arthur had already placed an order with Augustus for a copy of Noel Coward's *Blithe Spirit* and a rather obscure book on Victorian Spiritualism. Even with Arthur's remarkable recollections from his recent brush with the beyond, Augustus remained puzzled as to why he should be so interested in séances, considering he was still alive. The other requests were certainly more understandable – Turkish delight, a box of crystallised dates and a small hip flask of Cognac.

Chapter 12

As soon as Augustus heard that Arthur Plantagenet was back in his rooms, he went straight around, creeping up the ancient stairs to Arthur's door with the careful deference afforded to sick and sleeping children. He listened for a second to see if Arthur was alone, knowing full well that it would be quite impossible for Arthur to have an audience and not be talking at them. Hearing only a faint rustling noise, he knocked.

'Enter… '

'Good God, Arthur, what are you doing?'

Augustus entered the room to find his good friend peering into a packing case full of wood shavings. The atmosphere was thick with perfumed smoke emanating from a large walnut calabash pipe with a gleaming meerschaum bowl.

'Enjoying myself, dear boy.'

'But… but you should be resting, and when did you start smoking a pipe?'

'It arrived yesterday from London along with some supplies. A beauty, isn't it?'

Arthur had spent most of yesterday morning hiding in his room while he tried to teach himself the art of lighting and smoking a pipe. The two most important aspects of lighting a calabash pipe are long matches and patience – both of which Arthur lacked. The end result had been burnt fingers and several empty boxes of matches. Finally admitting defeat, he'd been forced to head to Mallards & Son, Purveyors of Fine Pipes and Tobacco in Turk Street, for guidance. He was discreetly chaperoned into the back room and Mr Mallard senior spent a very enjoyable hour teaching Arthur the art of pipe-lighting. The first lesson involved packing the pipe. Arthur, it turned out, had made the typical mistake of packing the pipe too tightly. To correct this he had been handed a glass of water and a straw. Once he had a sense of the slight pull required to drink through a straw, Mr Mallard allowed him to try packing his pipe with tobacco. Arthur then had to smoke his unlit pipe, loosening or packing the tobacco until the resistance to the flow of air was just right. Only then was he allowed on to the next step of lighting. After the first light, pulling the flame down with his breath, Arthur was instructed to lightly push down on the tobacco to make the pipe go out. Only then with the scorched tobacco properly prepared could the real lighting begin.

'Just about got the hang of it now. Fancy a puff yourself?' Arthur offered the pipe to his friend.

'Absolutely not. And why on earth are you smoking anyway?'

'All part of my grand plan, Augustus. As are these little beauties.'

Arthur then pulled out several small bottles of a dark-green liquid, which he passed to Augustus with great reverence.

'The original concentrated *elixir végétal* from Chartreuse. This is the exact recipe that Maréchal d'Estrées gave the monks in 1605. A secret elixir of life and even better than the normal green stuff I'd been trying. You were quoting Hippocrates at me before Christmas, let "medicine be thy food and food be thy medicine", well this is the drink version.'

'Sixty nine per cent alcohol! You think this will cure you before it kills you?'

'Of course it will cure me. I shall die a fragrantly flavoured death suffused with the best ingredients that nature and human ingenuity have gathered over the last two millennia.'

'How will it cure you if you end up dead?'

'Not cure in your meddling doctor way, Augustus, Cure with a capital C, a gastronomical cure. The pipe will help with the curing too. Like a fine smoked salmon I shall be perfumed with aromatic smoke. Do you like the smell? It's my own combination of A&C Peterson Caledonian mixture with a hint of Irish peat soaked in whiskey, then dried and crumbled. Fancy a puff? You're never too young to start smoking a pipe.'

'Or too sick, apparently,' said Augustus, falling into the lowest chair in the room to take advantage of the slightly clearer layer of air close to the ground. 'Arthur, you're not still talking about your crazy idea of donating your body to gastronomical science, surely?'

'Of course, I am even more determined now than I ever was. When I was over on the other side I realised this would be the perfect culmination of my life. I also realised that the spirit world exists, so I thought I'd like to invite Gordon Maxwell to our next dinner.'

Augustus looked at Arthur with concern and utter bemusement. This was surely all caused by the lack of blood to his brain while he was unconscious.

'Arthur, I know you came back, but Gordon died, so how can we invite him?'

'With a medium. Good God, there are times when you are slow on the uptake, my dear friend.'

Augustus sat back for a few moments watching Arthur rifle through his treasure chest of new supplies. He hardly recognised him as the same man that he had found half-dead barely a week ago. There is a lot to be said for the curative powers of enthusiasm.

Despite his delight at having Arthur Plantagenet back within the college walls, Augustus was more than glad to get back to the fresh air when he finally took his leave. As not even thoughts of cannibalism could put Augustus off his lunch, he headed to the senior common room parlour. Charles Pinker, as always the first to get to lunch, was already seated at the table with a glass of sherry in hand.

'Good day, Charles,' said Augustus, taking a seat beside the chaplain. 'You will be glad to know our patient is alive, well and still barking mad. His new-found interest in spiritualism shows no signs of waning, unfortunately.'

Augustus was spared what he sensed from the chaplain's unimpressed visage was a sermon in the making by the arrival of George Le Strang and Theodore Flanagan. Within a few minutes they had all been provided with bowls of the very presentable lobster bisque and after the usual climate-related pleasantries, the conversation inevitably turned back to Arthur Plantagenet.

'He's made a remarkable recovery. From the time I visited him in hospital to today when I saw him bustling across the quad, you wouldn't think he was the same man,' said Theodore.

'Well there have been moments when I thought he wasn't quite the same man,' rejoined Augustus. 'He seems even more determined to donate his body to gastronomic science and now he's into spiritualism as well. He just told me he wanted to bring along a medium so he could invite Gordon Maxwell back to the next dinner.'

'He can't be serious?' said Charles.

'Oh, he certainly is,' replied Augustus. 'He has piles of books on mysticism and all that hocus-pocus in his room.'

'No, I mean the bit about us having to eat him,' said Charles, now quite flustered.

'He is still convinced that is a marvellous idea, though I've no idea how he expects us to go along with his grand experiment if, God forbid, he does suddenly die on us,' said Augustus.

'You can lead a horse to the dining table but can't make a decent man eat it,' said Hamish, thoroughly pleased with his scrambled egg of a metaphor.

George Le Strang gave an enigmatic smile at this comment and seemed quite untroubled by talk of Arthur's grand experiment.

'I wouldn't worry about Arthur. If we just wait a week he will have another great plan to distract him.'

George did have a point. Arthur was a man renowned for intense but short-lived bursts of fancy. Charles and Theodore were only too glad to accept George's assessment of the situation. Augustus was less convinced of the fickleness of Arthur Plantagenet who on this occasion, seemed to possess a preternatural determination to follow through with his bizarre plan.

Chapter 13

The next morning, Augustus once again climbed the stairs towards Arthur Plantagenet's rooms. The smell of pipe smoke had been replaced by an odour that changed with each step from a puzzling, hard-to-pin-down impression to a full-out assault on the olfactory nerves. Acrid, fishy and fetid would describe the overall smell but words couldn't capture the brutal intensity that met Augustus as Arthur opened his door.

'Holy God, Arthur. What are you doing?'

'A bit of Roman cooking.'

'So what's that bloody awful smell?'

'Garum. Roman fish sauce, it is sometimes called liquamen. Almost every recipe in Apicius' *De Re Coquinaria* needs it. I've been trying out different ways of making it.'

'Was Apicius any good as a cook? This garum smells disgusting.'

'Marcus Gavius Apicius was a giant of ancient cuisine. Almost everything we know about Roman cooking we've learnt from this one man.'

'I'll take your word for it. What exactly is in this sauce, Arthur?'

'The best garum was supposed to be made with the livers of red mullet, but most of it was made from fermenting mackerel intestines with salt and a few herbs. I've just opened this jar of mackerel intestines that I sealed up in the summer and forgot about. It's perfect. Fancy a taste?'

'Do I have to eat this?'

'Well I don't think they ate it on its own. It was really a flavouring and I assume cooking mellows the taste a bit. You'll find out at the faculty dinner. I'm making some for that Roman food chap you've invited from Magdalen. I've got another little gem here which is a bit pongy as well.'

Augustus almost choked as the utterly different but equally awful smell was presented to his nostrils from a small jar that Arthur was thrusting into his face.

'Nearest thing left to the herb Silphium apparently. The Romans loved the herb so much that they ate it into extinction as it only grew in one small area around the ancient city of Cyrene in North Africa. They literally ate the stuff faster than it could grow.'

'This will have to improve a lot with cooking if you want me to eat any of your Roman recipes. What's this stuff called?'

'*Asafoetida* is the proper name, but the French have a more evocative name: *merde du diable*.'

'Devil's shit, well that about sums it up.'

'Still, very popular in India. It's meant to have great medical properties, excellent for flatulence apparently.'

'Probably just masks the smell. Anyway, talking of medical, I want to talk to you about your medical issues. I've been speaking with a cardiologist at the Radcliffe Hospital. He was explaining about these new pacemakers that Dr Pierce has recommended. You really should think about it.'

'Augustus, I know you mean well but believe me I have no intention of letting you or your friends meddle with my innards. In sympathy with Peru I'd rather eat a guinea pig than become one. Did you know they've always been just food over there? The painting of the Last Supper in the cathedral in Cusco even has Christ and the apostles tucking into plates of guinea pig. It's only us sentimental fools that treat them as pets.'

'Arthur, don't change the subject. I'm trying to be serious.

You'd rather die than receive help?'

'When you die, Augustus, and I dearly hope that it is many years away, would you wish it to be swift, peaceful and painless?'

'I suppose we'd all like that.'

'So you see I'm right to do it my way. The day my heart forgets to beat is the day I'm meant to die. A death that will be as quick and painless as fainting.'

'But rather more serious.'

'True, but we shall all be dead for a very long time. A fact that many people seem to forget while they are alive.'

When Augustus finally resurfaced into daylight he filled his lungs with the best tasting air he had ever inhaled. He had never really thought about tasting air before, but his senses seemed to have been heightened by Arthur's Roman experiments. Perhaps these ancient types were onto something after all.

*

'Potts, exactly the man I've been looking for.'

'Morning, sir. You're looking well today if you don't mind me saying.'

'Feeling very well too, Potts. Now I never got around to thanking you properly for your swift actions last term which probably saved my life, so here is a little something.'

Arthur thrust the bottle of whiskey into his hands despite Potts' protestations.

'Really, sir, I couldn't accept this. Really I couldn't.'

'Nonsense man, take it. Now, this ticker of mine isn't up to much and next time it might well be too late, so I've been making a few plans.'

Arthur thrust the letters into Potts' free hand.

'They are all addressed but they are to be delivered by hand on the day I die. Is that understood?'

'I think you'll live to an 'undred the ways you're looking now, sir.'

'Well if I do, don't forget to deliver those letters as you

may be a bit forgetful yourself by then.'

Arthur winked at Potts and headed off on his next mission.

*

Arthur Plantagenet was in truly fine form when a few hours later he strode out of the small courtyard of the Turf Tavern after going back to sample his favoured lunch as an undergraduate many years ago: pickled onions and a pint of bitter. He headed down Broad Street, gathering his thoughts for the forthcoming meeting. He'd awoken from a bizarrely vivid dream a few days earlier and since then, a plan had been growing and crystallising in his mind. He was now ready to convey this to the professional gentleman whose job it was to look after the details of such an undertaking.

He passed the door of the King Edward Hotel on the promise to himself of afternoon tea if all went well, and entered into the peaceful elegance of St John's Street. With fine houses and the brass plaques of the professional classes, it was a street for ambling along after escaping the busier, more commercial side of Oxford. As you approach the square at the end you would often hear birdsong during the middle of the day, an excellent antidote to the noise and fumes of St Giles that ran parallel to it. Arthur paused at the door of his physician, Dr Reginald Pierce. He entertained the idea of popping in to let Pierce know how well he was doing in putting the good doctor's advice into practice, but he had more pressing matters to attend to.

A few doors down he stopped at an almost identical door before crossing the threshold of Cragsworth, Cawl and Barringer, solicitors at law. He was ushered into the waiting room, William Morris wallpaper on this occasion but still adorned with *Vanity Fair* prints of great legal figures from the past. For possibly the first time in his life he was early, so he passed the time reading a translation of Petronius' *Satyricon* that he had been carrying around with him for the past few days. On the stroke of half-past two another door opened.

'Professor Plantagenet?'

'Indeed, Mr Barringer, I presume.'

'Exactly, now do come in.'

'Thank you, Mr Barringer. I must say I never cease to be amazed at why professional men are so attached to these accursed *Vanity Fair* prints. My doctor's waiting room is full of them too.'

'Much the same as schools of fish I suppose; safety in numbers coupled with a well-honed lack of imagination.'

Arthur was already starting to like Mr Barringer.

'Now, Professor. What can I do for you?'

'I'd like to make a will.'

'Excellent, excellent. Always good to be prepared. Now I need a little information from you and I'll be able to draw up a standard enough will in no time.'

'I've just a couple of questions first, if you don't mind.'

'Of course, fire away.'

'I presume what we discuss here will remain totally confidential until I die and indeed after?'

'Of course, Professor, our job relies on discretion and total confidentiality is guaranteed.'

'Very good, very good. Now my next question is about my executors. Are they legally bound to do what I ask? I mean do they have to deal with my body in exactly the way I ask?'

'It is a very serious undertaking being an executor and they are duty bound to follow your instructions to the letter.'

'Marvellous. Now I've got some notes here about what I want to happen on my death. I hope that is all right.'

'Oh, more than just all right, that is ideal. If only all our clients could be so organised and decisive.' Mr Barringer smiled across the table.

Arthur, on this topic at least, was certainly decisive. He listed the complicated arrangements he required after his death as fast as Mr Barringer could note them down. He then formally appointed all his fellow members of the shadow faculty of gastronomic science as joint executors before taking leave of Mr Barringer with a great load lifted from his mind. Mr Barringer, for his part, was left at his desk in a state of inner turmoil. Much to Mr Barringer's dismay and indeed horror, this was by no means a standard will.

Chapter 14

The final tasting meeting of the term had been scheduled for eleven o'clock that morning. With all the time wasted in hospital and the shadow faculty of gastronomic science dinner in less than a week, Arthur had no time to lose. So just after nine o'clock, he gathered up his letters, calabash pipe and a small shopping bag and made for the lodge. This bag contained a bottle of whiskey along with some of his recent research on topics as diverse as spiritualism and an obscure group of Buddhist monks from Japan. Arthur paused as he reached the road outside college to light his pipe, an action he was finally mastering.

Arthur's pipe and the associated cloud of pollution that accompanied it was becoming a familiar site around college and Oxford. He was even thrown out of the Bodleian library the previous week for lighting up in the middle of the manuscript room. While the popular image of pipe smokers was in a rocking chair by a stove, Arthur had found that smoking while walking briskly around town was a particularly pleasurable combination. So he was looking forward to this morning's tasks: a quick visit to his solicitor's office to sign his new will, a purely social visit to his physician Dr Pierce, and then onto the more enjoyable part of the morning, getting supplies for the tasting meeting. After a joyously polluting amble along Cornmarket and Magdalen Street, Arthur made a slight detour to have a rest on his favourite seat in the Ashmolean Museum. He sat on the green velvet-covered banquette surrounded by the armless statues of antiquity until one of the guards felt obliged to ask him to extinguish his pipe or leave. It was a simple decision.

*

After consulting *Country Life* for half an hour in Dr Pierce's waiting room he was finally called in, by which time the waiting room was thoroughly fumigated.

'Arthur, come in. Good God, what are you doing with that pipe?'

Arthur looked at his calabash with mock surprise.

'I do believe I am smoking it, Dr Pierce.'

'Take a seat, Arthur, and let's see where things stand,' replied Dr Pierce with a sigh of resignation.

Dr Pierce let Arthur sit before taking his right wrist and feeling the pulse for what seemed to Arthur to be an unreasonable length of time, even for a doctor.

'So far so good, Arthur. Any palpitations or fainting attacks since we let you go?'

'Not at all, been fit as a fiddle,' Arthur lied with perfect grace and confidence.

'Well if you start getting anything like that I want to know about it. Now, I want to talk to you seriously about the option of a pacemaker. I know you rejected the offer when you were in hospital... '

'Reginald, I appreciate the fact that you have my best interests at heart, excuse the pun, as does dear Augustus who has already tried in vain to convince me. I really have no desire to let anyone meddle with my heart with some electrical contraption. I'm rather enjoying my own treatment regime,' said Arthur, waving his pipe.

'Arthur, taking up a pipe is not a treatment. It is nothing short of folly for a man in your condition.'

'Dear boy, you have proposed a treatment which I have graciously declined. Without this treatment you say I have no chance of surviving more than a few months at best and weeks at worst. If I have no chance of surviving, how much less a chance could I have than that? So enjoying myself with good food and a fine tobacco seems the only logical course of action – *quod erat demonstrandum, QED.*'

'*Dulce et decorum est pro gastria mori?*'

'I do believe the word *gastria* is Greek rather than Latin, so it should be *pro ventre mori*,' beamed Arthur in response. 'But good effort and you're quite right. I'd rather die for my stomach than my country.'

*

On the home stretch, Arthur crossed the threshold into Benjamin and Sons, the wine importers, to collect his order of a range of obscure European liqueurs. Then he moved to the covered market for pickled walnuts, some Stilton cheese and fig jam. The most challenging of all was a source of ripe pears, but here too the gods were smiling on him, as he came across South African pears in Gough's greengrocers that were perfect.

Laden with bags and troubled with only the occasional skipped beat from his ailing heart, Arthur made his way back to college and headed straight to the kitchen cellars, reluctantly tamping out his pipe as he went. The rest of the shadow faculty of gastronomic science had already gathered around the makeshift table.

'Arthur, just the man,' said Hamish McIntyre. 'We were trying to decide whether either of these German *eiswein*s are worthy of serving at a dinner.'

'Excellent, let's put them to the test,' Arthur said, and started handing out the contents of his bags, delegating the tasks of slicing the pears and extracting the Stilton from its porcelain jar. Within a few minutes all six members of the faculty had on their plates a small tower with a slice of pear as the foundation stone, then fig jam, Stilton and a pickled walnut.

*Eiswein*s are made from frozen, almost shrivelled grapes

that must be picked at sub-zero temperatures well after normal grapes are harvested. This results in an explosive concentration of flavour and sugar. Combining the wines with Arthur's *hors d'oeuvres* was a triumph, with the sole dissenter being George Le Strang who stuck to his Gallic roots, agreeing with the official line in France that whatever this drink was, it wasn't wine.

Once the remnants of the Stilton had been cleared up, Arthur started emptying out his small bottles of spirits onto the table.

'Now, Gentlemen, I need your help in deciding which of these liqueurs would be best for pickling me. I've been experimenting with Chartreuse but I thought I better check out some others too.'

Arthur emptied the contents of his bag, which represented half a millennium of distillery expertise from the different monastic traditions. He placed the bottles of Benedictine, Trappistine, Carmeline and La Senancole triumphantly on the table.

'Literally or metaphorically, Arthur?' asked Theodore as he lifted the unfamiliar bottle of La Senancole for inspection.

'Oh, literally. You see I've discovered that humans can indeed be marinated while alive. I've been reading about these Shingon monks from the Yamagata region of Japan who can mummify themselves while alive by drinking special teas that dry out their bodies. By the time they die from hunger or boredom – I haven't worked out which – they are mummified.'

'I do hope you're not going to mummify yourself, Arthur,' said Charles nervously.

'The thought crossed my mind. That way I could ask in my will to keep attending the dinners rather like that Bentham fellow in University College London. But I think my original plan is better – to leave you, my fellow gastronomic explorers, to answer the question that no-one dare ask. Everyone seems to like asking big questions these days, such as why do I exist? And what is the purpose of life? But why does no-one ask, what do I taste like? So, as I announced at our last meeting, I'm donating my body to gastronomy and I want to make sure that I give myself the best possible flavour with these liqueurs.'

Augustus sat quietly shaking his head. He had already been through the stage of disbelief in Arthur's grand plan and realised its apparent inevitability. So he alone could appreciate the impact of these words on his colleagues.

'Arthur, I'm sure you'll be the finest-tasting Englishman who has ever died, but I believe a Frenchman would taste better.' George good-naturedly lifted a glass of Benedictine in toast.

'Thank you, George. A very kind offer,' replied Arthur with a smile curling on the corner of his lips as George look baffled.

'I presume you too mean to donate your body when you die so we can make a taste comparison. Excellent idea. I know you're only half-French, but it should give us some idea.'

It took Charles and Theodore several minutes to calm George down. He was verging on the apoplectic as much at the slur of being only half-French as at the thought of being eaten by the remaining Englishmen and an Irishman who would survive the double demise of Arthur and George. Hamish sat with tears of laughter rolling down his cheeks, leaving Augustus to fully appreciate the moment. Augustus then tried to deflect Arthur with an alternative plan.

'Arthur, I think I have a gastronomic challenge that will afford benefit to a greater range of gastronomes. After all, as wonderful or awful as you do or don't taste in the flesh, I don't think cannibalism is likely to prove popular.'

'Anthropophagy, please, cannibalism is such an ugly and etymologically unsound word,' replied Arthur, intrigued as to where his friend was going with his new challenge.

'Well, I don't think anthropophagy will be popular either – far too much of a mouthful. Now what commonly used ingredient tastes divine but causes some people concerns about the animal husbandry involved in its creation?'

'Veal?' offered Hamish, only to be met with a faint shake of the head from Augustus who had inadvertently slipped into tutorial teaching mode.

'*Foie gras*!' exclaimed the chaplain.

'Exactly, now Arthur, I suggest that you offer to make recompense to the geese that you may meet in the next world by being force-fed in the manner of a goose being raised to make *foie gras*.'

'How would appeasing geese help the cause of gastronomy?' said Arthur.

'It is certainly a matter of valid gastronomic enquiry. It would allow us to see what happens to the human liver under the same circumstances and how long a human can survive this diet. If the suffering proves too severe then the experiment can be stopped early as the answer will have been already found.'

The room fell silent as they waited for Arthur's verdict. Arthur's many chins stayed elevated for an agonisingly long time in the position that usually indicated an impending announcement. He finally gave his response.

'Augustus, my dear chap, I can't believe that you are telling me to commit suicide by overeating just to make yourself feel better about eating *foie gras*.'

Augustus took a deep breath to recover his poise and tried to use Arthur's own brand of logic against him, now more determined than ever to deflect Arthur from his stated plan.

'All right, Arthur, you seem more eager to answer your big gastronomic question than the rest of us. But to complete your grand experiment, you will inevitably have to die. As you will never know the answer, why bother?'

The murmurs of 'hear, hear' from around the table faded into expectant silence as Arthur pondered his reply.

'Elementary, my dear doctor, having been across the great divide and returned I know there is life beyond death. So with the aid of a medium I was rather hoping you could call me up after my death and tell me that I was right, that I tasted divine.'

'A medium?' asked Charles.

'Those clowns wouldn't know a spirit if it came up and kicked them in the goolies,' offered Hamish in his inimitable style.

'Do you really believe in those charlatans?' said Charles.

'No, I believe in my own experience,' continued Arthur, unperturbed by the hostility around the table. 'There are certainly clowns pretending to be mediums, but the spirit realm exists – of that I'm certain. If I can reach it and come back I don't see why a proper medium couldn't communicate with spirits. In fact I've just invited one to next term's dinner, a certain Thaddeus Rhymer who is greatly respected within the spiritual community. If I can see how mediums do it from this side, then when I'm on the other side I can tune in much better. I thought we could practise by calling up Gordon Maxwell.'

'An excellent plan, Arthur, I'm sure,' said Theodore. 'But of course you have to convince us to go along with your plan.'

'Certainly, Theodore, but I trust you all to do the right thing when the day of my departure arrives. Now George, why don't we try some more of that *foie gras* I see over there?'

With those words, the normal convivial atmosphere of these meetings was restored, with most members of the faculty taking Arthur's words to mean that by humouring him in life they might avoid having to eat him in death. Replacing the blue cheese on Arthur's pears with the *foie gras* produced an *hors d'oeuvres* which all agreed reached new heights. To do this combination true justice, George disappeared into the cellars on a mission to recover a bottle of Muscat de Rivesaltes and was rewarded by being victorious in a vote on Franco-German supremacy of sweet wines. All seemed well in the world of gastronomy.

Chapter 15

Gerard, the senior parlour scout, passed around the room lighting candles and laying out the menus. This term's faculty dinner was being held within the Master's lodgings. Arthur Plantagenet had been so impressed by the Master's expertise in the field of exotic fruits at their last meeting that he'd invited him as his guest. On accepting the invitation, Lord Faulkner had proposed the Harlaxton room as it was both a suitable atmosphere and far enough from prying eyes to afford complete privacy. The vice-chancellor had yet to follow through on his more outrageous threats to have the shadow faculty disbanded, but it seemed prudent to follow the Master's advice and not have the dinner in one of the more public areas of the College.

The dark panelled room was glowing with light from candles and the wood fire that burned in the vast stone fireplace. The fine Irish linen tablecloth was adorned with the best of the College's extensive silver collection. By electric light, polished silver could look a little brash, but by candlelight, the assorted collection was resplendent. Alchemists had for many years tried to transmute metals into gold and here, unnoticed by Gerard, the process was achieved: silver into burnished gold with the simple addition of burning beeswax. Gerard afforded himself a surreptitious glance at the menu. Although he didn't know the contents of every dish, he was reassured that there were no obviously poisonous dishes being served tonight. Rattlesnake fricassee had sounded rather hazardous a couple of years back, and, while not a culinary success, at least the members of the faculty and their guests were alive to discuss its failings after the event. There was a firm consensus at that dinner that snakes were punished by God for their meddling in the Garden of Eden not only by being forced to crawl on their bellies but also by having the worst-tasting flesh of all his creatures. Having said that, Gerard hadn't suspected any undue risks at last term's dinner, but the memory of poor Mr Tokoro's last laboured gasps still haunted him.

Once the table was dressed he looked to his next task, the preparation of the aperitif. Tonight's opening beverage was to be an absinthe martini. Successful preparation of twelve martinis single-handed was a significant challenge, but Gerard had rehearsed the sequence in his head and, as soon as he heard the first voices in the hall outside, he commenced. All twelve pre-chilled glasses were already lined up in a row and the eleven cocktail olives and single cocktail onion skewered on Georgian silver hatpins lay on a plate at the side. He started by pouring a generous measure of absinthe into the first two martini glasses and, with one in each hand, swirled them just fast enough to make the liquid rise to the lip of the glass without a drop being spilt. He then poured out the remaining spirit into the next two glasses and repeated this fine display of wrist control until all twelve glasses had a fine coating of absinthe on the inside surface.

He then drained the last remnants of water from the two mixing jugs of ice before adding first the French vermouth, Noilly Prat, and then the Booth's House of Lords gin in the requested 1:8 ratio. This was the best compromise the faculty could agree on between the dryness of Winston Churchill's martini, who famously preferred to bow in the direction of France before supping his glass of pure chilled gin, and Arthur Plantagenet's very un-dry martini. It was Arthur's grand notion that the gin to vermouth mix should mirror the dimensions of the Parthenon in Athens, approximately 1.618:1. This apparently insignificant number will be recognised by mathematicians and ancient Greek scholars as the golden ratio or golden mean. Although possibly a fine proportion for a temple, the rest of the faculty agreed it was an appalling way to make a martini.

Gerard stirred both jugs with long twirled silver spoons, just long enough for the ice to impart its cold but not long enough for any significant amount of water to dilute the mixture. He then poured the mixture through the ice strainer into each glass. The last hatpin plinked into the glass just as the door opened, disgorging the shadow faculty of gastronomic science and their guests. Each was duly issued with a perfectly prepared martini, the dew just starting to settle on the outside of the glass. Eleven glasses carried the classical choice of an olive; just one bore an onion. The onion-adorned glass, which for purists technically transformed the drink from a martini into a Gibson, was reserved for Augustus Bloom whose job it was to raise the first toast.

'To gastronomy and Jean Anthelme Brillat-Savarin.'

Once the final murmurs of the toast had settled, Augustus made his way across the room to rejoin his guest for the evening, Dr Peter Armstrong from Magdalen College, a noted classical scholar and expert on the food of ancient Rome. Dr Armstrong was at that moment being asked to adjudicate in an academic argument between Arthur Plantagenet and the Master on the closest living relative to the Roman herb Silphium. Augustus was intercepted en route by George Le Strang.

'Excellent martini, lovely extra dimension from the absinthe, don't you think?'

'Fine taste,' said Augustus with a tone of doubt. 'But I think I prefer my martinis clear.'

Seeing Hamish McIntyre close by he sought some moral support, which was always a wise move before disagreeing with George Le Strang.

'What do you reckon on George's new martini, Hamish?'

'Grand, quite exquisite in fact.'

The shocked look of betrayal on Augustus' face was cured by Hamish's trademark laddish wink. This uncharacteristically diplomatic and completely dishonest reply achieved its goal and, without further ado, sent a contented George Le Strang off around the room in search of more accolades. Le Strang was naturally convinced of this drink's superiority over the standard martini not only on taste but also on the grounds of numerical supremacy. Any drink where there are more ingredients from France than England must be a good thing to his mind.

'Lied through my teeth,' said Hamish once George had moved on out of earshot. 'I have to say a sad waste of a good olive. I wouldn't drown a witch in this stuff.'

'Could be worse, Hamish. Remember his Provençal lavender vodka martini from a few years back? How about this for a new law of martini-making: a martini mixed from three ingredients is like a woman with three eyes.'

Augustus smiled, enjoying his own wit and, in celebration of this new aphorism, forgetfully sipped the travesty he was holding. The involuntary shudder that followed proved the wisdom of his words. It was admittedly a somewhat derivative of Brillat-Savarin's sentiments on one-eyed women and cheese, but Augustus was sure the great man would have enjoyed the extension of this theme even if he had died the best part of a century before the uncertain and mysterious birth of the martini[5].

---

5   It is remarkable that even though at the time of this dinner there must have been innumerable people alive who had lived through the birth of the martini somewhere around the turn of the twentieth century, the exact origins of this quintessential cocktail have been lost. While etymologists favour a derivation from the Martinez, a mixture of sweet vermouth with a smaller amount of gin and a dash of bitters, they are poles apart in cocktail terms. No-one who has tasted both could countenance such a link. Although the obvious derivation from the Martini Company in Italy has been discounted as in America, the undisputed birthplace of the martini, this company was a minor player in the vermouth world and French vermouths are favoured by martini aficionados. A bartender from the Knickerbocker Hotel in New York, a certain Signor di Arma di Taggia has been credited with inventing the modern martini in 1912. As martinis are referred to in print before that date, this theory sadly also falls by the wayside.

'Not bad, Augustus,' agreed Hamish. 'But let me introduce Callum Morton from Monash University in Australia and a master of all the weird and toxic creatures that were dispatched to the colonies by Noah after the flood.'

'Pleased to meet you,' said Dr Morton, lightly crushing the bones in Augustus' hand. 'Must say, hard to beat the old line that martinis are like a woman's breasts: one is too few and three's too many.'

Callum Morton laughed rather too loudly for Augustus' taste and before he could think of a suitable reply a small bell sounded for dinner. This was indeed fortunate as there is no way of bettering this pinnacle of alcoholic philosophy even when it is told with an Australian accent.

The fellows and their guests began the search for their assigned seats. Theodore Flanagan had carefully marked each place with a small card. One of the unwritten rules of the faculty was that at dinner each faculty member should have their guests on their left-hand side. On this occasion, Theodore had invited a young visiting physicist from Trinity College Dublin, Dermot Keogh, who had a particular fascination with the physics of food preparation. George Le Strang was more than usually puffed up at having secured the acceptance of the head chef from the George V Hotel in Paris, Monsieur René Lemprière. Charles Pinker had invited Gascoigne Percival, from Yale, fresh from the academic success of his recent publication on food symbolism in Jonathan Swift's writings. It was truly a fine assemblage of gastronomes, with each guest having a love and knowledge of gastronomical matters that at least equalled, if not exceeded, their other academic achievements. If the guest list alone boded well for the dinner ahead, then the menu cryptically promised even more.

Shadow Faculty of Gastronomic Science
Michaelmas Term 1969

Aperitif

Absinthe martini

Amuse-gueule
Clonakilty pudding and girolle mushrooms topped with shaved white truffle
Served with La Gitana Manzanilla

Hors d'oeuvres
Desert prawns from Central Australia
Prairie oysters from Montana, USA
Served with Chassagne-Montrachet 1962

Roman surprise
Served with Mulsum

Entrées
Truffled turkey
Served with Château Petrus

'Napoleon's Revenge': A culinary puzzle from Belgium and Denmark
Served with Chambertin-Clos de Bèze Grand Cru 1962

Dessert
Saffron and nitrogen ice cream
Served with Muscat de Beaumes de Venise

Fruit
Miracle fruit and sweet limes
Served with a mystery wine

Cheese
Baked Vacherin Mont d'Or

Port
1935 Ramos Pinto

Once they were all seated, Gerard slid around the table collecting the martini glasses. Only George Le Strang felt the need to drain the last drop; the others gladly handed over glasses that varied from almost full to at most half-drained. In return they were offered a small glass of highly chilled fino sherry, a Manzanilla. This was so pale as to look like a white wine and a far cry from the evil sweet sherries poured at most Oxford tables. One sip of this dry resinous nectar is enough to tip a soul from peckish to ravenous. And so as soon as grace was said, they all fell upon the *amuse-gueule* of black pudding, girolle mushrooms and shaved white truffle like starved men. Even Monsieur Lemprière was grunting contentedly, much to the relief of George and the particular amusement of Hamish. The white truffle was a late addition, but one that met with universal approval. It had been added as the plates left the kitchen so that there was just enough heat to release the aroma but not so much as to destroy the flavour. White truffles are, after all, rather delicate creatures.

With the completion of these morsels, Augustus asked the guests who had provided dishes for the first course to present their wares. Without a moment's hesitation Callum Morton, Hamish's antipodean guest, rose to his feet.

'Gentlemen, I am truly honoured to be here tonight. If the rest of the food is as good as that amused girly thing, or whatever you call it, then it's going to be a great night. I've brought along a little treat that I'm sure hasn't been seen here in Oxford before. In the outback of Australia it would be called bush tucker and, rather than tell you the whole story now, why not have a taste and see if you can guess what they are. I like these raw and wriggling, but I've had your chef bake them for you. They're not half bad cooked either.'

After a discreet round of applause from some and a more restrained nod from others, a plate was passed around the table as each guest tried to select the smallest one they could find on the plate. They looked a little like segmented sausages, a good three inches long and almost an inch across with a yellowy hue, but enticingly browned by the skilled hand of Monsieur Roger, St Jerome's chef.

'Don't be shy now,' said Callum, picking one up with his fingers and biting it in half.

Slowly, knives and forks were wielded into action and distrust change into confused interest and a mêlée of gustatory mutterings arose from around the table. By the time the discussion was quietening down, most of the guests and fellows had managed to consume at least half of this morsel, with the notable exception of Charles Pinker. The chaplain had divided the creature neatly into pieces, but failed to overcome his deeply held belief that not all of God's creatures were put here for human consumption, particularly not the ugly-looking ones.

'So, can any of your refined palates work this one out? I'll disqualify Hamish on professional grounds, of course,' said Callum.

For his part, Hamish was delighted. A zoologist he might be but he still wasn't sure what these creatures were, other than the fact he was fairly certain that no prawns or any near relatives would be living in the Australian outback. He had his suspicions but out of politeness had tucked in and been pleasantly surprised. A brave few souls volunteered suggestions.

'Prawns, definitely a prawn flavour.'

'A bit like chicken, but it looks like some odd part of a snake.'

'Eggs and peanuts in there somewhere.'

'Prawn omelette, in some kind of odd skin?'

'No other offers?' asked Callum while smiling in his anticipated victory. Turning to his host he continued, 'So, Hamish, what's the answer?'

Hamish was absolutely flummoxed as his brain was happily idling in neutral having been earlier excused from proceedings, so his subconscious blurted out its suspicions without much thought for the consequences.

'Oh, gosh well, er... it's some kind of big maggot by the look of it, but it tasted jolly good.'

'I'll give you that, Hamish,' said Callum with a friendly pat on the back that almost made Hamish choke on the piece of maggot still in his mouth. 'They're the larvae of the cossid moth, to be precise, but maggot is close enough. We call them witchetty grubs because we find them in the ground under witchetty shrubs.'

Reactions to this news were certainly varied. Curiously, Hamish was as shocked as anyone. Until the words left his mouth he hadn't really taken his own suspicions seriously. Charles Pinker produced a nervous laugh that unintentionally helped to ease the mood around the table. In Gallic unity both Le Strang and his guest Monsieur Lemprière had struck on the strategy of drowning the bug in their stomachs with wine. This might indeed have been the first time in culinary history that a witchetty grub has bathed in such a fine white Burgundy as the 1962 Chassagne-Montrachet. Augustus was the only one to take another taste, his culinary curiosity far outweighing any squeamishness. Entomophagy, the eating of insects, was after all common in so many cultures that Augustus felt confident that maggots were unlikely to be poisonous.

Next up was the man from Yale, Gascoigne Percival. A man of many words who, although American in heritage and birth, leaned spiritually back to England.

'Gentlemen, I am happy to announce that the next dish comes from a large four-legged mammalian herbivore, so you can all relax.'

There were grunts of relief all around. Charles Pinker, still excessively jolly after his lucky escape from the witchetty grub, even started banging the table with his spoon in a rare display of rowdiness.

'I'm not sure how they ended up with the curious name of prairie oysters,' continued Gascoigne, 'but in the spirit of academic enquiry I shall again see if you can guess exactly which part of the animal we shall be eating. They are, as you'll see, coated in flour and pan-fried with *beurre noir*. Gentlemen, another treat from the New World.'

He raised his glass for a toast and, looking around, saw Arthur Plantagenet winking at him.

The general verdict was that these 'oysters' were not as interesting a flavour as Callum's 'prawns' – really more of a texture than a flavour and certainly not a patch on the real thing. A first opinion on their origin was also arrived at after the first mouthful.

'Badly cooked sweetbreads,' offered Monsieur Lemprière. 'At le George Cinq we serve sweetbreads properly in a truffled *Périgueux* sauce or a tarragon *velouté*.'

'And quite superb they are, Monsieur Lemprière,' said George Le Strang in support of his guest. 'I had the pleasure of tasting them myself just last year. Quite superb.'

Arthur chose his moment well, casting his eye around the table before speaking to ensure he had the floor to himself.

'Bollocks!'

'Pardon?' replied an affronted Monsieur Lemprière.

'An old English idiom, Monsieur, for testicles, which is exactly what we are eating. Isn't that correct, Dr Percival?'

While Yale was a fine university, it was certainly no match for Oxford and Arthur felt it his duty to ensure that a Yale man couldn't claim a victory here on Oxford's home turf, even against a Frenchman. Callum was excused from such one-upmanship in Arthur's eyes on the grounds that all Australian universities were so young that they deserved the latitude afforded a troublesome but charming nephew.

'With your indulgence, Gascoigne,' continued Arthur, 'I heard a rather funny tale about such oysters.'

The somewhat crestfallen Yale man could only nod in acknowledgement and let Arthur take control of the conversation as he was going to anyway.

'It is a tale of a young American travelling in Spain who discovers a tasty snack at a bar in Barcelona. On returning the next day he was disappointed to find the dish absent from the bar counter. The barman explained that this dish was only available when there had been a bullfight the night before. He suggested he come back the following day. When he returned the dish was back on the counter, though each piece was much smaller. They also tasted much sweeter than the previous time. He complimented the barman and asked what the difference was.' Arthur paused for theatrical effect and then, in an atrocious Spanish accent, continued, '"Signor, it iz not always the bull that loses."'

Arthur barely got the words out before erupting in laughter himself, then standing up to take a bow.

When the plates of chewy and rather tasteless testicles were cleared, Augustus turned to his guest Peter Armstrong with words of reassurance.

'Don't worry, I think you're on safe ground with Arthur, just don't forget to thank him for the garum.'

With considerable trepidation, Dr Armstrong rose to his feet.

'Gentlemen, as Juvenal said of the Romans: *Gustus elementa per omnia quaerunt*[6]. In the spirit of these words, I bring you a delicacy from the pages of the greatest food writer from the ancient world. While my fellow guests have tried to trick you and sadly failed, despite valiant efforts, I have placed my faith in the unique approach to food taken by Ancient Rome with their broad view of the edible. Marcus Gavius Apicius has provided the recipe and your esteemed Professor Plantagenet has recreated one of the key ingredients, a rather strong fish sauce which goes by the name of garum or liquamen.'

Arthur sat back in his chair, glowing with pride and anticipation.

The dish arrived on a large platter accompanied by an extraordinary aroma emanating principally from the sauce. It was clearly offal of some kind, on that all could agree. As to the exact nature of the meat, no-one even came close. That

---

6   They ransack all the elements for new flavours.

was not a reflection on their gustatory abilities as the sauce was so intense that texture apart they could indeed have been eating anything. Most of the diners managed a few mouthfuls when Arthur came to the rescue.

'Hold on, we're missing the wine,' shouted Arthur. 'Gerard, bring on the Mulsum.'

Gerard, looking thoroughly flustered, rushed around the table providing silver goblets and pouring the golden Roman-style honeyed wine. Arthur had chosen a Retsina as the base wine on the grounds that it was an ancient Mediterranean style of wine and because he couldn't bring himself to ruin a decent wine with the amount of honey required in the mix. Under normal circumstance it would have been barely tolerated, a cloying resinous brew of overpowering sweetness, but in the face of the intensely flavoured and salted Roman dish they were eating it was warmly welcomed. By masking the most disagreeable flavours of the sauce almost completely, it made the dish distinctly edible. Indeed Charles Pinker, assured by Dr Armstrong that the source of the meat was a common farm animal, even managed to clear his plate.

'Any last guesses?' said Augustus, casting his eyes around the table. 'Well, then I declare that Dr Armstrong has indeed baffled our taste buds. So Peter, would you care to tell what we have just sampled?'

'Thank you, Augustus. This was merely an unusual part of a pig with a decidedly unusual sauce made up of pepper, celery seed, mint, asafoetida root, honey, vinegar and garum.' He paused for dramatic effect, hoping someone would ask the obvious question as to the precise part of the pig involved. Charles duly obliged.

'Fascinating, really quite unusual. So which part of the pig, dare I ask?'

'Sow's womb: a particular Roman delicacy,' said Peter Armstrong proudly.

Charles Pinker nodded in acknowledgement and then drained the remnants of his Mulsum in the hope of eradicating the last lingering taste in his mouth. He mentally added the uterus to his ever-lengthening list of internal organs not worthy of human consumption.

Once plates and palates had been cleared by the scouts and the remains of the white Burgundy respectively, Gerard emerged through the double doors carrying a large platter covered with a huge silver cloche. The room was instantly filled with one of finest aromas on this earth. This was the fabled truffled turkey, a fowl elevated to epicurean heights by an extraordinary excess of black truffle. Indeed the very dish that had launched the shadow faculty on its gastronomic mission. The black truffle, *Tuber melanosporum,* being more robust than its more finely flavoured white cousin *Tuber magnatum*, has the advantage that it can be cooked without losing its flavour and so the whole bird can be imbued by the taste of this culinary gem. This particular bird had been lovingly prepared with its breasts filled with brandy-soaked sliced truffles and stuffed internally with more truffles, *foie gras*, veal and pork fat. The flavours had permeated the meat for two full days before cooking completed the transformation.

The eyes and noses of all but one of the diners had followed Gerard as he brought the plate to the table. Monsieur Lemprière's eyes had just spotted an empty bottle standing beside a full wine decanter that he fervently hoped held the contents of that bottle – Château Petrus 1947: a legendary vintage of an extraordinary wine. A wine crafted from the most pampered vines in France, with grapes picked only in the afternoon so that no remnants of dew could dilute the essence of each grape. The enveloping aroma of truffles and thought of this wine were enough to melt Lemprière's heart. He would surely have fallen in love with the first woman to enter the room at that moment, but finding himself in only male company the magic expressed itself as a wave of uncharacteristic forgiveness for the damage Arthur Plantagenet's garum had done to his taste buds and, indeed, he felt a sudden fondness for the whole nation of England. And this was before a single morsel or drop had passed his lips.

The '47 Petrus lived up to its immense reputation, from inspection of its regal purplish hue to a heavenly aroma and a taste constructed with the precision and complexity of a baroque cathedral. Waves of different tastes and aromas crashed over the palates of the fortunate diners and blended with the divine turkey flavours, leaving several of them in a state of near rapture. All pretence of manners and etiquette were abandoned as opinions were shared through full mouths, with aromatic dribbles of fat escaping and being left to fall unhindered by napkins. The fellows of the faculty had sampled this dish several times before, but on each occasion their memory had failed to retain the full intensity of the flavours. For the guests, with the exception of Monsieur Lemprière, this was a new experience and one that they would take to their graves.

The diners were left only with their memories of this exquisite combination as the table was cleared yet again, making way for George Le Strang to raise a toast to the magnificent truffle and its greatest admirer, Brillat-Savarin. He then went on to introduce his guest and the dish they had concocted together.

'I am honoured to present the *chef célèbre,* Monsieur René Lemprière from *le George Cinq en Paris*, *un chevalier* of the kitchen and creator of heaven on porcelain.' George changed effortlessly if somewhat pretentiously between an English and French accent. 'Together we have created a new dish, which is to be christened here tonight: "Napoleon's Revenge". If the events of June 1815 had been different and Napoleon had been victorious at Waterloo, then this would have been a fitting meal for a conquering emperor. It is served with Chambertin-Clos de Bèze, Napoleon's favourite Burgundy.'

The dish arrived on a long platter and was placed in front of Monsieur Lemprière for carving. It looked and smelt to the world and the assembled guests as a fine beef Wellington, a long-time stalwart of St Jerome's dinners. It did have a more elaborate decoration than usual with small *fleur-de-lis* all over the pastry, but that was not enough to make such a dish uniquely Napoleonic. George had kept the details of this dish secret, so its exact contents were a mystery even to the other members of the faculty, but Augustus felt forced to ask the question they were all thinking.

'A French beef Wellington, George?'

'Not *boeuf* Wellington or even *boeuf* Napoleon – rather *le cheval* de Wellington.'

Theodore Flanagan, who was famed for finding an Irish connection in the most unlikely settings, rescued another random fact from the recesses of his brain.

'Of course, both Napoleon's and Wellington's horses were bought in Ireland. Bonaparte's came from Ballinasloe, County Galway and Wellington's horse from the Cahirmee fair in County Cork... Copenhagen, that was Wellington's horse, wasn't it?'

'I think you missed an Irish claim there Theodore,' said the Master, 'Wellington himself was born in Ireland.'

'Of course, thank you Master. Another famous Irishman claimed by the English,' said Theodore.

'Now what was Wellington's famous dictum on being accused of being Irish?' countered George, irritated that the presentation of this dish was being interrupted. 'Oh yes, being born in a stable does not make one a horse.'

'*Touché*, George, *touché*.' Theodore acceded gracefully and consigned to his memory the thought that Arthur Wellesley, the 1st Duke of Wellington, was not worthy of being called Irish after all.

'As I was saying,' continued George, 'this is not beef Wellington but how the finest French chefs may have cooked the good horse Copenhagen in celebration.'

'You're not saying this is horse meat, are you?' said an incredulous Reverend Pinker.

'The finest flesh from the finest beast that graces this earth,

Reverend,' replied George. 'Marinated with garlic, thyme and port. Then baked in a fennel-flavoured *croûte*. With a heart of gold.'

As the first slice was placed on the plate, the soft unctuous heart of *foie gras* was revealed and, with the first mouthful of the finely flavoured flesh, most of the diners' initial reservations evaporated. The chaplain, the sole remaining dissenter, found solace in the glass of Chambertin-Clos de Bèze Grand Cru that had been placed in front of him, and as the expressions of delight around the table became too much, he picked up his knife and fork. Looking intently at the plate, he cut a piece of horse meat and raised it to his mouth. The table had fallen silent as all eyes were now watching the chaplain for his reaction. The chaplain's eyes were closed as he chewed, and then came the verdict.

'Good God, that's divine.'

A great cheer around the table and the French defeat at Waterloo was expunged temporarily from history.

Theodore Flanagan's guest, Dermot Keogh was looking decidedly pale and nervous as the table was cleared for dessert. Dr Keogh was on sabbatical from Trinity College Dublin and had begun to think he had the measure of Oxford, until tonight of course. The unusual parts of normal animals and normal parts of unusual animals had left him wondering whether it was such a good idea to offer ice cream as a dessert. Seeing him shifting in his seat as the time approached, Theodore took pity on the young man and rose to make the introduction.

'Gentlemen, may I present my guest Dr Keogh, with what I assure you will be a most surprising dessert: saffron and nitrogen ice cream.'

Dermot Keogh stood to polite applause and could sense the slight disbelief from some quarters that so simple a dish as ice cream was being offered in such revered company. Surprisingly, this dish did not contravene rule four of the faculty of gastronomic science's constitution. Seaweed ice cream had been served last year, but the unique nature of Dr

Keogh's dish had been deemed by the faculty to represent an entirely new departure. He nodded to Gerard across the room who opened the doors to let two scouts into the room. The first was carrying a large bowl of liquid with the most remarkably luminous yellow colour. This was a mixture of cream, milk, sugar, egg yolks, vanilla and saffron. As it was placed on the table, the weight of the bowl was almost too much for the small serving girl and the contents sloshed, revealing beyond all doubt that this was a liquid and most definitely not ice cream. Dermot Keogh heard George Le Strang mutter, 'They must like their ice cream runny in Dublin.' There were a few suppressed snorts at this, which were only silenced by a glaring Theodore Flanagan.

The second server brought a large stainless steel flask, which was placed in front of Dr Keogh. The arrival of this second component turned the amusement into curiosity, made all the greater when a large whisk was carried in by Gerard on a silver tray and placed beside the flask. The quaking doctor then lifted the lid from the vial to reveal a cloud of what looked like smoke pouring from its mouth and flowing over the tablecloth. Turning to his host for assistance, Theodore was recruited to pour the contents of the vial into the cream mixture leaving Dr Keogh free to rapidly whisk. This produced an almighty plume of smoke, fog or whatever it was, which engulfed both Irishmen for several seconds. The remaining diners were left with the clanking sound of the whisk in the bowl and dim outline of Dermot Keogh's elbow flailing in great circles.

A few seconds later as the air cleared, a beaming young physicist was holding a bowl of ice-cold, perfectly solid and luminous ice cream amid rapturous applause. The mysterious ingredient was liquid nitrogen, which boils at almost minus $200°$C. When it hit the warm cream, the liquid boiled away in a torrent of nitrogen fog, freezing the cream mixture so fast that the ice crystals were microscopic and the resulting ice cream filled with tiny bubbles. While all were impressed by the sense of gastronomical theatre, few thought the taste could live up to expectations. Bowls were passed around and, after a little suspicious prodding, the ice cream was slowly tasted by all. Monsieur Lemprière was nodding slowly to himself as he ate in total silence and one by one all the others fell silent in eager anticipation of his verdict. Finally he made his announcement.

'*Monsieur, ce n'est pas une glace… mais c'est magnifique.*'

As indeed it was in flavour, texture, conception and delivery. The French chef rose to his feet in tribute and the rest of the table followed, leaving a young Dr Keogh in a daze of success, the like of which he had never known.

The only guest left to offer a dish was Arthur's guest, the Master. You might think that at this stage of a dinner of such unbridled culinary range, he would be worried that his own offering might fall a little flat. There were certainly no signs of any external doubt as he in turn rose to his feet.

'Gentlemen, I can after these remarkable dishes offer you only two simple but unique fruits: the miracle fruit and a new variety of sweet lime I discovered on my travels with the foreign office which remains unknown to conventional or gastronomic science. I give them to you without any exotic preparation as, to my mind, the good Lord created them perfectly in the first place.'

The chaplain, finally feeling on safe ground gastronomically and spiritually, led the applause. The Master nodded with regal grace before adding, 'And don't forget to taste the miracle fruit first.'

A large bowl containing the shiny red miracle fruit and vivid green limes was passed around the table. The miracle fruit, despite its grandiose title, is not a particularly remarkable-looking fruit. More like large red olives than a proper fruit, they were too small to be impressive and too smooth-skinned to be surprising in appearance. Certainly their flavour aroused little excitement around the table, but few were brave enough to express this thought. George leaned across to his guest

Monsieur Lemprière and whispered his verdict.

'Quite tasteless, René; I'd stick to the wine.'

Heeding his advice, René passed on the miracle fruit and lingered instead on the dessert wine that had been served with the ice cream, a good but not a remarkable Muscat.

Then, one by one the faculty and their guests embarked upon the sweet limes. They were overcome by the novelty of an intense lime flavour without any hint of acidity. Piqued by their reactions, René Lemprière carefully sliced off the skin, halved his lime and popped one half into his mouth. His faced contorted into spasms of shock. A flood of citric acid assailed taste buds that his brain had prepared for sweetness.

'Pah, what is zis, one of your English jokes?'

Everyone looked truly stunned, except of course for the puckered Frenchman and the Master who was smiling beatifically and without a moment's hesitation offered an explanation for the confusion.

'I do apologise, René. Perhaps a normal lime had been mixed in with the bowl by mistake.'

George Le Strang, mortified by this mistake, without hesitation offered the remaining half of his own lime. He had tasted his and it was without doubt one of the Master's exotic sweet limes. In the same move he also removed the offending lime from Monsieur Lemprière's plate, who graciously accepted the error and brought a slice of Le Strang's lime to his lips, albeit briefly.

'But zis is the same, George. It is just a lime, 'ave you all lost you reason? Zis is like the Emperor's pyjamas – someone says it's sweet and you all believe.'

A baffled George tasted Lemprière's lime and then his own. Both tasted just as sweet.

The Master could contain himself no longer and burst out laughing.

'Forgive me, René, it seems you didn't taste my miracle fruit.'

'I admit I did not, but why does zat matter?'

'Try a little miracle fruit and then taste the lime again,' suggested the Master.

Lemprière took a bite of the mildly tasting miracle fruit and then cautiously took a slice of lime.

'*Incroyable*. What kind of magic is zis?'

'Miracle fruit is remarkable not for its taste but its effect. Once tasted, anything sour or acidic tastes sweet for an hour or so. So these are indeed not sweet limes but quite ordinary limes made to taste quite extraordinary.' The Master sat back triumphantly and signalled to Gerard to bring a small decanter to the table.

'Indulge me for one more test, in the spirit of gastronomic exploration. Everyone taste this wine and tell me what you think.'

Each person at the table was given a small glass of straw-coloured wine. The verdicts were similar and rather puzzled. All agreed it was a poor quality sweet wine and a little lost why the Master was so pleased to be offering it around. To resolve the mystery, Gerard was asked to bring in the bottle for inspection. With great solemnity Gerard brought in a bottle of white wine vinegar and placed it on the table to scenes of total amazement. The Master stood and took a graciously low bow to a stunned but wildly clapping audience.

As the dinner drew to a close the cheeseboards were laid out and the diners' glasses were refilled with more of the Chambertin-Clos de Bèze. Callum Morton's hand fell on his knife only to be stayed by the bear-like paw of his host Hamish. With his other hand Hamish raised his glass in the penultimate toast of the dinner.

'Gentlemen I give you cheese... '

To the surprise of all the guests, the rest of the faculty chanted in perfect unison another of Brillat-Savarin's bon mots.

'... a meal without cheese is like a beautiful woman with only one eye.'

This left the guests to raise their glasses and in far less unity, toast everything from cheese, beauty, women and, belatedly, the Queen of England. Dr Morton's knife was then free to dive into a divinely swamp-like Vacherin Mont d'Or, which had been baked and then gently de-roofed.

Arthur Plantagenet surprised the assembled company by rising to his feet.

'Gentlemen, it is an honour to dine with you all. If I were to die this evening I would die as the happiest, best-fed man in Christendom.' He held up a hand to quell the rising murmurs before they could trouble his flow of speech. 'As my colleagues here already know, I am not a well man.' Arthur enjoyed the total silence that fell on the room for a few seconds before continuing. 'Indeed I may not live to see the next of these extraordinary feasts, so there is no better place to announce my lasting gift to gastronomy.'

Charles Pinker placed his face in his hands and starting rocking backwards and forwards. Augustus, sensing impending disaster, tried to cut across Arthur.

'Perhaps this isn't quite the time or place, Arthur… '

'Nonsense. Gentlemen, the grandest experiment in gastronomy is to answer the simple question of what is the taste of human flesh. I have therefore decided to donate my body to gastronomic science so that this very question can be decided beyond all doubt upon my death.'

There was a stunned silence in the room that was broken by the voice of Monsieur Lemprière.

'I'd rather eat an Englishman's horse than any part of an Englishman. I couldn't imagine your flesh would even be edible.'

'And a Frenchman would taste better, René?' rejoined Hamish.

'Of course, a well-dined Frenchman would have eaten the finest food on God's earth and drunk the best wines, so of course he would taste better than someone whose body has been reared on beer and overcooked beef.'

'I think Arthur would fit your description of a well-marinated Frenchman rather accurately,' said Augustus, who found to his surprise that his national pride and friendship for Arthur were stronger than his moral objections to cannibalism. At this, the rest of the faculty of gastronomic science rallied behind Arthur with supportive clinking of spoons on glasses and grunts of 'hear, hear' and 'quite right' from all sides. *L'entente cordiale,* as George might have said, *était vraiment morte.*

'I hear one of your eminent countrymen was all for eating people, Theodore. A certain Jonathan Swift for one. Isn't that right, Gascoigne?' Arthur had, in a reversal of his early strategy, decided that even a man from Yale was better than a French horse chef. Pleased to be suddenly useful, Gascoigne Percival eagerly joined the fray.

'Oh, indeed, but it was ironic, designed to shame the English establishment for their neglect of the Irish poor.' He paused, suddenly realising he was in the English establishment and perhaps that wasn't the best opening gambit under the circumstances, but the clanking spoon of Theodore Flanagan came as a reassurance.

'Well said, that man.'

'Quite, quite, but do tell us what Swift proposed, Dr Percival,' Arthur said, starting into a quotation of the opening lines of Swift's pamphlet before the good doctor could reply. '"I have been assured by a very knowing American…"' Arthur paused to smile at the hapless Percival who felt obliged, against his better judgement, to complete the quotation.

'"… of my acquaintance in London, that a young healthy child well nursed, is, at a year old, a most delicious, nourishing and wholesome food, whether stewed, roasted, baked, or boiled." From that dubious starting point he suggested that the problems of the famine and excess children in Ireland could neatly be solved by having the Irish breed children as food. But as I said, this pamphlet was designed to highlight the problem of Irish malnutrition, not promote cannibalism.'

'Arthur, please tell me you are not serious. After all, cannibalism is a moral outrage perpetrated by heathen savages.' Charles tried to inject a note of prejudiced reason into the discussion.

'Charles, as you well know I prefer the term "anthropophagy" myself: fewer moral overtones. The word cannibal was created as a mighty slur on the Carib tribe and was used mostly as an excuse for far more immoral massacres of noble savage races by the ignoble English and Spanish invaders. After all, chaplain, does the Bible forbid cannibalism?'

'Good grief, Arthur, you are incorrigible. The Ten Commandments should cover it I think.'

'Nonsense. They just say "Thou shalt not kill", not "Thou shalt not die and be voluntarily consumed". I think the Bible is stricter on shellfish and pork than eating people.'

'Well… Leviticus does seem to ban certain creatures for Jews, such as pigs and shellfish… '

'And some lesser known creatures, such as camels, falcons and ostriches, but not, it seems, humans, isn't that so, Charles?'

'Well, I haven't read that chapter in a while,' muttered the browbeaten chaplain.

'I would strongly recommend chapter eleven of Leviticus; a very interesting chapter,' continued Arthur, now firmly in his stride and clearly unstoppable. 'It suggests some other good things to eat, such as locusts, grasshoppers and people. Then there is Leviticus 26:29: "And ye shall eat the flesh of your sons, and the flesh of your daughters shall ye eat", or Jeremiah 19:9: "And they shall eat every one the flesh of his friend".'

'Bravo, Arthur. Thirty–Love.' The Master joined in, entirely convinced this was all said in good fun. This was just the sort of well-chiselled academic sparring that he had hoped for on coming to Oxford.

Having won the religious argument, Arthur took on the law of the land.

'So Theodore, is there any law in the judicial system of England that forbids voluntary anthropophagy?'

'Er, well, now you mention it I don't think there is, at least not in English law… or any law as far as I know.'

'I rest my case.'

'Game, set and match to Arthur,' said the Master, clapping furiously. 'Now how about brandy and cigars in the drawing room?'

Chapter 16

Mr Potts began his morning inspection of the college just before dawn. The cold December night was on the wane, leaving the grass of the quadrangles coated with a thin white frost and the surrounding paths treacherous. This daily round always revealed some clues to the events that took place under cover of darkness. The frequent beer glass, infrequent but unwelcome pools of vomit and the occasional fractured branches from the trees along the boundary wall signifying an illicit exit or entrance. On occasion in the summer months there might even be an undergraduate in various states of undress pinned to the grass of the quadrangle by croquet hoops.

Passing the senior common room, Potts saw a light on. It had been a late night after the dinner at the Master's lodge. He'd heard Dr McIntyre singing his Flanders and Swann songs as he staggered off to bed at three o'clock in the morning, so he knew they had had a good time. Looking in to check all was well, Potts saw Professor Arthur Plantagenet fast asleep in his favourite leather chair, still in his evening finery, snoring gently. Potts smiled. In his mind, Arthur was exactly what an Oxford professor should be. The rest of the room was in its expected state of disarray. He'd get Gerard to tidy up first thing and bring in some breakfast for the professor. Leaving Arthur to sleep off the excesses of the previous night, he turned off the light and gently closed the door.

*

For Augustus Bloom, every hangover was a curse and a blessing. A curse as naturally no-one could relish the skull-wrenching headache and gastric ill-ease. It was also an annoyance for any logical being to find oneself making the same mistake over and over again. Lashing into brandy after midnight and continuing until almost 3 a.m. without the barest attempt at rehydration can only have one result. The slowest laboratory rat can learn the route through a new maze in a few trials and avoid the path leading to an electric shock. After several decades of adulthood, Augustus was showing little progress up the 'perils of brandy' learning curve. The pleasure that mollified the pain for Augustus was the research opportunity offered by every really cracking hangover. One of Augustus' more whimsical projects was his little black book of hangover cures. For over a decade he had tried a new remedy for each hangover.

One or two hangovers each term had provided sufficient research material to fill a small black leather notebook Augustus had purchased in Florence during his travels with Arthur. Befitting its origins, it boasted hand-painted marbled paper on the inside covers and the first contribution was made in the café at the top of the Uffizi gallery. After a very late night investigating the delights of Italian wines and an early morning start at the Uffizi to miss the crowds, Augustus had mutinied and insisted they go directly to the café before he'd look at a single painting. The café was situated at the very end of the gallery with a terrace on the rooftops overlooking the Piazza della Signoria but still over-shadowed by the huge tower of the Palazzo Vecchio. Arthur ordered a *caffè corretto alla grappa* for them both. A small intense espresso with a cover of brown velvety *crema* and a dash of grappa. The effect was rapid and dramatic, though sadly short-lived. The intense beverage lifted their hangovers like the lifting of the curtain at the opera and started Augustus on a new research endeavour. It is ironic that Italy, the country that gave Augustus the first

137

entry in his little black book, has no word in its language for hangover.

Over the years the exploration of other potential cures turned out to be a very broad-ranging exercise with every potential avenue considered from the weird to the potentially poisonous. The strangest to date, and certainly hardest to track down, were two types of coffee: *caphe cut chon* from Vietnam and *kopi luwak* from Java. These coffee beans were not unique in their horticulture or in terms of the type of tree, but solely in terms of where they had been. Before being prepared for coffee-making, these beans are hand-picked as berries by a small civet, a spotty cat-like creature. The animal is famed for only picking the best coffee berries; unfortunately they then eat them. So they can only be collected once they have been through the digestive tract, a process that is supposed to remove the bitterness from the coffee. By 'through' this really does mean all the way through and out the other end. The half-digested beans are collected from the droppings of this animal. They are then lightly roasted to complete the transformation. In the spirit of experimentation, Augustus had sought out both types of these bizarrely expensive coffee beans, only to discover they are no more effective as a cure for a serious hangover than coffee plucked from a tree.

The most poisonous so far had been *Nux Vomica*. This delightfully named herbal remedy has as its principal active ingredient a poison that was popular in Victorian times, namely strychnine. A little strychnine is claimed to stimulate an alcoholically paralysed stomach, though too much puts all the body's muscles into spasm and induces convulsions, leading to death. The herbal extract had proved passably effective for understandable physiological reasons, though it tasted fairly vile. Being an open-minded sort, Augustus had also tested the homeopathic version of *Nux Vomica*. This proved to be entirely ineffective at alleviating the symptoms induced by an evening comparing the aniseed-based liqueurs from across Europe, though one can fairly claim this was a particularly challenging test for homeopathy.

After examining individual remedies for many years, Augustus had recently turned to exploring the effects of mixtures of previously successful ingredients. He fumbled for the small book to see what he had noted down as the next combination. After each trial of a new treatment he would write down notes regarding palatability, level of symptom relief and the duration of that relief. Then he would write the next concoction to be tried as he assumed, not unreasonably, that in the throes of his next hangover his critical facilities would be so impaired as to prevent any meaningful thought on the subject. He was narrowing down on the ideal cure and was by now certain that it must contain ample quantities of liquid, salt, sugar and fat. He was as yet undecided about the merits of adding alcohol to this list of ingredients. After that it was just a question of getting the most effective and palatable combination. Surprisingly, the next combination he had noted down in his book at the end of the previous term was exactly what he felt like eating at that moment.

Getting up he crossed the gently rocking floor to the cupboard that hid Augustus' dirty little culinary secret. Taking down the jar, he set about creating this morning's curative preparation, pausing for a second to wonder why this little dark jar with a yellow lid held such sway over a man with otherwise refined tastes. For Augustus was afflicted by that uniquely English vice – a love of Marmite. Today's trial involved a fried egg in a sandwich made from buttered toast covered with Marmite and marmalade. All washed down with Earl Grey tea. Sophisticated? No. Exotic? No. Palatable? Extremely for a dedicated marmitophile and disgusting for the rest of the population. Effective? Augustus returned to his bed to find out.

*

For other members of the faculty, the morning after such a feast held a range of experiences. The chaplain, for all his outward nervousness, had the internal constitution of an ox and a liver to match. In a few short hours his prodigious internal organs had absorbed, processed, disassembled and eliminated all the alcohol and more destructive congeners – the associated range of complex chemicals that are the real villains of any hangover. By the time any of the others were even conscious he had awoken in rude good health, and completed a walking circuit of Christchurch Meadow with the aid of a key given to him by the Dean of Christchurch, in gratitude for one of his more exceptional organ recitals performed in the cathedral. He had then headed off to hall for a large cooked breakfast with the undergraduates. He was widely admired for these intermittent pastoral visits to the low table breakfast, as it was rare for fellows to mix with the undergraduates outside tutorials or formal events. His motivations were less pastoral than gastric, as the undergraduate breakfast was served an hour earlier than that in the senior common room parlour and, by the time he returned from his walk, he was always ravenous.

Hamish had more of a bear-like constitution, better suited to hibernation with a slow but steady metabolism. He would typically not wake up until early evening the following day, amnesic to all events after midnight, ravenously hungry but otherwise in fine shape. He would rise and head off to evensong before heading straight back into hall for dinner. Today was no exception and, as the day's events unfolded, they did so without the involvement or awareness of Hamish McIntyre.

George Le Strang had inherited his appetite from his aristocratic French father but unfortunately had inherited his liver from his waiflike English mother. This was a source of much distress for Le Strang as he was always reminded of this constitutional conflict on mornings such as this. His solution was a bath of such searing heat that it operated on a similar principle to a distillery. Le Strang would lie in the hot bath with alcohol forced out of every pore and mixing with the impenetrable fog that soon filled the bathroom. The vaporous alcohol would then condense on the windows, which were usually the coldest surfaces. Many a wandering spider or trapped fly has died an inebriated death at the hands of the condensation on Le Strang's bathroom windows.

The final member of the declining dining society, Theodore Flanagan, was more conventional in his morning-after habits, usually with more success than some of Augustus' more dubious efforts. He was taught his solution in the form of a rhyme as a young student while visiting the Galway oyster festival, and he had lived by it ever since.

If a hangover you wish to lack,
Take a pint of water before the sack.
A bottle of Guinness on rising from bed
And you'll start the day without an aching head.

*

While Arthur Plantagenet remained slumped in his chair in the senior common room, a select group did manage to assemble in the parlour for breakfast. This included Professor Le Strang and Theodore Flanagan, who were the only conscious and hungry members of the gastronomic faculty at that time. They were accompanied by the few guests from the previous night who were staying in college as they had travelled from outside Oxford: Reginald Morton, Gascoigne Percival and Monsieur Lemprière. The Master did not join them, taking his breakfast as usual in his study in preparation for tackling the *Times* crossword. Being hungover had only a slight impact on his completion times provided he had absolutely no other distractions. The assembled few were a very different group compared to the previous night. Then, they had been united in gastronomic delight and, of course, wine. This morning they were a somewhat bedraggled and internationally disparate group for whom the silence hung heavily between each stilted attempt at conversation.

Unusually they were served by the housekeeper, Mary O'Sullivan rather than Gerard, who had served them so expertly the night before. Although at this stage an old college retainer, Gerard had in fact attended St Jerome's coming up as a student in 1939 before enlisting in 1941. The war had taken a heavy toll on Gerard. He had been left a broken man after being pulled half-dead from under the bodies of the rest of his platoon who were killed when one of Rommel's Panzers rolled over their dugout in the Battle of Gazala in North Africa. He had not uttered a single word since. In 1946, he was finally discharged from the wartime psychiatric services at the Royal Victoria Military Hospital Netley, where Dr Watson of Sherlock Holmes had supposedly once worked. Word of Gerard's plight had been brought back to college as war-worn students returned to finish their degrees. Gerard was in no fit state to complete his studies, but was offered a job at St Jerome's in the library as it was considered that his lack of speech would be a positive asset in that environment. The thoughtless impatience of students had been hard on his nerves and he had finally found peace as the senior steward, a job he had performed flawlessly for such a length of time that no-one even remembered his surname any more. This made his absence today all the more remarkable.

Sadly, breakfast was as undistinguished as breakfast always was at St Jerome's: kippers, toast and over-poached eggs. The highlight was undoubtedly a black tea that Theodore Flanagan had brought back from a recent trip to Istanbul. This was brewed in an extravagant Russian silver samovar that took pride of place on the elegant Georgian sideboard in the parlour. This samovar had been donated to the college by Tsar Alexander I of Russia in 1814 when he visited Oxford with King Frederick William III of Prussia to meet the English Prince Regent and celebrate the fall of Napoleon Bonaparte, a little prematurely as it turned out.

*

Gerard's absence from the senior common room parlour, which was his first in over twenty years as he had never been known to have a single day off, was equally inexplicable to Mr Potts. As the cardboard kippers were being pushed around the plates, Gerard was sitting ashen-faced and shaking in the porter's lodge. When Gerard had arrived in a state of great distress a good half hour earlier, Potts had offered him the customary pencil and notepad with which Gerard communicated all messages that couldn't be conveyed by hand or eye movements. On this occasion, Gerard's hands were shaking so much he couldn't manage a legible word. That didn't stop him from writing pages of spidery illegible scrawl. His frustration at not being understood seemed to make him even worse. So Potts had reverted to his cure-all concoction of strong sweet tea and whiskey.

Slowly the sugar and whiskey infused into Gerard's blood stream and then finally reached the parts of his brain that were in such profound turmoil. Only then did his breathing start to regulate and tremor subside enough to make another attempt at communication. The words were still barely legible but when Potts read them out loud, Gerard started nodding his head wildly before collapsing into a pitiful bout of sobbing. Potts always had a problem when women turned on the waterworks, but he really couldn't cope with it from grown men. As shocking as the news from Gerard was, Potts was delighted to be able to leave the lodge and all that emotion behind him as he ran to the senior common room.

There, in the same chair, in the same position, was a motionless, silent and deathly pale Professor Plantagenet. Potts slowed to a more deferential walk as he approached the don. He tried a gentle shake of the shoulders before a sequence of 'sirs' from the quiet and expectant to the bellowing and frankly desperate. Arthur's skin was cold and clammy to touch and Potts was compelled to agree with Gerard's assessment of the situation. To gather his thoughts he took the unimaginable step of sitting down in one of the senior common room's chairs, his sense of the social order overwhelmed by the enormity of the situation. Then Potts spotted a silver goblet at Arthur's feet. He gazed at the shining goblet for a few moments, puzzled at why his mind was demanding he attend to it. Then it struck him. He grabbed the cup and, after brushing it frantically on his sleeve to a mirror-like sheen, held it over Arthur's nostrils and watched intently before rushing out of the door to locate Dr Bloom.

*

It was gone lunchtime when Augustus got back to college after accompanying Arthur to hospital. He was officially pronounced dead on arrival and transferred straight to the morgue, leaving Augustus sitting numbed in an empty cubicle in the casualty department of the Radcliffe Infirmary. On his return, he was met in the lodge by Mr Potts who asked the only question he needed to ask with the barest rise of his eyebrows and was answered with the faintest shake of the head by Augustus.

'In that case, sir, the professor asked me to give you this. Said it was important you got it on the day he died. It was like 'e knew 'e was about to go.'

'Thank you, Potts.' Augustus looked up from the letter and caught the sadness in Mr Potts' eyes.

Augustus spent the afternoon in his rooms where one by one the other members of the shadow faculty of gastronomic science had gathered for no other reason than to talk, knowing that when the talking stopped the real sadness would begin. Once everyone had departed, Augustus himself set off, reaching the Laboratory of Physiology in the late afternoon. A note had been left for him in his pigeonhole at the entrance of the building.

Package arrived for you. Placed in frozen storage as per instructions.

Augustus had no recollection of leaving any instructions or expecting a package on that particular day, so he duly stuffed the note in a pocket and slowly wound his way up the echoing 1930s stone-effect staircase. He deliberately hadn't yet read the letter that Potts had delivered this morning. When he finally reached his office he pulled the letter out of his tweed jacket pocket and examined the familiar handwriting. His name was spelt out in green ink from the over-sized fountain pen that Arthur always used, the words capturing the movement and life Arthur still had when he wrote them. Augustus couldn't see how reading it could change things for the better and assumed, rather presciently, that right now it was more likely to change things for the worse. He placed it behind his brass desk lamp, leant forward onto his folded arms and closed his eyes before tears could appear.

Chapter 17

It was a sad and beleaguered collection of Oxford dons that congregated the following morning around the long mahogany boardroom table in the first floor of Cragsworth, Cawl and Barringer, solicitors at law. Mr Barringer himself was presiding.

'Gentlemen, thank you for attending at such short notice. It was a particular request of the late Professor Arthur Plantagenet in his last will and testament that this will be read within a day of his death so that all the arrangements within it can be carried out while... ' His voice trailed off for a second before continuing, '... he was still fresh.'

Mr Barringer regained his composure, finding reassurance in the legal formalities. 'As you may or may not know, your good friend Arthur Plantagenet has no living close relatives and so he has named you five as the executors of his will and trustees of his estate. This legally binds you to an obligation. Think carefully before you accept this role... *very* carefully.' He looked at each of them in turn. Assuming they knew at least broadly the terms of the will, and that at least one of them if not all would refuse the onus about to be placed upon them.

'You are all willing to do this?' he asked incredulously.

They all nodded.

'Reverend?' He looked one last time at Charles Pinker,

hoping he at least would exempt himself from these bizarre proceedings – to no avail. Barringer had no choice but to continue.

'Do you, Dr Augustus Bloom, Dr Theodore Flanagan, Professor George Le Strang, Dr Hamish McIntyre and the Reverend Charles Pinker all agree to act as joint executors of Arthur Plantagenet's last will and testament and trustees of his estate?'

To a man they all agreed again.

'So that brings me to the conditions of the will itself.' A bead of sweat started to appear on Barringer's expansive forehead as he read on.

'I leave the totality of my estate for the purpose of enhancing the science of gastronomy. The sum of £250,000 is to be donated to the university for the creation of the post of Professor of Gastronomy and a further £50,000 is to be donated to St Jerome's College as an endowment to support the election of the Professor of Gastronomy as a fellow of St Jerome's. In the event that the university is not in a position to create this post, the funds are to be invested at the discretion of the executors until such a time as the university agrees to this eminently sensible proposition.

A few eyebrows lifted at this news, impressed that Arthur had such funds at his disposal. Human nature being as it is, several indecent expectations of a personal windfall were also born in that announcement.

I wish my funeral to be a quiet affair with only fellow members of the shadow faculty of gastronomic science in attendance. Subject to the provisions below I should like my remains to be cremated...

Profound relief came over the assembled dons at the mention of cremation. This seemed at a stroke to rule out the more unusual intentions Arthur had previously expressed for his corporeal remains.

... with the ashes to be divided into three parts. The first

part is to be dug into the roots of one of the magnificent Cypress trees in the island cemetery of St Michael in Venice, the second portion is to be scattered across the arena of the Coliseum in Rome. The remainder is to be placed...

At this point Mr Barringer paused and swallowed hard before overcoming his personal distaste for this particular will.

... within a truffled turkey which is to be dropped off a punt on the river Cherwell to the music of Rossini's Stabat Mater played on my beloved HMV Model 101 gramophone. After which I donate this gramophone and my collection of 78s to my good friend, Augustus Bloom.

To the solicitor's utter dismay, the audience seemed to approve wholeheartedly of these bizarre arrangements. Though a cultured and learned man, Mr Barringer was clearly unaware of the gastronomic importance of the truffled turkey, and the role this most fragrant of birds played in both Professor Plantagenet's and Gioacchino Rossini's life. After a heartfelt sigh he continued.

As a public event I would greatly appreciate a memorial service to be held in the college chapel. The sum of £5,000 is to be donated for the purchase of food and champagne with any excess donated to the shadow faculty of gastronomic science. I wish foie gras to be served with sliced figs and quince jelly. The champagne should be Dom Perignon 1962. I should also request that Charles Pinker play the Maestoso from Camille Saint-Saëns' Symphony No. 3 in C minor, Op. 78.

Barringer cleared his throat for a second time. Taking advantage of the grunts of approval at the arrangements for the funeral, he tried to deliver the next words with as much professional detachment as he could muster.

The most important provision of my will, is that I wish to donate part of my body to gastronomic science.

There were a few groans from the assembled dons, and Mr

Barringer paused to peer over his reading glasses to gauge the reaction. The Reverend Pinker's mood had changed from pride to dread, Hamish McIntyre was most definitely chuckling to himself, and the others merely sat in stunned silence.

To that end I have decided to donate my left leg to the shadow faculty of gastronomic science to prepare in a manner that will best answer the question of the gustatory virtues of human flesh. While I will leave the exact details of preparation to my friends and colleagues, I would suggest some form of dry curing in the spirit of Iberico or Parma ham.

The solicitor raised his hand without lifting his eyes from the page to quell the rising unrest of his audience.

I also require that the results of this culinary experiment be presented as one of the dishes at a dinner of the shadow faculty of gastronomic science. In the spirit of Eumolpus[7] and as a condition of my legacy to the university, I require that Dr Ridgeway, vice-chancellor of the University of Oxford, be invited to this dinner. Provided the vice-chancellor accepts the establishment of a faculty of gastronomic science, full payment of my endowment is to be presented to the university at this dinner.

This last detail was too much for Hamish McIntyre who literally exploded in laughter. Augustus tried to hold back the mental image of Dr Ridgeway being offered all that money and a plate of Arthur's left leg, before it became too much for him. George Le Strang was quick to follow. It took longer for Theodore who was curiously lost in thought about why Arthur had chosen to leave his left rather than his right leg. By the time he resurfaced from this introspective conjecture, the room was so filled with laughter that he too joined in. Charles fought very hard to maintain some grain of Christian

---

7 A character in the *Satyricon*, an ancient Roman work by Petronius, whose will required his legatees to eat him on his death if they wished to share in his inheritance.

decency, and was indeed succeeding until he caught sight of the astonished face of Mr Barringer, whereupon he too lost all semblance of composure. At this point in the proceedings, Mr Barringer abandoned all attempts to restore order and complete his reading of the will.

He ushered them all from the room and down the stairs. Standing on the pavement of St John's Street, they had just started to regain some grip on reality when Hamish suggested that they head up the street and tell Dr Ridgeway the good news straight away. That set them all off again until there were tears rolling down their cheeks. The first practical suggestion came, as ever, from Theodore Flanagan, who suggested that they visit a few of Arthur's favourite haunts before dinner. They set off on a long and circuitous journey back to St Jerome's college, starting first at the Eagle and Child in St Giles. This was a small but renowned establishment famous in former years for the meetings of the Inklings, the writing circle that numbered J.R.R. Tolkien and C.S. Lewis amongst its numbers. Tolkien, the Rawlinson and Bosworth Professor of Anglo-Saxon, had befriended the young Arthur Plantagenet when he had first been elected as a professor and Arthur was a frequent attendee at Inkling gatherings, strictly in a libatory rather than a literary capacity.

As the dons took their seats in the wood panelled back room, the ground rules were set: a different drink in each pub, no maudlin talk and no mention of the 'C' word. Charles Pinker requested a small amendment of the rules after the first pint, adding the 'A' word – anthropophagy, Arthur's preferred word for the legacy he had foisted on his colleagues, to the proscribed list. After the Eagle and Child, it was a short jaunt to the Lamb and Flag in the footsteps of the Inklings, then a thirst-inducing walk of at least five minutes to the White Horse on Broad Street, nestled between Trinity College and Blackwell's booksellers. This pub was a favourite haunt of Arthur's, who was well known for picking up a few books from Blackwell's and, without a moment's hesitation, carrying them unpaid out of the door for more detailed inspection in the White Horse. After a pint or two he would head back with the books he was going to buy, leaving the rest scattered around the table for the barman to return to the bookshop later in the day. After an excellent pint of Courage in the White Horse, the shadow faculty of gastronomic science were on the home run with a pint of Brakspear's old ale in the King's Arms, a hot port in the Turf Tavern, followed by a bottle of Guinness in the Wheatsheaf, at Theodore's insistence.

The final destination was the Bear in Blue Boar Street, one of the oldest and smallest pubs in Oxford. The walls and ceilings of this inn were, and indeed still are, covered by ties snipped off their former owners in return for a pint of beer, if they were lucky to have a tie not already in the extensive collection. It took them an age to locate the tie Arthur had parted with many years previously. Implausible as it seemed now, thinking of the recently departed Professor's substantial weight, Arthur had had an unusual time in the war as part of the heroic but largely forgotten Glider Pilot Regiment. As they sat down with the final pint of Arthur's particular favourite bitter, Old Speckled Hen, Augustus raised the toast in the words of Arthur's old regimental motto: *Nihil est Impossibilis*.

This nostalgic circuit of Arthur's favourite drinking places had taken a considerable amount of time, what with all the drinking, walking, talking and urinating that this amount of beer entails. Time had passed so fast that the dons were stunned to hear Tom Tower strike seven o'clock.

'Good God, we'll be late for dinner. Come on, lads.' Hamish leapt to his feet with an agility that defied expectation after four hours of committed drinking. The others tried to respond with similar determination but with less success. Charles Pinker was by this stage snoring gently in the corner and all attempts to rouse him failed. The sight of an ordained minister of the church unconscious from drink may appear rather shocking to the modern mind, but history favoured the chaplain. In the context of the long tradition of the Bear, which claims heritage back to 1242, this was positively seemly behaviour for a member of the clergy.

The others made their way back to college as fast as their legs and bladders would permit. After heading into the senior common room to collect their voluminous black gowns, they ran up the stairs to the great hall through the gloom of the night in various states of inebriation, only to burst in while one of the scholars was still reading grace. Summoning as much poise as they could manage, they made their way past the assembled lines of students to take their places at high table. The Master nodded disapprovingly at each of them as they sat down. The young scholar had the foresight to restart the long Latin grace from the beginning to restore a sense of order and decorum.

Augustus was last to reach the raised platform on which high table sat and so had to take the only available seat left, beside the Master.

'Glad you could make it, Augustus.'

'Sorry, Master, we had to attend Arthur's solicitor. A few details and arrangements to be sorted out.'

The mention of Arthur had the desired calming effect on the Master. It is hard to bear a grudge within the shadow of the death of a good friend.

'Tragic loss. I know you were good friends. Very sad altogether,' offered the Master in consolation.

'He knew it was coming, though perhaps not quite yet.'

'*For everything there is a season, and a time for every matter under heaven. A time to be born, and a time to die* – as the good book says. Mind you I certainly never knew Arthur was so well versed in the Bible until that dinner the other night. He ran rings around the poor chaplain. Where is Charles, anyway? He missed evensong completely.'

'Oh, he's a little… overwrought by the whole thing.'

'Understandable. Anyway, talking of overwrought, I had the vice-chancellor on the phone straight after Arthur was found dead.'

'How did he know?' asked Augustus in some shock.

'No idea, but he was convinced we'd poisoned him too. He seemed to find it hard to understand why someone seems to die at every one of your dinners.'

'Good God, that's a bit rich, isn't it? Anyway Arthur died after dinner rather than during it and he was hardly in the full of his health.'

'More or less what I told him,' replied the Master, 'but no doubt he'll keep going on about it for a while. Thoroughly unreasonable chap, the vice-chancellor.'

Augustus was sensibly abstemious during dinner, but further down the table his fellow faculty members were being less cautious. By the time they retired to the senior common room, Hamish was in roaring form. There was a point on Hamish's drinking curve when he would inevitably start singing. He passed that point just before dessert and had now reached his second level: singing *and* playing the piano. The entire canon of Flanders and Swann was in Hamish's repertoire, along with several profoundly less reputable compositions. He was just launching into the "Hippopotamus Song" when George Le Strang interrupted.

'You play and I'll sing.'

'Go, go George. I'm with you,' said a delighted Hamish.

'*Boue, boue, boue glorieuse, Il n'y a rien comme elle pour refroidir le sang*[8]... ' George delivered the entire rendition of the aforementioned tune in French. As the applause settled down, Hamish stood to announce the next song.

He started thumping the top of the piano in a primal rhythm.

'This is a little song called the "The Reluctant Cannibal" from Flanders and Swann's second album. In memory of our dear departed friend, Arthur.' Hamish then launched into the

---

8 Better recognised in English as 'Mud, mud, glorious mud. There's nothing quite like it for cooling the blood.' Flanders and Swann's masterpiece clearly rhymes better in English but is enjoyable in every language and was even recorded in Russian.

song, taking both vocal parts himself, delivering a remarkable impersonation of the original performers.

Seated one day at the tom-tom,
I heard a welcome shout from the kitchen:
'COME AND GEEEEEEEEEEET IT!'
Roast leg of insurance salesman!

'I don't want any part of it!'
What? Why not?
I don't eat people.
Hey?
I won't eat people.
Huh?
I don't eat people.
I must be going deaf!
Eating people is wrong.

The dazed chaplain then walked into the senior common room. He had been woken up a few minutes earlier by the barman at the Bear and sent on his way as it was now well past closing time. Charles Pinker stood in stunned silence looking on a room full of Oxford dons all singing about cannibalism. He slumped into a chair, consoling himself with the thought that even the worst nightmare doesn't last all night, and he would soon wake up in his bed and the world would have been restored to normality.

*

Down in the cellars of St Jerome's, a bottle of '52 Château Margaux slipped from the racks and disappeared into the dark solitude. It was as quiet as a graveyard down there, but if you had listened hard you would have heard the faint sound of laughter and someone humming snippets from Flanders and Swann's songs.

Chapter 18

The following morning, Charles Pinker did indeed wake up in his own bed with absolutely no recollection of how he got there, but otherwise none the worse for wear. On opening his eyes, he became aware of some faint, grotesque memories of singing and an image of a punt floating in his mind. As with most dreams, the more he wanted to remember the more these images slipped away. He went over to the window, which was nestled in the roof of Old Quad, and threw it open, pulling cold clean air from the bluest of skies into his lungs. At the moment of maximum inspiration he paused in wonder at the beauty of the world, and then he remembered. Arthur was dead. Slowly the air – warm, damp and now merely second-hand – escaped from the chaplain. Despite Arthur's garrulous eccentricity, Charles felt a huge emptiness now he was gone.

In memory of his friend, Charles decided to take his early morning walk in the Botanical Gardens, a place where they would often bump into each other and then sit for hours as Arthur would engage in his favourite pastime – disguising a soliloquy as a conversation. As it was fiercely cold, he took the shortcut across Christchurch Meadow to reach the gardens. Augustus was already halfway to the Botanical Gardens. He had taken the slower, more reflective route down Dodgson's Walk to the river. With term essentially over, there was no shouting from coaches or splashing of oars to disturb the peace. Only the swans were left, cutting a poetic swathe through the mist that floated on the Isis on mornings such as this. He saw Charles Pinker just ahead of him as he came up the winding path that led to the back gates of the meadows. Quickening his pace, he drew alongside and gently placed a hand on the chaplain's shoulder.

'Morning, Charles. How are you?'

'If truth be told I'm just plain sad, Augustus. Sad and, as Arthur might say, bloody freezing.' He managed a weak smile and his best Arthuresque accent.

'I miss the old sod too,' said Augustus trying to put a brave face on things and admiring Charles' honesty. 'Mind you, I could have done without that damned will,' Augustus continued after they had walked on for a few minutes in companionable silence. At the mention of the word 'will' memories started crystallising in the chaplain's mind: the room, the laughter, the chaos, the solicitor's shocked expression and sweating brow.

'That really happened, did it? The will. Arthur requiring that we eat him?'

'It certainly did, Charles. But it's not all bad. Remember the bit about being cremated?'

'Did it involve a truffled turkey, by any chance?' Details were now flooding back for Charles, pushing back the tide of his beer-induced amnesia.

'Oh don't forget the punt and Rossini on the gramophone, but I've thought of a way out of our dilemma,' said Augustus beaming.

'You have?'

'You see, Arthur left a letter for me with old Potts to be delivered when he died. It had lists of all sorts of things to do, people to call. This was one of the best-planned deaths you could ever imagine. He left all the contact details for the crematorium. So yesterday morning I'd gone ahead and booked the cremation for tomorrow morning before we'd even heard the terms of the will.'

'But how does that help?'

'Well, if we forget to collect dear Arthur's leg then our problem will have literally gone up in smoke by Saturday lunchtime.'

'But I thought we were obliged to carry out the wishes of his will.'

'If we can, of course. But if an overzealous cremator cremates our friend before we can carry out his wishes to the letter, then what can we do?'

'Brilliant Augustus, quite brilliant.'

In a state of mutual reassurance, the pair headed off to the nearest warm place in Oxford, the Palm House in the botanical gardens.

It was mid-morning by the time the chaplain returned to college, forsaking his usual short cut along Blue Boar Street without knowing why. The amnesia of excess had spared him the memory of his forceful ejection from the Bear. His subconscious mind was in turn being kind to him in guiding him away from the scene lest the sight of it should restore memories best left forgotten. He crossed the threshold and felt an enveloping security. He was met in the lodge by Mr Potts.

'These letters were just dropped in for you and all the other gentlemen.'

Charles thanked Potts and pocketed the crisp ivory envelope that was addressed to him before heading off to the chapel for a bit of organ practice. Before climbing the stairs to the organ loft he settled down on the first row of choir stalls, opened the letter and cast an eye over the impressive letterhead of Cragsworth, Cawl and Barringer Solicitors.

Dear Sir,

Despite the apparent amusement displayed at the reading of Professor Arthur Plantagenet's will, I am obliged to inform you of the serious and consequential nature of your responsibilities as executors of this legal document. You have all agreed to take on these *responsibilities and must now follow them through to completion with due diligence. In light of the worrisome content of Professor Plantagenet's will, I strongly urge you to take appropriate legal and indeed spiritual advice before completing your prescribed duties. I must emphasise that <u>no-one</u> at the offices of Cragsworth, Cawl and Barringer will be in a position to assist or advise you in this matter.*

I enclose a copy of Professor Plantagenet's will for your records. You'll note that the general hilarity on the day prevented me from reading the final clause, which I will leave you to peruse at your leisure.

Yours faithfully,
Mr C.P.P. Barringer, BCL MBE

This letter could easily have thrown the chaplain into a total tailspin. But buoyed up by Augustus' confidence that the crematorium would see off the moral and legal dilemmas bequeathed by Arthur, he could now look back at the recently remembered meeting in the solicitor's office with detached amusement. Charles noted with a wry smile that the words 'no-one' in the typed letter had been underlined in the same vivid green ink that Arthur was so fond of himself. He pocketed the letter and copy of the will and just as he rose to leave the chapel, he heard laughter. It was Arthur's type of laugh, as clear as day. His head spun towards the door, which was still shut, and he sat motionless, listening intently. Through the silence, random sounds permeated in from the quad as the end of term exodus from college continued, muffled certainly but audible. Then some more laughter, distant, not quite the same, but laughter nonetheless that clearly came from the quad outside. Charles sighed with relief and, remembering Arthur's wishes about his memorial service, decided to go in search of the music for Camille Saint-Saëns' third symphony. This piece required both an organ and a full orchestra, so Arthur had clearly not considered the full practical implications of having this performed in St Jerome's small chapel. Charles wasn't sure an arrangement for solo organ existed but failing that he could write his own arrangement – a fitting tribute to his departed friend.

*

The remaining members of the shadow faculty assembled the following morning at the small but eminently functional crematorium in Headington. At the express wish of Arthur, no-one else had been invited: all pomp and ceremony were to be reserved for the memorial service. They sat in complete solemnity in the small chapel. They had all heartily subscribed to Augustus' plan of saying nothing to the undertakers at the crematorium. Only when the coffin containing Arthur's remains was carried in and laid gently on the track did it finally seem likely that this plan might work. The service proceeded with an almost indecent haste and before they realised, the last final words were being intoned.

Into your loving arms, O God, we commend our dear friend Arthur Plantagenet, at the end of his earthly life. We commit his body to be cremated, earth to earth, ashes to ashes, dust to dust, in sure and certain hope of the resurrection to eternal life through our Lord, Jesus Christ. Amen.

With that, Arthur Plantagenet's coffin disappeared from view.

*

When Augustus got back to college he went over to Arthur's former rooms. As soon as he opened the door he was met by the stale smell of Arthur's pipe. As he looked around, every detail of the room exuded Arthur Plantagenet's personality, all apart from the silence. Every flat surface held a bottle of one of the many embalming liqueurs with which he had been preparing his body. It was clear that Arthur hadn't expected his end to arrive quite so soon. He had planned to start the process of collecting Arthur's belongings but this was not the day for that. Today was a day for slow reflection and Augustus always found he reflected best on foot.

Without much idea of where he was going, Augustus headed down the stairs, straight through the lodge and up the road to the High Street. There were too many people there so he cut up past the Radcliffe Camera. Normally one of the quietest parts in Oxford, this morning students were piling out the entrance of Brasenose College, forcing Augustus to cut across to the opposite side. He smiled ironically at the copy of the Bridge of Sighs at Hertford College and on past the King's Arms, promising himself a pint on the way back. He paused for a second to enjoy the view of the beautifully frosted lawns through the tall iron gates of Trinity College, before finding himself heading towards the science area and the reassuring peace of the Laboratory of Physiology. He was in as close to a state of contentment as was possible under the circumstances. The faculty of gastronomic science might not be able to fulfil all of Arthur's wishes, but they would organise the best memorial service Oxford had seen in decades. There would be no point in depositing Arthur's ashes in the Cherwell at this time of year, so that could wait until summer, with a full picnic to go along with the sacrificial turkey. The thought of Arthur's final funerary voyage was beginning to form an enchanting image in Augustus' mind as he reached the main entrance of the laboratory.

Picking up his post he found a small handwritten note in his pigeonhole from the departmental porter.

Dear Dr Bloom. Don't forget your delivery. It's a wooden box just on the left as you go in the cold store marked with your name.

He couldn't think who could be sending him a package requiring cold storage, but then thoughts of a Christmas hamper filled with *foie gras*, confiture of figs and bottles of Sauternes came into his head. A hamper had arrived last year from one of Augustus' old and generous friends from medical school, Henry Hyde, now one of London's leading surgeons with elegant rooms in Harley Street and a Bentley to match. This sumptuous gift was sent in gratitude for a slender act of courtesy on Augustus' part last year when he had met and offered a few words of encouragement to Mr Hyde's nephew who was intent on reading medicine at Oxford. With that nephew now safely ensconced in Magdalen College, a repeat gesture seemed the most likely reason for the delivery.

Augustus walked down the corridor to the basement stairs with a sense of eager anticipation. He swung open the heavy industrial door into the dark Siberian underworld of the laboratory's cold store. Pulling the cord of the light switch, he found the wooden box just as described with a note bearing his name. This was clearly no hamper. He flipped down the large metal catch and opened the lid to find a large plastic bag with crushed ice. Somewhat perplexed, he opened the top of the bag and cleared away the top layer of ice before recoiling in horror. As the lid on the box slammed down, his proposed escape route for the shadow faculty of gastronomic science was now in ruins. In the box, lay the unmistakable shape of a human thigh, undoubtedly that of Professor Arthur Plantagenet, lately of St Jerome's College Oxford.

Augustus' chest began to hurt as his panicked breathing pulled more and more freezing air into his lungs. Slowly, he managed to quell first his wild breathing and then his racing heart. It was then that he remembered the letter from Arthur that Potts had given him the other day. It was still sitting on his desk upstairs. Despite his better judgement, he pulled the plastic bag out of the box and headed back to his office.

The letter was sitting propped up against the lamp on his desk. He ripped it open and started reading. On the paper was the flowing and familiar script of his good friend. Arthur had clearly researched the topic in some detail as the two pages of closely packed writing contained detailed 'suggestions' as to how to prepare his leg in the style of air cured ham. While he had gallantly offered to leave the exact details for members of the faculty to decide, there was certainly no doubt about Arthur's seriousness in this endeavour. The first and most urgent step was to start the drying process by packing it in salt for two weeks. Arthur strongly advocated that it should be done as rapidly as possible, preferably on the day of receipt. Then the salt should be washed off and the leg dried in a cool dry place with good airflow. He was particularly adamant that the choice of drying location be selected very carefully. Although Iberico and Parma hams are only salt cured, Arthur had suggested that applying a cure of juniper berries and molasses might help to enhance the flavour of the meat, as he was no longer, as he put it, a spring chicken.

*

When the ashen-faced Dr Bloom returned to the reassuring security of college he was carrying Arthur's leg in the plastic bag, which was now dripping water. He was hailed by Mr Potts as he passed through the gates.

'Sir, could I have a word?'

'Not now, Potts.'

'It's important, sir. It's about the professor.'

Seeing the look in Potts' eyes Augustus realised he had no choice.

'We'd better talk in 'ere, sir,' said Potts, leading the way into the back room.

'The letters that the professor left for me have got me a bit... er... edgy-like, sir,' continued Potts when they were a safe distance inside the lodge.

'Letters? Like the one Arthur left for me?'

'Yes, but it wasn't just you, you see. There was a whole load of 'em and... one for me, too.'

'You know he had great respect for you, Potts.'

'Well, he had a few kind words for me in his letter, but the rest was instructions. I was sent off to the Radcliffe mortuary straight after it all 'appened. I gave this letter to the head man and 'e opened it there and then.' Potts, who had been talking to the threadbare carpet for the last few minutes, looked up as if asking permission to continue his confession. Dr Bloom's heart was now beating as weakly and unevenly as Arthur's once had, but still he managed a nod of dread thinly disguised as encouragement.

'Well, 'e read it and then just laughed, but not a normal laugh like... told me to wait half 'n hour and it would be ready. So I went off for a cup of tea and when I came back 'e had this box... with your name on it.'

The two men stood in brooding silence, the only sound the dripping of water onto the floor from the plastic bag. Finally Potts asked the question.

'What's going on, sir? It's all a bit... you know... '

'It certainly is, Potts. It certainly is. This is all Arthur's idea of a joke, I guess. One that is getting a bit out of hand, that's all.'

'Pulling our leg you mean... ' Potts started to chortle but on seeing the look of panic on Augustus' face, Potts stumbled on. 'I didn't look, 'onest. It was the mortuary man, he told me. I'll take it to me grave, won't tell a soul, promise.'

Augustus knew Mr Potts would do just that. He placed a reassuring hand on the porter's shoulder and turned to leave.

'There's one more fing.' Potts disappeared for a second, returning with two large sacks of salt. 'The professor said you'd know what to do wiv 'em. Shall I drop 'em up to your room, sir?'

'That would be very kind, Potts, but not for a while. I need... a little time to myself.'

Chapter 19

Potts was true to his word and several hours later the two sacks of salt were delivered to Augustus along with a smaller bag of saltpetre. Augustus was perplexed as to the purpose of the saltpetre, or potassium nitrate to give it its modern name, but assuming Arthur had provided this for a purpose, he consulted his bookshelves for guidance. A nineteenth-century tome from his private library entitled *Culinary Chemistry* solved the mystery, providing a suitably simple recipe for curing ham, which called for a pound of saltpetre, three quarts of fine salt and pepper. As he read, Augustus' mind slowly turned from moral turmoil to the more reassuring practicalities of the curing process.

Curing is a remarkable process that halts the ravages of decay with the simplest of ingredients and it is worthy of a short digression. The simplest form of all is salt-curing where salt draws out water and creates an environment in which the normal bacteria of putrefaction cannot survive. Once protected from rotting, the meat needs to dry to achieve the firm, translucent character of the best hams. This is a slow process traditionally performed in open-sided buildings in clean mountain air or in rafters of houses or barns. Smoking is commonly used in Germany, most notably in Westphalia. Smoking has the additional benefits of adding a new dimension to the flavour and providing additional preservation against bacteria, though at the price of a flavour that most connoisseurs of dried meats would consider too dominant.

Augustus locked his door and started clearing space in his cooking alcove in preparation for the task in hand. Only then did he remove Arthur's leg for inspection. The gentleman from the hospital mortuary who had removed the limb clearly had some training or, at least, innate skills in the art of butchery, as the thigh was well presented and neatly trimmed. The skin tone was unappealing in colour, but the flesh was impressively firm for a man of Arthur's age. He knew he should have felt at least some sense of revulsion, but having spent several of his formative years as a medical student learning anatomy from the formalin-scented remains of his fellow humans, Augustus had acquired a certain sense of composure when it came to death, or indeed severed limbs. So, as the hour approached midnight, Augustus set about the task of curing Professor Plantagenet, carefully drying the surface before rubbing in the salt and saltpetre mixture to which he had added a few additional herbs from his own collection.

Chapter 20

Hilary Term 1970

Patrick Eccles walked up from the station to college at the start of the new term. Over Christmas he had revelled in the adulation of his family as the bright young thing from Oxford. Patrick was one of only a small number of the extended Eccles clan that had ever been to university and the first to go to Oxford. Every arcane feature of college life was examined at the family table with doting aunts hanging on his every word. But the feeling he didn't deserve to be here lingered over him and turning into the gate, he felt as nervous as he had on his first day last term. In the lodge, Eccles almost collided with his tutor Dr Augustus Bloom, making conversation unavoidable for either of them.

'Ah, Eccles. Welcome back.'

'Oh, yes, sir... thank you... ' Eccles mumbled in the direction of Dr Bloom's knees.

'I'll see you later to go over last term's exams. Let's say eleven o'clock in my rooms?'

'Yes... yes... of course, sir.' Eccles paused, unsure whether to say anything about the death of the man who was clearly a good friend of his tutor. 'I heard all about Professor Plantagenet.'

A look of panic flashed across Augustus Bloom's face.

'Heard what exactly?'

'Well, about him dying and all that,' mumbled Eccles, suddenly fearful that the news of Professor Plantagenet's death at the end of last term had been no more than an inaccurate rumour.

'Yes, of course. Tragic, tragic… and a great loss to us all,' said a relieved Augustus. 'By the way there's a memorial service in the chapel at the end of the week. Perhaps you could let the rowing club know and anyone else who might want to come.' With that, Augustus Bloom, still rattled by the mere mention of Arthur Plantagenet, turned on his heels before Eccles could reply.

Eccles for his part was happy that their conversation proved to be so brief and hurried on to the sanctuary of his rooms. He was barely through the door when a voice stopped him in his tracks.

'Eccles, there you are,' said Kingsley-Hampton from one of the Chesterfield armchairs. 'Be a good man and nip out to collect a cake from the covered market. I'm expecting guests. After that make yourself scarce.'

Eccles turned as slowly as he could without looking surly and made for the door, but Kingsley-Hampton hadn't finished.

'Oh, and you know that dining club you so singularly failed to track down last term? I asked my father about that dead Japanese bloke over Christmas and he got rather vexed and told me not to meddle. So now I'm really interested to know who's behind it. The dinner was held in this college so someone in the kitchens must know something. Go and ask the chef while you're out.'

The thoughts going through Eccles' head as he let the door slam after him might offend the gentler reader and so perhaps are best left to the imagination. Needless to say, Kingsley-Hampton's final shouted request didn't help.

'Oh, and get some fresh milk, there's a good man.'

*

A few minutes later and against his better judgement, Eccles found himself climbing the stone stairs into the Great Hall. At meal times the place was thronging with students and chatter, but now there was an eerie calm about the place. He was suddenly aware of the extraordinary volume of noise coming from his shoes on the stone flags and started to tiptoe. He was looking around for a door that he knew logically must exist but had never seen, the door to the kitchens below. Just then an old oak door at the far end of the entrance lobby flung open to reveal a short but ample woman using her substantial bosoms to support the four huge silver candelabras she was carrying. She walked directly at Eccles who remained frozen to the spot. Moments before their seemingly inevitable collision she caught sight of him through all the silver and let out a squeal of shock, almost losing her load.

'Goodness, sir, you gave me dreadful fright creeping around like a burglar. Anyway you're too late for breakfast. You young men these days sleep until all hours, I don't know, really I don't.' After relieving herself of these observations she continued on her way, bustling past the still frozen Eccles who felt a guilty blush rush up his face as he tried to gather his remaining shreds of poise.

'I'm actually looking for the head chef.'

She looked back in surprise at the young man. Though trying to look masterly and businesslike, Eccles' lost-lamb look had a very beneficial effect on Mary O'Sullivan, the head housekeeper. For her, there were two types of students: the toffs and the ducklings. She was clearly looking here at her favourite type – a duckling, the ones that need looking after.

'Well then, we'd better be going and finding him. Now help me down with these candlestick thingies.'

Once the eighteenth-century solid silver candelabras had been laid to rest on a nearby table, Mary O'Sullivan took Eccles by the arm and led him off down the back stairs to the kitchens.

Eccles and O'Sullivan cut a fine figure as they passed down the large central aisle of the kitchen, arm in arm as if on the way back from the altar. Eccles was amazed at the scale of this underground world that students rarely if ever saw. He had never suspected so many people worked to keep people like him fed. He was naturally greeted by suspicious looks from some and giggles from the younger girls as they peeled biblical mounds of potatoes. He was finally brought through to a small room at the back where he was presented.

'Morning, chef, this 'ere young man would like a word.' She patted Eccles on the arm as she turned to leave.

'Good luck, love.' With a final smile and a wink she was gone, leaving Eccles standing in front of the head chef and fervently wishing he had never started on this mission. The chef sat quietly, ticking items off a list with a pencil, which he then rather surprisingly stuck behind his ear. He was wearing a gleaming white coat, a relic from his days at the Savoy Hotel, with his name embroidered on the breast, Paul Roger. By this time, the soles of Eccles feet were burning and the power of speech seemed a distant memory. Finally, the chef looked up to inspect what the housekeeper had brought in.

'So?'

'Oh, er, well, Mr Rodger, it's about… '

'*Rho-Jer*, my name is Monsieur *Roger*.'

'Oh, Monsieur Rho-jer, very sorry, yes, of course. Well I thought you'd be the best person to ask about an exotic dish that has come up in my studies.'

Flattery in any language, accent or country is generally well received and a slight softening could be detected on Monsieur Roger's stern visage.

'Indeed, and what is zis dish?'

'Fugu.'

Eccles finally managed to lift his head and look his interlocutor in the eyes.

'Fugu? Zis is not a French dish.'

'No. Japanese, I believe.'

'Well I zink you should be looking for a Japanese cook, no?'

'I heard it had been served here, at St Jerome's… last year.'

Monsieur Roger dropped his head slightly to peer over the top of his reading glasses.

'If such a dish 'ad been served 'ere I would be ze first to know, don't you zink?'

'Indeed, of course, er, thank you.' Eccles retreated, nodding until he was clear of the door and could make a dash for it.

*

When Eccles returned after a detour to collect the milk and cake, he received not a word of thanks from Kingsley-Hampton who sat in his chair engrossed in *The Times*.

'Bang the kettle on there, old chap,' Kingsley-Hampton said from behind the newspaper.

Eccles duly turned his attention to making tea. Though he resented being treated as a servant, he was more accepting of Kingsley-Hampton's gentler requests, which put him in the role of a surrogate valet. Eccles found solace in the indubitable truth that he, like most valets, was considerably more intelligent than the man he was now expected to wait upon.

'And?' asked Kingsley-Hampton when Eccles handed him a cup of tea. 'What did the chef tell you?'

'He didn't seem to know anything about Fugu at all. Suggested I go and find a Japanese chef.'

'What exactly did he say?'

Eccles thought back and tried to recreate the words from the abstracted shorthand form within his head called memory.

'Something like, "I'd have known" or "I'd be the first person to know".'

'So he didn't give a clear "no"?'

'Well… I thought it seemed pretty clear cut, but he didn't actually say "no".'

'I'd call that an evasive "yes". But who the hell was it cooked for? Who is the shadow faculty of gastronomic science? Did you ask that?'

Eccles shook his head in reply.

'Oh for God's sake, Eccles.' Kingsley-Hampton gave *The Times* a dismissive shake and hid his annoyance behind it.

'As they call themselves a faculty, it could be a bunch of dons, couldn't it?' said Eccles, trying to salvage some dignity from the conversation.

'Can't believe that. None of those old farts would have the balls to serve some toxic fish at a dinner. No it has to be some secret student club.'

'They must be pretty well connected to invite a Japanese diplomat.'

'No more connected than I am and as they haven't yet invited me then it's time to start shaking a few trees.' He started pacing the floor while Eccles struggled to find something constructive to say.

'Perhaps they all died of Fugu poisoning at the last dinner.'

'We know for certain that at least one guest died, but I doubt it was all of them. I managed to wrangle from my father that the cultural attaché at the Japanese embassy did die suddenly last term at a dinner in Oxford. When I pushed him for more details he got really stroppy. So someone around here went to a lot of trouble to keep that quiet, but the death of an entire dining society would be impossible to hide. So how do we flush them out? We need beaters.'

'Beaters?'

'Good God, Eccles, there are times when you're almost intelligent and others when you are implausibly dense. Grouse-beaters are locals that march through the bracken and send the birds up in the air where you can shoot them.'

Eccles had never seen a grouse let alone shot one and so could reasonably plead ignorance of the subtleties of shooting small defenceless birds.

'How about placing an ad asking for information about a lost menu for this shadow faculty? Perhaps even offering a reward. They'll know straight away that their cover has been blown. No-one else will bother to reply because we have the menu but they'll be bound to contact us to try and shut us up if it's that much of a secret.'

Kingsley-Hampton stopped in his tracks while his mind digested this plan. Although as a rule he always favoured his own ideas, on this occasion the lack of any thoughts of his own made him more receptive to the suggestions of others.

'Why wouldn't we just put up a notice saying we'd found this menu and offer to return it to its rightful owner?' Kingsley-Hampton asked.

'They could just ignore a notice like that. If we pretended we were one of them that would really get their attention.'

'Of course. If that were my dining society and someone like you pretended you were a member that would really piss me off. I couldn't let anyone get away with that. Excellent. I knew we'd crack this with a little effort. How about a small ad in *Styx* and a note on the union notice board. Something like: "Lost: one menu from shadow faculty of gastronomic science. Trinity term last year. Great sentimental value. £10 reward." Oh, and make sure your name is on it.'

Kingsley-Hampton paused, clearly in deep thought. 'Mind you that might link this back to me too. On second thoughts set up a post office box number for the replies. That should do the trick, and add a nice spectre of mystery to the whole thing.' He rubbed his hands in apparent glee.

'Now my guests will be here soon so head off and get that sorted. Oh, and thanks for the cake.'

*

Well past the appointed tutorial hour of eleven o'clock, Augustus dashed up the stairs with a loaf of bread and a small bag of groceries to find Eccles sitting patiently on the top step.

'Come in, come in. Sorry I'm late, Eccles. Grab a seat there.'

Eccles sat on the edge of the chair to the left of the fire where he always sat and awaited his fate, as his tutor launched into the now comforting ritual of preparing tea and at least one edible item during the first part of a tutorial.

'So these exams of yours. Not bad but a bit patchy in

places.'

Eccles nodded in agreement to Dr Bloom's back as Augustus starting slicing into a loaf of bread in the cooking alcove.

'Very good essay on reflexes, not bad on synapses, but a bit shaky on the humble action potential. Your exam papers are there on the desk by the window, have a look through them while I finish off here.'

Eccles walked over and picked up his essays, which to his pleasant surprise were not heavily marked in red ink. He had almost finished going over them when his tutor thrust a plate of fish-smelling toast and a cup of grey Chinese tea into his hands.

'Anchovy relish on buttered toast. It was one of Arthur Plantagenet's favourite snacks.'

Eccles nibbled cautiously as Augustus wolfed down several slices.

'You seem to have forgotten to mention tetrodotoxin in your action potential essay. Odd, seeing as you seemed so interested in tetrodotoxin and Fugu last term. The chef even mentioned to me that someone had been down in the kitchens asking about Fugu this morning. That wasn't you, by any chance?'

Dr Bloom looked across at his student who was fingering his toast and studiously avoiding eye contact.

'Me? No, that must have been someone else.' Eccles flushed as soon as the lie left his lips. Into his panicked mind came the image of what it would be like to die of Fugu poisoning, lying on the floor gasping for air like a goldfish. With a shudder of revulsion, Eccles managed to clear the image and look up, only to see the shocked face of his tutor looking back.

'Are you all right, Eccles? Is there anything you want to get off your chest?'

Augustus had just been fishing for clues. He had received a note from the chef barely an hour ago that someone had been down in the kitchens asking about Fugu. His first mildly paranoid reaction was that the vice-chancellor was sending in spies, but from the chef's description it must have been Eccles. So why would he lie about it?

'No, sir. Nothing at all. Sorry, I'm not feeling that well, I think it may be this fish paste. Would you excuse me?' With that, Eccles ran out of the room, exam papers in one hand and toast in the other.

Augustus' second and third-year student tutorials helped to take his mind off Eccles' bizarre behaviour. Thank God the rest of them seemed sane. It was with huge relief that Augustus finally made his way to the senior common room parlour for lunch.

'Charles, glad I caught you on your own,' said Augustus, taking the seat beside the chaplain. Charles mumbled his agreement through a spoonful of sherry-laced lobster bisque, as close to contented as his personality would allow. The chaplain was still of the belief that Arthur Plantagenet had been entirely cremated, thereby relieving them all of the more onerous obligations of his will. After setting in motion the first steps of the curing process, Augustus had been carrying the burden of the truth for them all during the Christmas vacation. With each passing day, sharing the news of the true fate and indeed location of Arthur's leg became harder and harder. With the start of the new term he had vowed to tell the rest of the shadow faculty come what may. Here was the perfect opportunity.

'What's on your mind Augustus?' asked the chaplain in his best pastoral tone.

'Well… er… ' Augustus hesitated for a fraction too long. Before he realised it he was talking about Eccles rather than Arthur's leg. 'Do you know my student Eccles? Young nervous sort with a mess of red hair?'

'Hmm, I think so.'

'Well, the truth is I think he is going off the rails a bit. Could you have a chat with him? Make sure he is all right?'

'Of course, of course, Augustus. I won't make a big thing

of it. I'll try and bump into him sometime or invite him to tea. See what's going on. First time away from home. A lot of temptations for a young man in Oxford.'

After that the pair sat in silence until the room filled with the voices and inconsequential chatter of other fellows of the college as they all filed in for lunch. Augustus began to doubt there would ever be a suitable time to explain to the others what he had been doing with Arthur Plantagenet's leg.

Chapter 21

The chapel was never designed for the crowd that assembled on that first Sunday of Hilary term. The whole of the senior common room were present of course, as well as a few select dignitaries from the faculty of ancient history. It was the number of past students that exceeded all expectations. The assembled mass of Arthur Plantagenet's past students had clearly forgotten the ritual humiliation of his tutorials and laboured humour of his lectures, so it could only have been the appeal of the man himself that had brought them back. Nostalgia and time had distilled and glorified their memories so much that if Arthur himself had come back from the dead to meet them they would hardly have recognised him. It wasn't just students of ancient history who had assembled: Arthur had also been popular amongst the students of other faculties too. This popularity arose at least in part from his enthusiastic support of the rowing and rugby clubs, which was expressed in the form of funding of their respective clubs' beer requirements each term.

The bulk of those brought back to Oxford by the announcement in *The Times* got no further than the grass outside the chapel on which they unconsciously assembled in groups by year, subject or, in the case of the products of the grander public schools, by their *alma mater*. Into the already overflowing chapel the Master arrived with his reluctant guest, the vice-chancellor. Those standing in the antechapel made way as the two men swept in wearing their gowns of office, allowing them to take their place in the reserved seats next to the dean of Christchurch.

The dean was presiding over the service to allow Charles Pinker to play the organ as specifically requested in Arthur's will. Charles still wanted to meet the congregation personally as they assembled, so St Jerome's current organ scholar was left to serve up an innocuous menu of Bach while the guests arrived. This was delivered in the flowing and entirely ignorable fashion of a pianist during tea service at one of the better hotels. The sound was absolutely right for the occasion and its absence would have been sorely felt, but those in the chapel were only subliminally aware of what was being played and the volume of Bach's *Cantata number 208* was just right to mask the murmur of conversation without in any way hindering it. When the chapel doors closed, Charles headed up the steep stairs to the organ loft.

The dean then rose for the welcoming remarks and opening prayers. The service moved onto familiar territory with a rousing chorus of 'Jerusalem' from the whole congregation. After the first few notes escaped from the heavy doors of the chapel, the congregation on the lawn outside rose to their feet and joined in. Charles had selected the readings himself and, steering clear of any selections from Leviticus regarding what one should and shouldn't eat, played safe with readings from the Book of Wisdom and one of St Paul's letters to the Romans. In an oblique tribute to Arthur's gargantuan appetite, he selected Luke 9:10-17 as the Gospel reading. Then Augustus Bloom rose to his feet and made his way to the lectern for the eulogy.

'The biggest tribute to our dear departed friend Arthur Ignatius Plantagenet has been the extraordinary number of his colleagues, students and former students who have gathered here today. When I think back over the time I have known Arthur, I realised that the times I spent with him have been some of the most enjoyable and worthwhile moments of my life. Thinking of the gospel we have just heard about how Jesus fed five thousand people with just five fish and five loaves, I have come to realise that Arthur could create such miracles with time. Five minutes with Arthur could be more memorable than a whole day with other mere mortals. So in tribute to Arthur I ask just one thing of you all. In his death let us keep and cherish the memory of every second we spent with him. If we do that he will never leave us.' Augustus waited for the murmurs of agreement to abate. 'In his will he requested that his good friend and our chaplain Charles Pinker play the organ at this service. He also requested a specific piece: the *Maestoso* from Saint-Saëns' third symphony. This piece is Arthur incarnate into music. I can think of no better tribute than for all of us to listen and remember.'

With the magnificent opening chords, the chapel was filled with a triumphant wall of sound that even stirred the souls of the several committed atheists who had attended out of loyalty to Arthur or, as in the case of the vice-chancellor, duty. The chaplain's arrangement of this piece required the full range of organ, many of whose more unusual pipes had been airless for years. As the deepest notes rumbled through the floor rather than the air, a strangled rattling sound could be heard. On the first occurrence it was hard to be sure it had really happened, but each time Charles' left foot hit the low C on the pedal board it was there. With each blast of air sent into the great thirty-two foot diapason organ pipes, the rattling got louder. For most of the congregation, the music was barely impaired by these sonic blemishes, though two people did seem unusually affected. In the organ loft, Charles was wincing but couldn't stop hitting the offending note without losing the whole spirit of the piece. In the stalls below, Augustus sat with his head in his hands trying to conceal the grimace that each distorted organ note delivered. Those around him interpreted this merely as a sign of his distress at the loss of a dear friend. Augustus alone suspected the real reason for the organ's curiously specific malfunctions.

The rest of the service passed without incident and the organ performed perfectly as Charles accompanied the choir in an arrangement of Fauré's *Requiem*. The dean delivered a homily which was spiritually well intended, but his audience were challenged to find the link to Arthur. This was not surprising as there was none. The congregation earlier in the day at the morning service in Christchurch cathedral had been equally confused by the glowing tribute to a former professor of ancient history most of the congregation had never heard of. It was a great sense of relief to all concerned to clear the lungs with a few more rousing hymns before the final prayers for former fellows.

At the end of the service, Mr Potts found himself beside Augustus as they waited to file out of the chapel. One question had been troubling the head porter and he finally plucked up the courage to ask it.

'It wasn't something 'e ate, was it, Dr Bloom? I mean like that Japanese man that died at your previous dinner?'

'Oh no, Potts, it was everything he had ever eaten.' Augustus smiled at Potts who, uncomfortable with such gestures of simple human kindness from any of the fellows, felt obliged to look away. He was starting to warm to Dr Bloom even though he had no idea what he was talking about. Augustus had somewhat cryptically told the truth. Arthur's death was indeed the sum of every rich morsel that he had consumed. Arthur had loved every mouthful and enjoyed every moment of his life spent at the dining table. Mr Potts and Augustus stepped out into the quad, leaving the open-mouthed Patrick Eccles a few paces behind.

Following Arthur's wishes, all those who attended were invited for restoratives in the form of toasted brioche laden with *foie gras*, sliced figs and quince jelly. The jelly had been prepared appropriately by Monsieur Roger using Arthur's own harvest from the Botanical Gardens. The chef had insisted on extending the menu to include a few of Arthur's favourite *hors d'oeuvres*, fine slices of juniper-flavoured dried duck breast, as well as slices of apple topped with Stilton and a walnut. In addition to several cases of Dom Perignon 1962, the fellows had also agreed to open the cellars to offer a young but fragrantly flavoured sweet Jurançon to complement the *foie gras* and Stilton. More spectacularly a Château Lafite-Rothschild 1955 Grand Cru Classé Pauillac was provided as the perfect accompaniment for the sliced duck breast, though this was reserved for the fellows of the college and their more important guests.

The task of escorting the vice-chancellor naturally fell to the Master. The stilted conversation between the two men was thankfully eased as soon as they reached the hall by the champagne and exquisite *hors d'oeuvres*. The Master waxed on lyrically about the food, expecting no reply, while the vice-chancellor stayed silent wishing some proper food had been provided. Finally, the Master decided to broach the subject of Arthur's bequest. Naturally the executors of Arthur's will had not divulged the full details of this unusual document to the Master, but they had delivered the pertinent details of the donation to the university, along with the requirement that it should be presented to the vice-chancellor personally at a meeting of the shadow faculty of gastronomic science.

'Now, Dr Ridgeway, you may be unaware that Professor Plantagenet was an independently wealthy man and in his will he made a number of bequests to the college and indeed one to the university.'

Dr Ridgeway's sullen demeanour was suddenly transformed. Despite the riches of the colleges, he had been shocked on his appointment to discover the parlous state of the central coffers of the university.

'Really, I had no idea. What scale of donation are we talking about, Lord Faulkner?'

'A very generous offer indeed: the endowment of a new professorship in fact, with support for his election here at St Jerome's as a fellow.'

'Excellent, a wonderful legacy. In what faculty would this chair be, or would the university decide?'

'Oh, he was quite specific but also wishes the bequest and all the details to be presented to the university at a dinner here in college. I understand this was a condition in his will, so we are obliged to honour that, of course.'

'Of course, indeed. I fully understand the need to follow the letter of his will.'

'So we will have to organise a dinner here in college that you can attend on behalf of the university to accept this bequest. You've met a number of our fellows already so that should be a jolly affair.' The Master indicated that this was the end of the conversation with a broad and indulgently unctuous smile. The vice-chancellor reciprocated with a pale, thin-lipped imitation, which was cut short as he saw Augustus Bloom hovering nearby.

After mingling with the guests exchanging memories of Arthur's finest moments, the surviving members of the shadow faculty had started to gather near the door closest to the kitchens. Augustus Bloom was the last to join them. He had been attempting to eavesdrop on the conversation between the Master and the vice-chancellor while avoiding being seen by either, but had failed on both accounts.

'Gentlemen. A toast to the old boy.' Augustus greeted his fellow gastronomes with his glass raised in deference to Arthur.

'Not a bad send off. I must say an impressive turnout,' said George Le Strang, for whom, like many of those present, Arthur's memory was more appealing and less infuriating than Arthur the man. After nods of agreement they fell into silence and Augustus took the opportunity to address them all.

'I think it would be a good moment to share something with all of you. Something Arthur left behind.'

Seeing the expectant look in Hamish's eye, who clearly presumed this to be some exotic and rare vintage wine, Augustus was forced to cut to the chase.

'I'm afraid it relates to the little problem he left us in the will that I had suggested would disappear with his cremation. You see, it turns out that without my knowledge he had made arrangements even before his death to ensure the success of his plan.'

'I thought… but you said… Oh God!' Charles Pinker's exuberant mood at the success of his service was gone.

'So where the hell is it now?' asked a shocked Hamish McIntyre.

'Curing in salt, according to Arthur's express wishes.'

Charles Pinker couldn't cope with this news and gravity at the same time and slumped onto the wooden bench that ran along the walls of the Hall. Theodore Flanagan's contribution was apposite and revealed once again his tendency to revert to his Irish roots under stress.

'Jesus, Mary and Joseph. I don't believe it.'

'But where?' asked Hamish again, apparently more troubled about the location of the leg rather than its existence.

'Perhaps I should show you?' Augustus had hoped sharing this secret would have eased the burden on his own shoulders, but looking around at the emotions etched on the faces of the group he realised it had just made things worse. Augustus led the group out of the dining hall and back into the gloom of the quadrangle at twilight.

As they passed along the gravel path, not one of them noticed the figure sitting on his own on one of the old wooden benches that lined the quad. Patrick Eccles didn't register their existence either. His mind was racing trying to reconcile the irreconcilable. His tutor must be part of this mythical dining society upon whose existence his roommate had stumbled. Now they've gone and killed Professor Plantagenet. If the story got out, God knows what might happen. Looking up, Eccles caught sight of a shaft of light cutting across the grass from the open chapel door through which he saw the chaplain disappear.

Inside the chapel, Augustus led the group up to the organ

loft. To Charles' great surprise Augustus went behind the organ and, with gentle pressure on the edge of the panelling, opened the secret door that the chaplain thought was known only to him. The men climbed the narrow stone staircase and emerged into the cool darkness of the room above. Augustus lit the candle he had taken from the organ loft, revealing the beams high in the ceiling and the letters carved on the gable wall H T B MDCCL. The chaplain glanced nervously at the pile of faculty documents he had hidden in the corner, which, to his great relief, looked undisturbed.

'Wow, what a brilliant place,' said Hamish, his enthusiasm obliterating the memory of why they were here. 'What does this HTB mean? And the year, seventeen hundred and er… ?'

'1750 is the year, so I think the other letters must stand for Hieronymus Theophilus Bloch, who was the chaplain at the time,' explained Augustus.

'The cellar ghost? Excellent,' said Hamish.

Theodore Flanagan gave a mannered cough. 'I believe there is something here you wish to show us Augustus?'

Without a word Augustus handed the candle to Charles Pinker. The golden stone walls of the room shuddered as the flame flickered from the shake in the chaplain's hand. Augustus knelt down on his knees and peered into the top of one of the longest organ pipes that protruded through the floor, a 32-foot diapason. He then pulled on a small rope. During previous inspections he had felt no resistance, but the object at the other end of the rope was firmly wedged into the organ pipe, amply explaining the strange sounds that this pipe had made during the service. A firm yank with both of his hands was required to lift the muslin sack holding Arthur's thigh into view.

Leabharlanna Poiblí Chathair Baile Átha Cliath

Dublin City Public Libraries

Chapter 22

The following morning, the five remaining members of the shadow faculty assembled in their tasting kitchen within the cellars. For the first time since these meetings started, no food or indeed wine graced the makeshift table. Without the usual culinary odours, the air was heavy with a dank musty smell. Charles Pinker's shoulders shuddered with the cold as he tried to pull the collar of his winter coat even tighter.

'So?' started Charles valiantly.

'So we are in a right pickle, legally and morally it seems,' offered Hamish before the table fell silent again. They all looked at each other, all except Augustus Bloom who was staring intently at the floor. Eventually George Le Strang could take it no more.

'Oh, for goodness sake, will you look at yourselves. It was all a bit of a lark, but it is time to thank Arthur for his entertaining prank of a will, bury the damn leg and get on with our lives.'

'I second that,' added Hamish.

'I'm not sure we can. As executors of his will we are obliged to follow his wishes... to the letter,' said Theodore.

'But, if he'd said "go and throttle the vice-chancellor and throw him off a punt" we wouldn't have to do that, surely?' asked Hamish.

'Well, I'd join you in that, Hamish. I'll throttle him and

you can throw him in. Better than eating Arthur's leg at any rate,' said George.

'Thankfully Arthur didn't ask us to murder the vice-chancellor, but if he had our obligations under the will would be waived as that would be illegal,' said Theodore.

'We can't surely be asked to commit the equally illegal – and might I add immoral – act of cannibalism just because a dead person asked us to?' asked Charles.

'That is true, Charles, but as Arthur pointed out at dinner last term, it's not illegal and in the absence of a law, morals carry no legal weight,' said Theodore.

'What's not illegal about it?' asked Hamish.

'Cannibalism isn't illegal, at least not in this country,' repeated Theodore.

'Don't be daft, it must be,' said Hamish. 'There must be some ancient law or other. I heard witchcraft was illegal, so cannibalism must be.'

'The laws against witches were repealed in 1951, but there really isn't a law against what Arthur has asked us to do,' said Theodore, slipping into the comfortable mode of law lecturer. 'I've done a bit of research and the best recent paper on cannibalism was published in the *Harvard Law Review* twenty years ago. It was the hypothetical case of a group of people stranded in a cave, 'The Case of the Speluncean Explorers', but the discussion centred on whether killing someone is ever justified if it is the only way for others to survive. It didn't address the act of eating someone.'

'There must have been real cases of cannibalism in the courts, surely?' asked Charles incredulously.

'The most famous case of cannibalism that came to court was *Regina vs. Dudley and Stephens* back in 1884. After they were shipwrecked they openly admitted eating one of the crew to survive, but the act of cannibalism was never in question – it was just the fact that they *killed* him in order to eat him. The offence of murder catches most wanton or criminal cannibals.'

'Well laws apart, it is certainly immoral,' said Charles.

'It is usually deemed so,' continued Theodore, who was starting to sound as if he were discussing an erudite topic in a tutorial rather than the rights and wrongs of eating their dear and recently departed friend. 'But, as Arthur pointed out, it is not immoral in the eyes of that usual model of moral authority in these lands, the Church. The Bible really doesn't offer much positive guidance and the Eucharist itself is essentially cannibalistic. Emperor Nero had even accused early Christians of cannibalism to turn the Roman mob against them. I'm surprised that Arthur didn't bring that up at the last dinner.'

'Last dinner, last supper,' chortled Hamish, digging Augustus in the ribs to try and lighten the atmosphere. He failed and received a withering look from the chaplain for his efforts.

'That's just a metaphor,' continued Charles. 'It's only wine and a wafer that you actually eat.'

'Not in my part of the world, Charles, or Rome or indeed in most of the Christian world,' replied Theodore indignantly. 'Wars have been fought in defence of the physical reality of transubstantiation: the idea that we are really eating the blood and body of Christ.'

Charles, puce with the exaggerated outrage of someone who knows the argument is slipping away from them, rose to his feet and started pacing the floor before stopping opposite Augustus Bloom.

'Augustus, come on, speak up, a good dose of common sense would do nicely right now. Surely there must be some medical dangers in cannibalism?'

Augustus slowly looked up and met the expectant gaze of his partners in this apparent non-crime.

'Well, there is a fatal disease called Kuru that is thought to be spread in Papua New Guinea by cannibalism within the Fore tribe.'

'There you have it, a perfectly sound reason not to pursue this ridiculous idea,' said Charles triumphantly.

'Yes, but only the women and children caught the disease from eating the offal including the brain. The men-folk of the Fore tribe ate the flesh and never seemed to come to much harm. So as Arthur died of natural causes and is only asking us to eat his leg, there should be no medical risks… '

'Oh Lord, give me strength. This is Lent: we're supposed to be basing our next dinner on a Lenten feast and avoiding meat, and you're saying we should just slap Arthur in the cooker and serve him up? Heathens the lot of you,' said Charles in total exasperation.

'We can't just serve him up anyway at this next dinner, Lent or no Lent,' offered Augustus.

'We can't? Excellent, finally a grain of sense, Augustus,' said Charles with a sense of relief.

'Well… He wouldn't be ready yet. Dry-curing takes months and months. He couldn't possibly be properly cured until next term at the very earliest.'

'Oh Christ forgive us!' Charles slumped back in his seat.

'Now, come on, Augustus, old chap; you can't really be agreeing with Theodore that we just have to get on and eat him?' asked Hamish.

'I think it's what Arthur wanted and as long as it's not illegal then… Then I think we are obliged to follow the express wishes of his will. Isn't that right, Theodore?'

'I'm sorry to say that I think it is. As executors we are obliged to administer the estate of the deceased in accordance with the terms of the will and according to the law. Unless we petition the House of Commons to introduce a law to outlaw cannibalism I see no option but do what Arthur asked of us.'

'So let's do that!' said Charles.

'I think that would draw more attention on us than you might like, Charles. It would certainly do little to endear us to the vice-chancellor,' concluded Theodore.

'Arthur's money will keep the vice-chancellor off our backs,' said Augustus. 'Talking of which, don't forget Arthur's will also requires us to invite the vice-chancellor to dinner to receive his bequest to the university and unwittingly to join in this grand gastronomic experiment.'

'I still don't see why we can't just keep the will secret and forget the whole daft idea. I know you explained about executors and all that, but who would know?' asked George.

'Well we've already told the Master about the money and he's told the vice-chancellor. So the existence of the will is already well known. If we take the money and ignore Arthur's other requests we are certainly acting illegally. Each provision of a will has equal weight in law,' explained Theodore.

'Why can't we declare that Arthur was not in sound mind when he made the damn will? That sort of thing must happen all the time,' asked Charles.

'It's not really fair to tarnish Arthur's memory by saying he was crazy, Charles,' said Augustus. 'That would be the height of disloyalty.'

The rest of the table nodded their assent. All, that is, apart from the chaplain.

'Well, I think you are all mad, quite certifiable,' said Charles, sitting back in his chair and folding his arms in a weak attempt at defiance.

*

By the time the five dons had resurfaced, no avenue of escape had been identified. Theodore and Augustus were strangely resigned to following through with the requirements of Arthur's will. Hamish was a little squeamish, but the idea had germinated a spark of curiosity in him. Add to that the truly delicious thought of watching the vice-chancellor tuck into Arthur's leg and Hamish was not far from becoming an eager accomplice. George was opposed to eating his former colleague primarily on the basis that he would most probably taste awful, while the poor chaplain was in a state of extreme theological turmoil. As Charles crossed the quad, muttering to himself, he was spotted by Patrick Eccles who was sitting in the window seat of his room ostensibly reading over his latest essay. Eccles sprang to his feet. By the time Eccles had hurtled down the stairs to reach the flagstones of Old Quad, Charles Pinker had reached the first step of his own staircase.

Eccles slowed to a more casual pace, trying to look as if he were merely going for a stroll, but a biting wind and the lack of an overcoat made this pretence almost impossible as he shivered around to the other side of the quad. Sheltering inside the stone entrance of the chaplain's staircase, Eccles paused to gather his thoughts and practise his opening words in his head. He started to climb the wooden stairs, wincing at each creak and trying to adapt his gait to make the next step quieter. By the time he reached the top, his legs were spread to each side of the stairs in the vain search for solid, non-creaking wood. He paused again outside the door, listening before raising his hand to knock. He could hear muffled voices, the chaplain's mostly. The words Eccles first made out were 'Arthur', 'Hell' and 'Sin'. Then after a brief silence, Eccles could have sworn he heard the voice of the recently deceased Arthur Plantagenet himself. Before he could hear anymore, the silence of the stairwell was broken by the sound of heavy footsteps on the lower steps. Eccles spun on his heels and tripped down the stairs, just managing to find his balance before colliding with Augustus Bloom who was on his way up. The pair passed each other in total silence with only the briefest nod of acknowledgement.

Augustus didn't pause at the door. If he had stopped to listen, he would also have heard the intense conversation from the other side. Instead, he hammered insistently on the door. As anxious as he was to calm his friend's nerves, more pressing was the need to make sure the chaplain didn't do anything that might expose them all. With his knock, all sounds from the chaplain's room stopped and then the door opened by a small crack, revealing an ashen-faced Charles Pinker.

'Augustus, er... can't talk now. Can I see you later?'

'Are you all right, Charles?'

'Fine, really fine. Just got someone here now, a bit delicate. I'll see you later.'

Augustus nodded in assent and slowly wound his way down the stairs.

Charles closed the door and leant against it in relief with his eyes closed. Then, after a deep breath he opened his eyes.

'Arthur!' he hissed scanning the room. 'Where are you? Come back, you old bastard, I hadn't finished yet.'

On getting back to his rooms, Augustus Bloom collapsed into his favourite armchair, mentally going over the morning's events. For Augustus, the sooner they completed the tasks Arthur had bequeathed them the sooner life would return to normal, so from that perspective things had gone passably well. Augustus looked up at the urn on his mantelpiece that contained Arthur's ashes, well the ashes of most of his body at least. His mind turned to the more practical aspects of Arthur's last will and testament. The picnic with the truffled turkey could wait until the first fine weekend of next term. As to visiting Rome and Venice to deposit the rest of the ashes, that would have to wait until the long vacation. Once he had mentally resolved these more pragmatic issues, Augustus was left looking at the urn. After a long period of reflection his mind returned to the question of serving Arthur at dinner. He looked up and addressed the urn.

'Arthur, have you any notion of the mayhem you are creating down here?'

Chapter 23

Dr Ridgeway, the vice-chancellor, turned over the pages of the newspaper on his desk with disdain. He held the pages cautiously in just one finger and thumb with his other fingers held as far away from the paper as anatomy permitted, as if he were afraid of catching a morbid disease from its pages. The editor of this particular publication was at that moment being escorted up St John's Street by one of the university proctors, accompanied by two bowler-hatted assistants, or Bulldogs as they are commonly called. Rupert Atworth had been publicly hauled out of the junior common room at Worcester College just after breakfast, protesting violently and incoherently about the freedom of the press and the fascist forces of the university establishment. Whilst sharing these very valid sentiments, not one of the other undergraduates felt the need to support Atworth in any significant or practical manner. They nodded, tutted and a few even clapped in what they had hoped was an obvious sign of support for their fellow student. Unfortunately, this was interpreted by the Bulldogs as support for their actions and by the student in question as treasonable disloyalty.

Atworth was manhandled through the door of Dr Ridgeway's office, truly baffled as to which of the glib and inconsequential stories about undergraduate life had been deemed so dangerous.

'Gentlemen, please. There is no need to be so... rough.' He smiled sycophantically at Atworth before continuing. 'Now Mr Atworth... May I call you Rupert?'

Atworth looked back at the vice-chancellor in a blank and unresponsive stare. Even the difference in age and status between them was not enough to assuage the inalienable sense of superiority that Rupert Atworth felt over the vice-chancellor by virtue of his breeding. Unbeknownst to the vice-chancellor, the student who had been frogmarched into his office was the second son of Field Marshall Atworth and thirty-fifth in line to the throne, further deaths and breeding amongst those closer in line notwithstanding. Somewhat thrown by the icy defiant stare, the vice-chancellor continued more cautiously.

'I must apologise for the harshness of the proctors. I had merely asked that they bring you along to my office. This is really just an informal chat.'

'My father won't be impressed, you know.'

'Indeed. Now I need some more information about a certain advert that was placed the other week in your publication: this one.' He tossed the copy of *Styx*, an unofficial undergraduate newspaper, across the table. At the open page, one particular advert had been circled in red.

Lost: One menu of great sentimental value relating to a dinner of the Shadow Faculty of Gastronomic Science. Reward of £10 if returned.

'Only a post office box number is given in the advertisement for contact. I merely need to know who placed this advertisement.'

'Do you know who my father is?'

'The problem I have is that when I approached the post office they could only tell me that all mail was being forwarded on and I would need a court order to be told to where and to whom.'

'Field Marshall Atworth. He served in the Royal Fusiliers with the real Chancellor, you know.'

Ridgeway was a little taken aback at this news and the curiously disconnected conversational style of this young man.

'A most esteemed military gentleman whom I am sure would be most keen for you to assist me in my duties.'

'Yeah, sure.' Atworth tried to sound surly, but unfortunately Dr Ridgeway had secured an unexpected direct hit with his last comment. The Field Marshall was extremely unimpressed that his son was dabbling in journalism. If he were in the room at this moment he would undoubtedly clip him over the head and order a detailed statement of everything his son knew about whatever sordid affair he was mixed up with, even if he wasn't.

'This is a delicate matter with ramifications that extend far wider than you could possibly imagine. It is certainly a matter that I wish to keep the police and judiciary well away from.'

'I don't know any more than you do, sorry.' Atworth was now more perplexed than angry. How could a small ad like that cause this much trouble?'

'But you're the editor. So… '

After a pause of several interminable seconds, it was the editor of *Styx* that gave way. 'So you want me to find out who it is?'

'Precisely. Shall we say Monday morning, back here in my office?'

*

Once Atworth had been ejected onto the street of Wellington Square, the vice-chancellor afforded himself a smile. When elected he had high hopes of sweeping away a thousand years of complacent academic torpor within his first year of breath-taking reforms. Now he had, with a little guidance, lowered his sights to merely winning each skirmish that came his way and moving the mountain teaspoonful by teaspoonful. Spurred on by this latest small victory, he picked up the phone to call Lord Faulkner, Master of St Jerome's.

'Lord Faulkner? Kenneth Ridgeway, the vice-chancellor here.'

'And?' Phone etiquette was never one of the Master's strong points and he was really in no mood for small talk.

'Well, it's about the late Professor Arthur Plantagenet and his legacy to the university.'

'Oh, the money. I was wondering when you'd get back to me about that.'

'Oh, you misunderstand, Lord Faulkner,' said the vice-chancellor in his gentlest tones. 'I fully appreciate that these things take time and I wouldn't dream of calling you about the details. My office can take care of that when the time comes. No, the problem is that Arthur's legacy is in peril of being tarnished by the activities of his former colleagues in this ridiculous gastronomical club. Something has appeared in one of the student newspapers, which suggests the story about Mr Tokoro we both worked so hard to suppress may be about to raise its ugly head.'

'Oh I wouldn't worry about any repercussions from last year,' replied the Master with the delight of a man holding a pair of twos who has been dealt three aces.

'I can't share your confidence. This could still reflect very badly on the university, and of course Professor Plantagenet. I don't think we've heard the last of it yet.'

'Well, I have just received a letter from the Japanese ambassador which I think brings the matter to a satisfactory conclusion. He was extremely gracious in thanking all the members of the society for their kind letters about the incident. So there is really no problem for you to be worrying about.'

'The ambassador wrote a letter of thanks? Oh well that is encouraging, but that wouldn't stop a disreputable journalist trying to make hay.'

'I'm sure there are far better things to talk about than a dead diplomat. Now, what was in this student rag?'

'An advertisement asking for information about a lost menu from the... what do they call themselves? Oh, yes, the shadow faculty of gastronomic science.'

'A menu? You're worried about a lost menu? Good God

man, haven't you anything better to do?'

*

It took no more than ten minutes for Rupert Atworth to reach the gates of St Jerome's. He sped through the lodge and cut straight across the grass of Old Quad. The 'Oy, you! Keep off the grass!' from Potts barely reaching his ears before he had reached his old school friend's staircase. Matthew Kingsley-Hampton was still sitting in pyjamas in front of a blazing fire when Atworth burst into the room and was confronted by a wall of heat.

'Christ almighty, Mattie-boy. I don't know what you're up to but it must be big.'

'For God's sake, Rupert, sit down. And please don't call me Mattie-boy. I'm not one of your Labradors, you know. Now what has you so hot and bothered?'

'Why is it so damn hot in here?' said Atworth, displaying his talent for random thought association.

'Just burning some old menus collected by my idiot roommate. Now, do you want to explain why you just burst in like a madman or do I have to guess?'

'Oh, yeah. Well I was having breakfast in the junior common room when these pair of bloody Bulldogs dragged me out, right up St John's Street to the vice-chancellor's office. The vice-chancellor's office for Christ's sake.' He paused for dramatic effect, but, disappointed by Kingsley-Hampton's complete lack of reaction, gave up and carried on talking. 'All because of your bloody advert.'

He suddenly had Kingsley-Hampton's complete attention.

'You're kidding. What did he say?'

'Oh, "major national importance", "didn't want to bring in the police". All very hush-hush.'

'He must've explained why?'

'Well, he didn't seem to be in an explaining sort of mood.'

'Did you ask for an explanation?'

'Oh, well not in so many words.'

'In any words?'

'Er, no,' admitted a crestfallen Atworth. It was like being back at school again. He had spent his schooldays on the receiving end of these sorts of schoolmasterly put-downs. It seemed he was destined to spend much of his adult life in the same position. In contrast, his school friend Kingsley-Hampton was clearly destined for the life as a barrister in the high court, if the urge or need to work for his living ever reared its ugly head.

'So what did you tell him? Did you tell him it was me?'

'No, of course not.'

'But… '

'Well, I sort of agreed to find out who placed the ad and tell him on Monday.'

'Holy crap, I'm surrounded by idiots.' Kingsley-Hampton cradled his shaking head in his hands for a second. 'Well, next time you see your friend the vice-chancellor, tell him it was Patrick no-bloody-middle-name-because-I'm-boring-and-middle-class Eccles.'

Atworth stared back blankly.

'My cretinous roommate. The ad was his idea and all we got in return is a room full of effing menus and a request for the £10 reward. They've kept the fire burning nicely for a week, but provided absolutely no information about this damn Russian roulette dining society.'

Between the vice-chancellor and the now ranting Kingsley-Hampton, Atworth was more than a little out of his depth. It was therefore a great relief when Kingsley-Hampton calmed down enough to explain about the menu and the death of the Japanese diplomat. This explanation took a while, but eventually Kingsley-Hampton managed to hammer a coherent picture of events into his interlocutor's head. As Atworth gazed at the original menu retrieved from Kingsley-Hampton's trunk, his journalistic spirit came to the fore.

'Look, if you can't entice them out, let me flush them out. I'll run it on the front page of the first edition next term. Big headline: "Russian Roulette Dining Soc Kills Japanese

Ambassador. Who will die next?"'

'Don't you think the vice-chancellor might get a little pissed off? Not a very hush-hush approach.'

'Oh, stuff him. Christ, I could get a job at *The Times* on the back of this.'

In the room beside them, Patrick Eccles had been lying on his bed reading a book, banished from the front room by Kingsley-Hampton for crimes unspecified. When he overheard the start of Atworth's story, he'd sat up on his bed waiting for the right moment to walk nonchalantly out of his room and join the conversation. It soon became clear to him that no such moment was likely to arise. By the time Atworth finally took his leave, Eccles doubted leaving the room would ever be a good idea.

Chapter 24

Augustus Bloom sat waiting for evensong to begin in the chapel at St Jerome's. He had arrived early to guarantee a place in the back row of the flamboyantly canopied choir stalls. These seats were enveloped by carved wood embellishments that looked far more pagan than Christian, with unicorns, cloven-hoofed elephants and faces contorted in anger or pain or both. These canopies served to isolate the inhabitant very effectively. This spared Augustus from the need to interact with those seated on either side, which was a great blessing for Augustus who much preferred evensong as a solitary experience. Even better were the ornately carved misericords underneath the hinged seats of this back row. These small shelves that derive their name from the Latin word for mercy had the merciful benefit of allowing those attending services to take the weight off their feet, by resting their posteriors when the seat was folded up yet appear to be standing.

Although generally fiercely loyal to his college, Augustus Bloom preferred the greater majesty and certainly better choirs of other colleges. Magdalen College's evensong was by far his favourite, followed by New College, with Christchurch as a reasonable third choice if he was running late, as it was the closest of the three. But this evening he had arranged to meet the chaplain to finalise the guest list and menu for this term's dinner. Although the setting was not quite so atmospheric nor the choir as ethereal as it might have been, he was looking forward to the distinct pleasure of hearing the voice of God, as Charles Pinker liked to describe Bach's organ works in his more lyrical moments, played by one of Oxford's finest organists.

The service turned out to be far better than Augustus had expected. An excellent *introitus* by Tomkins. The *magnificat* and *nunc dimittis* by Orlando Gibbons was ably executed but the anthem, Palestrina's *Exultate Deo* was quite sublime. As the service came to an end, Augustus settled back and closed his eyes to listen to the organ voluntary. As the last momentous notes echoed away into the cold silence of the chapel Augustus, a confirmed agnostic, felt he had at least glimpsed 'the peace that passes all understanding' that the chaplain kept trying to convince him was at the heart of all spirituality. When he finally opened his eyes, the last pairs of feet were leaving the chapel and the door clunked heavily behind them. Rising to his own feet he saw that Charles Pinker was still sitting at the organ.

Charles collected his music and spun his legs over the bench seat. 'Augustus. Don't just sit there, come up and give me a hand.'

By the time Augustus reached the organ loft there was no earthly sign of the chaplain. Seeing the secret panel door at the side of the organ swinging on its hinges, he knew in an instant where Charles had gone. He was about to head up the stone staircase to the room where Arthur's leg lay in rest when the chaplain appeared from behind the organ, arms laden with boxes of papers.

'There you are, Charles. I must say fine evensong tonight and I loved that last organ piece. Bach, I presume.'

'Who else? Bach's *Passacaglia* in C minor,' said Charles testily. 'Now, if you wouldn't mind, could you collect the rest of our archives from upstairs? They can't be left here.'

'Why not?'

'Well if you already know about this room then probably

half the college does. On reflection I reckon they'll be safer from prying eyes back in my rooms. At least I can lock my own door.'

'Okay, if you say so, but why are they here in the first place? I thought they were always kept in your room?'

'I thought they'd be safer here after Dr Ridgeway started kicking up a stink.'

'I think we are safe on that score now, Charles, what with Arthur's legacy.'

'Oh yes, of course. All thanks to Arthur's bloody will. Where would we be without it?'

Augustus knew better than to reply to that particular question and headed up the stairs in silence to collect the last of the shadow faculty's records from the room above, followed by the muttering chaplain. Within the stone walls of the chapel, the ethereal figure of the Reverend Hieronymus Theophilus Bloch looked down on Dr Bloom and the current chaplain with a certain annoyance. The Reverend Bloch had learnt of the shadow faculty of gastronomic science just a few months ago when the archives had been fortuitously delivered within his sphere of movement. He was, by the curiously fickle and unpredictable spectral rules of ghosts, limited to the wine cellars and the chapel. These menus were the discovery of the century for Bloch, possibly only surpassed when the college started laying down Château Petrus at the end of the nineteenth century. Bloch was therefore not unreasonably upset with the prospect of losing such vicarious gastronomic delights. Charles Pinker suddenly shuddered, struck by an overwhelming sense of foreboding. Fortunately for Charles Pinker the Reverend Bloch's interaction with the corporeal plane of existence was, by those same curiously fickle and unpredictable rules, limited to bottles of wine in the cellars. So all Bloch achieved as he tried to block Charles Pinker's path was to make the current chaplain shiver with cold and hasten his desire to escape. Charles thrust the nearest box of documents towards Augustus and, gathering the rest in his arms, hurried down the stairs.

It wasn't until Charles Pinker had crossed the threshold into the safety of his rooms in Old Quad that he admitted to Augustus that one of the menus had gone missing.

'Oh, come on Charles. It's bound to be in this pile somewhere.'

'Trust me, I've checked and double checked.'

'Which one?'

'It was one from last summer's dinner, so I know for certain that I had it here somewhere.'

There was a knock at the door.

'Who is it?' said Charles, leaping to the door and holding the handle in case anyone tried to force their way in.

'Mr Potts, sir. I've a delivery from Taylor and Sons, the framers.'

'Oh, Mr Potts do come in. Sorry, I wasn't quite sure who it was,' said Charles.

Potts ambled in with a large parcel immaculately wrapped in brown paper.

'There you go, sir and I'm sorry to disturb you and… Oh, Dr Bloom, good day to you too. It's this er… napkin thing of yours what that clot broke when 'e bashed into you, chaplain.'

Charles Pinker pulled off the wrapping to reveal the re-framed constitution of the Faculty of Gastronomic Science, the original having been damaged in his impetuous transfer of the faculty archives to the chapel.

'Good God, Charles, what happened to it?'

'Well, I er… ' The chaplain's explanation ground to a halt, but Mr Potts filled in the details.

'It was that clot Kingsley-Hampton – walked right into the chaplain, he did. Not looking or caring where he was going as usual.'

Mr Potts was generally very accepting of the class divisions that Oxford and indeed English society was built upon. After the trials and tribulations of his chequered military career, Potts was delighted to have the status of head porter and felt it only right and proper that he had to defer to clever young upstarts, mostly but not entirely born into a level of society that Potts felt was far above him. But the likes of the honourable Kingsley-Hampton rankled with Potts. He liked proper toffs but Kingsley-Hampton had only acquired his 'honourable' title last year when his father Edmund was made a life peer for political services, despite being born into a family with a small corner shop in east London: a fact known to all as the story had been covered in depth in the *Oxford Times*. A scholarship to a good school and an even better marriage into the Kingsley's of Richmond had catapulted the young Edmund Hampton into parliament and eventually the offspring of this union, Matthew Kingsley-Hampton, into Oxford University.

'Charles, how did this character end up damaging our constitution?' asked Augustus Bloom.

'Well, it was all in this confusion about moving our archives. I had a small collision in the quad.'

'The missing menu couldn't have been lost at the same time, could it Charles?'

'I'm sure, no, I'd have… Potts, you didn't find a menu by any chance that day?'

'No, sir. It was just the broken glass on this here framed whatever-it-is.'

'Potts, this Kingsley-Hampton chap, where are his rooms?' said Augustus.

'Staircase five, at the top, room three, sharing with that new boy, Eccles. He's another queer one too, getting sack loads of mail.'

'Good God!'

'Sir?'

'Oh, that's fine, Mr Potts, excellent in fact. Many thanks.' Augustus ushered the confused Mr Potts to the door before turning his attention again to the chaplain.

*

After leaving the chaplain's rooms, Augustus made his way to the porter's lodge. He found Mr Potts in the back room of the lodge sorting through a large pile of envelopes addressed to Mr P. Eccles.

'Potts, I have a slight problem that I hope you might help me with.'

'Course, sir. What can I do for you?'

'It's this Kingsley-Hampton chap, I have reason to think he picked up one of the menus for our little dining society when he collided with the chaplain. It seems he's been getting my student Eccles to nose around and ask questions. With all this business with Arthur still going on, we don't want anyone snooping into the affairs of the shadow faculty right now.'

'Oh no, indeed not, sir.'

'You wouldn't be able to get one of the scouts to keep an eye out for it would you? It would look just like this.' Augustus showed him an elegant ivory-boarded menu from an earlier dinner bearing St Jerome's crest with the pages behind held in place with black and purple ribbon.

'I'll take care of that myself, Dr Bloom; wouldn't want anyone else getting wind of this.'

'Thank you, Potts.' Augustus headed off to the senior common room parlour for a badly needed sherry before dinner.

Potts collected his bowler hat and black coat and ambled out into the cold night. He stood on the worn stone step between the lodge and Old Quad, surveying the scene while rocking backwards and forwards on his heels. He looked up at the lights coming from staircase five, letting out a little smile as the room on the second floor went dark. A few minutes later, Kingsley-Hampton and Eccles started their way across the quad: straight across the quad, in fact, ignoring the signs to avoid the grass. As they drew near Potts called out.

'Good evening, Mr Hampton, Mr Eccles. Take care on the grass there. Bit slippy this time of year.'

'It's the *honourable* Kingsley-Hampton to you, Potts, and I'll walk where I damn well please, thank you very much.'

'Indeed, sir. Have a good dinner. Oh… and Mr Eccles,

there's another bag of letters here when you've got a chance.'

Eccles nodded an acknowledgement only to be rewarded by a clip over the back of the head from Kingsley-Hampton's hand as they headed out of the quad and towards the Hall for dinner.

After a few more minutes of watching the college empty into the Hall, the time was right. Potts slipped almost silently around the stone flags and disappeared into the entrance of staircase five. At the door he removed a small ring of skeleton keys. Of course he had keys to every room in the college on huge metal rings back at the lodge, but he liked to keep his skills up. Entering the dark room he pulled a large torch from his coat and started the search, only to be met by towers of paper and card casting wild shadows on the walls behind.

'Bloody 'eck, the little blighter's gone bonkers.'

Almost every flat surface was covered with stacks of menus of every style and persuasion, from handwritten to badly typed, and a few formal printed menus from dinners and weddings. Eccles' plan had not gone well from the point of view of rousing the members of the shadow faculty of gastronomic science, as not one of them had seen the notice at the union or the advertisement in the *Styx*. These efforts had nevertheless revealed a surprising lust for the £10 reward and an enthusiasm for amateurish forgery amongst the undergraduates of Oxford.

Potts searched all the piles looking for the crest and ribbons in the style he'd just been shown by Augustus. After a fruitless search, the sounding of the nearby bells on the half hour disturbed him. If they skipped dessert, Eccles and Kingsley-Hampton could be back in a few minutes. Potts tidied up the piles and after a final check left the room and headed back to the lodge, grabbing all the letters bulging out of the 'E' pigeonhole before heading inside to put the kettle on. Five minutes later he was sitting with a cup of tea and two suspicious envelopes addressed to Patrick Eccles that had been expertly steamed open. The first contained a poorly typed menu and a handwritten note.

Dear Sir,
I saw your notice on the union notice board. I'm sure
this is the menu you have misplaced. I look forward to
receiving my £10 reward.
Yours faithfully,
Norman Linkslip
Balliol

The other note was from a young and sympathetic lady from St Hilda's College by the name of Jean Emily Stancheon.

Dear Sir,
I was terribly sorry to read about your loss in Styx.
I hate losing things myself. Only last week I lost my
fountain pen, which once belonged to my grandmother,
so you can imagine how upset I was. Anyway I can't say
I've found your menu, but your dining society sounds
terribly good just from the name and I'd love to join up.
Do write and let me know how I can become a member.
With the very best wishes,
JS
Jean Emily Stancheon
ps I have rooms at 43a Banbury Road, please write to
me there.

Chapter 25

To the great relief of Mr Potts, the curious flurry of mail forwarded by the post office for Mr Patrick Eccles dried to a mere trickle by the end of that week. After being alerted to the problem, he had taken the precaution of discreetly inspecting the contents of all envelopes of sufficient size to enclose the sort of menu shown to him by Augustus Bloom. Each revealed only irrelevant offerings from entirely forgettable dinners that had long been ingested, digested and abluted. The pain of failing in the mission given to him by Augustus Bloom was exacerbated by the impact on Potts' hands. As expert as Mr Potts was at this task, the occasional contact between steam and fingers was unavoidable. The ensuing blisters had been concealed behind plasters, but the effect on Potts' mood was all too obvious to any poor undergraduate who vexed the porter in any way during that week.

At the requested hour, Potts made his way to the kitchen cellars to meet Augustus and the chaplain. Augustus had decided that there was no need to brief the whole faculty on the loss of the menu and his student's investigations. With each further menu that arrived in the post, it seemed less likely that he or his roommate could have any idea of the significance of the one that Charles had lost.

'So Mr Potts there has seen no sign of the menu that Charles thinks might have fallen into the hands of Mr Kingsley-

Hampton?' asked Augustus.

'I'm very sorry, Dr Bloom,' replied Mr Potts. 'I did get back to their room a few times but I couldn't find 'ide nor 'air of it, but it's clear they've been burning most of them.'

'Most unfortunate. I really don't know what we'll do,' said the chaplain, whose already delicate mental state had crumbled further in recent days. 'Imagine if the story of Mr Tokoro gets out and then Arthur. If they start asking questions the whole thing could explode in our faces. Arthur and his bloody will and the rest of it.'

'Charles,' said Augustus in a reassuring tone, 'really there is nothing to worry about. If they wanted to cause any trouble, why would they bother collecting all those other menus?'

'So what is your explanation, Augustus?' asked Charles.

'Well all I can think of is that Kingsley-Hampton did find the menu and this triggered an interest on the part of his roommate Eccles to collect as many Oxford menus as he could. I do seem to recall from his entrance interview that he collected stamps, so he must have that sort of personality.'

'Barking you mean?' offered Potts, trying in vain to lighten the atmosphere.

'He seemed quite normal when I had him in for a chat at the start of term. At your suggestion, Augustus, I might add,' said Charles. 'Which begs the question, if there is nothing to worry about, why were you so concerned about him at the start of term?'

'That was when I discovered he was asking questions about Fugu.'

'What? You never told me that,' said Charles.

'I didn't want to worry you. Look, as far as I can tell, no harm has been done, so why don't we just keep a close watch on the pair of them, particularly Eccles as the menus were clearly addressed to him. I see him every week anyway for a tutorial.'

'Why don't you just ask him straight out?' asked Charles.

'That would really spook him. Even if he does have our

menu, he clearly has no idea of its significance. It probably just caught his attention because I happened to be teaching about action potentials and tetrodotoxin and he'd come across puffer fish in his studies. I'll certainly avoid that particular topic from now on. Now, Mr Potts, I'm sure we can rely on you to keep your eyes and ears open. If anything peculiar happens don't forget to let me know.'

'Absolutely, sir, you can count on me.' With that, Potts nodded his head in deference and headed off through the kitchens back towards the lodge.

'Perhaps you could keep a pastoral eye on Eccles too, Charles, just to be sure.' Seeing the uneasy combination of doubt and annoyance in Charles' eyes, he added, 'Everything will turn out fine, you'll see.'

'Oh I'm sure this menu will turn up somewhere; it's our eternal souls you should be worried about,' said Charles with sudden passion.

'We've been through this a hundred times, Charles. We really have no choice, and what harm can it do?'

'Harm? Just because some daft old sod writes a will doesn't mean we should risk eternal damnation by becoming cannibals.' With that Charles rose to his feet and headed off into the cellars without a backward glance.

'I think Arthur would have preferred the term anthropophagists,' said Augustus into the darkness of the cellars.

*

Over the next few weeks, the relationship between Augustus and Patrick Eccles, though strained, returned to a semblance of normality. Both felt they knew more than the other suspected, so neither said or did anything that might arouse suspicion. Fortunately, Augustus had no need to directly raise the issue of tetrodotoxin again in tutorials. With the new term the time had come to move on from teaching about the nervous system. Augustus taught his first-year students on a different system of the body each term: the nervous system in Michaelmas term, cardiovascular system in Hilary term, followed by the respiratory system in Trinity term. With this new term he had moved Eccles onto the apparently safe topic of the cardiovascular system as planned, though this forced Augustus to be teaching about the very subject that had caused his dearest friend's death. It hadn't escaped Augustus' notice that education was mirroring tragedy term by term: death by nervous paralysis at the end of last Trinity term, and death by a failure of the normal heart rhythm at the end of Michaelmas. Though a devoutly non-superstitious person by personality and training, a small part of Augustus did worry what dire suffocating fate might befall someone he knew as he moved on to teach about respiration next term.

The chaplain did indeed take Eccles under his wing, inviting him to a Christian fellowship tea party to observe him at close hand. Being rather constrained affairs at the best of times, it was unsurprising that the chaplain sensed nothing untoward in the young man's behaviour. Equally this was hardly the venue for Eccles to unburden himself about his suspicions regarding his tutor's involvement in a secretive and clearly dangerous dining society. Nevertheless, Charles Pinker found reassurance in Eccles' behaviour but heeding Augustus Bloom's concerns, urged Eccles to pursue the rowing career he had started the previous term. Over the years, Charles had discovered that while prayer was a great solace for the older generation, physical exercise worked best for the young. And so it turned out for Eccles who was promptly recruited by the crew of the college fourth rowing VIII, which at that moment were in some difficulty as they numbered only seven.

As much as Eccles found escape through physical exertion on the river, his greatest blessing was the non-appearance of the threatened article about the cursed menu in *Styx*. Even his recurring nightmares about being poisoned with Fugu-tainted fish paste and lying paralysed on his bed gasping for breath began to subside. With the publication of the next edition of *Styx*, Rupert Atworth was summoned by Kingsley-Hampton to explain why reporting on a speech by the vice-chancellor about the need to admit women to the traditional all-male colleges was of such importance compared to the promised but unpublished article on a secretive, murderous dining society.

'So Rupert, your role as defender of the truth is looking a little tarnished from where I am sitting,' said Kingsley-Hampton, ensconced in his favourite chair by the fire and waving the front page of *Styx* at his guest.

'Don't worry, I'll run that story of yours soon. Just doing some background checks. Not that I've found out any more. Still, need to check sources, you know? That's what responsible journalism is all about.'

'Don't talk bollocks, I am your source. What else do you need?'

'Well, some of the editorial committee are a bit dodgy about running a story like that.'

'I thought you were the editor, Rupert. Tell those pathetic creatures that this is the first decent story they've ever had.'

'Oh, they know it's a good story. It's that Emma Bellingham girl from Somerville, her dad's a top QC in London, so she says we need to take legal advice.'

'Oh, for God's sake. Just sort it out, Rupert, you spineless sap.'

Kingsley-Hampton was still riled at the thought of an elitist dining society existing right under his nose. Worse still, one that hadn't thought him worthy of an invitation. While Atworth stared into his teacup, Eccles took advantage of the uneasy silence to recharge the cups of tea and bring across the cucumber sandwiches he'd made earlier. The last time Rupert Atworth had been in these rooms, Eccles was struggling to hear the words through the closed door of his bedroom. But the world had moved on since then. The Honourable Matthew Kingsley-Hampton was by now graciously tolerating Eccles solely in his capacity as valet, though he found Eccles' frequent absences to attend lectures irksome. Domestic staff to the ruling classes were assumed to be models of discretion and endowed with selective deafness. So Kingsley-Hampton had openly conducted his life in front of Eccles without any attempt to include or exclude him. What he had failed to grasp was that loyalty from domestic staff was based on mutual respect, something that could only be earned, not demanded.

*

Patrick Eccles' new-found equilibrium was short-lived as Rupert Atworth had been true to his word on at least one front. After persistent pleas for a little more time to investigate, he had eventually provided the vice-chancellor with the name and college of the man who had placed the advertisement about the menu. As a result, Patrick Eccles was sitting in the very same chair where his tutor had sat a term before, ashen-faced in front of the vice-chancellor. With the relaxed manner of a man who already knew the answers to the questions he was asking, Ridgeway started his cross-examination of this poor unfortunate.

'So, Mr Eccles. Do you know why you are here?'

'Well, er… not exactly sir.' ·

'The editor of *Styx* was kind enough to supply your name as the source of a recent… advertisement.'

'I see.'

'Relating to… ' the vice-chancellor theatrically lifted the open copy of *Styx* on his desk, 'oh yes. Relating to the 'shadow faculty of gastronomic science.' Can I take it that you are a member of this group?'

'No, sir,' said Eccles, his head lowering with each utterance, much to the delight of the vice-chancellor.

'No? So why on earth were you trying to appear so?'

His question was met with an improved view of the crown of Eccles' head and silence.

'What possible interest could you have in a menu from this society? Well? Answer me.'

'My room… er… ' Eccles ground to a halt and then made the fatal mistake of looking up. He was met by the stony-faced vice-chancellor and his meagre defences crumbled. His tongue, which seconds before had seemed unable to generate the most basic of sounds, suddenly gained a mind of its own, and he found himself gabbling away at high speed. 'I found the menu by accident and I was interested in Fugu because my tutor had just set me an essay on action potentials. Tetrodotoxin, which is the poison in the puffer fish, was important in working out how nerves work and well, you see, Fugu is a dish made from puffer fish.'

'Yes, yes. Now excuse me the lecture on the details. I've had that already. So who is your tutor, dare I ask?'

'Dr Bloom, sir.'

Dr Ridgeway stared at the young man in front of him and saw the mocking face of Augustus Bloom looking back.

'Of course. Who else could it possibly be?' The vice-chancellor paused to gather his thoughts amidst the wave of irritation launched by the mention of Bloom's name. 'So what was the purpose of the advertisement?'

'Well I thought someone from this shadow faculty might contact us, I mean me. I wanted to know who its members were… I thought it might be fun to take part in one of their dinners.'

'I doubt it would be, but did they contact you?'

'Well, I got a lot of menus but no-one from this dining society replied.' In the short silence that followed, the thought that the vice-chancellor may be a member suddenly struck him and, unfortunately for Eccles, this thought also reached his vocal cords. 'Unless this all means that you are a member of course.'

'Don't be impertinent, and no I am not. So what does this dining society have to do with the fish you just mentioned?'

'I… I… '

'Spit it out boy.'

'I think someone died of Fugu poisoning at one of the dinners last year. A Japanese man called Mr Tokoro.'

Dr Ridgeway tried hard not to reveal how much this statement had thrown him off balance.

'And what makes you think that?'

'Well, his name was on the menu saying he'd brought the puffer fish.'

'So what made you leap to the conclusion that it had killed him?'

'I found his name in an obituary in *The Times*.'

'I see. Quite the little Sherlock Holmes, aren't we? Did *The Times* mention this university, by any chance?'

'No, I don't think so.'

'No it did not, and do you know why?'

Eccles merely shook his head.

'Because I spent a lot of time and effort to make sure the name of this university was not brought into it. Who else knows about your discoveries?'

'No-one, sir.' Eccles muttered to the floor.

'Don't lie, I heard you say *we* before.'

'Really, I haven't told anyone.' Eccles' insides were churning at the idiocy of this deception, but he couldn't seem to stop himself.

'Do you know what will happen if this story gets out? What will happen to you?'

'No, sir.'

'You'll be lucky if you are reading for a BSc in sewer management from the University of Bognor Regis, because you certainly won't be reading for one here. Do I make myself clear? Now go.'

Eccles shuffled out the door. Dr Ridgeway reached across to the gunmetal-grey tray that held his correspondence and pulled out the letter that had arrived the previous day from Augustus Bloom.

Dear Dr Ridgeway,
Lord Faulkner asked me to write in relation to Arthur Plantagenet's generous legacy to the university. One of the stipulations in Arthur's will was that the details and bequest itself be presented to you at a dinner to be held in St Jerome's College. Due to a range of unforeseen

circumstances arising from other aspects of Arthur's legacy, this will need to be deferred until Trinity term. Once arrangements have been finalised I shall be in contact again.

I remain yours faithfully,
Dr Augustus Bloom, MB BS MA DPhil (Oxon)

Knowing full well that one shouldn't look a gift horse in the mouth, the vice-chancellor pondered the possibilities of giving this particular gift horse a short sharp kick up the backside. If he couldn't get at Bloom directly, he could certainly annoy him intensely by having one of his students sent down. He just needed a little more rope than this advert provided.

*

That evening, Patrick Eccles was lying on his bed considering the ceiling and his fate when he heard the arrival of Kingsley-Hampton and entourage in the sitting room outside. He could hear boastful snippets of how excessively each of them was planning to spend their weekend, but the volume and inconsequentiality of their chatter made it easy to ignore. There was then a loud hammer on his bedroom door.

'Eccles, be a good chap and go down to the buttery for some teacakes and milk.'

There was then a poor attempt at a northern accent braying 'Eccles cakes' before the group dissolved in laughter. It was all a bit rich seeing as Patrick Eccles actually came from Bristol, but at his roommate's bidding he rose to his feet. He could always get a job as a waiter at the King Edward Hotel when he was sent down, so a bit more practice serving tea cakes to the ruling classes wouldn't go amiss. He consoled himself with the thought that he could find lodgings in Oxford and pretend to his family he was still at college.

Chapter 26

After the trauma of Arthur Plantagenet's death and the ensuing events, the pace of life thankfully eased as term progressed. For no-one more so than Arthur himself. The bulk of his mortal remains stood quietly in an urn on Augustus Bloom's mantelpiece. The remainder had a less peaceful, though just as sedentary, existence within the low C diapason organ pipe in the chapel. The chaplain had demanded its immediate removal when Augustus had first revealed the hiding place he had chosen for Arthur's leg. Despite much discussion, no better location could be found and so the leg remained. Charles Pinker only finally acquiesced when Augustus repositioned the leg within the pipe to ensure that the organ could at least be played without any recurrence of the problems experienced during the memorial service. So, with the aid of Charles Pinker's daily practice, Arthur's leg slowly cured, benefiting from the regular drafts of air through the pipe.

For members of the shadow faculty of gastronomic science, the genteel pace of the curing process of Arthur's leg had an undoubtedly beneficial effect by allowing them to avoid thinking about the unthinkable. Add to that the unique abilities of the human mind to adapt to new circumstances and one has an explanation for the surprising calm that fell upon the shadow faculty as each day passed. Theodore Flanagan stopped poring over old acts of parliament relating to the use and misuse of the human body, now convinced that at least legally they were on firm ground. George Le Strang's mood became positively buoyant on the foot of the surprise dish he was testing out for the forthcoming end-of-term dinner: so much so that he gave poor Arthur not a second thought. Sadly for Charles Pinker the moral dilemma that Arthur's will had created was never far from his mind and he added to his burden by taking up the task of praying for all their souls. Hamish had been thoroughly distracted by a pretty new librarian who had started work in the Zoology department. As for Augustus, he had become absorbed with monitoring the curing process itself. Indeed Augustus had just finished one of his now regular inspections of Arthur's leg and was on his way down the stairs to the organ loft when a booming voice filled the entire chapel.

'Augustus, you up there?'

'For God's sake, Hamish,' he hissed in reply. 'You could wake the dead with a voice like that.'

'Talking of which, how is our old friend Arthur?'

'Doing very nicely thank you, Hamish.'

'Excellent. Now I brought a spare coat because I knew you'd be late. It was bloody freezing down at the river yesterday.' Hamish tossed the coat at Augustus when he appeared from the organ loft. Hamish opened the door of the chapel with a flourish and the words, '"Lead on Macduff", as Arthur used to say.'

'"Lay on",' corrected Augustus.

'What?'

'"*Lay* on Macduff" is the actual quote.'

'Nonsense, Augustus. Lay on doesn't even make sense. Now come on or we'll miss the whole damn day's racing,' said Hamish as he marched out the door first.

Hamish was right about the temperature at least. It was indeed bloody freezing as the two men wandered down Dodgson's Walk towards the river and the last day of Torpids. Hamish filled his coat amply and cut a fine figure as he strode down the gravel path. Augustus, lost in the voluminous garment he had been given, looked rather less impressive. Although hardly trim himself, he certainly lacked Hamish's Falstaffian girth. Coming in the opposite direction was a steady stream of lightly chilled spectators and clusters of rowers from the lower divisions. It was not hard to determine the success or failure of their crews from their demeanour. The unsuccessful crews ambled slowly and disconsolately, any conversation punctuated by long, cold silences. The successful bounded along in incessant chatter.

'Hi, Dr Bloom,' called Patrick Eccles from a one such group of happy rowers as they passed by.

'One of my first years,' explained Augustus. 'Got off to a rocky start but seems to be getting it together now.'

'Sounds like most of my lot,' replied Hamish.

'Well there might have been a bit more to it than that. I don't think I told you that Charles Pinker lost one of the menus from last summer's dinner.'

'No, but does it matter?' asked Hamish quite unconcerned.

'Well, we think it got into the hands of that lad we just passed because he was asking questions around the place about Fugu and collecting menus from all over the university.'

Hamish stopped short and looked at Augustus. 'You might have thought of mentioning that.'

'Well, the chaplain was all in a tizzy about it at the time. He was so stressed about Arthur and was blaming himself for losing the menu in the first place that I thought I'd let sleeping dogs lie. Nothing seems to have come of it.'

'Good,' said Hamish striking out again for the river. 'Anything more from your friend the vice-chancellor?'

'Oh no, I think he's been well bought off with the promise of Arthur's money.'

'Only because he doesn't know it's for a professor of gastronomy,' laughed Hamish. 'Are we really going to invite him along to join in on Arthur's grand experiment?'

'Of course. I sent him a letter a few weeks ago.'

'You've really bought into this will thing hook, line and sinker, haven't you?'

'The way I see it, Hamish, we're obliged to do it and it won't harm anyone, so why not?'

'I must say, Augustus, you have to wonder, don't you?'

'Wonder what?'

'What we do actually taste like.'

An uneasy silence fell upon them, finally broken by Hamish.

'And I can't wait to see the vice-chancellor's face when I tell him he's just eaten a slice of Arthur's leg.'

'You better bloody not tell him anything,' said Augustus, hitting Hamish's chest with the back of his hand. Their conversation was interrupted by a muffled bang in the distance.

'Christ, that must be the second division starting already,' said Hamish setting off at a healthy trot. 'Come on, Augustus, we'll miss the whole shebang with your dawdling.'

*

After dinner, Matthew Kingsley-Hampton made his way back to his rooms. As he approached the entrance to his staircase he was confronted with a large group of rowers. The finishing touches were being put to the chalk markings on the wall that recorded St Jerome's only vestige of rowing success in that year's Torpids. Eccles' crew, the usually far from successful fourth VIII, had not only bumped that day but on each previous day of Torpids, earning them their blades. As the only member of the crew with rooms in Old Quad, Eccles' staircase was selected for decoration with the traditional chalk drawings of crossed blades and the college crest. Kingsley-Hampton came up to the group.

'When you've finished defacing the walls I'd like to get to my room,' said Kingsley-Hampton with contempt.

'Sorry, Matthew,' said Eccles, clearing a path. 'Let him through lads.'

In thanks, Kingsley-Hampton offered his roommate a withering stare.

'Only a few people can call me by my first name... and you, Eccles, are not one of them.' Kingsley-Hampton set off up the stairs.

There was a stunned silence for a few seconds until one of Eccles' crewmates, Roger Sinclair, issued a low 'Eeww' that rose steadily in pitch and volume as the others joined in.

'Is he always that much of a prick?' asked Sinclair.

'Yeah. Pretty much. So who's for a pint in the Bear?' Eccles replied.

*

Several hours and more than a few pints later, Eccles was standing at the top of his staircase, his ear to the door listening for any signs that Kingsley-Hampton had company. The unfortunate combination of his impaired balance and a weak lock made the door burst open, leaving Eccles sprawling on the floor. Kingsley-Hampton, sitting in his preferred armchair with a glass of brandy in one hand and a Montecristo no. 4 cigar in the other, acknowledged Eccles' arrival with surprising calm.

'Close the door, Eccles. There's a bit of a draught.'

Patrick rose to his feet, mumbling an apology and duly obliged. He then headed for the safety of his bedroom.

'By the way, Eccles, Felipe Banzarro is coming back at the start of next term,' said Kingsley-Hampton, turning to look at Eccles who responded with a blank stare.

'The chap who should be sharing this room with me. He had to take a year off because of his accident last summer, so that's why I got lumbered with your useless self. Officially he's not starting until next year, but he's bored in Buenos Aires and frankly I'm bored with you. So he's coming back for a bit of R and R here in Oxford for the summer. I've had to take out a lease already to secure my rooms out of college next year, but I'd rather be in college for Trinity term. So you'll be moving out next term to make space for Felipe and staying in the rooms I've leased above the Mitre Hotel.'

Chapter 27

Arthur's death had cast the preparations for the end of term dinner into disarray in more ways than one. Even though Arthur was no longer a member of the shadow faculty, his presence within the organ pipes of the chapel cast a long shadow. There was firstly the question of Mr Thaddeus Rhymer, the renowned medium, who Arthur had invited. It seemed discourteous to un-invite a guest merely because the man who made the original invitation had died. With this turn of events being extremely rare, no established form of etiquette exists to handle it, so it was decided Mr Rhymer would have to be accommodated in the absence of his host. Fortunately the chaplain's original guest, a distinguished organist from Germany, had to cancel at short notice. Although not thrilled at the prospect of having a spiritualist as a guest, Charles accepted his task with impressive grace.

In another deviation from normal, several culinary questions usually settled in the tasting meetings were left unresolved as the discussions were frequently diverted into legal and ethical debates about their dear departed colleague's leg. With the question of the best way to serve oysters still unanswered a week before the end-of-term dinner, the faculty decided to put the challenge to their guests. The best way to eat this most fragrant mollusc would be decided at the dinner itself, so each guest was asked to present a recipe to the chef by return post. With all his recent inner turmoil, Charles had also neglected to have the menu printed. He would normally have been mortified at such an oversight, but Charles took this in his stride and merely created a single handwritten menu for the faculty archives. Indeed the anticipation of this dinner had with each approaching day lifted the spirits of all the faculty members to an almost giddy excitement, an understandable release of tension considering recent events.

The guests themselves, in keeping with previous dinners, spanned an exotic range of backgrounds and gastronomic interests. Hamish had invited an American marine biologist from the Scripps Oceanographic Institute, Chad Zimovic, who was a world expert on jellyfish. George Le Strang, inspired by the chaplain's suggestion of making this Hilary term dinner into a Lenten feast, had invited Monsignor Alfonse Poitier from the University of Avignon, who was the leading authority on the culinary history of the Catholic Church. Theodore Flanagan had invited Myles Holohan, a surprisingly young man who had risen through the ranks of oenology to become wine critic of *The Irish Times*. Augustus Bloom's guest was, under the circumstances, a rather eerie choice but one that had been made before Arthur's death. Dr Geoffrey Altmann was an expert in the phantom limb phenomenon, a curious quirk of nature where amputees can get sensations from a severed limb decades later. He was also an excellent chef who owned a farm that specialised in preserving unusual species of duck.

The night of the Hilary dinner was now upon them and so, with the vice-chancellor apparently mollified with the promise of money, they returned to their traditional dining room overlooking the fellows' garden. This room was filled with the paintings of past fellows who hadn't merited hanging in the great hall, either because of their limited impact on history or the limited skill of the artist chosen to create their portrait. The portrait of one of their past members, Gordon Maxwell, was already hanging in the room. A space would soon have to be created here for Arthur too when his portrait was finished, unless of course the Master approved his inclusion in the Hall.

Augustus had inherited the remnants of Arthur's large supply of *elixir v*égétal de Chartreuse, so it was no surprise that this complex potion found its way into their introductory cocktail. After the subtle green martinis had been handed out, Augustus picked up a spoon and tapped his glass to get the attention of the diners for the toast.

'To gastronomy and Jean Anthelme Brillat-Savarin.'

After the murmurs died down, Augustus spoke again.

'Some of our guests may be unaware of the recent loss of one of the founding members of the shadow faculty of gastronomic science, Professor Arthur Plantagenet. In the words quoted by Brillat-Savarin, *Omnia mors poscit; lex est, non poena, perire*[9]. In remembering him, let us strive only to try and enjoy this remarkable meal with as much enthusiasm as Arthur would have, even if he can't be with us tonight.'

'Amen,' muttered Charles, raising his glass while looking nervously around the room.

Arthur's name was toasted while the guests sampled the unusual botanical concoction of herbs in their martini glasses. It was, all agreed, an unusual taste with the verdicts varying from appalling, through medicinal to really rather good. Taste apart, it was certainly good enough to evaporate the sombre mood left by the mention of Arthur's death. What more could you possibly ask of any cocktail?

After Charles had explained that the evening's dinner aimed to exemplify the very best food one can eat while maintaining a Lenten fast from meat, he delivered the college grace with his usual ease and indeed speed. As soon as he had finished, Gerard, accompanied by a swarm of scouts, swept in with the *amuse-gueule*. To Hamish's great pride his squills had been brought into service but transformed beyond his wildest expectations by the college chef, Monsieur Roger. Each plate arrived with a single squill that had been steamed in vermouth. The light crustacean odour mixing with the scent

---

9 Death claims us all; it is the natural law, not a punishment.

of the Noilly Prat caused all the diners to inhale deeply and savour their splendid aroma. The little creatures' edges had been neatly trimmed and a small ribbon tied around their tails. The guests looked in admiration at their plates and then at their hosts looking for guidance to the next move.

'This little creature gives me faith that God exists,' said Hamish rising to his feet. 'No-one but a generous, beneficent being could bring into existence a crustacean that tastes so good and is so easy to eat.' With that, Hamish lifted the small ribbon and the whole carapace rose up, revealing the creature's muscular tail bathed in foaming hollandaise. He hoisted the contents into his mouth, his table manners temporarily overcome by culinary lust. The others followed suit and within seconds this morsel had put every taste bud in the room on notice of even greater delights. Monsignor Alfonse Poitier was even heard to murmur, *ad majorem Dei gloriam*, to the greater glory of God, before clinking his glass with the chaplain's in a moment of unity.

Then, George Le Strang rose to his feet to introduce the next gastronomic challenge.

'Gentlemen, we shall next be serving several dishes that are designed to answer two simple but fundamental questions in gastronomy. The first is whether to cook or not to cook one of my dearest friends the oyster and the second related question is what ingredients best enhance the incomparable briny flavour of an oyster. You have all proposed a method of preparation of oysters that our chef has followed. One of you,' George nodded towards Theodore's guest, Mr Myles Holohan, 'has also added the extra dimension of what best to drink with oysters. Let the games commence.'

George clapped his hands with the imperious hauteur of a Roman emperor in the Coliseum and nodded at Gerard who was positioned with his hand on the door handle. With the signal given, the serving scouts carried in ten silver platters, each adorned with ten oysters, two of each flavour, so that first impressions could be checked and clarified before the pronouncement was made. Gerard also discreetly laid out ten pencils and notepads while the cellar steward brought forth the liquid accompaniments. Each diner received a glass of a simple youthful Entre-Deux-Mers, a 1959 Pol Roger Champagne and a large sherry schooner filled with a tiny but expertly poured Guinness.

'Would you be so kind as to describe your selections, Gentlemen?' said George, extending an open palm towards his own guest, Monsignor Poitier.

'*Merci, Professeur.* I have chosen a method favoured in the Vatican in the nineteenth century: oysters coated in a champagne *volouté* flamed under the hottest grill for the shortest possible time.' A polite but impatient round of applause came from the table as the diners eyed the plates in front of them, then it was the turn of Hamish's guest Mr Zimovic.

'These, my friends, are Oysters Rockefeller, the finest dish ever invented in America, created in 1899 in Antoine's restaurant, New Orleans, by Jules Alciatore. The real recipe has been kept secret for the past seventy years, but in my youth I had what in Oxford you might call a dalliance with Jules Alciatore's granddaughter. So you are all blessed with the authentic recipe, of which I shared with your chef under a pact of total secrecy. But I can tell you that the intense green colour does not involve spinach.'

Dr Altmann was next to rise to his feet.

'I share my dear friend Augustus' love of the martini, so in marrying the finest drink with the finest crustacean I give you an uncooked oyster coated in a *frappé* of ice soaked in gin with lemon zest and a drop of vermouth. I can guarantee you all that even if this isn't the best-tasting oyster you'll ever have eaten, it will certainly be the happiest.' Dr Altmann sat down to the best reception so far and then it was the turn of Mr Rhymer, the medium.

'As an allegory of our short lives and inevitable death, nothing comes close to the demise of the oyster, one of the few, perhaps only, animals routinely eaten with a still-beating heart.' The room fell silent; none of the other diners had even considered the circulatory system of an oyster and certainly never envisaged swallowing a beating heart. 'This oyster will die a death befitting Cleopatra in a warm bath of star anise scented cream. If I were an oyster this is how I would like to be eaten.' With a gentle round of 'hear-hear', Mr Rhymer gave the floor to Mr Holohan.

'Gentlemen, fine words but a finer mollusc sits before you. Naked, awaiting lemon juice, pepper and your tonsils. Eat on!' With that he picked up his own raw oyster and glooped it down his gullet, followed by the entire miniature glass of Guinness. After taking a deep bow to the acclaim of his fellow diners, Mr Holohan took his seat. The games were truly afoot.

The eating and enjoying was by far the simplest part of this challenge. The scoring and ultimate rankings were inevitably more divisive. The question was ultimately answered in favour of the uncooked oyster. Poor Chad Zimovic was truly deflated that his nation's greatest creation came last, though Hamish's generous refilling of his glass with the divine vintage of Pol Roger was some recompense. Monsignor Poitier could distance himself in the knowledge that in recent years, the Vatican had favoured simpler treatments of the oyster, but he was still surprised to finish fourth. Of the three recipes without heat, Mr Rhymer's was highly commended but was undoubtedly marked down by his unnerving introduction. This left the naked oyster and the martini oyster for the final judgement. It was a close call but by a single vote, Dr Altmann prevailed with his martini oyster, a rarely prepared but exquisite combination where the brininess of a dirty martini[10] was obtained from the salty oyster liquor. Myles Holohan should really have won but just before the vote he created a Black Velvet, a Guinness champagne mixture, for George Le Strang. Although the taste was in George's mind

10 Despite its curious name, a dirty martini is merely one made with gin and a teaspoon of brine from a jar of olives.

an improvement over pure Guinness, the disrespect shown to this memorable vintage champagne was too much for George who changed his vote in silent protest.

Once the remains of the oysters were cleared, the table was set for the main courses. First up was a dish that George Le Strang had managed to keep secret even from his colleagues in the shadow faculty. He had bragged this would be the very best dish one could possibly eat during Lent. Served *sous cloche*, it was presented to the diners in perfect synchrony with the ten silver cloches lifted off the plates to reveal both the visual and olfactory delights of this dish: Sole stuffed with truffle-scented lobster or Sole Walewska. This dish was one of Escoffier's finest creations and for decades was a favourite at the Casino in Monte Carlo, though no gambler had ever tasted as fine a version as Monsieur Roger presented on this night. A neglected classic, Sole Walewska was first created for the bastard progeny of the liaison of Napoleon I and Marie Walewska, a certain Alexandre Florian de Walewski. Alexandre's mother was wooed by Napoleon and forwent her honour to spare her country from the destructive military forces of France.

The sole induced a state of near delirium amongst the diners and when Myles Holohan rose to his feet to propose that a bottle of the Pol Roger be sent to the kitchens in gratitude, the response was unanimous. When the plates returned to the kitchen, Monsieur Roger always reviewed them for signs of success and failure. He could only smile to see that not a morsel remained on a single plate. Indeed the plates were almost as clean as they had been before this unusual dish had been served upon them. He was a little perplexed with the arrival of the full but uncorked bottle of champagne, initially fearing the worst, until Gerard rushed into the kitchen and with upturned thumbs tried to convey to Monsieur Roger the extent of his triumph as well as one can in the absence of words. By the time Gerard had forced Monsieur Roger to accept a glass of this exceptional champagne, the full extent of his victory was apparent. The chef sat back and took a deep draft of champagne. It was doubtful that Napoleon himself had ever felt as content in his achievements as Monsieur Roger did at that moment.

The accompaniment to this dish was also showered with great praise, both for taste and inventiveness: jellyfish noodles deep-fried and coated in a fine cream and tarragon sauce. Chad Zimovic revealed the secret of their preparation: fresh jellyfish squeezed through a potato ricer straight into a pan of oil. As unpromising as the starting materials were, the result was a triumph and the failure of his oyster Rockefeller recipe in the face of stiff opposition was all but forgotten. How the great Escoffier would have felt about the pairing of Sole Walewska with jellyfish is a matter of conjecture, but he would certainly have approved of the foaming cream sauce.

The lack of a printed menu added a certain frisson of interest when the plates for the next course arrived. There were some puzzled faces amongst some of the guests as the silver cloches were lifted off. On their plates was a dish that looked and indeed had the aroma of an excellent beef stroganoff, but according to the chaplain's introduction this dinner was, within the traditions of Lent, devoid of all meat. Smiling with mirth at the consternation his dish had created, Monsignor Poitier rose to his feet to explain.

'Gentlemen, what you have in front of you is a dish that appears to contain meat but in keeping with Papal decree is in fact fish. Back in the time when the papacy was less inclined to forgo the physical pleasures of the table, meat was still unacceptable during Lent and only fish could be served. As an alternative to the repetition of fish dishes, the tail of the beaver was given the honorary status as fish, seeing as it bore scales and spent most of its time under water. I present to you a unique dish, beaver-tail stroganoff.'

The announcement of this extraordinary gastronomic creation was met with the clinking of spoons on glass, one of the highest accolades the faculty bestowed on such announcements. In terms of a gastronomic icon, this dish shone as brightly as any star. As a dish it sadly failed to excite the palate to the same degree. Fortunately another vestige of a more sybaritic papacy saved the day. The wine accompanying this dish was a remarkable Clos de Papes Châteauneuf-du-Pape, a style of wine first created for the Pope while the papacy was located within France at Avignon.

By the time the far from empty plates of beaver tail were being cleared away the conversation broke away from discussions of the food into polite interchange. Charles Pinker, having failed to make much headway with his guest Mr Rhymer, tried Augustus' guest who was on his other side.

'So, Dr Altmann… '

'Geoffrey, please.'

'Geoffrey, what is it that you do?'

'I'm a neurologist in Queen Square now, but I worked here in the physiology labs with Augustus for a while. Phantom limbs are my special interest.'

Charles blanched visibly but etiquette required that having started the conversation he was obliged to follow through with the topic that Dr Altmann had chosen.

'Could you explain to a simple clergyman what a phantom limb is?' Charles asked with a certain trepidation.

'When a limb is amputated, the patient can have sensations that feel completely real in parts of the limb that have been removed. An itch on the big toe can drive you crazy if there is nothing you can do to reach it.'

'An amputated limb can haunt the patient? How dreadful. Can a limb haunt others too?' asked Charles.

'No, it's not supernatural – just the brain reacting to signals from cut nerves. Everyone else is quite safe.'

'Well, that is excellent news. Please excuse me. I better go and remind Gerard to open the port in good time.' Charles rose to his feet, desperately hoping that there were no external clues to his inner turmoil. Fresh air would help.

He reached the door only to meet the dessert course on its

way in. Charles passed through the sensuous clouds of smells rising from each plate, but indicating to Gerard that service should continue in his absence, he headed out of the door in search of a moment alone.

The dessert was a sublime soufflé with a perfectly crusted top. The diners were still admiring their individual dishes when the servers came around with small jugs and miniature glass funnels which they placed into the top of the soufflé and then poured in a mixture of Chartreuse and molten dark chocolate. It was a dish for which it was impossible not to close one's eyes after the first mouthful. When the eyes reopened a small glass of a port-like wine had appeared as if by magic in front of them. Myles Holohan took a cautious sip while the other diners waited for his reaction.

'Banyuls: brilliant, quite brilliant choice.' Mr Holohan raised his glass in a toast. 'Gentlemen, this is the science of gastronomy raised to the level of an art form.'

The other diners raised and sampled the almost inky red L'Etoile Banyuls in their glasses. The lingering complex flavours of the soufflé exploded into exotic fruit when this much-neglected red dessert wine reached their taste buds.

After the last morsels of the chocolate and Chartreuse soufflé passed his lips, Augustus turned to Mr Rhymer, trying to engage the remarkably taciturn medium in conversation. He had barely spoken a word after introducing his oyster dish, though Augustus understood that attending a dinner after the death of one's host had placed Mr Rhymer in a difficult position.

'A fine spirit, this green Chartreuse; don't you think, Mr Rhymer?'

'Indeed, but I must say that there are far stronger and more erudite spirits within this very room.'

Augustus found himself looking to the sideboard to see what other liqueur bottles had been laid out before Mr Rhymer clarified his meaning.

'Spirits that have never graced the inside of a bottle, Dr Bloom.'

The strange compelling intensity of Mr Rhymer's voice had drawn to a close all other conversation around the table, a fact that did not escape the medium's attention. So raising his voice, Mr Rhymer addressed the whole table.

'Gentlemen, this room, this occasion and the tragic recent death of Professor Plantagenet have created a spiritual vortex the like of which I have never encountered. Forgive my lack of polite conversation, but I have been deafened by certain spirit voices that are clamouring to be heard. I understand that the professor died suddenly. Although his heart was known to be weak, he passed on without his dearest friends being able to say a final farewell and with one unanswered question. I am sure that there are people in this room that would like to have a final word with Arthur, because he is here in this very room waiting for us to contact him.'

'Like a séance? Excellent idea,' said Hamish without a moment's thought.

'I see that one of our number, the chaplain, is temporarily missing,' continued Mr Rhymer in a voice that was becoming increasingly hypnotic. 'This is an auspicious moment because nine is a far more spiritual number and I sensed a certain negativity to my profession from the chaplain over dinner. Shall we begin?'

Before anyone could offer a sensible objection, the table was cleared of all the plates except the chaplain's soufflé, which Mr Rhymer asked to be left as an offering at the centre of the table with a glass of the Banyuls. Mr Rhymer rose to bring over the silver candlesticks that had been standing on the sideboard. All the serving scouts had the good sense to leave the room unbidden before the doors were firmly closed. The diners were then asked to join hands.

'Repeat these words after me,' instructed their medium. 'Our dear departed Arthur Plantagenet, we offer you these gifts. Commune with us, Arthur, and show us a sign of your presence.'

There followed a nervous silence, broken only when Mr

Rhymer began chanting again.

'Commune with us Arthur and show us a sign.' These words were repeated slowly over and over again until all the diners had joined in. Then came the knock.

'Is that you, Arthur Plantagenet?' chanted Mr Rhymer. Two rather muffled knocks came from the centre of the table. Then Mr Rhymer convulsed and fell forward onto the table. The circle of hands held firm while the diners watched and waited. Then Mr Rhymer sat up as if pulled by strings, a different looking man than the one that had slumped forward a few seconds earlier.

'Gentlemen, I told you it would work.'

These words emerged from the medium's mouth, but with every nuance and vowel it was Arthur Plantagenet.

'Augustus, dear chap, don't look so stunned. Fine job on dinner though, I would have certainly fancied tasting those martini oysters. Looked much better than that oyster and Laphroaig creation we came up with last year.'

With these last words all hope of trickery on the part of Mr Rhymer vanished. He could not possibly have known about the last oyster dish they had served up at the start of the ill-fated dinner of Trinity term last year. Augustus finally managed to speak.

'Arthur, I, well… we have something to ask you.'

'Ask away, dear boy, I have all the time in the world. I'll be dead for quite a while after all.'

'Well before I ask it, remember that there are guests in the room and not just members of the shadow faculty.'

'For God's sake, Bloom I'm dead, not blind and stupid! And I know what you want to ask and the answer is yes.'

Such a perfectly Plantagenet-esque reply confirmed the veracity of this apparition, at least to the four members of the shadow faculty around the table.

'Yes?'

'Yes, I did mean what I wrote in my will, and no it doesn't break any laws, so I think you have to get on with it. If you don't I'll never be able to properly join the spirit world. It's a big thing here this crossing over.'

'Don't worry, Arthur. We will do as you ask,' said an ashen-faced George Le Strang.

'Oh, y-y-y-yes,' stuttered Theodore, suddenly reverting to his childhood handicap.

'Arthur, it's Hamish and it's great to hear you again and God we miss you around here.'

'I knew I could trust you. I see Charles isn't here; just apologise for my dropping in on him a while back and tell him he's not going crazy.'

In the corridor outside, straining to hear through the closed door, the chaplain slumped to the ground in a combination of relief and shock and leant heavily against the door, which suddenly opened. Augustus and Chad Zimovic both let their grip loosen as they turned involuntarily to the door. The circle and moment was broken and Mr Rhymer let out a strangled cry before collapsing onto the table. Dr Altmann leapt to his feet and rushed around to Mr Rhymer's chair but by the time he arrived, the medium was already starting to rouse.

A stiff brandy was forced on Mr Rhymer and whispered comments began to be shared amongst the guests. The chaplain took his seat and Augustus pulled the soufflé and glass of wine back to their original place in front of Charles. Rather sheepishly, the chaplain stuck his spoon into the soufflé only to have the entire thing collapse. Flipping up the crusted lid, the contents seemed to have vanished. Charles caught Gerard's eye and another stiff brandy was delivered to the table. The almost immediate arrival of the cheese and port was a true blessing. All the diners were far happier talking about cheese than they were trying to acknowledge what they had all just experienced.

Once the port decanter had completed its last circuit, the guests and dons dispersed into the night after the strangest dinner that the shadow faculty had ever hosted. The chaplain crossed the quad to the chapel, carrying with him one of the still-lit candlesticks from the table. When he reached the chapel he continued up the stairs to the organ loft. Placing the candlestick beside him, he settled down on the wooden seat, closed his eyes and lost himself in a trance of pure Bach. The music echoed around the building, the quad and the cellars below, the melodious air rushing through the low C diapason pipe swept over Arthur's surviving corporeal remains. Despite the fact that all the doors and windows were closed, a gust of wind emerged out of the darkness and blew out the candles. The Reverend Pinker played on in total darkness, more at peace with the world than he had been for a considerable period of time.

Chapter 28

Every member of the shadow faculty of gastronomic science was altered in some way by the events at the end of that Hilary term. For Augustus, the impact was certainly the most rapid, the consequences appearing within hours of the séance. In the molluscan version of roulette played by every lover of oysters, there are inevitable losers. The oyster's dietary habit of scooping up detritus from the ocean floor is decidedly less selective than the humans that are fond of eating them. On this turn of the wheel it was Augustus who lost. He was pulled awake in the small hours of that April night by the unavoidable visceral sense of impending gastric emptying. He staggered to the sink in his room with beads of sweat emerging on the back of his neck and waited for the inevitable. It would be a while before Augustus would willingly tuck into an oyster again.

For the others, the effect was profound but somewhat slower. Each of them withdrew into their personal, familiar routines assisted by the onset of the Easter vacation. The most notable outward change was that visits to the chapel became a far commoner occurrence for the faculty members, often at the most peculiar times. This change in behaviour was not due to an increased intensity of religious feeling brought on by the séance, but rather a greater respect for Arthur's mortal remains. Arthur had clearly set his sights on completing the great gastronomic experiment, so they each took it upon themselves to keep a close check on Arthur's leg for fear of putrefaction. If the curing process failed, the experiment would fail. The reader may consider this an entirely honourable escape for the faculty. Indeed at one time, before the séance, this would have been true. Charles Pinker for one would have leapt at this chance to avoid the moral turpitude of coerced cannibalism. The séance had changed everything. Failure of poor Arthur's great experiment might prevent him from crossing over properly and leave him in spiritual limbo in perpetuity. Worse still was the prospect of further ghostly manifestations of Arthur's trapped spirit. A thwarted ghost, particularly one as irascible as Arthur Plantagenet, roaming the quads and staircases of the college, was not a prospect that any member of the shadow faculty of gastronomic science relished.

As well as taking care of the physical state of Arthur's leg, each member of the faculty would take time to commune with their departed friend. These conversations in the quiet of the secret room above the organ served a valuable therapeutic role for all of them. The one exception was Augustus, who spoke to Arthur from the comfort of his own rooms as Arthur's ashes remained on his mantelpiece. The truth is that the fellows rather enjoyed these conversations. For the first time each could tell Arthur what they really thought without fear of interruption or correction.

With a sudden run of a few clear days in the week before the start of the new term, Augustus decided it was time for the shadow faculty to reconvene. There were other obligations laid upon them by Arthur's will, which might prove easier to swallow. So for the first time since the séance, the five surviving members of the declining dining society met together in Augustus' rooms. Although the memory of Arthur Plantagenet and recent events had rarely left any of the members' minds in the last few weeks, his name had never left their lips. When two or more of them met, the conversation was jolly but inconsequential with everyone hoping that no-one would raise the topic just yet. Events as unusual as those of the previous term must be decanted with care into one's memory, letting the distressing sediment settle far from the conscious mind and leaving a reassuringly clear supernatant on top. After such an intense experience, an unexpected discussion could wreak as much havoc to the natural process of re-equilibration of the human mind as shaking a bottle of fine wine while it is being decanted. But it was now time for the faculty to face their responsibilities and memories.

Augustus had arranged for Gerard to bring tea and sandwiches to ease the awkwardness of the task in hand. The table was already laid out with a spread of Earl Grey tea, cucumber sandwiches and cakes. It was not the exotic or ground-breaking spread they usually aspired to, but met the needs of the occasion perfectly. So well in fact that half an hour later, Augustus felt guilty about raising his spoon to force the conversation to the intended topic. By the third clink on his now empty teacup, the room fell silent.

'Gentlemen. If I can have your attention, it seems that we still have some unfinished business to attend to.'

To a man, not one of them received Augustus' gaze, preferring to examine remnants of their sandwiches, empty teacups or the cake crumbs on the carpet between their feet.

'First of all we have to fulfil one of Arthur's last wishes to have a portion of his ashes deposited in the Cherwell within a truffled turkey. I thought a picnic outing on a punt might fit the bill.'

'Oh, yes, definitely,' chimed up Charles Pinker, delighted that Augustus had started with one of Arthur's simpler legacies.

'Thank you, Charles. I assume you would think up a suitable form of service for the occasion?'

'Oh, indeed. Not a normal sort of event of course but I could get a few suitable words together, I'm sure.'

'George,' continued Augustus, 'I was hoping you could provide the truffled turkey?'

'Oh, yes, of course, Augustus. I'd be delighted,' replied George.

'And Theodore, could I ask you to arrange the punt?'

'Certainly, Augustus. What day are we thinking of?'

'I thought Saturday lunchtime would be good if the weather holds.'

'I could arrange the drinks if you like,' volunteered Hamish who had grown increasingly nervous as the tasks had been allocated. In his mind, the images of ramming Arthur's ashes up the rear end of a turkey were proving deeply unsettling.

'I've been working on a brilliant new summer cocktail. Might be the perfect occasion for its first run out.'

'Thank you Hamish, that would be excellent.' Augustus rose to his feet and picked up the urn on the mantelpiece. 'That just leaves Arthur. I'll make sure he gets there on time for once.'

*

As the day of the picnic approached, each took to their appointed tasks with relief, grateful that the more time they spent in preparation, the less time there was for reflection on the plight that Arthur had bequeathed to them all. Augustus had already taken possession of the wind-up portable HMV gramophone that Arthur had left him, along with an extensive collection of 78s. Augustus had allotted himself the task of locating the best preserved and most appropriate discs of Gioacchino Rossini's music for the event. He was planning the faculty's picnic as a re-enactment of a scene in the life of the famous composer. Rossini had once been reduced to tears by the accidental loss of a truffled turkey into the waters of the river Seine during a picnic trip. It was therefore only fitting that Arthur should sink beneath the waters of the Cherwell River to the sound of Rossini's music played on Arthur's own gramophone. A few test playings suggested that the needles were far from their prime and the only playable Rossini recording in Arthur's collection was a scratchy version of the *William Tell Overture*. So Augustus headed off in search of new gramophone needles and the more challenging task of locating a playable version of Rossini's *Stabat Mater* on an old 78.

Hamish McIntyre was eminently suited to his task of bringing the libations. He could merely have visited the wine cellars, but Hamish had a different plan – to unveil his Pimmtini. The entombing of a person's ashes within a truffled turkey and dropping them into a river was a unique event in gastronomic and possibly human history, an event that could only be adequately honoured with the invention of an entirely new drink. The invention of a new drink, like any invention, first needs some knowledge of the topic lest the inventor creates the unusable or merely reinvents the obvious. This knowledge Hamish could certainly claim from an extensive practical experience on the subject of alcoholic drinks. The second requirement is that inexplicable spark of imagination. This spark had come to Hamish one morning as he lay under the covers contemplating the misery of college rooms in winter. Examining the faint clouds of moisture coalescing in the cold air from his warm breath, a vision of summer warmth in a chilled glass emerged fully formed in his mind. He had closed his eyes to savour the moment when the imaginary drink touched his lips. Hamish knew it was a masterpiece just waiting to be delivered to a suitably appreciative audience.

For George Le Strang, locating one of the principal *dramatis personae* for the outing, a truffled turkey, was no simple matter. These birds were an erudite culinary creation even at Christmas and at the start of summer almost unheard of as fresh truffles were not in season. Fortunately, black truffles can be preserved with moderate success and George pulled out all the stops. Within no time he had succeeded in arranging for the Savoy in London to send up a pre-cooked truffled turkey on the appointed day. Although not expressly requested, he also took it upon himself to bring certain other culinary treats for the picnic.

When the Saturday came, Mr Potts knocked on the door of Augustus' rooms just after ten o'clock. The fragrantly scented bird had arrived on the early train from London.

''Ere you are, sir.'

'Thank you, Potts. Pop it on the table there.'

Potts cast an eye around the room, which was stacked high with napkins, glasses and cutlery from the senior common room parlour.

'Anything else you need, sir?'

'Oh, I think we're almost there, you couldn't give me a hand packing this lot into these cases could you?'

'Certainly, sir.'

After a few minutes, the tableware was neatly packed into two wicker hampers and Potts headed down the stairs with them. As soon as Potts had left, Hamish burst in with a large stainless steel box from which seeped a white fog-like vapour.

'What in God's name is that, Hamish?' asked Augustus.

'The ingredients for my new creation. It's going to be great, just you wait.'

'What is it?'

'A surprising and totally new drink. If I say so myself, a brilliant one.'

'Doesn't it just come in a bottle?'

'Oh the box, that's just to allow me to assemble everything on the punt.'

'Christ, that'll sink it.'

'Nonsense, Augustus, now let's get going. I've just got delivery of my new motor. She's an absolute cracker.'

'Hold on, Hamish. There is just one more thing to get ready: this turkey. Now how do you suppose we get these ashes into it?'

'No better man to work that one out than you, Augustus. I'll just bring down this gramophone here and get Vanessa loaded up.'

'Vanessa?'

'Oh, I've christened her Vanessa, my car. She is truly gorgeous.' True to his word Hamish grabbed the old gramophone in one hand and the mysteriously smoking metal case in the other and with great relief launched himself down the staircase. He had no desire to see or assist in the entombing of Arthur's ashes within the fragrant fowl that sat on Augustus' table.

It would have been simpler to have had Arthur's ashes mixed with the truffled stuffing before cooking, but it was too late for that. Augustus sat at the table in front of Arthur's urn and his soon to be culinary sarcophagus. Like a master chess player, he surveyed the options in his mind. A thick dusting of ashes would be simple but not in keeping with Arthur's will. A vision of the dust lingering on the surface while the turkey fell to the depths was sufficient to completely dispel that plan. The ashes had to be concealed within without making an almighty mess. Augustus took to his feet and started pacing the floor. Pausing at the small alcove that served as his kitchen, he spied a narrow jar of capers recently purchased and still unopened. Considering that Arthur had rather unusually chosen to have his ashes deposited at three different locations, the jar, though small, would fit the bill nicely.

Emptying the contents of the jar into a mug, Augustus scanned for something that would serve as a funnel. There was certainly nothing intended for the purpose of funnelling human ashes, though that is perhaps not altogether unsurprising in the rooms of an Oxford don. What is never lacking in such a room is paper, stacks of loose sheets and journals covering most available horizontal surface. So the creation of a funnel came down to the choice of the correct piece of paper. One might imagine that this should depend on the physical properties of the paper, its size and rigidity and such like. For Augustus, his sense of academic decorum dictated that Arthur's ashes should only slide down a piece of paper adorned with words of a suitable subject matter. After several minutes of indecision, he felt that a page from a review he was writing on the medical benefits of monastic herbal liqueurs would be ideal. After carefully decanting a portion of Arthur's ashes onto the title page of his manuscript, Augustus rolled up the page to let Arthur slip into the jar. The final stage required some hands-on rearrangement of the turkey and sadly the sacrilegious loss of some of the stuffing, but after a few more moments of ungainly shoving, one of Arthur's resting places was ready for its final voyage.

*

Augustus arrived in the lodge with the turkey and walked into what resembled the base-camp for a Victorian exploration. The stone flags were stacked high with the two wicker cases from his room and several more besides, a gramophone, assorted rugs and Hamish's strange-looking scientific equipment. His fellow faculty members were nowhere to be seen but he could hear Hamish's enthusiastic tone. Walking through the gates he discovered his colleagues being instructed by Hamish in the delights of his new motor vehicle. Although motor cars carried little fascination for most of the faculty, Hamish's infectious enthusiasm resulted in the curious sight of four Oxford dons admiring the engine of his brand new Jaguar E-Type 2+2.

For George, Theodore and Charles, this was the first car engine they had ever been forced to examine in detail. They were running out of suitable adjectives and devoid of any technical knowledge that might guide a relevant question, so the arrival of Augustus was met with general delight. All the more so when he proved able to pass an informed comment about the challenges of balancing the triple carburettors of such cars. With that, the bonnet was clicked back into position with the two elegantly curved chrome handles restoring 'Vanessa' to her full curvaceous glory.

Two rugs and a single hamper were squeezed into the boot upon which Charles volunteered the opinion that they probably wouldn't all fit in. After a little more debate on the topic, he returned to ask Potts to call a cab.

'On its way already, sir. I guessed you wouldn't all be fitting into that little car,' said Potts with a deferential tap on the edge of his black bowler hat with his finger, leaving an impressed chaplain to return to the throng outside.

'Smart fellow that Potts,' said Charles on his return. 'He'd already called a cab. I don't know what we'd do without him.'

'Excellent! You lot take the cab,' said Hamish. 'Augustus and me will head on up to the boathouse and get the punts ready.' Hamish achieved the apparently impossible task of squeezing himself into the driver's seat and fired up Vanessa, who roared to life before settling into a throaty purr. Augustus, being of a lighter frame, fitted easily into the passenger seat and cradled the turkey on his lap. Theodore Flanagan stood shaking his head disapprovingly as Vanessa departed into the warm April sun, 'Augustus and *I*... Augustus and *I*... '

*

By the time Hamish rolled Vanessa's shining blue frame into the yard of the Cherwell boathouse, the others were already there. Hamish hadn't been able to resist the urge to show off his new toy to Augustus, so the route included several circuits of Oxford's landmarks. A heavily laden punt was already tied up but still only partly loaded with the picnic hampers. With the installation of the last hamper, the remaining members of the shadow faculty took their places. There were only seats for four, but George had already taken charge of the punt pole and positioned himself at the stern, so two empty seats remained. One might imagine that telling the stern of a punt from its bow should be a simple matter, but it is an issue curiously complicated by geography. In Oxford, the stern is located at the opposite end to the platform called the box, which is also more cryptically known as the 'till'. Confusingly, the till is the stern in Cambridge, and one stands on it to punt in defiance of all logic. The smallest amount of water combined with a poor choice in footwear can spell disaster, with the punter inevitably sliding off the till into the water. As there is no navigable waterway from Oxford to Cambridge, thankfully punters are spared the challenging question of exactly where on a journey between these two eminent university towns to change ends.

George expertly guided the punt into the stream. They made quite a sight passing down the Cherwell with the sides of the craft perilously close to the water line. Hamish's steel container gave the craft the appearance of a comically flattened Thames steamer with a steady flow of smoke-like vapour trailing back along the punt. The first instalment of Arthur's ashes lay within the turkey, which was cradled on Augustus' lap. The gramophone had been lashed with rope to the top of the till for safety.

Although made to seem like a complicated art by generations of hapless tourists and new students, punting is a simple but enjoyable activity once a few basic rules are understood. The principal secret of punting is how to steer. In skilled hands this appears to happen miraculously without any human intervention and in the absence of any mechanical steering device. The trick is in the gathering of the pole. After each push the skilled punter leaves the pole trailing in the water, appearing to admire the scenery but in reality during these moments slight movements of the pole provide the effect of a rudder. Only once the punter is happy with the direction of the punt will he start to gather back the pole. Once gathered, the next common mistake is to lower the pole at an angle hand over hand. This leaves the novice grasping onto the very end of the pole while the punt continues to move forward. The skilled punter has the pole vertical before letting it drop through the hands. In a moving punt this produces the correct angle of the pole by the time it reaches the riverbed. After a gentle push comes the final twist which is done imperceptibly a few seconds before the pole needs to be lifted. This clears the pole from the mud beneath or at the very least alerts the punter that he may require more force to free the pole before disaster strikes. Therein lies the most visually entertaining mistake in punting; slavishly hanging onto a pole that is stuck in the mud as the punt moves forward. The poor unfortunate is left suspended for a few agonising moments before sliding or falling into the water.

Naturally, George Le Strang had mastered all these and many other finer points of punting. At the start he was punting masterfully, but when they approached Parson's Pleasure the boat started to rock as he changed his stance. Parson's Pleasure was a gentleman's bathing area located on the River Cherwell, where distinguished senior members of the university could rest and swim unencumbered by a swimming costume. More exhibitionist members would sit on the bank trailing legs and anything else lacking support over the edge, entirely immune to the sniggering hoards of undergraduates punting past. This had been a favourite summer haunt of Arthur Plantagenet and indeed the place where he and George Le Strang had first become friends, despite their wildly disparate personalities. While Arthur made no secret of his love of Parson's Pleasure, for George it was an unspoken pleasure. The appearance of punt-loads of thrill-seeking ladies from Somerville or St Hugh's always served to accentuate their diametrically opposite response to almost any situation. Arthur would merely lift his book a little higher, leaving the rest of his Neronic physique on full view. George would instinctively reach for a towel or, in the absence of that refuge of decency, cover his privates with his hands. Arthur always maintained a logical superiority in such situations, claiming with undoubted veracity that most people recognised him by his face rather than any other part of his anatomy. Covering one's face was therefore the only reasonable action to spare one's own blushes.

The cause of George's sudden punting difficulties was Professor Henrik Olsen, an eccentric and voluble friend of Arthur who would most certainly recognise George and attempt a conversation across the watery divide. George had therefore turned his back on Parson's Pleasure and was attempting to punt on his left-hand side, contrary to his usual custom. This caused the punt to veer from side to side and shake with sudden and unpredictable tilts to port or starboard. Despite some glances and mutterings between Hamish and Theodore on George's sudden loss of punting skills, the plan worked and Henrik Olsen remained in rapt conversation with the self-consciously contorted young man with whom he was sharing a bench.

When Parson's Pleasure was well out of sight, Charles Pinker made a discreet cough to gain his fellow punters' attention. George left the pole trailing in the water behind, and the others sat up in preparation for the ceremony. Charles sat for a few long seconds with his eyes closed and then, in his chapel voice, intoned his oration for Arthur Plantagenet.

'Dear Lord, I commit this son of Adam to your care. The parents of the human race were forced to leave paradise for an apple, what would they have done for a truffled turkey? In tribute to Arthur Plantagenet we leave his ashes in gastronomic paradise inside such a creature and commend his soul to you.'

A stunned silence followed these words. To a man they were expecting Charles to speak for much longer and with a more ecclesiastical tone. A flick of the chaplain's eyebrows in the direction of Augustus gave the signal for the turkey containing Arthur's ashes to be released into the water beneath. Augustus lifted the plate and Hamish obliged with the gramophone lowering the needle onto the recording of *Stabat Mater*. With a gentle nudge, Augustus sent Arthur's unusual sarcophagus slipping into the green waters to the crackling bass tones of the *Pro Peccatis* from the gramophone. For the briefest of moments the dull green glint of the bird could be seen descending through the water. Then it was gone.

No-one could think of anything else to say and after a few moments they fell into a respectful silence, all apart from George who was singing quietly along with the gramophone. After the last notes from the gramophone faded, the chaplain intoned the last words of the *Stabat Mater*.

'*Quando corpus morietur, fac, ut animae donetur paradisi gloria. Amen.*' Seeing the rather blank look on Hamish's face, Charles obliged with a translation, 'When my body dies, let my soul be granted the glory of Paradise. Amen.'

'Amen,' the small floating congregation intoned back.

'Now, anyone thirsty?' asked Hamish after a decent interval which he had cut as short as decency allowed. Not waiting for an answer he turned around and hoisted his mysterious casket onto his lap and started pulling out its contents.

'Theodore, if you would be so kind as to hold this jug and the bottle of Pimms.' Then Hamish pulled out a bottle of Gilbey's gin containing a suspicious green liquid that looked decidedly un-gin-like and a steaming flask.

'Dare I ask what the green liquid is?' said Augustus, hoping desperately that it wasn't more Chartreuse. Ever since the séance, even the smell of Chartreuse had left him with a sense of foreboding.

'Gin infused for a full week in crushed cucumber skins then filtered. You'll love it. Now Charles, get the glasses ready.' Charles duly rooted for the martini glasses while Hamish decanted the entire bottle of cucumber infused gin into the mixing jug. He then added a small glug of Pimms before handing the jug back to Theodore for stirring. Then he opened the steaming flask and shook a few white pellets of dry ice into each glass.

'Theodore, would you like to pour?'

Theodore poured the green liquor into each glass, causing a torrent of boiling fog to pour over the edge of each glass.

'Gentlemen, I present to you the cucumber Pimmtini,' said Hamish, holding his glass high in a toast. 'To Arthur.'

It was a concoction of alcoholic and theatrical perfection and Hamish sat back victoriously sipping his Pimmtini and admiring the nugget of dry ice that danced in his glass and the mist tumbling down over the stem.

'Congratulations, Hamish,' said George. 'Perhaps I could offer a small *hors d'oeuvres* as an accompaniment to this fine drink? Have a look in the top of that hamper.'

Hamish lifted the lid and cooed with delight before passing around the bowl of boiled quails' eggs.

No reasonable and otherwise caring person should spend too long thinking about the common human practice of eating the unborn eggs of birds. It is not after all a practice that will bear up to deep moral inquiry when compared to the protection we offer our own children, but anyone with an aesthetic soul can only marvel at the glorious colours on the outside and especially the inside of a quail egg. It is one of the great mysteries of nature why, under luckier circumstances, a quail chick develops inside a vault of such a divine blue-green. A colour that is hidden from the world until the egg is opened and discarded. These particular eggs were shelled with due admiration of their colour and then the conversation tumbled on, turning naturally to memories of Arthur, recounting phrases that were quintessentially his own. One by one they bit into their eggs with casual disregard, only to be brought up short by the explosion of flavour from the still soft yolk.

'Heavens above, George,' spluttered Hamish, 'these eggs are outrageously good. Where in God's name did you get them?'

'My own dedication to Arthur, a quail laid them but I humbly improved them.'

George smiled down the punt, relishing the next round of comments and accolades.

'But how?' spluttered Augustus.

'The eggs were cooked for 2 minutes 45 seconds in gently simmering water, cooled in running water and then injected with a tiny volume of a mixture of Worcestershire sauce and truffle-scented oil into the cooling but still liquid yolk. I used those fine hypodermic syringes you kindly gave me last year Augustus when we were experimenting with brandy injected bananas.'

George gave a small bow in acknowledgement of the applause and popped one of the eggs into his mouth. With gentle pressure of the tongue against the roof of his mouth he released the fragrant yolk onto his taste buds. No Roman emperor had ever tasted anything so exquisite. Sadly neither had Arthur Plantagenet, not in this life at least.

Chapter 29

'So Mr... what was your name again?' asked Detective Inspector Granger.

''Ogarth. Frederick 'Ogarth.'

'Mr Hogarth,' replied the policeman, emphasising the 'H'.

'That's what I said, 'Ogarth.'

'Good, now we have that cleared up perhaps you could explain why one of my constables found you at five o'clock this morning in the deer park at Magdalen College with a rope and large meat cleaver.'

'Trying to look after my nearest and dearest. Meat don't grow on trees, you know.'

'Indeed, Mr Hogarth. An accurate biological statement but I understand you are in employment. I would suppose therefore that you are able to purchase meat as a normal person might rather than steal it in the middle of the night.' The inspector looked down at the notes on the desk in front of him. 'You are a mortuary assistant at the Radcliffe Infirmary. Is that correct?'

'And proud of it. Still, hard to support a family on them wages. Anyway it's not like they'd miss a deer or two.'

'Your family are fond of venison, I take it?'

'Look, meat is meat. In a pie a deer tastes as good as a cow in my book.'

'So, can I take it that you admit to attempting to steal a

deer from Magdalen College?'

'Well, you can't blame a man for trying. But as I didn't kill anything I can't be done for nothing.' Mr Hogarth sat back with a satisfied smile on his face. He was not unfamiliar with the ways of the law and fully expected to be released with no more than a caution.

'Oh, let's see. Three months for aggravated trespass on private property. Resisting arrest. Let's not forget threatening a police officer with a cleaver… '

'I didn't threaten no-one. Can't say I was too chuffed being caught, but well, when you're nicked you're nicked, ain't ya?'

'Succinctly put Mr Hogarth. Unfortunately, as Magdalen College have lost several deer in the last few months they seem quite insistent that we charge you with something. Did I mention I was once a student of Magdalen? No? Well never mind, why don't we cut to the chase. One of my sergeants has prepared a statement. If you could look it over and sign at the bottom we'll leave the charges at trespass and, despite your ample criminal record, I don't suppose her Majesty will need detain you too long.'

'I ain't being put away for walking around a deer park.'

'With a meat cleaver?'

Silence fell on the two men who glared at each other from opposite sides of the table and indeed opposite sides of society.

'Look, inspector. There's bigger fish than me. What if I could help you catch one?'

'I hardly think you are in a position to do any kind of deal, Mr Hogarth.'

'What if I said I knew that one of these college types was stealing body parts… from dead people like.'

The Detective Inspector sat back in his chair, looked at Mr Frederick Hogarth, then shook his head in disbelief.

'Very imaginative, I must say, but under the circumstances I hardly think a judge would give your evidence much credence. The only offer on the table is to sign this confession and save us all a lot of time and effort.'

'Well, I've got proof. Now, why do you suppose I was asked to chop off some dead bloke's leg and deliver it packed in ice? The instructions was very clear that the leg 'ad to get there fresh like.'

'Are you saying this was someone from Magdalen College?'

'Oh no, inspector. St Jerome's.'

'Thank God for that at least.'

Chapter 30

Trinity Term 1970

When Eccles arrived back at St Jerome's on Monday of noughth week for the start of Trinity term he walked straight through the lodge to gaze across Old Quad at his former staircase. The window boxes were now in full bloom with crimson geraniums and the golden stone glowed in the summer sun. He looked at the still fresh-looking chalk markings over the arch of staircase five that signified the greatest sporting achievement of his life; the four bumps that had earned the fourth VIII their blades. On the back of that and with the forthcoming final examinations for some of the better oarsmen, Eccles had been promoted to the second crew for the summer bumps, a significant accomplishment for a first-year novice rower. Looking up above to the windows of his former room he was brought back to the searing unfairness of his eviction by Kingsley-Hampton.

Despite Eccles' doubts, Kingsley-Hampton had followed through on his promise and an envelope was waiting for him in the lodge. The keys were small and unimpressive looking, much as he expected his new lodgings to be. Eccles made his way out of college and headed down the cobbled street. When he arrived at the Mitre Hotel he wandered up and down looking for the grey door described on the scribbled note that came with the keys. When he finally located it, it turned out to be the strangest door he had ever seen, barely five foot high sitting in a crooked frame. The pavement was a good six inches above the bottom of the door giving the appearance that the door had sunk under the weight of the building above. Although it looked as if it hadn't been opened in years, the lock clicked and the door swung inwards with the gentlest push.

The door led into a small dark corridor with a steep staircase at the end. Climbing the stairs he came into a room flooded with light that defied his every expectation. All his books and belongings had been brought up from college and were neatly stacked. The room was huge, far larger than he ever imagined, with furnishings bordering on the elegant. He threw open one of the windows and let the noise and heat from the High Street fill the room. A small plaque caught his eye beside the window.

In Max Beerbohm's classic Oxford novel Zuleika Dobson, *The Junta met in these rooms and the Duke of Dorset leapt from this very window.*

Eccles decided he would have to get a copy of Beerbohm's book. The smell of cooking from the Mitre Hotel, which was located a few doors down, caught his nostrils and diverted his thoughts to more practical issues like food. With a hotel next door and the covered market almost on his doorstep, he would be well provided for on that front. Eccles was starting to think that this arrangement might work out rather well. He stood mulling over the airy, literary and geographical virtues of his new rooms and found himself feeling guilty about how much he had cursed his former roommate over the Easter holidays about this move. It was, after all, the Honourable Kingsley-Hampton who had set him up in such style, albeit to suit his own purposes.

While the young medical student relaxed in his new accommodations, he was rapidly becoming a minor celebrity around Oxford. Trinity term's first issue of *Styx* was being delivered to the lodges and junior common rooms of Oxford. The editor, Rupert Atworth had finally managed to get the story about the mysterious dining society printed, despite the reservations of the other members of the editorial committee. Miss Bellingham's father, a barrister, had indicated that publication was defensible provided there was solid written evidence to back up the story. The existence of the menu was deemed sufficient and Atworth had finally prevailed. His original title with the words 'Russian Roulette' was deemed inappropriate as it may create a diplomatic row with two countries rather than merely one. Atworth stuck to his guns on the reference to the Japanese ambassador as he felt sure that his readers wouldn't care who exactly died and it gave the story more gravitas than it would with the death of a mere cultural attaché. Atworth was also true to his word in placing the story prominently on the front page.

Compared to the normal story run in *Styx*, this front page created quite a stir as the news started to disperse around the city. Eccles had decided to take his lunch in the covered market in celebration of his new accommodations. He was sitting in Martha's café, in a state of perfect contentment, with the remnants of a cheese and pickle sandwich in front of him and reading a second-hand copy of *Zuleika Dobson* he had picked up half an hour earlier in the bookshop next door. He hadn't read a novel since he had left school, and at school it was a matter of necessity not choice. This was therefore the first adult work of fiction he had ever read for simple amusement and for simple amusement there could be no finer place to start.

'Eccles, thought it was you,' the shaggy-haired Simon Cavendish, one of his fellow rowers from the Torpids fourth VIII, pulled out the chair opposite and sat down.

'Hi Simon, good vac?' replied Eccles, looking up. They were an unlikely pair. Cavendish, in keeping with the fashion of the time, sported a pink paisley print shirt and a mop of hair, while Eccles was part of a dying breed, the clean-cut student in a tweed jacket.

'Yeah, not bad. Too much family, not enough drink; apart from that it was okay. Christ, you're reading a book?' said Cavendish yanking it out of Eccles' grasp before dropping it on the table. 'I didn't think medical students had time for that kind of thing. *Zuleika Dobson*. Oh God, you're not in love or something horrible, are you?'

'No, it's just… '

'Anyway, sod the book. Listen, you're famous. Look at this.' Simon Cavendish shoved an already crumpled looking copy of the *Styx* into Eccles' now empty hands.

Mysterious Dining Soc kills Japanese Ambassador. Who will die next?

Evidence has emerged of the existence of a dangerous dining society within our midst. Though no members of this arcane organisation have come forward, reporters for Styx *have uncovered details of the dinner in Trinity term of last year that led to the death of the Japanese Ambassador. This death arose from the serving of Fugu, a delicacy made from puffer fish, which is revered in the orient but if improperly prepared can be fatal, as it proved to be on this inauspicious night. Medical student Patrick Eccles told our reporter that this dish contains tetratoxin, a deadly poison more toxic than cyanide. Senior figures in the university have sought to suppress this story in the apparent hope of preventing an international incident. Certainly it is remarkable that the circumstances surrounding the death of this diplomat have been so thoroughly obscured from public view.*

The exotic nature of the food served at this dinner proves that this society is hell-bent on a dangerous culinary path that will surely place others in mortal peril unless this society is stamped out. Despite extensive undercover research by Styx, this newspaper has been unable to track down any members of the university who will admit to membership of this dangerous dining society. What is known from the discovery of a menu, the key evidence in breaking this story, is that this fateful dinner was held at St Jerome's College. It is therefore likely that several members of this bizarre dining society are lurking in the midst of this ancient college. If anyone has any information that might assist Styx in preventing further loss of life, please contact the editor.

Patrick Eccles started reading down the front page. As the words sank in, his eyes stopped scanning and started skating over the page in a panic.

'Look, you're there,' Cavendish thrust his finger to the relevant passage.

'Medical student Patrick Eccles. How cool is that?'

'Oh God.' Eccles slumped back in his seat for a second before launching for the door, hoping that he could reach the street before his stomach contents reached his mouth. Simon Cavendish looked after him, bemused, and after stuffing the remnants of his friend's sandwich in his mouth, rose to his feet only to meet Martha demanding payment for a cheese and pickle sandwich and two cups of tea.

A well-placed bin allowed Eccles to recover some semblance of dignity by hiding both the act of vomiting and his face from passers-by. Wiping his mouth with the back of his hand, he stumbled into a cautious run towards college, picking up speed down the narrow lane leading from the High Street. At first he was unaware why he was running, but a plan started to emerge in his troubled mind as the fresh air rushed past his head and filled his lungs. He rushed through the lodge when he reached college and sped across Old Quad to the chaplain's staircase. At the top, he paused only to catch his breath and then knocked on the door. Hearing nothing, he knocked again. He stood in silence, his heart and breathing returning slowly to a more normal rate. He turned and lowered himself down onto the top step. He would wait. The chaplain had to come back some time. He sat in state of suspended anxiety, hearing the sounds of the comings and goings filtering up from the quad below. After ten minutes spent trying to calm the mental maelstrom in his head he could stand it no longer and he set off down the stairs. He emerged into the bright sunlight and met the last person on earth he wanted to see just then.

'Eccles! So how is my former valet finding his new quarters?' Kingsley-Hampton was accompanied by an olive-skinned young gentleman with a noticeable limp and an elegant, silver-tipped walking cane.

'Fine, thanks,' said Eccles who tried to continue on his way but Kingsley-Hampton stretched his arm out to lean against the wall and block his path.

'May I introduce my new roommate, Felipe Banzarro.'

When Eccles out of politeness offered his hand to Mr Banzarro, Kingsley-Hampton cut him short, 'Felipe, I wouldn't bother,' before offering Eccles a disdainful facial movement that resembled a smile and turned to leave. At the last moment he paused to secure the last word.

'Oh, I think the vice-chancellor might want a word with you after this scurrilous article in *Styx* with your name in it. Enjoy whatever dead-beat red-brick university you end up in.' Kingsley-Hampton threw the copy of *Styx* so it landed just short of Eccles.

'Come on, Felipe, I'm parched. Let's get some refreshments.'

Kingsley-Hampton strode on, and had to pause for a second for Mr Banzarro to catch up.

'Who was that?' asked Banzarro when he drew alongside.

'No-one important. Just that Eccles deadbeat I threw out so you could come back.'

'The one who was trying to find your mysterious dining society for you?'

'The very same, but he couldn't find his nose to pick in

the dark. He was mildly entertaining, even useful for a while, but then he grew rather tiresome. The final straw was when he started inviting his new-found rowing trolls over to *my* room.'

'Well, maybe we should just start our own dining society, The Dangerous Dining Club, sounds rather good.'

'Now you're talking. After that article in *Styx* that other crowd aren't going to last long… God, it's good to have you back in Oxford, Felipe. It's been very dull so far this year.'

*

Kingsley-Hampton had unwittingly helped Patrick Eccles in providing the perfect antidote to his state of hopeless anxiety. In that curious way that anger can cure despair, Eccles stooped to pick up the copy of *Styx* from the flagstones and, as he regained his full height, found that his mind was clear. Eccles walked into Chapel Quad and caught sight of the man he had been looking for. The chaplain was standing at the chapel door struggling with keys. In the time it took for Eccles to reach him, Charles Pinker had managed to lock the door, walk away and return to check and relock the door all over again.

'Chaplain, could I have a word?'

'Oh, er… Eccles. Of course, of course, young man. Now what is it?' said the chaplain, struggling to clear his mind of thoughts of Arthur's leg after the long one-sided conversation he had just had with it. With a sudden mini-heatwave in the making, all the members of the shadow faculty had been taking extra care to ensure that the curing process didn't go awry. Heat could be beneficial to the process of air-drying, but only in moderation.

'Well, it's a bit delicate and I'd rather tell you in private. If you don't mind?'

'Not at all, come to my rooms and have a cup of tea. Nothing a chat and a cup of tea can't help, I'm sure.' Charles smiled at Eccles, delighted at the distraction of some nice simple pastoral issue that he assumed was troubling the young man.

In the chaplain's rooms, Eccles settled himself in one of the armchairs. Reverend Pinker busied himself with preparing the tea while keeping the conversation to safe topics such as the state of the window boxes, the weather and the refreshments.

'Lapsang okay for you, er… Patrick, isn't it?'

'Perfect, thank you, Reverend.'

'I'll call for some cucumber sandwiches too, Gerard will be able to knock them up in no time.'

Charles swirled the small pot trying to hasten the process of infusion and then opened a small miniature bottle of whiskey, which he tipped into the pot. He always found fortified tea was an even better restorative in difficult situations and that resinous Chinese teas like Lapsang masked the flavour of the whiskey rather well.

'So let's get this tea poured and you can tell me what's troubling you,' said Charles Pinker bringing the tray across and placing it on the table in front of them.

'Oh, I must call Gerard for those sandwiches.' He poured the tea and then made the brief telephone call to the senior common room parlour.

'Now, what do you think of this tea?' asked the chaplain.

Eccles took a large slug of tea and had to admit that it was one of the finest cups of tea he had ever tasted.

'Now,' said the chaplain, 'where were we?'

'Well it seems I may be in some trouble because of this article that's just appeared in *Styx*.'

'Sticks and stones may break your bones, but names will never hurt you, dear boy,' said the chaplain as he unfolded the newspaper that Eccles thrust anxiously at him. Eccles waited for the chaplain to read down, but after a second or two of silence couldn't help defending himself.

'Of course, it's all wrong. They quoted me but I've nothing to do with this story really, and they've got all the names wrong.'

The chaplain remained silent, staring at the front page of *Styx*.

'It's my roommate, Matthew Kingsley-Hampton. He found the menu and bullied the editor of *Styx* into publishing this story… You see he wanted to know who was in this dining society because he felt he should have known about it. Well, he really thought he should have been invited to join.'

The chaplain was now shaking his head, but still showed no signs of imminent speech.

'I'm afraid that my tutor Dr Bloom might be involved because I overheard a conversation at Professor Plantagenet's service, and I don't want to cause any trouble for him… or the college… so I thought you might know what to do?'

'I see,' the chaplain said before running out of words. The tension was broken by a knock on the door, as Gerard brought in a plate of cucumber sandwiches and small cakes.

'Thank you, Gerard,' said the chaplain while Gerard made a discreet exit. 'Oh, Gerard, could you do me a favour and see if you can track down Augustus Bloom and ask him to join us. I last saw him in the fellows' garden.'

Gerard nodded, gave a small bow and left the chaplain and an ashen-faced Eccles to their cucumber sandwiches.

Chapter 31

Into the warm silence of an unsuspecting summer morning in St Jerome's came an unwelcome intrusion – the sound of hobnailed boots. In the lodge the sound grew louder second by second until it was suddenly silenced as the source came into view. Potts lifted his bowler-hatted head to the rare sight of two more bowler hats gazing back and four now silent boots. The hats and boots belonged to two Bulldogs. Potts had a comradely respect for these university policemen as long as they didn't trespass into his college, but they were now standing firmly on college ground.

'Mr Percival Potts. Long time no see,' said Brian O'Donnell, the thicker necked and older of the two Bulldogs, who was an old acquaintance of Potts.

'Indeed,' said Potts in reply.

'The vice-chancellor has sent us to personally deliver this letter to a Mr Patrick Eccles and I've got another for his tutor, Dr Bloom,' continued O'Donnell while his companion remained in silent solidarity, which was clearly the only role he intended to play.

'Leave it with me and I'll see that they get them,' said Potts.

'I'm afraid the vice-chancellor was quite specific. We aren't to leave until we have personally delivered them both.'

'Well, they're not 'ere so you'd best just leave them with me,' Potts replied, stretching out his hand which hung in the air for a few moments before he finally realised the resolve facing him.

'As I said, Mr Potts, the vice-chancellor's in a bit of a steam about this so if you could just tell us where Mr Eccles' and Dr Bloom's rooms are we will go and wait for them to return.'

'Like I said, Eccles ain't here. If you wait here for a minute I can see if I can find Dr Bloom. But I'm warning you, 'e won't be too impressed by this sort of palaver.'

Potts stormed out of the lodge to find Augustus Bloom. He was in such a state that he didn't notice the small man lurking just outside the gates. Once Potts was gone, the little man slid through the gate and walked unnoticed into the college.

Potts sped up the stairs to Dr Bloom's room and hammered on the door with even more force than usual.

'Is it urgent, Potts?' asked Dr Bloom when he opened the door. 'I'll be finished this tutorial in another ten minutes.'

'Sorry, sir… yes… '

'Good God, man, what's happened?'

'Vice… ' wheezed Potts, barely catching his breath.

'Vice what?'

'Chancellor… Bulldogs,' Potts pointed in the direction of the lodge. To his great surprise Augustus seemed quite unsurprised.

'Hmm. A little faster than I expected, but let's see what they want.' Augustus excused himself and led the way back to the lodge.

*

When Augustus reached the lodge he held out a hand to introduce himself.

'Good morning, Gentlemen, Dr Bloom. Is there anything I can do for you?'

Rather than the expected handshake, his outstretched hand received only the letter that the Bulldogs had been ordered to deliver. Augustus looked at the familiar envelope and crest and, to Potts complete consternation, smiled. The past few months had taught Dr Bloom a great deal about hiding one's inner feelings.

'And what can I do for our illustrious vice-chancellor?' asked Augustus.

'I believe it's about one of your students, Mr Patrick Eccles. The vice-chancellor's ordered him to be gated pending a disciplinary hearing for bringing the university into disrepute,' said Mr O'Donnell.

'An order? Well as this is my college and Mr Eccles is my student I will consider the vice-chancellor's… request,' said Augustus, pocketing the letter unopened inside his jacket.

The vice-chancellor had forewarned his trusted constables that Dr Bloom was a slippery character and armed them with the ammunition they needed.

'If you read this extract of the university regulations you will see that the vice-chancellor has the right to gate any student in the university.' The Bulldog thrust the piece of paper with the relevant regulation at Augustus.

Augustus scanned over the piece of paper with well-hidden surprise.

'I see. Well thank you for your assistance with the regulations,' said Augustus, handing back the piece of paper and turning to leave. He had taken a few paces when he stopped and turned to look back at the still motionless Bulldogs.

'Was there anything else?'

'We have a letter for Mr Eccles too.'

'I'll see that he gets it,' said Augustus.

'I'm to deliver it in person,' said O'Donnell, visibly bristling.

'I know the vice-chancellor very well at this stage and I am sure he would accept my assurance that Eccles will receive it.'

Seeing O'Donnell's hesitation, Potts seized his chance and the letter.

'Right, Gentlemen, job done. Time to go home.' With that, Potts herded the two Bulldogs out of the gate with his outstretched arms and down the cobbled street that lay beyond the gate lodge. When Potts returned, Dr Bloom was still standing there.

'Well done, Potts. Now I'd really appreciate if you could find Eccles and bring him to my room.'

Bloom was thoroughly relieved to find his room empty on his return. His student had taken the opportunity to cut short what had been proving a rather challenging tutorial. Bloom placed the letter on the mantelpiece, moved to the small kitchen alcove and filled the kettle. He had just received a small package of jasmine bud tea from a former student who was working in Hong Kong. He had placed it aside, keeping it for a special occasion. Now seemed like an excellent time, if only to try and soften the bitter pill sent by the vice-chancellor. As the kettle groaned into life, he picked up the two letters and opened the one addressed to him.

Dear Dr Bloom,

As you may be aware, a certain matter has again been brought to prominence in the student publication Styx. *The article in question firmly identifies Mr Patrick Eccles of St Jerome's College as a prime source of information and willing informant. This article has the potential to cause untold damage to the good standing of the university. In light of this I am imposing an immediate gating of this student pending more draconian sanctions that will inevitably follow once this matter has been fully investigated. Be assured that the activities of you and your colleagues will not be immune from this investigation.*

Yours sincerely,

Dr K W Ridgeway

Augustus crumpled the letter and launched it into the fireless grate. Even though it was summer it felt more emphatic than throwing it in the waste-paper bin. He glanced at the accompanying letter addressed to Mr Eccles, but doubting it held any surprises placed it on the mantelpiece next to

Arthur's ashes. Returning to the alcove he lifted the lid on the shiny red octagonal box he had recently received to inspect the curious grey balls within. He dropped a few of them into two cups, added hot water and waited to be surprised. The tea was still infusing when Eccles arrived at his threshold.

'Patrick, come in and try this new tea of mine.'

Eccles' mental state had improved considerably after his confessional meeting with the chaplain and his tutor a few days earlier. He had been reassured that the college would handle the matter in return for his full cooperation in their own investigations into the authorship of the fateful article in *Styx* and of course the recovery of the menu. So apart from the surprise at being summoned by the head porter from his new rooms on the High Street, he arrived in a state of unsuspecting calm. This feeling was further enhanced by the strange and fragrant smell from the cup that was handed to him as he crossed the threshold.

'A type of jasmine tea made from buds,' explained Augustus, passing the cup under his nose. 'Smells promising, but I think it will benefit from another minute or two of infusing.'

Eccles followed suit in inhaling the vapour from his cup, now familiar with the eccentric culinary diversions of his tutor.

'Now, a little issue has arisen with the vice-chancellor. Grab that letter there on the mantelpiece will you?'

Eccles rose to gather the letter and went to pass it to his tutor until it became clear that he was meant to read it himself. While Eccles was reading and rereading the letter, Augustus absent-mindedly peered into his cup. The small buds had burst out into a mass of folded leaves. He was about to take a taste when Eccles interrupted his reverie.

'Gated? What does that mean, Dr Bloom?'

'Well, technically it means that you must remain within the walls of the college until further notice. Really it is a form of house arrest, but not as serious of course.'

'Oh,' said Eccles initially relieved. It took a moment for him to appreciate the full implications of this ruling.

'But what about rowing?' Eccles asked. 'And lectures... '

'I think we can put lectures down as essential college business,' replied Bloom. 'Mind you, rowing might be more problematic, but we'll see what we can do. What the vice-chancellor doesn't know won't hurt him.'

'But I don't live in anymore, so how can I stay inside the college at night?'

'What?' asked Bloom suddenly caught off guard. 'Of course you do. With that Kingsley-Hampton character who has caused us all so much trouble.'

Eccles chronicled the details of his eviction to suit the social needs of his former roommate. On hearing this story his tutor became more and more agitated until he suddenly rose to his feet and marched out of the door. Eccles sat in the oppressive silence for a few minutes, until he remembered the strange tea that had been offered. The worm-like mass at the bottom of the cup looked rather unpleasant but the taste was, even to Eccles' untrained palate, rather good. His attention then returned to the letter. The phrase *draconian sanctions* stared back at him from the page.

'Oh God,' he muttered to himself as he began pacing the floor until he could stand it no longer and he too marched through the door.

At the bottom of the staircase, he was forced to a halt by a small balding man with a camera. He stood impatiently behind the man who was taking an inordinate length of time lining up a photograph.

'Excuse me,' Eccles said eventually.

'Very sorry, young man, I didn't mean to delay you. But if you have a minute?'

'Really, I have to be off and the college is closed to tourists during term, so you really shouldn't be here.'

'Oh, I'm not a tourist. I'm with the *Daily Mail*,' the man said proudly. 'Following up a story about the killing of some Japanese bloke. Would you mind if I asked you a few questions?'

Eccles stared back in a state of disbelief bearing an expression more commonly seen on a fishmonger's slab. He was rescued by Augustus Bloom on his return from the Master's lodge who had overheard the reporter's description of his assignment.

'A mere April's fool,' Augustus said, taking the man firmly by the arm and marching him towards the lodge. 'You of all people should know the dangers of believing what is written in newspapers.'

Chapter 32

Patrick Eccles was sitting out of view in the back room of the porter's lodge on his tutor's instructions. Mr Potts had received an unwelcome earful from Augustus Bloom about his complicity in evicting Eccles from his room. It was Potts who had moved all of Eccles' books and possessions during the Easter vacation. In penance he, along with Eccles, had been recruited to recover the accursed menu from Eccles' former roommate Matthew Kingsley-Hampton. It was for this reason that Eccles was receiving such deferential treatment from Potts, though Eccles could have done without another cup of tea. The strength of tea can be gauged in many ways and the English language has been amply stretched to meet this challenge. From 'weak as gnat's piss' to the more obscure imagery favoured by Potts of 'mouse-trotter' which refers to the ability of being able to trot a mouse along the surface of a decently strong cup of tea. Potts made and drank proper mouse-trotter tea, which, as Eccles discovered, was an acquired taste he had yet to acquire. With this particular cup, Potts had exceeded even his high standards, and Eccles found his digestive biscuit broke in this brew in the same manner as a shovel hitting hard ground.

Matthew Kingsley-Hampton strutted through the lodge with Felipe Banzarro, who was struggling to keep up. His bones had only recently healed after his accident on the glacier last year and he had yet to adjust fully to the challenges of bipedal locomotion, especially at the unearthly hour of nine o'clock in the morning.

'Morning Potts… Good morning, Potts,' repeated Kingsley-Hampton, determined to extract a response.

'Good morning, sir,' muttered Potts, barely lifting his head.

Kingsley-Hampton marched on out of the lodge to have breakfast in Worcester College with Rupert Atworth. Atworth, as the editor of the *Styx*, had received the same fate as Eccles in being gated by the vice-chancellor, but his college was taking a rather stricter view of this punishment. For the time being, Kingsley-Hampton had avoided censure by keeping his name out of the press. So out of solidarity he had arranged to visit Atworth to alleviate the worst of the boredom of gating.

'They've gone,' said Mr Potts as he handed Eccles the key to his former room.

Subterfuge did not come naturally to Eccles, but he took a particular delight in crossing the threshold into his former yet still rightful abode. During the time that Kingsley-Hampton had been treating Eccles as a curious fusion of acolyte, Eton fag and valet, Eccles had learnt most of his roommate's habits and customs. Kingsley-Hampton had a range of hiding places for objects that were precious, illegal or a possible source of temptation to others. A secret compartment at the base of his travelling trunk concealed his ample collection of erotica, the preferred term for pornography amongst the ruling classes. The only functional role for the riding boots that Eccles had been forced to polish at regular intervals was as a hiding place for a bottle of absinthe in the left boot and a slender hookah in the right.

Eccles started with the trunk. The distant echoes from the bells of Tom Tower brought him back to his task half an hour later, wide-eyed from his voyeuristic excursion into unsuspected realms of human activity. For all the exotic activities included in Kingsley-Hampton's erotic archives, fine dining was certainly not one of them. A quick check of the boots revealed only their usual contents, but he noted with displaced pride that without his assistance they had lost their Napoleonic lustre. At a loss, he started checking, book by book, the densely packed bookcase. After checking a complete shelf of curiously random books, from William Blake to Ian Fleming, he came to an old atlas. He had often seen Kingsley-Hampton disappear into his bedroom with this book without passing much thought as to the reason for such a secretive devotion to geography. Inside this volume, he discovered the pages were stuck together and had been carefully dissected to create a secret compartment. Inside was a bag containing a block of a brown resinous substance that Eccles didn't recognise and, thank God, the menu.

*

In another panelled room in another college, a young man was pacing the threadbare carpet.

'Relax, will you Rupert,' said Kingsley-Hampton, casually sitting side-saddle on a threadbare chintz armchair and drinking tea from one of his host's ancestral china cups. 'This will be a defining moment in your journalistic career if you can just keep your nerve. There was even a man from the *Daily Mail* sneaking around college looking for Eccles the other day.'

'Really? Well that would be a scoop. Mind you, shame it wasn't a decent newspaper. What did you tell him?' asked Atworth.

'Oh, I just spun him a yarn. Told him Eccles had been sent down as he couldn't pay his bills. I don't want that toerag getting any more publicity. I gave the reporter one of my cards to give to his editor. Told him in no uncertain terms that I'd only talk to the editor himself. Of course, I'd prefer *The Times* or *Telegraph* to pick up on the story, but we might yet get a few quid from an exclusive interview in the *Mail*.' Kingsley-Hampton was rarely without his expensively embossed cards that he had had printed in a little place off Bond Street as soon as he'd heard of his elevation to the title of 'The Honourable'.

He lavished them on everyone from serving girls in tea shops to the porters at the train station, usually in place of a tip.

'Perhaps this story does have legs. Mind you, there have been times when I've wondered why I let you talk me into this. Most notably when the vice-chancellor's goons burst in on me.'

'Don't worry, we can handle the vice-chancellor. We are on the side of truth and transparency, Rupert. For all his pomp and office he is no better than some communist apparatchik.' Kingsley-Hampton delivered these words in a voice he usually reserved for speeches in the Oxford union. He rose to his feet and kicked the outstretched legs of Felipe Banzarro who had fallen asleep. Felipe awoke with a squeal as the pain of the kick rattled his healing bones.

'Come on, Felipe. If we are going to make it for lunch in town we'd better get moving.' As they made their way to the door, Kingsley-Hampton threw one last question back at Atworth.

'Any good leads come out of the story yet? It must have stirred someone other than the vice-chancellor.'

'Oh, nothing apart from a paranoid freak who claims that all the college kitchens are run by elves who will poison anyone who threatens to reveal their secret.'

'Excellent, you should run that story in the next edition.'

He ducked just in time to avoid the complex swerving path of the piece of toast that Atworth threw across the room.

*

Meanwhile, Mr Potts had been sitting at his post in the lodge watching out in case Kingsley-Hampton should return, ready with a pre-prepared if fictitious letter demanding that Kingsley-Hampton report immediately to the Master. Potts was most certainly not expecting the person who did arrive.

'Good morning, sir,' said the police officer. 'I'm looking for a Mr Potts. One of the porters, I believe.'

'Well, well,' said Potts who was not especially fond of Her Majesty's constabulary, 'and why would you be looking for 'im?'

'Just a routine enquiry. Probably nothing really, but I've been asked to investigate by my superiors. You know the way it is.'

'Well, I guess you are looking for me then. You'd better come round to the side door,' said Potts. 'We can talk insides.'

Sergeant Jenkins declined Mr Potts' offer of both tea and a chair.

'So, Mr Potts, the reason I am here is that a certain Mr Hogarth, employed by the John Radcliffe Hospital until his recent arrest for aggravated trespass and other offences, gave us your name. He is claiming that you were instrumental in removing certain body parts from the mortuary at dates unspecified last year.'

'No I bloody well weren't,' said Potts indignantly.

'No I bloody well weren't,' repeated Sergeant Jenkins, noting Mr Potts' words in his notebook.

'Do you have any knowledge of the whereabouts of body parts? In particular a human leg?' asked Sergeant Jenkins.

'No I don't,' said Potts emphatically.

This denial was duly noted by the policeman.

'Well then, thank you, Mr Potts. That's all I needed to know.' With that, and seeming quite satisfied, he took his leave of the porter. Once on his own, Potts went into the back room to get the small bottle of whiskey he kept for emergencies. He poured a large glug into his teacup, which he drained in a single draught before heading off to find Augustus Bloom.

Chapter 33

It was well past midnight when Augustus Bloom, unable to sleep, slipped down the stairs into the quadrangle below. He had stood up to the strain of recent events with remarkable resilience, but the news that Potts had delivered that morning had thrown him. The vice-chancellor's rants were one thing, but the prospect of a police investigation was quite another. The cool night air weaved itself through every thread of Augustus' dressing gown, soothing his frayed nerves but making him shudder involuntarily in the cold. He paused at the foot of the staircase taking in the scene. The world is a different place after midnight and the Cinderella effect had worked its magic on the stone walls, distorting familiar shapes into angular shadows. A partly clouded gibbous moon offered just enough light for Augustus to navigate through the dark alley towards the chapel. Inside the building it was another story entirely. When Augustus closed the doors of the chapel a suffocating darkness enveloped him. He stood motionless, waiting for his eyes to adapt to the meagre scraps of light that found their way through the stained glass window high over the altar. Then he crept forward, holding one hand along the wall for guidance, until he reached the wooden choir stalls. Suddenly, his breath was taken away by an assault on his ears from the organ pipes above.

After the first moment of shock had subsided, Augustus'

racing heart slowed to a more normal pace. He didn't recognise the piece but was completely convinced that it was being played by Charles. He let the resonance of the last chord fade into silence before starting to clap.

'Bravo, Charles,' Augustus called up to the organ loft. As there was no reply or acknowledgement he called again.

'Charles?'

The heart in Augustus' chest was the only thing in the chapel to respond; a gentle crescendo in force and a progression from calm adagio to a decidedly edgy allegro.

'Charles, talk to me.'

The silence mocked him back. He slowly made his way to the door. Augustus closed the door and stepped back into the quad. Under the circumstances his planned communion with Arthur Plantagenet's leg could wait until morning.

*

The following morning over breakfast, Augustus engaged the chaplain in the usual polite topics that are considered safe at such a time of day. Needless to say Augustus hadn't told the chaplain about the interest of the local constabulary in their affairs or indeed anyone else.

'That was you playing last night in the chapel, wasn't it Charles?'

'What time was that?'

'Oh, some time past midnight.'

'Not me. Are you sure it was coming from the chapel rather than a wayward gramophone?'

'Oh, no. I was in the chapel at the time.'

'What were you doing there at that time of... ' Charles' voice trailed off as the question did not need to be asked. There was only one reason these days why any of the members of the shadow faculty of gastronomic science would be in the chapel at odd hours.

'… and how was Arthur?' asked Charles pointedly.

'Doing fine when I checked this morning.' Augustus looked at Charles and was taken aback by the intensity of his gaze.

'Listening to you and the others, you'd think we were pondering on whether one can serve cucumber sandwiches on brown bread in decent society. We are walking blindfold into a darkness beyond forgiveness.'

'Well, that's a bit strong, isn't it?' said Augustus.

'Strong? I can't see why you are so accepting of that daft old sod making... ' Charles leant over and hissed the word 'cannibals' into Augustus' ear before continuing.

'... of us all and laughing all the way from here to Hades, where he certainly deserves to spend the rest of his days.' At that, he forced a large pile of overcooked scrambled eggs into his mouth. Augustus scanned the faces around the far from empty senior common room parlour looking for a sign of a reaction, an elevated eyebrow or the inclination of an eavesdropping head.

'This probably isn't the place for that conversation, Charles. We are meeting at lunchtime after all. I was just wondering who was playing the organ last night.'

'What was being played?' said Charles.

'Oh, it sort of went, di di di di di di di di daa daa darghhh,' replied Augustus with a reasonable rendition of the rhythm but only the vaguest sense of melody.

In reply, Charles hummed and trilled a far more musical reprise and continued on for several more bars.

'Exactly, that's it.'

'Bach, *Fantasia* in C minor BWV 906.' He then rose to his feet and, with a last glug of tea, he headed out of the room without a backwards glance. It was a piece that Charles knew well. As much from playing it as hearing it. He had never sat in the stalls and heard it as Augustus had, but for the last few months he had often heard snatched bars across the quad on approaching the chapel. As soon as his hand touched the door the music fell silent. At other times, he would be practising the organ only to find himself playing this piece rather than the one he had intended.

*

There was a loud and distinctive knock on Augustus Bloom's door.

'Come in, Mr Potts,' shouted Augustus. He was sitting with Theodore Flanagan recounting what Potts had told him the day before about the policeman's visit. It had seemed perfectly clear to Augustus until Theodore had started asking questions, so Mr Potts had been summoned to fill in the gaps in the story.

'Have a seat there, Mr Potts,' said Augustus, pulling up one of the chairs usually used for tutorials. 'Can I offer you a cup of tea?'

'Oh no, sir, I mean thanking you kindly for the offer, but I'm fine… thanks,' said Potts, looking nervously across at Dr Theodore Flanagan.

'I've been explaining to Theodore about the policeman's visit, Mr Potts,' said Augustus. 'It's never a bad idea to get legal advice early in matters such as these, even if nothing comes of it.'

'So, Mr Potts,' said Theodore. 'It is clear from what Augustus has explained that the police have been told some of the details of what happened to Arthur's leg. Now what can you tell me about this Hogarth character?'

'He's a snitch for a start, the dirty little toerag,' said Potts.

'Indeed, but let's go back to the time you met him in the mortuary after Arthur died. What exactly happened?'

'Well, before he died, the professor gave me all these letters for different folk, me included. In my letter, the professor, God rest his soul, asked me to deliver a letter to the mortuary. When I gave this letter to 'ogarth 'e went off and come back with the box which I delivered to Dr Bloom's laboratory, the box with Arthur's… ' Potts voice trailed off.

'Excellent, Potts. Now did you say anything to him apart from giving him the letter?' Theodore leaned forward on his seat, waiting for the reply.

'Well just the normal sort of chit-chat. When 'e came back with the box 'e tried to crack a joke or two.'

'So how did the police know to find you here, Potts?'

'I probably introduced myself, so 'e could have remembered my name from that,' said Potts.

'The letters, well mine at least, was on St Jerome's notepaper,' interjected Augustus.

'Did he give you the letter back when he gave you the box?' continued Theodore, silencing Augustus with a single look.

'No, I'm sure I just got the box.'

'Hmm. Did this Hogarth character know where the leg was going to be delivered?'

'Oh… er… yes. Yes 'e did because it was 'im that wrote the address. All that must 'ave been in the professor's letter,' said Potts.

'I see,' said Theodore, sitting back in his chair now the interrogation was complete. 'Well thank you, Mr Potts. That was very helpful.'

'I'm really sorry about all this, but I was just doing what the professor asked. I told the police it was all rubbish. I didn't admit to nothing.'

'I know, Potts,' said Augustus, standing to open the door. 'Don't worry, we'll get everything sorted out.'

After Potts had left, a serious-looking Theodore Flanagan looked across at Augustus.

'You know what this means, Augustus? It is likely that Hogarth has a letter describing every gory detail and it has your name on it. This could all get rather messy.'

There was a profound silence as the implications of Theodore's words soaked in. It was Augustus who spoke first.

'Yes, but that makes it completely clear that it was all at the specific request of Arthur. All that matters is whether any law has been broken. Are you sure what we're doing isn't illegal?'

'As sure as I can be, Augustus.'

'So why did the police come around?' asked Augustus, more in puzzlement than fear.

'They'd have to investigate a thing like this to make sure there was no foul play and I don't suppose Potts denying all knowledge of it is going to help.'

'Look, Theodore, should we go to the police and explain we were just following the instructions of an eccentric old friend and put the matter to rest?'

'Let's not do anything rash. Give me a few days to double-check the laws on bodily bequests first. As for the rest of the faculty, I think we should keep this to ourselves until we know what we're up against.'

'Agreed. At least we have one good bit of news to report to the faculty,' said Augustus, opening the drawer of his desk. He then waved the long-lost menu at Theodore. 'Skilfully retrieved by one of my students with Mr Potts' help. We can now claim that the whole article in *Styx* was a fabrication. Without this bit of evidence they have nothing to support their story.'

'Wouldn't that be lying, Augustus?'

'Not really, we'd just be saying that the editor of *Styx* was lying and offer him the chance to defend himself.'

'Which he can't do because we stole the evidence,' said Theodore.

'He can still defend himself and anyway you can't be accused of stealing your own property. Seems perfectly fair to me.'

'I think that is stretching the concept of fairness to breaking point.'

'Any better ideas of how to get this story retracted?'

Theodore shook his head.

'Well then that settles it,' said Augustus. 'Come on, we'd better get to this tasting meeting. Hamish has another new concoction he's all excited about.'

*

The meeting of the shadow faculty of gastronomic science had been called for noon with the intention of setting some sort of shape on that term's dinner. The atmosphere lacked the usual convivial cheer of such gatherings. Augustus and Theodore Flanagan were the last to arrive. Charles Pinker, George Le Strang and Hamish McIntyre were already huddled around the makeshift table in the kitchen cellar in morose silence.

'Well, Gentlemen, at least one glimmer of good news,' said Augustus, dropping the retrieved menu onto the table.

'A bit late, isn't it?' said George. 'I mean the cat is well out of the bag at this stage.'

'And sticking a cat back in a bag is a noisy, unpleasant affair,' added Hamish, displaying his zoological knowledge. Charles picked up the menu that he had lost so many months before and, deep in his own thoughts, slowly turned it over. He read down, smiling as he remembered the whiskey-soaked oyster. Arthur had been right, the whiskey was too dominant to blend with the subtle flavours of the oyster, but the sea urchin with fennel was exquisite and the '64 Condrieu served with it was divine. After the turbot was the cursed Fugu, and there was poor Mr Tokoro's name too. Charles closed his eyes and rested his head on the table.

'Well, I was expecting a bit more gratitude than that,' said Augustus, crestfallen. Hamish patted him on the shoulder and in wordless congratulation handed Augustus a glass filled with his latest experiment: the lemon thyme and basil mojito.

'A toast to small mercies, Gentlemen?' Hamish raised his own glass. Once it was clear that he would stay in that position until the others relented, he was joined by everyone except the chaplain, who remained in his pensive, sullen mood. The ice in the glasses clinked and the herb-infused rum started weaving its magic in the cool darkness of the cellar, which had robbed the day of its summer warmth. It was a simple but masterful twist on a classic recipe: white rum, the normal fresh mint mixed with lemon thyme and basil, lime juice, sugar, angostura bitters and topped with champagne.

'After all,' continued Hamish, 'it's only a story in a student rag. I mean it's not like anyone has died or anything.'

George turned to Hamish with a look of consternation that in an instant broke into a smile. Augustus caught Theodore's eye and the pair of them fought hard to suppress a laugh. That was it. Four grown men sitting in a dark cellar with tears of laughter rolling down their cheeks. To any reasonable observer, they appeared on the brink of madness or beyond.

Charles Pinker alone remained immune. His head, weighed down by spiritual responsibility he bore for them all, lay slumped on his hands. He muttered a prayer.

'Forgive them, Lord, for they know not what they do.'

Chapter 34

'Christ, look at the time,' Kingsley-Hampton broke into a run, sped through the lodge and across the grass. He was halfway up the stairs before Potts got to his feet to see who had just run across the grass in defiance of the ample signage. Felipe Banzarro was still in no state to run anywhere. The considerable amount of Pimms that he had consumed in the punt certainly didn't help. He had been excused punting duty on the grounds of his convalescence, so he was in charge of keeping the glasses charged with this innocent-tasting but alcoholic drink. A certain class of Englishmen and indeed well-bred Argentineans feel compelled to drink Pimms whenever they are in the proximity of fresh water during the summer months. Strangely saltwater does not seem to have the same effect; drinking Pimms at the seaside would be most eccentric. The effect of all this was to slow down Felipe just enough so that as he entered the gates alone he came face to face with Mr Potts.

'Oh, it's you Mr Banzarro. So that must 'ave been Mr Kingsley-Hampton running through 'ere like a lunatic.' Potts glared for a second at the Argentinean. If he had little time for Kingsley-Hampton, Potts positively resented having to be polite to foreigners with airs and graces.

'An' tell 'im to keep off my grass in future.'

*

By the time Mr Banzarro had negotiated the stairs, his roommate was in quite a state.

'Potts sends his regards, and told me to tell you to keep orf 'is grass.' Despite his Argentinean origins, years in an English boarding school had given Felipe faultless English diction that allowed him to offer an excellent rendition of Potts.

'Screw Potts, the grumpy old peasant. I've bigger worries than him. I can't find this bloody menu. Remember I showed you last week? Not that you took a blind bit of notice.'

'Oh, yes the dodgy dining society.'

'Did you put it somewhere, Felipe?'

Felipe Banzarro collapsed into a chair after his exertions up the stairs.

'Me? No. You put it back in your atlas after you showed me. That one,' he helpfully pointed to the atlas sitting on the top shelf of his bookcase. This useful tome had been hand-crafted and glued in Kingsley-Hampton's last year at Eton. The last vestiges of the British Empire and former colonies had been neatly cut out to create a storage place for Moroccan hashish, which was Kingsley-Hampton's sole remaining interest in matters geographical.

'That's the first place I looked. Atworth will do his nut if I've lost it.'

'Just get Atworth to tell the Master he's protecting his sources so he can't produce the actual menu, but as fortieth in line to the throne he vouches on his honour to its veracity.'

'Atworth couldn't protect his own arse, let alone his sources,' Kingsley-Hampton continued his frantic search. 'Oh and he just told me that he's now thirty-ninth in line, the Marquis of Devon, who was at number fourteen, died.'

'Excellent, so we just throw a dinner party for the other thirty-eight, poison them all and bingo, one of our amigos is the King of England.'

'Very funny Felipe, but this is serious, so perhaps you could get out of that bloody chair and help me look.'

*

Everyone was gathered in the Master's study. It was past the appointed hour, almost two fifteen. Immune to the rising tension in the room, Rupert Atworth was sitting confidently defiant in one corner. He had tried to position himself next to Matthew Kingsley-Hampton for a quiet word before proceedings began. Augustus Bloom had thwarted that plan by sidling in between the pair on a divide-and-conquer strategy. Augustus, the sole representative of the shadow faculty, maintained a composed but serious appearance. The vice-chancellor, Dr Ridgeway, was sitting in the corner on his own looking almost as confident as Rupert Atworth. He could hardly believe his luck when he heard the Master of St Jerome's proposal: the shadow faculty of gastronomic science would immediately be disbanded if they couldn't prove that the story in *Styx* was false and force a complete retraction. From the vice-chancellor's experience with Mr Atworth, this meant it was only a matter of time before this annoying charade of a 'cooking' faculty was no more.

Eccles then entered the room and took the last remaining chair, which was directly opposite Rupert Atworth. Eccles was rewarded by a finely chiselled look of distaste from the aristocratic editor. Finally, the Master made a deliberately dramatic entrance in full robes and took no time in taking his place on the other side of his expansive desk. As the Master started his enquiries, he made it amply clear to the vice-chancellor who was running this mock trial.

'Now, Mr Atworth, let us see where we are regarding your article in the *Styx*. Who suggested its publication?' The Master looked disapprovingly at Atworth.

'Well, I am the editor but we have an editorial committee, so we decided together.'

'I see. But did anyone in this room who wasn't a member of the editorial committee provide information, suggestions or influence you in any way about publication?'

'No.' Atworth could always lie rather convincingly when he felt he had the upper hand.

'Really? Well I have a letter here from my very good friend, Mr Oliver Bellingham QC. I understand that his daughter Emma is on this editorial committee. She seemed quite vexed that a certain Matthew Kingsley-Hampton was trying to force publication of this story for his own ends. Is there anyone by the name of Matthew Kingsley-Hampton in this room, Mr Atworth?'

'Yes, yes there is,' muttered Atworth, whose confidence was waning by the second.

'So I take it that he did provide some guidance in this story?'

'Yes, no, well, we talked about it… a few times,' said Atworth.

'So much for protecting sources,' muttered Kingsley-Hampton.

'I take it that you are the aforementioned Kingsley-Hampton character,' said the Master. 'Do you have something to share with us?'

'No, please carry on,' said Kingsley-Hampton as he tried to catch Atworth's eye but Dr Bloom did an excellent job of leaning forwards at just the right moment.

'So, you accept that Mr Kingsley-Ham – '

'The Hon… ' The Honourable Kingsley-Hampton stopped short in his defence of his title in response to a withering stare from the Master.

'… that *Mister* Kingsley-Hampton provided information and also pressurised you into publication?'

Atworth sat, staring at the inside of his eyelids in silence.

'I will take your silence as a yes. Now as editor, though I personally doubt that you deserve that title, do you stand over the story as published or not? I will, I'm afraid, require an answer on this point.'

'Yes,' muttered Atworth.

'Sorry, not everyone in the room is endowed with perfect hearing.' The Master looked across to smile at the vice-chancellor.

'Yes. Yes, sir, I do. I stand over every word.' Atworth, spurred on by the slight to his journalistic standing, found a sudden vein of courage and lifted his head to hold the Master's gaze.

'Excellent,' the Master smiled back. 'Now let us see what merit this story has. First, do you have proof to back up your accusations? Oliver Bellingham also shared the legal advice he gave you, on an informal basis. I understand he advised that the story should not be published without written evidence that would stand up in court. Otherwise, *Styx* could be in peril of an action for defamation from either the university or St Jerome's College.'

'Indeed and I have personally seen the menu described in the article, which is in the possession of the Honourable Kingsley-Hampton,' said Atworth, recovering his confidence.

'I see. Well that puts a different complexion on things,' said the Master with a reasonable impersonation of concern. The vice-chancellor, for his part, released an involuntary snort of delight.

'So, Mr Kingsley-Hampton, may I see this menu?' said the Master.

'Er, I haven't got it with me exactly,' Kingsley-Hampton said. 'I did have it but it seems to have disappeared.' He spat out this last word and glared at Eccles.

'So, Mr Atworth, it seems that you don't have documentary proof and, from my correspondence with Mr Bellingham, it seems the committee were never shown this document but relied on your assurance that it existed.'

'It does exist, I've seen it!'

'You can see a mirage, Mr Atworth, but you cannot hold one. As this mythical menu cannot be offered in proof, we shall take that as one count of falsehood in this article. Now, the death of the Japanese Ambassador. Within the last few months I have also had correspondence with this esteemed gentleman who has been in his post for five years. So it seems that your description of his death must be an... exaggeration, Mr Atworth?'

'Well, Mr Tokoro died, and I thought he was the ambassador.'

'Well, it is a matter of record that Mr Tokoro was never the ambassador. I believe he did die almost a year ago, but as his obituary was published in *The Times* newspaper that was hardly a secret. Be that as it may, there lies the second falsehood. Now this deadly poison and your interview with Mr Eccles. Did you or any of the staff of your publication actually interview Mr Eccles?'

'Yes. Well, I'd met him in his rooms. He shares rooms with Mattie, I mean Matthew Kingsley-Hampton.'

'Shared, I believe is the correct tense. I understand the Honourable Kingsley-Hampton has evicted Mr Eccles to make space for one of his friends who had supposedly gone down for a year: an unseemly affair that we shall deal with later. Now, Mr Eccles was present in the same room as you, but did you interview him and take notes as a journalist should?'

'No, not really.'

'Mr Eccles,' the Master turned to address Patrick. 'Did you ever grant this man an interview or speak to anyone of his staff in a formal way?'

'I absolutely did not,' Eccles answered in a clear and confident tone. In advance of this meeting, Augustus Bloom had tutored him in how to handle each question.

'I see. And Mr Eccles, this tetratoxin, have you heard of this deadly toxin?'

'I'm not aware of a toxin of that name, sir, no.'

'Dr Bloom, does tetratoxin exist?'

'No, Master. I might guess from the context that the author meant to write *tetrodotoxin*, but what was actually written is factually incorrect.'

'Factually incorrect. Did you hear that, Dr Ridgeway? So, if I may conclude, we have a story which was published without documentary proof, against legal advice which contains two other major falsehoods.'

'Well, Lord Faulkner, with respect, they may pass as

typographical errors.'

'Having the wrong person killed with an imaginary poison is not typographical, it is culpable,' replied the Master, raising his voice for the first time.

'But my concern is for the university and the damage this article has done. Particularly if the national press pick up on the story,' said Ridgeway.

'That won't be a problem, will it, Mr Atworth?' replied the Master.

Atworth shook his head, unaware exactly what he was acknowledging.

'Because *Styx* is going to publish a full retraction, on the front page.'

'Well, I'll have to talk… '

'Mr Atworth, nothing short of a full retraction will prevent an action of defamation being launched by this college against the *Styx* and you personally. So do you want to reconsider?'

'I think in light of the errors that we made, a note of correction might be appropriate,' said Atworth through clenched teeth.

'Not a correction, Mr Atworth, a complete and unequivocal retraction with an admission that the whole thing was a spoof. A belated April Fool's prank, perhaps.'

'But parts of it are tr – ' One glare from the Master was sufficient to silence Atworth.

'Legal action for defamation or a retraction. The choice is yours, Mr Atworth.'

'I'll retract the story,' muttered Atworth.

'Excellent. Well I think we can conclude this story is well and truly dead, Dr Ridgeway,' concluded the Master.

'Well, that would be a… satisfactory resolution,' muttered Ridgeway in muted response. 'Apart, of course, from the sanctions against the students involved. We can't forget that damage has already been done to the reputation of both the university and St Jerome's. Perhaps we could dismiss the undergraduates so that we can discuss their fate in private.'

The three undergraduates filed out and passed down the dark passageway from the Master's lodging in total silence. Only when they reached the Old Quad did Kingsley-Hampton turn on Eccles.

'If anything happens to us Eccles, you're dead, you conniving little bastard. Now piss off out of my sight.'

This was the first of Kingsley-Hampton's orders that Eccles was only too glad to follow.

Chapter 35

It took several drafts for Rupert Atworth to produce a retraction that was acceptable to all concerned. Clinging onto the last vestiges of his journalistic pride, he initially tried to claim that *Styx* had been misled by its sources and tricked into publishing the story. Needless to say this first draft left a certain Mr Eccles fully in the firing line. Under duress from the Master and threats of legal action from Mr Oliver Bellingham to protect the good name of his daughter, Atworth surrendered into an admission that the entire story was a fabrication intended as an April Fool's prank for which he took sole responsibility. Publication was further delayed by the fact that his editorial committee had resigned on mass and formed a competing publication, the *Rubicon*, which is still published to this day under the highest code of journalistic ethics.

What did eventually appear was published on the front page of *Styx* under the headline 'Apologia'. It read as follows:

In our last edition, we ran a story about the alleged activities of a secret dining society claiming this was responsible for poisoning certain foreign dignitaries. Furthermore, we implicated St Jerome's College and suggested that the university was involved in suppressing information about its existence. We would

*like to confirm that that story was merely a spoof
intended to entertain our readers and, as Editor, I
Rupert Atworth take full responsibility for any distress
caused to any party. Furthermore, certain quotes
attributed to a Mr Patrick Eccles were fabricated as
part of this report and Mr Eccles, while he is a medical
student at St Jerome's College, took no part in the
publication of this story.*

Such is the power of journalism that even though this was
the last edition of *Styx* ever published, the legacy of this once
proud publication would live on in the form of several dining
societies that modelled themselves on a story declared to be
entirely fictitious. The first of which even boasted the disgraced
former editor of *Styx* as one of its founding members.

The publication of this retraction lifted the spirits of the
shadow faculty, most notably for the chaplain, Charles Pinker.
None of them relished the prospect of unwanted attention
from the vice-chancellor or journalists, especially in light of
Arthur's legacy but, as Charles considered himself responsible
for the crisis with the initial loss of the menu, it was he that
benefited most by this resolution. One can reasonably wonder
why the publication of this retraction had such a beneficial
effect on the chaplain and the others, when they were
facing what would seem a far greater moral challenge in the
fulfilment of Arthur Plantagenet's will. For Charles Pinker it
seemed that a straw had been lifted from the back of a camel,
leaving him with enough strength to carry the weight of his
own conscience as well as those of his fellow gastronomic
travellers. Needless to say, Augustus still had not shared with
Charles the news that Her Majesty's constabulary were taking
an interest in the whereabouts of Arthur's leg.

During these days, Charles prayed a great deal more and
at night, alone in the chapel, these prayers increasingly took
the more informal style of a conversation with a friend who
is happy just to listen – prayers delivered with an innate

confidence that they were being heard.

One night, Charles was kneeling before the altar, once again rhetorically exploring the moral dilemma they were facing.

'Lord, I'm sorry to trouble you again. I know I have talked about this before. It's just that I have been taught to believe that the Eucharist is symbolic, but I am facing a challenge that will be easier to accept if your words were meant to be taken literally as they do in Rome. You see if… ' Charles was brought up short by the definite sound of a cough from the altar. He looked up and then over his shoulder as the acoustics of the chapel were notoriously fickle. Just as he had convinced himself he was imagining things, he heard a voice as clear as his own.

'Charles, I have heard your prayers and I know what worries you.' The voice was strangely familiar and clearly emanating directly from the altar. Although distinctly English in accent, the voice had a disembodied and ethereal nature. Charles didn't doubt for an instant that this was the voice of God.

'You do? Oh, I'm sorry, of course you do, Lord,' said Charles, bowing his head a little lower.

'Your soul and the souls of those that travel with you are not in peril. You have been asked to help a soul of the departed in his eccentric but personal quest. Far worse has been done in my name. Curiosity is no sin as long as no-one suffers. Go in peace.'

'Thank you, thank you, Lord. May I call on you again?'

'You are most welcome, and thank you for all your prayers. I may not always reply, but I shall always listen.'

That God had taken to replying to his prayers was a great solace to the chaplain, though it would lead most men to doubt their grip on reality. True to his word, God never replied again, but Charles prayed every day for the rest of his life. On this one occasion when God did reply it was no more than a spiritual subterfuge but a well-meaning one. Arthur's spirit resided mostly within the walls of the chapel and it was within these four walls that the chaplain's deep distress was most obvious. In the months since his death, Arthur had seen Charles flounder in despair and, on particularly bad days, waver on the edge of madness. Compassion was unfamiliar territory for Arthur in death as it was in life, but it was compassion rather than devilment that drove him to impersonate God, though it would only be fair to admit that a fondness for the stories of Don Camillo played a part too.

It was only later that Arthur pondered on the consequences. After all, for a soul that has died but not passed over, impersonating God to a member of the clergy could be considered foolhardy in the extreme. The consequences might at worst last for all eternity. But, far from upsetting God, Arthur made an important step towards his own salvation that day by concluding that whatever the consequences for himself, restoring Charles' peace of mind was more important. God indeed moves in mysterious ways.

Chapter 36

Eights week arrived that term with indecent haste. In a terminology that no-one in Oxford finds in the least confusing, Eights week, an entertaining interlude where the bump races are held on the river Isis, is generally held in the fifth week of Trinity term. These are similar in most respects to Torpids, the rowing races held in the previous term, except for a few details. The rules of how the races are conducted are somewhat different and more importantly the weather is generally better which makes these races far more attractive to spectators. For the faculty of gastronomic science the arrival of Eights week came as a reminder that time waits for no man. By this stage of the term they had never been so lacking in preparation. The only practical result from their last meeting was an almost unanimous vote for Hamish's Royal Herbal mojito as the aperitif. So another meeting had been hastily called.

'Perhaps we should start with a status report on Arthur,' said Augustus, launching the meeting with a gentle tap of an upturned spoon. He cast a concerned eye at Charles as he uttered these words.

'I know we have all been keeping an eye on things, but I must say I think he survived the mini-heatwave last week very well, not that I am an expert in curing, of course,' replied Charles without hesitation.

'Coming on nicely, indeed,' chimed in George Le Strang

to fill the silence that met the chaplain's surprisingly upbeat assessment, while the others expressed their agreement with vigorous nodding and mumbled agreement. None of the surviving faculty had any prior knowledge of curing, but were all now well-versed on this topic.

'So how exactly do you think Arthur wished to be served?' asked Theodore, taking the opportunity to get straight to the question that had been ignored for far too long.

'With horseradish perhaps? An old English trick for masking the taste of bad meat,' said George, who remained secretly convinced that being of aristocratic French lineage he would beat Arthur in a head-to-head taste comparison.

'I was thinking of a taste comparison of different types of cured meat. We could slip Arthur in unannounced, so to speak,' replied Augustus.

'Oh my goodness, the guests!' said Charles, suddenly losing his new-found equanimity about the whole affair. 'We surely can't tell them, but we can hardly force them to… to… '

'Share the experience?' Hamish offered.

'Couldn't we just get it over and done with down here before the actual dinner?' Charles looked around the table for support. The only person who met his eye was Theodore Flanagan who put the matter to rest.

'I'm afraid Arthur's will was painfully clear on this point Charles. Luckily we have no obligation to tell the guests of this experiment, which has the added benefit of making the whole thing more objective. Our palates will all be tainted by the knowledge of what we are eating.'

'Who rather than what,' Charles corrected Theodore. With the conversation turning towards guests, Augustus seized his moment to reveal his own particular coup on that front. He had been holding back on this announcement, waiting for a good moment, something that had been in very short supply in recent times.

'On the topic of guests, I have someone rather special coming along to this dinner. M.F.K. Fisher has finally accepted my invitation after years of badgering.'

'Fisher? Why do I know that name?' said a puzzled Hamish. Augustus had come prepared and from under his seat produced a copy of their spiritual mentor's book – Brillat-Savarin's *The Physiology of Taste* bearing in large type M.F.K. Fisher on the cover.

'Only the translator of the best edition of *The Physiology of Taste* produced in the English language,' said Augustus sitting back triumphantly.

'Well done,' said Hamish patting him on the back. 'Mind you I thought the chap was long dead by now.'

'Oh, she's far from dead. Quite a live wire, in fact.'

'A female guest? Well, well. Is that allowed?' asked Charles.

*

The gating of Patrick Eccles, which was still in force while the vice-chancellor stubbornly tried to get at Augustus Bloom by punishing his student, had not proved too limiting on account of a simple subterfuge. A rangy little black and white cat that had taken residence in the porter's lodge at the end of Hilary term was duly christened Patrick Eccles. This creature roamed the college at night and spent all day asleep under Potts' desk in the lodge, allowing the head porter to confirm to the vice-chancellor's office on a daily basis that Patrick Eccles was indeed still within the confines of the college. This allowed Patrick, at his own request, to remain in his new accommodation, and as long as he was discreet, to go wherever he wished. Sitting in his elegant rooms on the High Street, Patrick Eccles glanced down at his watch. He should have been down at the boathouse ten minutes ago, but he only had another few pages of *Zuleika Dobson* to finish, so he stayed glued to his book. He had never met a lady like Zuleika in life or in fiction, but didn't doubt such a creature could exist. Worse still, even though he had almost reached the end of the book, far enough for most sensible folk to have an accurately low opinion of Zuleika, he was already in love with her. He flew through the last few pages with his head

Ian Flitcroft

spinning. Once at the end he sat turning the book over in his hands looking for a few more words to keep him away from the real world and closer to Zuleika. His reverie was broken by a shout from the street below.

'Eccles! Eccles! Are you in there?'

Eccles leapt to his feet and looked down through the open window. 'Oh Christ, sorry I'm late.'

'Too bloody right, you are,' said Sinclair, the stroke of the second VIII who had frantically peddled up from the boathouses.

'What in God's name were you doing?'

Eccles had the good sense to know that reading a book was not an acceptable excuse for being late amongst rowers.

'It's a long story,' he said.

*

Augustus Bloom grabbed his bicycle and headed off down St Aldgate's to the Isis. He had missed the lower divisions who race first, but still hoped to get the second and first division races. Eccles and the second VIII were racing in division two, but if they bumped up today could reach the first division. The trouble Eccles had caused couldn't dent Bloom's support for any college boat. He made for the towpath on the far side, away from most of the spectators who flooded in across Christchurch Meadow. The towpath was by far the most interesting side of the river for rowing enthusiasts. From there you could see the start and follow the whole race if you were brave enough to cycle at breakneck speed along the towpath.

Bloom was still cycling up towards the narrowest part of the course, the gut, when he heard the gun announcing the start. Upriver, the coxes released the wooden blocks on ropes that held the boats in position in the anxious minutes before the start. The once-still waters were churned by brightly painted blades as the boats jerked into motion. He turned his bicycle and waited with his pedals poised for a fast take-off. Within seconds he was engulfed in noise as the Worcester first VIII came past a good two lengths ahead of St Jerome's second VIII. St Jerome's in turn were barely a canvas ahead of the chasing boat, Christchurch's first VIII. Bloom took off as fast as he could as the boats drew level, but he could only keep up with them for a few seconds before he was overtaken by bicycles ridden by students with far less concern for their own safety or for the safety of others. Forced to a halt, he watched the crews down the wide straight section of the river that led towards the finish, knowing the pain of every stroke from the memories of his own undergraduate races.

St Jerome's rowed over, not quite victorious but undefeated on the day and the highest positioned second VIII on the river. Eccles lay slumped over his oar, his windpipe laid raw by the implausible volume of air his body had demanded during the race and his legs burning.

'Jerome, Jerome, Jerome... ' The chant grew louder and louder from supporters on the banks. Sinclair took up the chant from the stroke's seat and the chant's primal enthusiasm swept away the pain as the entire crew joined in. Overtaken by a transcendent happiness and possibly a shortage of oxygen to the brain, Eccles saw an image of the boat from above and instantly knew this was the high point of his existence. Into his mind came the image of the Duke of Dorset, straight from the pages of *Zuleika Dobson*, looking upwards towards the light from the bottom of the river. Eccles unstrapped the buckles that fixed his shoes to the boat and slowly raised himself up until he was standing poised for his grand gesture. This is by no means a simple feat in a boat designed for maximal speed and minimal stability. 'Gentlemen, St Jerome's... ' with those words Eccles was launched head first into the Isis by a sudden lurch of the boat. He had hoped for a longer speech, but these simple words had a galvanising effect on the crew. One by one they leapt into the water shouting their college's name. Instinct, natural buoyancy and the sobering effects of cold water all served to ensure that Eccles was the first to resurface, his attempt at a noble sacrifice now looking like no more than high spirits.

In the final race of the day, St Jerome's first VIII crossed the line victorious as the head of the river for the first time in over half a century. The St Jerome's boathouse erupted in a tumultuous scene of celebration. The recently disembarked second VIII watching from the pontoon and while still dripping, led the chant once again.

'Jerome, Jerome, Jerome…'

On the balcony of the boathouse, Kingsley-Hampton looked down in contempt at his former roommate Eccles, who was at that moment being carried lengthways on the shoulders of his crew.

Chapter 37

Augustus stood in the small alcove in his rooms preparing tea. His heart was leaping in his chest and he struggled to steady his hand.

'Do you take sugar in your tea, inspector?'

'No thank you, Dr Bloom, just a drop of milk.'

It had been several weeks since the police had called on Mr Potts. With each passing day, the threat of any action had seemed to wane and Augustus had no longer felt the need to cross the street when he saw a policeman. Theodore had managed to convince both himself and Augustus that they had done nothing illegal, but in the interests of not attracting unwanted attention had advised against attempting to clarify matters with the police. Mr Potts had used his contacts to discover that the mortuary attendant Mr Hogarth was being held on remand in Oxford gaol, making it unlikely that the potential witness was held in high regard. It was therefore a true shock for Augustus to find Detective Inspector Granger waiting for him in the lodge when he returned one evening from the laboratory.

'Very sorry for dropping in on you unannounced, Dr Bloom,' said the inspector, sipping his tea. 'I thought you might prefer an informal chat rather than being brought down to the station for questioning.'

'Very thoughtful of you, inspector. So how can I help you?'

'We've been investigating certain discrepancies relating to

the death of a friend of yours, Professor Arthur Plantagenet. I understand from the crematorium that you are his executor and it was yourself that received his ashes. Is that correct?'

'I am one of his executors. Is there a problem inspector?'

'Could you tell me where Professor Plantagenet's remains are at this moment?'

Augustus looked up at the mantelpiece in silence.

'Dr Bloom?'

Augustus stood up and walked over to the small urn.

'Here they are, inspector. Do you wish to inspect them?'

'If I may?' Much to Augustus' surprise the inspector took the urn and opened it to inspect the contents.

'I understand that Arthur Plantagenet was… not a small man,' said the inspector. 'This urn doesn't seem to contain enough ashes.'

'He had varied requests about where his ashes should be distributed and we have partly met those wishes, so some of his ashes have already been deposited in their final resting place. He has also requested that some be spread in locations overseas. We haven't had time to meet that request.'

'So originally this urn held all his remains?'

'That's right,' said Augustus. He had intended to explain about the will but the words had left his mouth before his conscious mind could stop them.

'So his entire body was cremated?' The inspector looked directly at Augustus and smiled.

'I… believe so.'

'Quite. Now my problem, Dr Bloom, is that I have a statement from a mortuary attendant that Professor Plantagenet's leg was removed and dispatched to you before his cremation. What do you say to that?'

'Oh,' said Augustus.

'Oh indeed. Now perhaps you could explain this extraordinary turn of events.'

Augustus took a moment to gather his thoughts and then in a wavering voice began his confession.

'Arthur's leg was delivered to me, but not by my choice. The whole thing with the mortuary was apparently arranged by Arthur before his death. Until the leg was delivered to me, I had no knowledge of what was going on. It's all part of Arthur's rather eccentric will.'

'And what, dare I ask, does this will require you to do with the professor's leg?'

'He had his own private wishes.'

'Dr Bloom, if you are just complying with your duties as executor of Professor Plantagenet's will, then why not share the details with me and we can have this matter all cleared up in no time.'

'Am I accused of committing a crime, inspector?'

'Not yet,' said the inspector, showing the first signs of irritation. 'But at the very least we could charge you with handling stolen property. There are also laws regarding the proper disposal of human bodies, which you are clearly flouting. I don't suppose it would impress the university authorities or indeed the medical council if you were convicted of grave-robbing?'

'I see,' said Augustus almost inaudibly.

'Well then, we have finally made some progress. I will need to have you down at St Aldgate's police station at noon tomorrow for formal questioning under caution. That gives you a little time to reflect on your position concerning the secretive will of Arthur Plantagenet. We will take your statement then. Can I rely on your attendance without the need to send one of my constables?'

Augustus nodded his assent. 'I presume I can bring along a solicitor?'

'Under the circumstances, that would be very wise, Dr Bloom.'

*

'Good morning, Gentlemen,' said Mr Barringer. 'Please take a seat. I hope you will be able to maintain more dignity than you managed last time you were in my office for the reading of Professor Plantagenet's will.'

'I do apologise for that. I'm not sure what came over us,' said Theodore.

'Sorry,' mumbled Augustus.

'Apologies accepted. Now I had indicated that I couldn't assist any further in relation to this most bizarre will, but I understand something rather pressing has come up?'

'Indeed,' said Theodore, as Augustus sat back in his chair looking thoroughly wretched, clearly not intending to take much part in proceedings. 'As I mentioned on the phone this morning, Augustus is due down at St Aldgate's police station in less than two hours. Inspector Granger has made some veiled threats to Augustus in relation to Arthur Plantagenet's will.'

'Inspector Granger. Dear old Cornelius. I was at college with him many years ago. How is he these days?' asked Mr Barringer.

'Rather aggressive, quite frankly,' replied Augustus. 'He more or less accused me of grave-robbing.'

'Good God, please tell me you didn't actually dig up Arthur's grave?' Mr Barringer brought both hands over his face and directed the question at Augustus through his fingers. Theodore nobly interceded on Augustus' behalf.

'Of course he didn't. Arthur left Augustus specific instructions for his body to be cremated and we thought that would be the end of it.'

'And why wasn't it?' asked Mr Barringer, reassured but clearly perplexed.

'He was cremated, but it turns out Arthur also left instructions for his left leg to be removed by one of the workers at the hospital mortuary before the rest of his body was released to the crematorium. It was the mortuary attendant who told the police.'

Mr Barringer reclined back in his chair, his face fixed in a thoughtful frown. This scene was soon replaced by a view of Mr Barringer's bald patch as he swivelled in his chair to face the window.

'What happened to the leg after it was removed?' said Mr Barringer to the windowpanes.

'It was delivered to Augustus at his laboratory, packed in ice.'

Mr Barringer suddenly turned to face Augustus again. This time it was clear he wished Augustus himself to answer.

'And what did you do with it, Dr Bloom?'

'Oh... well... exactly what Arthur had instructed,' replied Augustus.

'You don't mean you actually cooked it and... '

'Oh no, no,' Augustus reassured him. 'No. It was moved back to college... for safekeeping.'

'And it's still there?' asked Mr Barringer.

Augustus merely nodded. An oppressive silence then fell upon the room. Distant sounds from the street outside seemed suddenly amplified. Augustus looked at the ground. Theodore gazed at Mr Barringer, who in turn stared at the bookcase at the back of the room. Meanwhile the large grandfather clock ground out each tick as if it were its last. Mr Barringer finally broke the tension. With impressive agility for a man approaching sixty years of age, he leapt to his feet and made directly for the book he had spotted. A small red cloth-bound volume with gilt lettering edited by William Roughead on the trial of Burke and Hare, the notorious Edinburgh grave-robbers of the eighteenth century. He flipped through until he seemed to find what he was looking for.

'Now, what exactly did the inspector threaten you with, Dr Bloom?'

'He mentioned charging me with handling stolen property first. To be honest, I think the threats about grave-robbing were more to rattle me,' said Augustus.

'Well, he seems to have succeeded in that at least. You say the leg was delivered in ice, entirely unclothed?'

'Yes,' said Augustus, baffled at the line of questioning.

'Well that puts paid to any question of stolen property,' said Barringer emphatically. 'Under common law no-one owns a dead body. Now where is that passage?' Barringer's finger ran down the page. 'Ah, yes. The only lawful possessor of the dead body is the earth. So if no-one owns a body, one can't by definition steal one.'

'Excellent, that's exactly what I'd told Augustus,' said Theodore, springing to his feet and starting to pace the floor. 'But what about this grave-robbing threat?'

'For the same reason grave-robbing is not a crime unless possessions of the dead are removed such as jewellery. Burke and Hare were convicted of murder, not robbing graves. They introduced an act after that infamous case to regulate the use of bodies for anatomy, but that was not what the professor had in mind, as I understand from his will.'

'Indeed not,' said Theodore quietly.

Mr Barringer's well-endowed eyebrows elevated in silent comment. He then replaced the book on Burke and Hare and ran his fingers along the spines of a large series of volumes, Halsbury's Statutes of England and Wales. He pulled out a volume and brought it back to his desk.

'In relation to the use of this limb, that should fall under the Human Tissues Act 1961. Now let's see what that says.' Barringer busied himself in locating this particular Act of Parliament while Theodore and Augustus sat in impressed but anxious silence.

'Yes, here we go. *If any person, either in writing at any time or orally in the presence of two or more witnesses during his last illness has expressed a request that his body or any specified part of his body be used after his death for therapeutic purposes or for purposes of medical education or research, the person lawfully in possession of his body after his death may, unless he has reason to believe the request was subsequently withdrawn, authorise the removal from the body of any part or, as the case may be, the specified part, for use in accordance with the request.* It is clear from his will that Professor Plantagenet intended his leg to be used for... research, so this act seems to provide a legal basis for your actions. Provided of course that the professor hadn't changed his mind since signing his will.'

'Definitely not. He even announced it at dinner the night before he died,' said Augustus.

'Good. So we have some witnesses. Any relatives who might object?' said Barringer as he read on.

'Both his parents have definitely passed away and I'm almost certain he has no brothers or sisters,' said Augustus.

'Well, there is your defence,' said Barringer, sitting back triumphantly.

'Really? So we've nothing to worry about legally?'

'Oh there's plenty to worry about. I can't guarantee Inspector Granger won't try and charge you. After all, it's not for the police to determine if you are guilty, that is for the courts. He just needs to have evidence that suggests you may have committed a crime. What evidence does he have?'

'The evidence of the mortuary assistant who removed the leg,' said Augustus. 'Oh, and possibly the letter from Arthur himself asking for the leg to be delivered to me.'

'Oh,' Mr Barringer sat back, his lips frozen into the pursed shape they fell into at the end of that ominous comment.

'So the facts are clear. It will just come down to the question of whether what you have done in accepting this... object... and what has happened since, has broken any laws.'

'But you just said everything was fine on the basis of that 1961 Act?' Theodore burst in.

'As an academic exercise I am confident that, distasteful as this whole situation is, you have perfectly good grounds for your actions. But Inspector Granger might have a different viewpoint, so be careful.'

Mr Barringer rose to his feet, clearly indicating the meeting was coming to an end. 'Unfortunately I won't be able to come with you to the police station. Mind you, as the inspector and I have some... history... my presence might prove counterproductive anyway.'

'Of course, I quite understand,' said Theodore. 'I can

handle this myself. Would you have a pen and paper? I wouldn't mind jotting down those points. It was the 1961 Human Tissue Act, wasn't it?'

*

On arrival at St Aldgate's police station, Augustus and Theodore were shown into one of the interview rooms. Inspector Granger made a point of leaving them a good half hour to 'stew in their own juices' as he was wont to say. Before entering he looked in through the small, reinforced glass window and was surprised to the see the two men chatting away and not looking as stressed as he'd hoped to find them.

'Good afternoon, Gentlemen,' said the inspector as he entered.

Much to the inspector's delight, Augustus stood up as he entered the room, a courtesy rarely shown by the criminal classes. Theodore felt no such compunction. Not because of any base criminality, but on account of his antipathy to the British constabulary after the Bogside riots the previous year.

'May I introduce Theodore Flanagan,' said Augustus once Inspector Granger had taken his seat on the opposite side of the small interview table.

'Your solicitor?'

'No, he's the law tutor at St Jerome's and a fellow executor of Arthur Plantagenet's will,' explained Augustus.

'Welcome, Dr Flanagan,' said the inspector, clearly rather amused. 'Though I should say, Dr Bloom, that in light of the seriousness of the situation you may wish to contact a *proper* solicitor when we do formally charge you.'

'I don't believe that is a likely event, inspector,' said Theodore, bristling at the inspector's pointed emphasis on the word proper.

'Really? Well let's review the facts surrounding the theft and disappearance of Professor Arthur Plantagenet's leg, shall we? A mortuary assistant by the name of Frederick Hogarth has told us that he was requested by Mr Potts, porter of St Jerome's College, to remove the professor's leg prior to the body being released to the undertakers. It was then taken by Mr Potts to you, Dr Bloom, at the University Laboratory of Physiology and at present the whereabouts of this limb are unknown. Isn't that correct, Dr Bloom?'

'I'm afraid you are mistaken in several important details, inspector,' said Augustus. 'Firstly, from my discussions with Mr Potts, the request for the removal of the leg was made in writing by Arthur Plantagenet himself prior to his death with Mr Potts merely delivering a sealed letter. The mortuary attendant was apparently instructed by this letter written by Arthur to pack the limb into a box and address it to me.'

'I see,' said the inspector, taking notes. 'We will of course have to verify that with our own witness to these events, Mr Hogarth.'

'Hardly a man of good character by all accounts,' interjected Theodore.

'Perhaps not, Dr Flanagan, but his extensive criminal record is no shorter or longer than that of your own Mr Potts. Be that as it may, Dr Bloom, you do not seem to dispute the fact that you received the dismembered limb of one of your colleagues and have so far refused to explain its whereabouts.'

'I did indeed receive the leg according to Arthur Plantagenet's will and it is in safekeeping until we can comply with the wishes in his will.'

'Ah yes, the secretive will,' said the inspector. 'I can scarcely imagine what possible will would require one's leg to be removed after death and delivered on ice to a laboratory of physiology. It all sounds rather Frankenstein-like, does it not, Dr Bloom?'

'Some people donate their bodies to science. Others like Arthur decide to donate just one part of their body, as he is quite entitled to,' said Augustus.

'Yes, but it is the manner in which it was done that raises suspicions, Dr Bloom. May I see this will?'

'I don't believe there is any need for that,' interjected Theodore.

'Well I do,' said the inspector, becoming irritated with the whole carry-on.

'Under the 1961 Human Tissues Act,' continued Theodore, ignoring the inspector's last comment, 'a person can request in writing that any part of their body be removed after their death for medical purposes, teaching or research. Arthur Plantagenet's written wishes were conveyed to Mr Hogarth in writing.'

'That may be so, but did you ask the hospital's permission? No, you did not. So there is the question of theft and handling stolen property. I propose to press charges on that score at least.'

'I think you will find that under common law no person actually owns a dead body as it belongs to the earth. As a body is not property it cannot legally or logically be stolen.' Theodore concluded his case by sitting back in his chair and smiling at the inspector, which only infuriated the poor man even further.

'You clearly both think you are very clever, as I'm sure you are in your own fields of study, but rest assured what happened here is indecent, immoral and undoubtedly illegal. Dr Bloom, I am not yet ready to bring formal charges… '

'So I am free to go?' Augustus interrupted.

'For now. But I am formally cautioning you not to leave Oxford as I fully expect to have you charged and brought before the courts within a matter of weeks.'

Chapter 38

The entire senior common room had assembled in the college cloisters and were struggling through glasses of sherry that were overly sweet and entirely lacking in quality. The reason for their fate was revealed when Mr Potts, who had been standing on guard by the door, made his announcement.

'Gentlemen, the victorious first VIII.'

The first VIII, in their full rowing regalia of cream blazers trimmed in purple silk, entered to polite applause from the dons. Their success at Eights week had earned the whole college a bumps supper and the crew a congratulatory drink with the senior common room, though in deference to final examinations this had been deferred a few weeks. Despite their temporarily elevated status, this was no reason to change the tradition of offering only the cheapest sherry at any event where undergraduates were present, even those of sporting prowess. George Le Strang, who had never as much as touched an oar in his entire life, had just engaged the stroke of the first VIII, a classicist who went by the unusual name of Atticus Plunkett in a polite if slightly stilted conversation, when Hamish McIntyre sidled up.

'Come on lads, time to pour that filth into the flower beds.' Hamish's words were explained by the appearance of a battered pewter hip flask. At this, George Le Strang discreetly discharged his glass through the glassless stone window onto the innocent but now doomed bedding plants that lined the walls of the cloisters. Atticus Plunkett, realising that the instruction was meant to be taken literally, followed the lead set by George and held out his now empty glass.

'A pleasant 1949 Armagnac that just happens to be a similar colour to this disgrace of a sherry,' explained Hamish to his grateful audience.

'Thank you, quite a treat. 1949, goodness I hadn't even been born then, er, Dr… ' stuttered young Plunkett.

'McIntyre, Hamish McIntyre, zoologist extraordinaire at your service,' said Hamish offering one of his bear-like hands that swallowed the not insubstantial digits of the young rower. The glowing burn of the first sip of Armagnac had barely reached the end of their respective oesophagi before Gerard came and shook the handbell that called the guests to dinner.

They filed out of the cloisters in a straggling line and made their way across Chapel Quad towards the Hall. While the members of the senior common room and their guests filed in past the standing ranks of undergraduates and members of the lesser crews, the choir intoned the college song 'Floreat Sanctus Jeromiensis' from the balcony in a new four part arrangement prepared especially for the occasion by the Reverend Pinker. This performance was met with respectful silence. As raucous as the members of the boat club could certainly be on occasion, they were, at least in the early part of any evening, all gentlemen.

After grace, the doors opened to let in the swarm of scouts carrying plates. This process of food delivery happened as if by magic for the diners, as they generally had only a subliminal awareness of the scouts at such moments. The hall exploded into conversation and as the food arrived, the members of the college were lost in the needs of their stomachs. On this occasion they should, however, have paid more attention. Amongst the wiry old men and stocky grandmother figures that made up the usual servers a young girl of eighteen moved gracefully forwards.

In a college entirely bereft of young ladies and full of young men in the vigorous flush of incipient manhood she should have created a sensation, instead she passed through the hall like a mirage. Invisible to all except one young man sitting with his back against the carved oak panelling, mute and unresponsive to all questions. He was transfixed by this young lady as she made several forays to serve the tables on the other side of the hall. Walking fast without rushing, she exuded grace amid the bustle. Eccles had to imagine her long blond hair. It was pinned up but for a few enticing locks that fell down from beneath her cap and onto her gracefully curved neck. He suddenly knew why his grand gesture in the river had failed. The Duke of Dorset had sunk to the bottom of the Isis, dragged down by the weight of unrequited love and a vision in his mind of Zuleika Dobson. Here in front of his eyes was a woman to die for. Eccles was brought back from his reverie by a solid dig in the ribs from a fellow member of his crew, Roger Sinclair.

'Eccles, have you heard a word I said?'

'Of course, but did you see that girl?'

'What girl?' asked Roger, craning his head.

'One of the scouts. God knows what she's doing here, but she's gorgeous.'

'"Shall I compare thee to a summer's day? Thou art more temperate and beautiful,"' quoted Roger, showing off the meagre educational gains he had acquired in his years at Oxford. 'But really, Patrick, a scout? There are probably laws against that sort of thing.'

Before Patrick could utter any words of defence, Roger shouted down the table.

'Guys listen to this, Eccles fancies one of the scouts!'

This was met by a chorus of jeers from the rest of the table.

'Come on lads, we'll have a whip-round and send him off to Mollie's[11]. Clearly a bad case of full bag encephalopathy,' said

---

11 An infamous, but possibly mythical brothel that frequently came up in undergraduate conversations, even though no-one seemed to have had any first-hand experience of the delights supposedly on offer.

Luke Blandford, one of Eccles' fellow medical students and crewmate who had a fine line in spurious medical diagnoses.

'Full bag what?'

'A form of brain rot caused by excessive sexual abstinence, very dangerous altogether. You either go mad or your scrotum explodes, very messy either way. Here Eccles, have my pint. You clearly need it more than I do.'

A pint of beer in a battered silver pot slid down the table as his fellow rowers banged their spoons on the table. In the spirit of the moment he downed the beer in a single draught.

*

As the first plates reached high table, Hamish let out a quiet but indiscreet, 'Yes!' The reason for his excitement was sitting on his plate partially hidden by a slice of sea-bream terrine. There, lay five plump spears of the king of vegetables – asparagus – and with it the chance for an asparagus race. What more fitting occasion for an asparagus race could there be than a dinner dedicated to a boat race. Once all on high table had been served, Hamish cast his eye around and declared to the entire table.

'I see the princely shoot has arrived.'

This was met by a mixture of bemused looks and polite nods from most of the diners, but knowing smiles from members of the declining dining society. The rules of the St Jerome's asparagus race are fairly simple. There is no formal starting gun for an asparagus race; such races are carried out by subterfuge under the very noses of those gastronomically less enlightened dons who might regard it as rather childish. Amongst the members of the shadow faculty, a race can be declared by any member with the words uttered a few seconds earlier by Hamish McIntyre. To be a race it naturally requires at least two competitors, so in accepting the challenge one replies with the innocuously cryptic response: 'Indeed, and would you have the correct time?' This curious interchange serves the very practical purpose of allowing all participants to synchronise their watches. After this is done, those who accept the challenge will wait with fork raised until all have been served. To ensure that all participants take their first mouthful at the same time, they must all wait for the nod of whoever declared the race before any asparagus can enter their mouths.

Once the race has commenced it continues without any visible manifestations until the first competitor stands and excuses themselves to allow a visit to the toilet facilities. As soon as the first competitor leaves everyone else remains seated until he returns either victorious or shaking his head in failure, in which case another competitor can take up the mantle. The nature of victory? To be the first to pass water laced with the rich aroma of asparagus. It is of course a gamble whether to go early in the hope that one's kidneys are working fast or bide one's time to be sure that the aroma has reached one's bladder in sufficient concentration to be detected. It is also highly dependent on what else has been consumed earlier in the meal and the state of one's bladder when a race is declared.

For the shadow faculty of gastronomic science an asparagus race was a very serious event, but one which Charles Pinker could barely comprehend, as he was born with a complete inability to smell the chemical that is excreted in urine after eating asparagus. It is remarkable that the potent scent of asparagus-scented urine, so vivid to most, can be entirely undetectable to some. A few unfortunate souls even lack an ability to smell the specific aroma of truffles, and so go through life blind to the delights of gastronomy's finest fungus. Needless to say, no-one in the shadow faculty of gastronomic science was afflicted by this most extreme form of culinary blindness. Augustus' attempts to explain this medical condition, a form of specific anosmia, to Charles, did little to increase the chaplain's understanding of an asparagus race, which remained as incomprehensible to him as a game of musical chairs would be to a deaf man.

The plates had barely been collected from high table

before Hamish rose to his feet only nine minutes into the race.

'The enthusiasm of youth,' muttered Theodore Flanagan to his neighbour George Le Strang who glanced at his watch nervously. If Hamish's kidneys could deliver this prodigious feat of metabolism, Le Strang's own record would be shattered.

'Folly was the word you were looking for,' replied Le Strang, as all the faculty's eyes followed Hamish down the length of the hall.

The delivery of new glasses and a fine Pomerol distracted their attention to such an extent that Hamish was almost back to his seat before he was spotted. His movement and stance said it all. He had, in athletics parlance, crashed into the first hurdle and sprawled on the track was now out of the race. George Le Strang made a modest if unsuccessful effort to conceal the smile that was forming on his lips as he moved his chair back in anticipation of taking up the challenge.

'Your record is safe,' said Hamish as he passed behind Le Strang and gave him a comradely pat on the back. The brief turn of the head that Le Strang gave in acknowledgement was enough to let Theodore rise to his feet ahead of him.

When Theodore returned down the hall a few minutes later it was clear that victory was his. One might reasonably wonder how victory was judged in the absence of an umpire at the urinal. After all, even the gentlemanly game of cricket requires two umpires. An asparagus race was of course a game of honour and, as victory without honour is worse than an honourable defeat, there was never a need to doubt a result. The only question that was adjudicated was the time. Charles Pinker, by dint of his olfactory handicap, was the unspoken timekeeper.

'Sixteen minutes and twenty seconds. I think that equals the record doesn't it?' said the chaplain as Theodore sat down.

'Congratulations Theodore,' said Le Strang, raising his glass. 'To the supremacy of French and Irish kidneys over weaker English organs.'

After this toast, which caused an understandable degree

of consternation amongst the other guests at high table, the chaplain congratulated himself on maintaining détente by declaring a dead heat in a race that could have been reasonably called either way. For all his magnanimity, Le Strang was furious at Hamish, convinced that his pat on the back had been a deliberate piece of gamesmanship rather than well-meaning bonhomie. As for the victor, Theodore Flanagan, next time he vowed to walk back to the table a little faster.

Gastronomically speaking the rest of the dinner was unremarkable. That is not to say it was a dull occasion. The captain of boats' speech was a veritable tour de force, the eloquence of Cicero combined with a base humour that would have made Nero blush. The cancan, performed by the third VIII from the balcony complete with stockings and heavy layered skirts, obtained at short notice by the ever resourceful Mr Potts, received great acclaim. The greatest cheer was reserved for former coach of the first VIII and deeply missed patron of the boat club, Professor Arthur Plantagenet. As Augustus Bloom invited glasses to be raised in the final toast to their recently departed friend, a chant started in the far corner of the hall.

'Planty, Planty, Planty… ' This chant, Arthur's nickname since his own undergraduate days, spread around the hall as everyone rose to their feet. Every available piece of silverware was recruited to provide a percussive accompaniment to this chant. As the spoons became flatter with every bang on the table, the chant got faster and faster until it broke down into a monumental roar that reached across the quad to shake the very organ pipe where Planty's left leg now hung. Thanks to the Master, Arthur Plantagenet witnessed this scene for himself. Lord Faulkner had ordered the hanging of Arthur's portrait in the hall, a decision that had met with general approval despite the fact that the artist had left Arthur with an uncharacteristically serious expression. Had anyone been looking at Professor Plantagenet's portrait during the chant, they might have noticed his initially sombre features ease into what almost looked like a smile.

Rather than retire directly to the senior common room parlour after dinner, the diners from high table had gathered at the foot of the stone staircase that lead to the hall enjoying the last light of a fine summer evening. Gerard was offering around strawberries and glasses of white port as Patrick Eccles came alongside Dr Bloom. Augustus had, in light of recent events, been understandably rather subdued for most of the evening. A fact most amply demonstrated by the fact that he hadn't even attempted to take part in the asparagus race, a sport he normally excelled in. He had, of course, risen to the occasion when asked to raise the toast for Arthur but he was now standing silently lost in his thoughts.

'Dr Bloom, I, er… well some of the crew were wondering if we could buy you a pint.'

'Patrick, well… why not? I'd be delighted.'

Eccles duly led on as his tutor followed with gown billowing, a strawberry in one hand and glass of port still in the other. It had been a long time since Augustus had been into the college bar, a small subterranean world with feeble light and, by that time of night, floors tacky from spilt beer. He was soon feeling like he'd never left the place.

It was almost midnight by the time the barman managed to convince everyone to leave. As a decidedly worse-for-wear Dr Bloom teetered across the quadrangle, Eccles veered off towards the toilets only to collide with Kingsley-Hampton and several of his entourage.

'Eccles, you pisshead. Look what you've done!' said Kingsley-Hampton, inspecting a few damp spots on his shirt while still holding an almost full pint glass in his hand.

'Sorry,' mumbled Eccles as he tried to avoid eye contact and sidle past the group, only to find his path firmly blocked.

'Goodness, it must be past your bedtime Eccles,' said Kingsley-Hampton. 'What time is it anyway?' With that, he lifted his left hand that held his pint glass over Eccles' head while theatrically rotating his wrist to see the time on his watch.

After the laughter had eased and the pack had finished harrowing their dripping prey, their leader spoke again.

'Now, what is the punishment for breaking the curfew, Eccles?'

'What curfew?' he replied, perhaps a little too defiantly under the circumstances.

'The curfew for annoying little pricks like you, Eccles. Let me see, Gentlemen, do you think we should educate Eccles in the finer points of croquet?'

With this, a bemused and bedraggled Eccles was manhandled through the alley towards the college gardens. There, at the foot of the large majestic horse chestnut tree, he was unceremoniously stripped and held down while four croquet hoops, one over each limb, were firmly hammered into the ground with a croquet mallet. Felipe Banzarro gallantly offered up the remains of his own beer to allow Eccles to be re-doused from head to toe. There he was left, dripping with beer, spread-eagled, stark naked and face up. Croqueted.

If you are ever subject to the indignity of such a fate the very best you can hope for is a clear starry night. For apart from awaiting rescue there is very little else to do once croqueted. After the futility of escape has been realised and the pain from the associated grazes on ankles and wrists has waned, a sense of peace often falls on the victim. Only when this stage has been reached can you start to appreciate the true wondrous beauty of a clear starlit night.

Eccles recognised most of the summer constellations and so could appreciate the allegorical symbolism of lying beneath the constellation Cygnus – a swan in flight with outstretched arms. Next to Cygnus was the shining pearl of the star Vega in the constellation Lyra. Without warning the stars began to take the shape of a human face, a girl's face. The girl serving in the hall. How had he forgotten her so easily? He didn't know her name, but he didn't need to. Whatever earthly name she had been given, she was Vega. The cooling night and alcohol still eking into his bloodstream conspired with his nakedness to produce a mild state of delirium. Like the Duke of Dorset he too could now die with dignity, with the name of the girl he loved on his lips and her image in front of his eyes.

Chapter 39

'Come in!' Augustus shouted over the sound of the boiling kettle.

Patrick Eccles duly shuffled in, followed by a miasma of mothball-scented air. He was still wearing the old clothes Potts had given him that morning. The porter had discovered Eccles during his predawn circuit of the college grounds. The restorative tea provided in the lodge had been laced with so much whiskey that Eccles was still under the influence as he entered Augustus Bloom's room for a tutorial. Augustus didn't notice anything amiss and merely busied himself by pouring hot water into two mugs filled with stringy roots.

'We'll leave those to stew for a while,' he said, while placing the cups on the mantelpiece before slumping into his armchair. 'Now… good God, you look as bad as I felt when I woke up this morning.'

'I feel fine, really I do,' replied Eccles, the persistence of circulating alcohol giving the words their truth.

'Trust me, hangovers get worse as you get older. Quite a night last night. Mind you, worth the celebration.' Augustus sniffed the air trying to place the odour that was fighting with the ginseng root aroma, spreading out from the cups on the mantelpiece.

'Now try some of this ginseng tea. Supposedly good for hangovers.'

Eccles smelt the earthy vapour rising off the cup with suspicion before trying a sip. Augustus closed his eyes before taking a draft of his own cup.

'Ham sandwiches on white bread with lots of butter,' said Eccles.

'Sorry?'

'My favourite hangover cure. Ham with thick white bread and sweet tea.'

With that, Augustus rose to his feet and opening his desk pulled out a small black book to note down his student's suggestion. Not spectacular from a culinary perspective, but plausibly effective. It had all the right components for a hangover cure, something to absorb residual alcohol together with fat, salt, sugar and fluids.

'Excellent. Now what were we supposed to be talking about today?'

'Respiratory reflexes.'

'Oh, of course. Off we go then.'

Augustus settled into his chair with his eyes closed while his student stumbled through his essay on the various respiratory reflexes. The occasional sip from his cup and grunt of affirmation reassured his student that he was still awake. Eccles finished with a flourish on the mythological origins of Ondine's curse. When he stopped talking, Augustus opened his eyes.

'Excellent. I think you've got the hang of that. Now, as I'm not feeling the best and have an important guest arriving this morning, would you mind if we called it a day there?'

'No, not at all.'

'Thanks. We'll catch up with any questions you might have on Friday. Now do you have any lectures today in the science area?'

'Yes we've got a pharmacology practical I think.'

'You wouldn't mind dropping this envelope into the vice-chancellor's office, would you? Don't worry, it's just a dinner invitation.'

Eccles headed out of the room with invitation in hand and Augustus rose to his feet and emptied the contents of his cup into the sink. He then picked up the phone.

'Gerard, you couldn't see if the kitchen could rustle up a ham sandwich could you? Plenty of butter, thick white bread and some tea... normal tea will do fine. Oh, and could you bring a little white sugar with that too?'

*

Matthew Kingsley-Hampton was flipping through the contents of the 'K' pigeonhole when Mr Potts came up behind him.

'There's a letter here from the Master. Asked me to deliver it in person.'

Kingsley-Hampton looked at Potts and then the letter. He stretched his hand out, fingers and thumbs poised to grasp the letter. Then with a slight hesitation and supercilious smile he unfolded his hand and waited for Potts to place the letter in his outstretched palm.

'But seeing as you're 'ere, I'll just pop it in the pigeon'ole,' said Potts, relishing this rare victory over Kingsley-Hampton.

This allegory of the modern tensions in the English class structure was interrupted by the unusual intrusion of an American voice, a female American voice to boot.

'Excuse me, are you Mr Potts, by any chance?' she said addressing herself to the aforementioned. 'Augustus, I mean Doctor Bloom, told me to ask for you.'

Potts turned to look at the disarming smile of Mary Frances Kennedy Fisher, renowned translator of Brillat-Savarin's magnum opus *La Physiologie du Goût* or *The Physiology of Taste*. That was the book's short title. It also bore the impressive subtitle of *Méditations de Gastronomie Transcendante; ouvrage théorique, historique et à l'ordre du jour, dédié aux Gastronomes parisiens, par un Professeur, membre de plusieurs sociétés littéraires et savantes.*[12]

---

12 *Meditations on Transcendental Gastronomy; theoretical, historical and topical work, dedicated to the gastronomes of Paris by a professor, a member of several literary and scholarly societies.*

'I am indeed, Madam. Let me show you to 'is rooms. Can I 'elp you with them bags? They look a bit 'eavy for a lady like yourself.'

'Oh, why thank you. That would be most kind.'

There were times and places where Mary Frances would have resented such an assumption of female helplessness and struggled with her own bags. This wasn't one of them.

'You've been booked into a guest room in the Master's lodging, Ma'am, so I'll drop your bags up later after I've shown you up to Dr Bloom.'

Mary Frances took the few free seconds while Potts pulled the bags into the lodge to drink in the scene. Fresh-faced young men sidled past, oblivious to her presence and to the history around them. In her youth, she wouldn't have been invisible to men like these or as unimpressed by the scale and history of the honeyed stone walls. She stepped into the quadrangle and felt the gentle warmth of the morning sun. Another group of young men walked past. At the fore, a pimply-faced youth was walking backwards trying to break into the conversation. Not one of them paused to notice the scene that was enthralling Mary Frances in the middle of the quadrangle. A duck walked at heel behind the figure of a man dressed in archaic clerical garb as he strolled across the grass.

'Now, Ma'am, this way.'

Mary Frances turned to follow. When she glanced back the man and the duck were gone.

Augustus recognised the tenor of knock on his door and jumped to his feet, only to regret his haste as his brain crashed from one side of his cranium to the other. The tea and ham sandwich had had a beneficial effect on the gastric symptoms of his hangover but the contents of his head were still in a delicate state. He pulled open the door.

'Mary Frances, you've arrived; how splendid.'

He offered his hand.

'Oh God, you English,' said Mary Frances, deftly avoiding his hand to plant a kiss on both cheeks, a habit ingrained from her many years in France but thoroughly alien to Augustus. Then she swept in to explore the room.

'Augustus, white bread and rubber ham? What's happened to my champion of gastronomy?' she said, picking up the corner of a half-eaten ham sandwich with the deference usually given to soiled undergarments.

'An experiment… Part of my hangover research.'

Mary Frances sniffed the air. Her acute olfactory apparatus picked up ginseng, a strong ketotic beer smell and something else entirely unexpected.

'What is that other smell? A chemical sort of scent.'

'Smell?' asked Augustus, suddenly worried that his Anglo-Saxon approach to hygiene, with a bath on Sunday nights, might be falling short of American standards.

'Mothballs, that's it. I must say Augustus, it looks as if I've arrived just in time to save you. You are looking wretched.'

This meeting was not going quite as Augustus had planned and certainly radically different to their last meeting in the bar of the Waldorf Astoria in New York. That conversation, fuelled on a diet of olives and martinis, had, at least in Augustus' memory, been a flirtatious meeting of minds. Augustus had felt he had finally found a woman who shared his passion for the gastronomic side of life. In the intervening few years his memory had shaved years from her face and inches from her waist. But what were a few decades if you found someone truly special? Now here was that same woman taking on the role of a well-meaning aunt intent on reforming a wayward nephew who was old enough to know better. The combination of a wicked hangover and weeks of sleepless nights had certainly taken its toll on Augustus.

'Sorry, you've caught me on the hop. Bit of a big night around here last night, bumps supper. We're back head of the river.'

'Bumps?'

'A type of rowing race, Mary Frances.'

'Your college won the race last night?'

'Not exactly. Come on, let me show you around and I'll explain all about it.'

'Perfect, Augustus. You can show me Oxford and tell me about your love life at the same time. You're not still pining about that woman from the British Museum, I hope?'

Taking his arm firmly in her own, she led Augustus out of the door.

*

'I'll have the Tournedos Rossini. Very rare. Absolutely dripping in fact, or even twitching if possible.' Matthew Kingsley-Hampton sat in a dark corner of the Elizabeth restaurant, one of Oxford's better dining establishments, for a celebratory lunch.

'Make that two,' said Felipe Banzarro sitting across the table. 'Mind you Mat, one of these days I'm going to get you over to Buenos Aires for a decent piece of meat.'

'You're on. Now what to drink? A bottle of Bollinger straight away and decant a bottle of your '59 Hermitage for later,' said Kingsley-Hampton, dismissing the waiter with a subliminal flick of the hand.

'So what's the celebration, Mat?'

The Honourable Matthew Kingsley-Hampton, one-time scholar of St Jerome's College, fished the letter out of his jacket pocket and offered it to his friend.

'All the weak saps could think of to do to me was take away my scholarship.'

'Is that a good thing?'

'Look, academics earn shit and die poor. The way I see it, I've just quadrupled my earning capacity by abandoning a scholarship and learning to take the odd risk here or there.'

Felipe could only smile, shaking his head as he read over the letter again. '… reckless abuse of college regulations in evicting a fellow student on a whim… manipulating and hiding behind others in an attempt to smear the good name of the college… ' It took a profound sense of self-belief to receive such a letter and celebrate. Two champagne flutes appeared and the waiter offered Kingsley-Hampton the first taste. After the customary nod, the waiter filled the glasses just a little too slowly for Kingsley-Hampton's liking.

'As the good bard said, better to have scholared and lost than never to have scholared at all.'

'I'll drink to that,' said Banzarro, clinking glasses across the table. 'And I think you came out better than that squealer Eccles. Wouldn't fancy a night staked to the quad stark-bollock naked even in what you English call summer.'

'Revenge is the sweetest wine, my dear Felipe. Who said that?'

'I think you just did.'

'I have my moments. Now grab that bottle Felipe and pour some more of that champagne. That damn waiter seems determined to have me die of thirst.'

*

By the evening, Eccles was back in his old clothes with the last vestiges of his delayed hangover finally lifted. He was sitting with his back to the panelled wall of the Great Hall. He was still surrounded by rowers picking over the bones of last night's events, but oblivious to their banter as he scanned the faces of the scouts bringing in armfuls of soup plates. He was looking for the girl he had christened Vega during the cool hours of captivity under the stars.

'Enjoy your game of croquet last night, Eccles?' said Kingsley-Hampton as he sauntered in late as usual and still wearing his long flowing scholar's gown, as Felipe followed behind in the far less impressive commoner's gown that barely reached his waist. No reply was expected and Eccles for his part had no intention of delivering one.

'Patrick, what was that ponce on about?' asked Roger Sinclair.

'Oh, nothing much. Just the usual Kingsley-Hampton crap. I'm used to it now.'

'I heard someone was croqueted last night. That wasn't you, was it Patrick?'

'Oh, it was nothing really. Potts had me out of there in no time.'

'Jesus, that guy is dead,' said Roger as he turned in a whisper to his neighbour. Within a minute the whole table had heard the story and were to a man bent on revenge.

'Ok lads, tonight Kingsley-Hampton's face down on the Master's lawn with a daffodil sticking out of his arse,' said Gareth Jenkins in his Welsh brogue and customary linguistic flair.

'Appealing image, but wrong season Gareth, a bit late for daffodils. Mind you, a well-barbed rose might work better,' said John Metcalfe, surprised to have finally found a practical application for his studies in Botany. 'What do you think, Roger?'

'Oh, I have a far better plan,' said a smiling Roger Sinclair. 'A little more complicated, but perfect. Now we'll need a few bits and pieces, starting with chloroform. I'll nick that from the labs today. Anyone got easy access to a nightdress, preferably pink?' asked Sinclair. From the tone of his voice he might as well have been asking someone to pass the salt.

*

It was well past midnight before the plan was put into action. Eccles led the rest of the second VIII up the staircase, pointing out the quietest part of each stair. He opened the door with the key returned to him by Potts and then stood back to let his crew members flood into the room, each bearing a torch and fully briefed as to the layout of the room and their respective tasks. Within seconds, both Kingsley-Hampton and Banzarro were rendered incapable of resisting with the aid of Sinclair's chloroform. Banzarro was tied to his bed and his door screwed shut. Another fate was planned for his roommate. Eccles was given the task of ensuring continued anaesthesia while the others lifted every item of furniture down the stairs into the quad outside. Finally Gareth Jenkins, a horse of a man at the tender age of twenty, hoisted the unconscious Kingsley-Hampton over his shoulder.

In the corner of Old Quad, Patrick Eccles' former sitting room was reassembled with breathtaking accuracy from the threadbare rug to the dusty aspidistra. Kingsley-Hampton's bed was placed alongside the rest of the furniture from his bedroom in just the right location, taking into account the fact that the only thing not moved were the walls and doors. An appropriate pink nightdress had been procured with disturbing ease and pulled over the head of Kingsley-Hampton's unconscious and semi-naked form. Finally, a pair of handcuffs and chain were placed to ensure there would be no easy escape. After a final draught of chloroform was delivered through a well-soaked handkerchief, Eccles and his crew vanished into the night with a plan to convene early for breakfast.

Mr Potts came across the scene just before dawn. He was out collecting the relics left over after summer examinations: empty champagne bottles, discarded mortarboards and white *sub-fusc* bow ties. As he approached, he quickened his step in mounting fury. Then he saw the body in the bed, already exhausted from futile struggles to escape, and had a change of heart. Recognising the occupant, he stopped and smiled, taking time to relish the scene. He turned back towards the lodge. Only one person would be drinking whiskey in their tea that dawn, and it wasn't going to be The Honourable Matthew Kingsley-Hampton.

Chapter 40

Mary Frances woke early, as was her custom. After reading for a while, she wrote a long letter to an old friend in London whom she hadn't seen for years and took a fancy to visit before heading back to America. She may never get the chance again. It was not quite seven o'clock in the morning by the time she had exhausted the recreational possibilities of her small room, so she decided to explore the college again. Augustus had conducted a brief tour yesterday but she wanted time to relish it on her own. Mary Frances had, in her later years, grown very fond of quiet moments. She would go to the Met in New York just before closing and find an empty gallery to sit quietly in a vacant attendant's chair. Her advancing years allowed her to take such liberties, and taking liberties was one of the few perks of age she did enjoy. She would remain in the settling silence until finally ushered out, allowing her to amble through deserted galleries as if they were her own.

The college at this hour had that same serene feel as an empty art gallery. The grassy quadrangles were free of the celebrating finalists soaked in flour and champagne that she had seen the day before. The croquet hoops sat empty and unused. Dark shadows and honey-coloured glints highlighted the curves and crevices of the stone walls. Dew remained on the fleshy leaves of red geraniums in the still-shadowed window boxes. As she traversed a passageway between Old

Quad and Chapel Quad the unwelcome sound of voices intruded into her meditative wander. In a few more steps the source was apparent. The leather chairs sitting incongruously on the grass were filled with young men drinking tea with plates stacked high with toast. Others were sitting on the backs of the chairs and others still were standing in groups. They were surrounded by bookcases and a standard lamp stood at a precarious angle, its lead plugged into the grass. She wandered over for a better look, trying to second-guess the nature of this strange gathering. She still seemed invisible to the strange and insular group of young men who inhabited this college. The snippets of conversation she could grasp seemed bizarrely normal, ranging from a ball-by-ball discussion of last weekend's cricket match, to plans for a punting trip later that day. When she drew near, Mary Frances saw a young lady in a pink nightdress lying in a bed, handcuffed and chained to the ancient but solid square lead drainpipes. All sense of charm evaporated immediately to be replaced by outrage. Then the young lady screamed at the assembled crowd in a most un-ladylike manner.

'Okay, you bastards, you've had your fun. Now get me out of here.' Kingsley-Hampton tried another futile attempt to dislodge the chain from the drainpipe. 'You do realise who my father is, don't you? I'll have you all arrested for this. Especially you, Jenkins, I'll get you deported to the colonies.'

'Will you really? For what crime?' called Gareth Jenkins over his shoulder.

'For the worst crime of all, being a fat Welsh git!'

'You know what, Roger,' said Jenkins to the man in the chair opposite. 'It's a damn shame there weren't any daffodils still around this time of year.' With that, he kicked off his shoe and pulled off one of his socks. Walking by Mary Frances he gave her a polite nod of acknowledgement and went over to the bed.

'Now you should watch your language, Kingsley-Whatsit, there's a real lady present,' and he stuffed the dirty sock into Kingsley-Hampton's mouth.

'Could I offer you a cup of tea?' Jenkins turned to Mary Frances with a huge smile and a wink.

'Oh… why not?' replied Mary Frances.

'Come on lads, where's your manners? Offer the lady a seat.'

*

The phone rang on Inspector Granger's desk.

'Granger,' he barked into the phone.

'I've got the inspector of anatomy on the line, sir,' said the girl at the switchboard. 'From the Home Office in London.'

'Excellent. Put him through… '

*

An hour later, Mary Frances and Augustus were sitting in the small café in the covered market where he and Arthur used to meet and put the world to rights. Martha finally ran out of flat surfaces to wipe with her damp grey cloth and so came over to take their order.

'Yes, love?'

'Two full breakfasts, with tea please, and could you bring the tea straight away?'

'Two breakfast and tea,' she shouted across the café then wiped the already clean table with the dirty cloth. Mary Frances recoiled slightly, her American sense of hygiene deeply troubled by the smears left on the table. She picked out a paper napkin from the chrome dispenser and dried the table in front of her.

'So what do you think?'

'Of this place?' Mary Frances panicked in trying to hide her inner cultural crisis. When Augustus had suggested the café in the covered market for breakfast she had pictured a gleaming white and chrome diner. Instead there were yellow net curtains, curling linoleum, ashtrays filled with cigarette butts and Martha's bacteria-laden cloth.

'Well I meant Oxford, really.'

'Oh Augustus, Oxford is simply divine. Bizarre, dysfunctional, but divine.'

'We English prefer the term eccentric.'

'Well this morning was certainly an eye opener. Does your English eccentricity cover chaining apparently unwilling transvestites to their beds in the middle of the... what do you call them... quadrants?'

'Quadrangles. And as for our friend in the pink nightdress, that was just a bit of harmless fun.'

'Dare I ask what he had done to deserve such a fate, Augustus?'

'Oh, we've had a few problems with that particular young man, but I'm not sure quite how he upset the boat club so much.'

'Mind you, they were perfect gentlemen to me.' Mary Frances caught Augustus' eye for a moment before continuing. 'Has it ever occurred to anyone that excluding women may be bad for the mental health of the students?'

'Bad for them? Why on earth would it be bad for them?'

'Tea,' Martha said as she banged a large blue and white striped teapot and two cups on the table.

'Oh Augustus, you definitely need a woman to sort you out.'

'Are you offering your services?'

'Me?' Mary Frances laughed. 'Heaven forbid, no. But I might just give you a good shove in the right direction.'

'I need a good shove?'

'Oh, definitely. Now I'll pour the tea and you'll tell me all about this gastronomic dining society.'

'Goodness, where should I start?'

'At the beginning will do nicely. There you go.' Mary Frances handed over a cup of tea and sat back in anticipation.

'Well, it all started a few years back with a truffled turkey George Le Strang had sent over from Paris. You'll meet him at dinner. Can be a bit standoffish, but a good chap when you get to know him. Well, your good friend Jean Anthelme Brillat-Savarin's name came up in the course of this dinner.'

'I would expect no less in such academic company.'

'Indeed, and as many of us were well-versed in his writings and similarly gastronomically inclined, we all agreed with him that gastronomy should be granted proper academic status. So there and then we decided to found a shadow faculty of gastronomic science which would remain in existence until we could convince the university to set up a proper faculty.'[13]

'What a marvellous idea. I'm sure Jean Anthelme would have been delighted. So who's in this secret gastronomic faculty of yours?'

'Well there are only five of us left now but we started with nine.'

'My goodness. How on earth did you lose so many?'

'Three have died and one had to leave after breaking one of the rules.'

'Three dead? Well you know Brillat-Savarin died only two months after *La Physiologie du Goût* was published. You don't think there might be a curse on the poor man that has affected your dining club too?'

'Not at all. I don't believe in that sort of superstition. Do you?' Though boldly spoken, Augustus felt a strange prickle down his neck as he uttered these words.

'Oh no, just teasing.' Mary Frances smiled and squeezed his hand across the table. 'So why not get a few new members? Couldn't I join rather than just be your guest?'

'Well unfortunately we set it up with a rather tightly worded constitution. So all members must be members of the college and we've no mechanism for electing new members or it seems changing the rules.'

'Why that's plain silly.'

'Perhaps a little short-sighted, but there was a lot of absinthe involved in the inauguration.'

'So your faculty will just fade away to nothing. Then where will gastronomy be?'

'Well this dinner tonight might change all that. You see our constitution says we will disband once the university

---

13 For a more complete description of the founding and early history of the shadow faculty of gastronomic science, please see the appendix.

founds a faculty of gastronomic science. Do you remember that I wrote to you about Arthur who died last term of a heart complaint? Well he's left an endowment for a professorship in gastronomy. The vice-chancellor will be there tonight to receive this legacy, so you might be witness to a momentous night in the history of gastronomy. Not that we exactly see eye to eye with the vice-chancellor after a certain Japanese diplomat died last year at one of our dinners.'

Mary Frances, looked understandably alarmed, but the question she was dying to ask hung silently on her lips.

'Fugu. He insisted on preparing it himself. Terrible shock to us all,' Augustus explained.

'Should I update my will before dinner?'

'Oh, I think you should be safe enough tonight. Nothing poisonous on the menu this time. Talking of which, I'll need to abandon you for a good bit of the day.' Augustus glanced at his watch. 'I'm really sorry but I've a few details to sort out today in relation to tonight's dinner. Is there anything you'd particularly like to see around Oxford? I could point you in the right direction at least.'

'I hear the Ashmolean Gallery is a nice place to wander around, so that will keep me entertained for a good while and I've been told by the hosts of this morning's tea party that I must see the shrunken heads in the Pitt Rivers Museum. That should fill the day nicely. What time do you need me back?'

'I'll collect you from your room at say, six thirty this evening?'

And with that, two plates of England's finest breakfast spread arrived on the table along with a bottle of HP sauce. Mary Frances looked at the plate with a certain suspicion.

'It is important, Mary Frances, in appreciating the finer points of gastronomy not to forget the simpler pleasures of eggs, meat, offal and grease,' said Augustus, deftly stacking a small column of egg white, bacon and black pudding onto his fork.

*

Charles Pinker and Hamish McIntyre were waiting in the senior common room for Augustus. The stark reality of what they were about to do in the name of gastronomy and under the legal obligation of their former colleague was now unavoidable. Until this moment, the whole affair had seemed reassuringly abstract. They now faced the decidedly concrete issue of bringing Arthur's final contribution to gastronomy from the organ pipe to the kitchens for its final preparation.

'Charles, it's gone twelve o'clock. Looks as if we are doing this by ourselves,' said Hamish pacing the floor.

'Where on earth has Augustus got to?' asked Charles. 'It's not like him to be late. Do you think anything has happened to him?'

'Chickened out, most likely. Come on, let's get it over and done with,' said Hamish rising to his feet and stuffing a roll of muslin that had been left on the sideboard into his pocket.

The pair made their way across to the chapel. Charles Pinker was by far the calmer of the two. The remarkable conversation with God of a few weeks past was still etched in his mind and was the source of his current serenity. For Hamish, this had all been rather a lark until today. Once inside the chapel, Hamish made a rapid search for unwanted guests while Charles wandered up to the altar. When this meeting had been arranged, Hamish had been allocated the task of watch duty and Augustus was supposed to be getting Arthur's leg. No specific part in this enterprise had been given to the chaplain but he had expressed a wish to be present and so he was.

Once Hamish had satisfied himself that they were alone he started up the stairs to the organ loft. He paused by the organ to catch his breath before proceeding through the concealed door. When he reached the small room above the organ itself he went down on his knees to peer into the pipe and locate the rope, from which Arthur's leg was suspended – no easy task in the pale light filtering through the louvred opening above. When he did finally manage to pull the leg out of the organ pipe, the dim light that had proved such a hindrance became

333

a blessing. The leg looked far less disturbing than he had remembered from his last visit when he had thought to bring a torch. Hamish lifted the leg to his nose for a final sniff of reassurance that the curing process had completed its magical transformation.

'Not bad,' muttered Hamish making his way down the stairs and folding the leg in muslin as he went, leaving the spirit of Arthur Plantagenet who had been watching from above, apoplectic in outrage at this meagre description of his great sacrifice to gastronomy.

*

Augustus had, in fact, arrived back at St Jerome's in good time to assist in the removal of Arthur's leg but got no further than the lodge. A policeman was standing just outside the gates when he arrived, a man Augustus recognised from his last visit to the police station. Unfortunately the recognition was mutual.

'Dr Bloom, just the man. I've been waiting for you,' said the young policeman.

'Really? Well what is it this time?' Augustus said, his heart registering a greater sense of fear than his voice.

'The inspector needs you down at the station.'

'Again? I thought we sorted all this out. Can't this wait until tomorrow?'

'I'm sorry, sir, if you'd like to come with me?' The policeman placed his hand under Augustus' upper arm as a signal it was time to leave.

'Oy, hands off,' cried Potts, appearing from inside the porter's lodge. 'Sorry Dr Bloom. I told him he couldn't come into college without a warrant but he insisted on waiting for you outside.'

'It's okay, Potts,' said Augustus smiling at his would-be saviour. 'Officer, the thing is I have an important dinner tonight and a guest who has come all the way from America. So just let the inspector know that I'll be down at the station first thing tomorrow morning.'

'Dr Bloom, if you won't come voluntarily I've been instructed to arrest you,' said the policeman, eking out another inch of height from an already substantial frame and placing his free hand on the leather pouch containing his handcuffs.

'On what charge?' said Augustus defiantly.

'Breaches of the 1832 Anatomy Act with respect to the illegal handling of dead bodies, sir. Now, do you want to do this here or at the station?'

'Perhaps we should head down then,' said an ashen-faced Augustus. 'Will this take long?'

'That all depends, sir.'

'On what?'

'On the inspector.'

Chapter 41

It was well past five o'clock in the evening and the Master was fretting about two things. Firstly, fifteen down. Irreversible botanical flow, five letters. Something H something something E. He hadn't failed to complete a *Times* crossword by dinner time for over twenty years so this last unsolved clue was extremely galling. Secondly, Dr Ridgeway the vice-chancellor was due that evening for dinner. This required him to make a speech and be civil to the vice-chancellor. Making speeches was something the Master could do effortlessly and with a little preparation. Being civil to Dr Ridgeway was something that no amount of preparation would make any easier, so the knock on the door did nothing to improve his mood.

'Enter,' he shouted.

'Sorry to disturb you, Master.' Hamish's head appeared around the door. 'We're just setting up the cocktails out in the garden here and, er… '

'And?'

'Well, I'd appreciate your opinion on the taste.' The rest of Hamish emerged from behind the door carrying a Victorian etched-glass tumbler glinting green and gold as it passed through a shaft of light from the window.

'What is it?'

'A departure from our usual martini variants. I'm trying to capture the essence of a summer evening with this new twist on the mojito.' Hamish placed the glass in the Master's outstretched hand and continued talking.

'I'm still tweaking the balance of flavours, but I got this fantastic old white rum from Bewick's in London and I hope you don't mind but I've used one of the '59 Bollingers. A bit extravagant for a cocktail, but it is a tribute to Arthur after all. I've had the herbs grown for the occasion by that chap Benson in the Botanical Gardens, Arthur's old friend.'

As he spoke, the Master had lifted the glass to admire the kaleidoscopic effect of the crushed ice, herbs and golden liquid. Then he raised the glass to his nose and inhaled as wave after wave of different aromas hit his olfactory organs, and finally he took a sip.

'As well as the white rum and the normal mint I've added lemon thyme and basil, lime juice, sugar, Angostura bitters, and topped with the champagne.' Hamish completed his description while the Master's eyes were still closed and waited for the verdict.

'Exquisite Hamish. You are completely wasted in academia.'

'Any suggestions? Are the basil and thyme too dominant?'

'No, I think it's perfect.'

After Hamish had retired beaming from ear to ear, the Master sat back in his chair. Fifteen down. Irreversible botanical flow, five letters… Thyme. Time indeed waits for no man but on this occasion, the Master's impressive record for completing crosswords remained unblemished. That left only the insoluble challenge of how to be true to himself and civil to the vice-chancellor at the same time.

*

When Inspector Granger looked into the interview room he was delighted to see Dr Bloom pacing the floors. Augustus' detainment had been handled during the day with a deliberate lack of urgency, each passing hour adding to his distress. Priming is what the inspector called this process of preparing a detainee for questioning, a technique based on the old medical notion of only lancing a boil when it is ripe. In the four hours since his arrest, Augustus had most certainly ripened.

'That's more like it,' said the inspector under his breath and then swung open the door and marched in with Constable Trent at his heel.

'Dr Bloom, terribly sorry to detain you. The constable here mentioned you had a dinner this evening, but I'm afraid you will have to send your apologies as you are likely to be detained overnight. Would you like to make a phone call?'

'This is preposterous,' fumed Augustus.

'Shall I take that to mean you don't wish to make a phone call?' The inspector usually tried to annoy his interviewees as much as possible. Anger loosens careful tongues far better than anything else he had ever discovered.

'I certainly would like to make a phone call,' said Augustus through clenched teeth.

'Very well. Constable Trent will you escort the *prisoner* to the telephone at the front desk.'

'Theodore,' hissed Augustus into the receiver.

'Augustus? Is that you?'

'Of course it is. Now listen, I've been stuck in the police station most of the day and they are threatening to hold me overnight. Even if they can't, I'm certain to miss dinner… '

'You stay right there, Augustus, I'm coming straight down. Don't say a word until I get there… '

'Theodore, listen. There is no point in both of us missing dinner and I need you to tell Mary Frances that something has come up and escort her to dinner. Please, as a friend, just look after her.'

'What shall I tell her?'

'Oh, I don't know… Look, tell her one my students has been arrested and I'm stuck down in the police station sorting it out. I was going to call at her room at six thirty to bring her to the drinks reception, so don't be late.'

'Augustus, are you sure you don't want me to come down?'

'Positive. There'll be plenty of time tomorrow to get this

sorted out. I think the inspector just wants revenge for last time.'

*

True to his word, Theodore was at the door of Mary Frances' room at the appointed hour. He gathered his thoughts before knocking timidly on the door.

'Come in,' Mary Frances shouted through the closed door.

Theodore entered and found himself facing an almost, but not quite fully dressed Mary Frances with her back turned to the door.

'Could you be a sweetie and zip me up the last few inches, Augustus,' she said while fiddling with her earrings. Theodore stepped up and did what was asked only to have Mary Frances let out a scream when she turned around to thank him.

'Oh my God, who are you?'

'Terribly sorry, let me introduce myself. Theodore Flanagan, one of Augustus' colleagues. He's been detained at the police station, one of his students is in a spot of bother and he has to sort it out. So he asked me to escort you to the Master's lodge for the drinks reception.'

'Is he coming later?'

'He hopes so but it rather depends on the police.'

Mary Frances looked Theodore up and down. A little short for her liking but very well turned out otherwise. She took Theodore by the arm.

'Well, you'll do for now. Shall we go? I could do with a drink after a day looking at shrunken heads in a dusty museum.'

*

The Trinity term dinners of the shadow faculty of gastronomic science always had a very different feel to those in Michaelmas and Hilary terms as they traditionally started outdoors. The scene that met Mary Frances' appreciative eyes when she and Theodore entered through the low arch into the Master's garden was one of an idyllic English garden party. Surrounded by the vivid colours of one of Oxford's finest herbaceous borders, the gentlemen were arranged in small black and white groups. A string quartet completed the picture. Mary Frances, aware she was the first woman to grace a dinner of this august society, particularly appreciated the impact her arrival had on the assembled gentlemen. The hum of conversation was silenced for a few moments and the poor cellist hit a note that Mozart could never have intended. A few moments later, once equilibrium had been restored, Theodore led Mary Frances towards the first group, which included the Master, the vice-chancellor and George Le Strang.

*

'Lord Faulkner,' said Theodore. 'May I introduce one of our distinguished guests best known from her writings as M.F.K. Fisher.'

'An honour to meet you Ma'am, I have heard and read a great deal about you,' said the Master, lifting Mary Frances' hand to within a whisker of his lips before delivering the perfect diplomatic air kiss. Mary Frances visibly flushed and unusually flustered by the Master's gesture, made an attempt at a response that was halfway between a bow and a curtsy. Lord Faulkner, ever the perfect diplomat, picked up on her confusion and tried to put her at ease.

'Welcome to our college and my little oasis of a garden, though I can't take credit for that personally.'

'Why thank you, it is truly an honour to be here,' said Mary Frances, recovering her poise.

'Now,' continued the Master, 'may I introduce our Professor of Modern History, George Le Strang.'

'Mrs Fisher,' said Le Strang, offering his hand. 'The honour is all mine. Your translation of Brillat-Savarin has a special place in my bookshelf.'

'Why thank you, but please call me Mary Frances.' Before George could reply the Master gently guided Mary Frances towards the vice-chancellor.

'May I introduce the vice-chancellor of our fine university, Dr Ridgeway. A man on a mission to modernise Oxford and bring us all into the twentieth century before it's all over. Isn't that right?' He smiled with perfect insincerity at the vice-chancellor.

'Indeed, but I hope it won't take another thirty years,' Ridgeway said offering his hand to Mary Frances who, whilst admiring his reforming agenda, was disappointed with his limp handshake. She was spared the conversational challenge of talking to the vice-chancellor by the arrival of Hamish McIntyre who had grabbed three of his herbal mojito's from Gerard's tray and rushed over.

'Now, first treat of the evening,' he said, proudly offering a glass to Theodore and Mary Frances.

'Where's Augustus?' asked Hamish, holding out a third glass for his clearly absent friend.

'He's been delayed,' explained Theodore.

'Oh well, his loss,' said Hamish taking a slug from the mojito in his hand.

'Wow,' said Mary Frances suddenly bereft of words when the cocktail hit her parched taste buds.

'My thoughts exactly,' said the Master. 'Now I think apart from Augustus, most people are here, so I'd better say a few words.' With that, he tapped his glass discreetly and cleared his throat.

'Gentlemen and esteemed Lady,' he said bowing his head towards Mary Frances. 'I should first like to welcome all our guests. Tonight's dinner promises to be another fine adventure in gastronomy, a barely explored continent of human experience. Sadly I shall not be joining you tonight. You have been invited over me as you are all experts in some aspect of this fine science, except of course for our vice-chancellor who is here for another purpose entirely.' The Master relished the pained expression these words carved on the face of the vice-chancellor. 'For their part, your hosts are a group of devoted gastronomes who have recently lost one of their dearest colleagues, Professor Arthur Plantagenet. He left a magnificent legacy, which I have the great honour of announcing this evening. This legacy amounts to a quarter of a million pounds to the university and a further fifty thousand to this college.'

The vice-chancellor led the applause, which the Master had to quell with a raised hand.

'The sum he donated to the college was to create the post of Professor of Gastronomy and as Master I hereby confirm my commitment to make the first appointment to this chair in the next academic year.'

A far more voluble response met this announcement from all, apart from the vice-chancellor whose expression turned decidedly icy.

'In relation to the donation to the university,' the Master pulled out a cheque from his jacket pocket and held it up, 'this magnificent sum is to be donated on the condition that a Faculty of Gastronomic Science is set up within the university, to which I am sure the vice-chancellor can have no objections.'

All eyes turned to the vice-chancellor.

'A magnificent donation indeed,' he said holding out his hand for the cheque, 'which the university will duly take into consideration depending on other priorities.'

'Of course,' beamed the Master, 'and until such time as your considerations are complete and the new faculty is inaugurated, his executors will look after the cheque. Perhaps you could take this cheque for now Theodore. You can talk this over with the vice-chancellor over dinner. Now may I propose a toast to Arthur Plantagenet and to Gastronomy.'

After the toast, Gerard appeared at the entrance of the garden and rang a small silver bell. The shadow faculty knew this was their cue to assemble their guests and make their way to dinner. As for the Master, he settled himself onto a bench nestled within the flowerbed to enjoy the evening sun, mojito in hand.

*

In stark contrast to the Master, Augustus Bloom was sitting in a dimly lit room and the very picture of abject misery. Across the table sat Inspector Granger.

'I had a most interesting conversation earlier today with the Inspector of Anatomy from the Home Office in London. Dr Bloom, do you know what the Inspector of Anatomy does?'

Augustus remained silent, assuming correctly that the question was a rhetorical one.

'He supervises the operation of the 1832 Anatomy Act,' continued the inspector, oblivious to Bloom's silence. 'An act that was introduced after an epidemic of grave-robbing in the early nineteenth century. The advice I have received from the inspector is that you are in breach of this act and hence no better than a grave-robber. Do you have anything to say before I formally charge you?'

'Can you at least tell me what exactly I am to be charged with? It certainly can't be grave-robbing as Arthur doesn't even have a grave,' asked Augustus.

'Of course. I shall be charging you under the 1832 Anatomy Act of illegally receiving body parts for the purpose of anatomical examination without a licence.'

'But Arthur didn't leave his body for anatomical examination. If he had he would have donated it to the department of human anatomy.'

'If that is your only defence, Dr Bloom, perhaps you could explain why Professor Plantagenet donated his leg to your laboratory?'

'For research… scientific research.'

'Research requires examination and examination of any part of the human body is to my mind anatomy. So, quite frankly, Dr Bloom, you are wasting your breath. You will have to argue your case in front of a judge and jury. By the way, if found guilty there is a prison sentence of up to three months, which seems rather lenient to my mind.'

There was a knock on the door then and a young constable stuck his head around the partially opened door.

'Sorry to interrupt, but there's a man at the front desk who says he's Dr Bloom's solicitor. He's demanding to be present if you are questioning his client.'

Augustus glanced at his watch. Almost quarter to seven. He hoped to God it wasn't Theodore otherwise Mary Frances was stranded and tonight's dinner was turning into a complete shambles.

'Dr Flanagan, I presume. Well, show him in,' said the inspector with an irritated sigh.

When Mr Barringer was shown into the room, the inspector's demeanour changed beyond recognition.

'Cornelius, long time no see,' said Mr Barringer holding out a hand, which was studiously ignored by the inspector.

'Mr Edgar Barringer. Well, well. It has certainly been a few years.'

'Time marches on Cornelius. Now I wish to speak to my client in private. Five or ten minutes should suffice.'

When they were alone, Mr Barringer opened his leather briefcase and pulled out a notepad and pen.

'I didn't expect to see you here,' said Augustus. 'I mean I'm delighted you are but I thought you wanted your name kept out of this mess.'

'Theodore Flanagan is a very persuasive man when he wants to be. As he pointed out when he phoned me earlier, if this gets to court my role will be fully exposed. I'm afraid I was tied up in court most of the day so apologies for leaving you in the lurch for so long. Now I'm here my mission is to make sure we get you off whatever trumped-up charges dear old Cornelius Granger is trying to stick on you.' Mr Barringer uncapped his fountain pen with a flourish.

'Sounds good to me,' said Augustus.

'What has he charged you with?' said Mr Barringer, getting straight to business.

'Well he hasn't charged me yet but he was about to when you came in. Something along the lines of receiving body parts without a licence under the Anatomy Act. I told him it was nothing to do with anatomy but… '

'First things first, Dr Bloom. The Anatomy Act? That was back in the eighteen hundreds.'

'I think he said 1832,' offered Augustus.

'That's preposterous.'

'I'm sure he said it was 1832.'

'No, the idea of it, not the date. How about the will? Has he asked about that?'

'I was questioned for at least an hour earlier this afternoon by another police officer, but I refused to say anything other than we are following Arthur's instructions to the letter.'

'If it comes to it, Dr Bloom, we may have to explain exactly what Arthur has asked of you.'

'Are you daft?'

'The most important thing is that we convince the inspector not to press charges and avoid a court case. Showing him the will is a last resort but we may have to. I've brought a copy just in case.'

'I'm sorry, Mr Barringer, I couldn't betray Arthur's trust just to save my own skin. If it comes to that I'll just plead guilty. He said the maximum sentence was three months. With the summer holidays coming up I could be out for the start of next term.'

'Dr Bloom, you can't be serious?' Mr Barringer looked across the table and realised immediately from Augustus' eyes that he was deadly serious. 'All right, well we'd better find some other way to get us all out of this predicament. Let's get the inspector back in and see exactly why he thinks he can charge you with this alleged crime. Remember, don't say anything unless I ask you to. You are not obliged to answer any of his questions.'

'So Cornelius, do you mind if I call you Cornelius or should I call you Inspector Granger under the circumstances?' asked Barringer smiling.

'Either is fine.' The inspector muttered in reply.

'Good. Now could you explain why you are holding my client and exactly what he is alleged to have done?'

'This isn't an alleged crime, Edgar. We have ample proof.'

'Of what?'

'Of receiving a portion of a human body in the absence of an anatomy licence or certificate of release and of failing to notify the inspector of anatomy within the required 48-hour period that Professor Plantagenet's body was to be used for anatomical studies. As proof, we have a sworn statement from one of the mortuary attendants at the John Radcliffe Hospital indicating that the leg of the late professor was delivered to Dr Bloom on Friday, 5th December 1969.' The inspector rattled off this information without a hint of hesitation.

'These charges are being brought under the 1832 Anatomy Act, is that right?'

'That is quite correct, Edgar. Dr Bloom is in breach of the regulations set out in sections I, IX and XI.'

'I see. Well in that case do you have a copy of Halsbury's Statutes I can consult to check on the details of this act? I am quite familiar with the history behind the passing of this act but rather sketchy on the details. Until today, none of my clients have been charged under this act. I should also like to see the statement made by this mortuary assistant.'

'I've told you which parts of the act Dr Bloom has contravened – that should suffice.'

'Cornelius, I don't think it is an unreasonable request.'

There was an uncomfortable silence until the inspector relented.

'Jenkins, show him up to my office. You'll find a full set of Halsbury in the glass cabinet behind my desk, Mr Barringer. Jenkins, stay with him while he's checking that the details I have given are correct. And get him a copy of the Hogarth statement too.'

Mr Barringer reappeared after an agonising delay of almost thirty minutes carrying the relevant volume of Halsbury under his arm.

'Cornelius, if I may I wish to read out section VII of the 1832 act: "And be it enacted, that if any action or suit shall be commenced or brought against any person for anything done in pursuant of this act the same shall be commenced within Six Calendar Months next after the cause of action accrued."'

'What does that mean, exactly?' said Augustus.

'It means that the inspector has no reason to detain you any longer. You are a free man, Augustus. Isn't that so inspector?'

'If I may?' Inspector Granger held out his hand. Mr Barringer offered the volume in his hands to the inspector. While he read, Mr Barringer continued talking.

'Arthur Plantagenet passed away sometime between the night of December 3rd and the morning of December 4th. As you have already indicated the alleged crime of receiving Professor Plantagenet's leg occurred on December 5th 1969. As it is now June 10th 1970, six months and five days later, no charges can be brought under this act.' At that, Mr Barringer wisely stopped talking, leaving the inspector to read and re-read the relevant section of the act. Finally, Inspector Granger broke his silence.

'So it seems. Fortunately we have other charges to lay before Dr Bloom under the Human Tissues Act of 1961.'

'I am quite familiar with that act Cornelius and it quite clearly allows Professor Plantagenet to leave parts of his body for research as he did. I can't see what crime has been committed under that act.'

'The 1961 act clearly states that any body part should be removed by a registered medical practitioner. It clearly was not removed by a registered medical practitioner but a mortuary assistant.'

'You can scarcely be considering charging my client with *not* removing the leg of Professor Plantagenet.'

'As executor of the will and a registered medical practitioner he should have ensured that he or another doctor removed the limb.'

'As the statement from your witness, Mr Hogarth, clearly states, my client was not present at the removal of the leg and indeed until the leg was delivered he had no idea that these events were taking place. Therefore he can be no more held responsible for not removing Professor Plantagenet's leg than any other doctor. If my client is guilty of not removing Professor Plantagenet's leg then by extension so is every registered medical practitioner in the land. The only people who could possibly be charged of this supposed crime, are the professor himself who made these arrangements and the man who did remove the leg, your Mr Hogarth. Since Mr Hogarth was acting under direct instructions of Professor Plantagenet, the guilt lies clearly with the professor. Sadly, Arthur Plantagenet is now dead and unable to be charged with any crime other than being a fine example of an English eccentric.'

'Eccentric? Do you think that justifies this bizarre behaviour? It is an outrage to have bits of bodies stored wherever people want. I've never heard the like of it.'

'Really? There are some eminent precedents.' Barringer paused and smiled at the inspector. 'Weren't you a member of the Benthamites when we were at Magdalen College all those years ago?'

The inspector glared at his adversary in disbelief at the mention of what he had hoped was a long-forgotten chapter in his life.

'As you must remember your hero, Jeremy Bentham donated his body to be preserved in a glass case in University College London. I believe you were part of a group that managed to steal his head on one occasion.' Mr Barringer looked at the inspector waiting for a response. When he received only the most cursory humph he continued.

'Arthur Plantagenet and Jeremy Bentham were both remarkable men who shared eccentric wishes for how their bodies were to be dealt with after their death. It would be a sad day if we were to lose our admiration for eccentricity

Cornelius. We've lost most of the empire and seem intent on misplacing the rest. Last week we even lost Tonga[14]. If we end up discouraging all forms of eccentric behaviour then we might as well give up and call ourselves American.' Mr Barringer smiled across the table.

The inspector stood up, his face contorted with anger, and opened the door.

'Do I take it that my client will face no charges and is free to go?'

The inspector, temporarily lost for words, nodded.

Augustus had been held at the police station for barely half a day, yet on stepping out that evening he discovered a quite unsuspected new taste, freedom. Undoubtedly this is one of the most pleasurable tastes that man and nature conspiring together can create. Sadly one can only truly savour it by being incarcerated first. Most of us, who have never lost our freedom or like Augustus feared its loss, wander through our liberated existences as oblivious to our freedom as a blind man walking through a picture gallery is to the beautiful art all around. For that intense moment as he stood on the pavement in the slanting summer sunlight Augustus' eyes were wide open to delights of liberty.

'Well, that was a close call, Dr Bloom,' said Mr Barringer appearing from inside the police station.

'How can I repay you? You were brilliant,' said Augustus, enveloping Mr Barringer's right hand in both of his own.

'Please, call me Edgar, and as for repayment, a promise never to invite me to one of your dinners will suffice.'

'You've no idea what culinary delights you'd be missing,' laughed Augustus.

'As you must now be,' said Mr Barringer. 'I dare say if you hurry you might make it in time for the main course.'

Augustus looked at his watch, barely quarter past seven.

---

14 Tonga left the British Empire on June 4th 1970, gaining independence after seventy years of colonial rule.

He'd easily catch the *hors d'oeuvres* if he hurried but first he had to satisfy his curiosity.

'By the way Edgar, who were the Benthamites?'

'In his first two years at Magdalen, Cornelius Granger was a member of a hedonist dining society dedicated to Jeremy Bentham, a philosopher of the utilitarian school who held that pleasure is the only universal good and that as humans our goal should be to ensure the greatest happiness for the greatest number of people. There are stories from that time that Cornelius would undoubtedly wish to be kept quiet considering his current profession. I wondered whether playing that card was the right thing to do. In the end it seems to have brought things to a most satisfactory conclusion.'

'Is that why he gave you such a frosty reception when you came in?'

'It was probably more to do with a young lady we both knew and even came to blows about; a lady who is now Mrs Emily Barringer, my wife. I don't believe Cornelius ever forgave me or forgot her.'

'Hard to imagine Granger devoting his life to the pursuit of happiness and fighting with his bare fists for a lady. He's a nasty piece of work now.'

'Bitterness can do that to a man, Augustus. In the end I think Bentham was right. There is no shame in wishing to be happy and no fate better than being happy.'

'Arthur would certainly have agreed with that. Though his legacy has created more grief than happiness so far,' said Augustus reflecting on the torment of the last few months.

'I'm sure in a few years' time this whole story will bring great delight in its retelling. Perhaps over dinner, and talking of which, shouldn't you be at yours?'

Chapter 42

The table had been laid as beautifully as ever, the college silver catching the early evening light streaming through the huge bay window at the end of the room. A large bouquet of lilies and white roses adorned the sideboard. This was an unusual addition to the room but Gerard had been informed that a lady would be present, and, despite knowing little of the gentler sex, he knew they appreciated flowers. The candlesticks were primed and the wicks trimmed to just the right length but still unlit. Arthur's portrait, brought in from the Great Hall for the occasion, looked down from the walls enjoying a peace that no living soul can experience, the solitude of a completely empty room prepared for a feast.

This was potentially the final dinner of the shadow faculty of gastronomic science. Rule seven of the constitution of the shadow faculty states that 'The Shadow Faculty will remain in existence until the University of Oxford inaugurates an official Faculty of Gastronomic Science'. If the vice-chancellor could be prevailed upon to accept the conditions of Arthur Plantagenet's bequest during the course of dinner, this would be a sad day for the shadow faculty but a momentous one in the history of gastronomy. As the Master had indicated, the guest list, with the exception of the vice-chancellor, included a very distinguished group in terms of gastronomic expertise. Mary Frances Kennedy Fisher, though most famous for her translation of Brillat-Savarin, was a distinguished food writer with a long list of publications that included such intriguing titles as *How to Cook a Wolf*. Hamish had invited a young chemist by the curious name of Credo Ottwater who had a particular fascination for the baffling relationship between chemical structure and smell, whose interests spanned from perfumes to food additives. George Le Strang had invited an historian from Christchurch by the name of Oliver Liddell who was researching a book on dining rights through the ages. Charles Pinker's guest, Reginald Hargreaves, was an expert on Caravaggio and Italian still-life paintings from the Courtauld Institute in London. Theodore Flanagan had drawn the short straw. He had not chosen a guest by the time the invitation to the vice-chancellor was issued, so he had the honour of hosting the good Dr Ridgeway as well as looking after Mary Frances.

The door burst open with Hamish McIntyre leading the way. Several hours of cocktail-testing had left him in voluble form and he was regaling his guest Credo Ottwater with a song about a centipede.

A centipede was happy quite,
Until a frog in fun said:
'Pray tell which leg comes after which?'
This raised her mind to such a pitch,
she lay distracted in a ditch...

On entering the room, Dr Ottwater took his chance to distance himself from his host's rendition to bury his nose in the flowers. As he lifted his head he discreetly plucked one of the roses and gently placed it inside his jacket pocket. Sadly, the lady for whom the flowers had been intended was oblivious to their charms, due to her sudden delight in seeing her own host Augustus Bloom standing on the far side of the table.

'Augustus, you made it.' Mary Frances rushed around

the table and, somewhat liberated by the effects of Hamish's mojitos, threw her arms around Augustus.

'So you sprung your student from the sheriff's clutches,' she said with an exaggerated American accent once they had disentangled themselves.

'Oh indeed, snatched from the gallows.'

'Was it the same boys as this morning? What were they up to this time?'

'Oh, it's a long and rather complicated story, Mary Frances,' said Augustus, his desire to explain any further suppressed by the appearance in the doorway of the vice-chancellor himself, who glared across at Augustus with a novel blend of contempt and surprise.

Theodore rushed over to the pair of them.

'Well done Augustus, you made it. You had me worried on the phone. How did you get off?' Seeing the puzzled look on Mary Frances' face, Theodore corrected himself, 'I mean get him off?'

'Old Barringer came down himself, thanks to your call. He played a blinder as you would say, Theodore.'

'Brilliant. Look you can tell me all the details later but now you're here you'd better look after Arthur's cheque.' Theodore pulled the cheque from his pocket under the watchful eye of the vice-chancellor and gave it to Augustus.

'Enough of this chit-chat,' said Mary Frances, taking Augustus' arm. 'Let me tell you about my new book.'

As they made their way across the room to the dining table, the vice-chancellor tried to cut in.

'Dr Bloom, could I possibly have a word before dinner?'

'Unfortunately I think we are just about to start. Now you'll be sitting here, vice-chancellor.'

Augustus moved around the table to his own seat, which was several places further on, ushering Mary Frances to his left. That should have placed the vice-chancellor at a safe distance with Hamish and his guest Dr Ottwater in between. The vice-chancellor had other plans and, as soon as Augustus had turned his back, he deftly swapped his name card with Dr Ottwater's and stood back from the table to let events unfold. Gerard moved around the table filling one of the two champagne glasses laid out at each setting with vintage Bollinger champagne. When Augustus took his place he had the unpleasant experience of finding the vice-chancellor on his right.

'So glad you could join us, Dr Bloom,' said the vice-chancellor. 'I noticed you were delayed. Nothing serious I hope?'

'A little misunderstanding, but my solicitor sorted it all out,' Augustus replied with a barb in his voice, certain that the vice-chancellor was behind it all.

'That is good news I'm sure. Now about this cookery faculty… '

'Faculty of Gastronomic Science,' Augustus corrected him.

'Well, titles apart, we obviously can't set up this faculty without spending time and a little money first in research and resource planning. So if you could just hand me the cheque at an appropriate moment during dinner, I will of course provide a full account of our progress but it would naturally be a slow and possibly expensive process.'

'A vote approving the setting up of the faculty at Hebdomadal Council would suffice. Until then the cheque is quite safe,' said Augustus patting his jacket. Then he raised his glass and announced the first toast of the dinner, which was dedicated to the man who had first inspired their endeavours, Jean Anthelme Brillat-Savarin.

'Who is this Jean whatsit we are all toasting?' the vice-chancellor asked.

'A dead Frenchman you have clearly never heard of,' said Augustus shaking his head in disbelief before draining his glass entirely. Fortunately, Gerard was on hand in moments to immediately refill it.

'Best sort to my mind,' said the vice-chancellor.

'Not as good as a dead vice-chancellor,' muttered Augustus

under his breath as Charles said grace and set the scene for George Le Strang to describe the theme for this particular dinner.

'Lady and Gentlemen,' George began. 'Tonight's dinner explores every aspect of gastronomy to exemplify the breadth and significance of this neglected science, in the hope that our ancient university will have the foresight to accept Arthur Plantagenet's legacy and create the world's first Faculty of Gastronomic Science. With the experience of our distinguished guests, I hope we can explore the visual, olfactory, historical and literary facets of dining. In the spirit of exploration may I present a first challenge, a comparison of the taste of champagne from a modern champagne flute with the traditional coupe.'

'I thought the flute has been determined to be best because it helps to keep the bubbles. It's all about surface area isn't it?' offered Reginald Hargreaves, showing a remarkable grasp of physics for an art historian.

The discussion was then taken deep into the realm of science by a rather tedious analysis of the nucleation process for bubbles and carbon dioxide content of champagne, led by Credo Ottwater who seemed momentarily to forget he was at dinner and not in the lecture hall. Mary Frances sat back in her chair sipping her champagne from her preferred coupe glass. When the conversation on the physics of bubbles petered out she entered the fray.

'Gentlemen, Gentlemen. You are missing the point. The only person who would want to keep their champagne fizzy for longer is someone who drinks it very slowly. To my mind anyone who drinks a glass of champagne slowly shouldn't be allowed to drink it in the first place.'

George Le Strang, a firm enthusiast for the flattened coupe, banged the table in agreement.

'And besides,' continued Mary Frances. 'This glorious design is more fun and to my mind the more fun you are having the better any champagne will taste.'

'How about this Mary Antoinette and her… ' Hamish stopped mid-sentence.

'Breasts?' said Mary Frances.

'Exactly, are these glasses really shaped on hers?'

'Well, as the only person in this room who has a pair of breasts may I say that she must have been a strange-shaped gal.'

'You are quite right to cast doubt on this story, Madam,' said Dr Liddell. 'History does not accurately record the shape of her breasts but this design of glass first appeared in England in 1663, almost a century before the young lady was even born.'

'And did you know she was betrayed by that most powerful of the gastronomic senses, smell? On attempting to escape Paris after the revolution dressed as a commoner she was pulled from the crowd on account of her fine perfume,' said Credo Ottwater who, having spotted Mary Frances yawn during his earlier pronouncements on bubble nucleation, was keen to redress the tone of his contributions.

'One of the lesser-known lessons from the French Revolution: better to drink like a queen and smell like a peasant, than drink like a peasant and smell like a queen,' said Mary Frances, raising her glass. She was beginning to enjoy this dinner. In contrast, Augustus was starting to show some signs of nerves and hoped the conversation might flow into calmer waters. From where he was sitting the surface area of champagne glasses and bubble nucleation seemed to be a perfect topic of conversation.

The arrival of the *amuse-gueule* offered to provide an antidote to the surfeit of champagne. On each plate was a piece of San Daniele ham rolled around a fig that had been soaked in a mixture of cassis and brandy for several days. Inside each fig a core of Stilton had been carefully inserted so as to conceal its presence from casual inspection.

'Devils on horseback, just what I felt like,' said Hamish pulling out the silver pin that was securing the ham.

The vice-chancellor poked the object on his plate with

a fork in the same way a young boy applies a stick to a cadaverous bird found on the road.

'Please tell me this isn't anything to do with a horse.'

'Not at all,' said George Le Strang with his mouth full. 'Mind you, we did serve up a wonderful horse dish last Christmas.'

Charles Pinker then rose to his feet to get the attention of his fellow diners and introduce his guest.

'Gentlemen and Gentlewoman. May I introduce my guest Reginald Hargreaves from the Courtauld Institute in London: an art historian with a particular interest in the visual aspects of food.'

'Thank you, Charles,' Dr Hargreaves replied with a gracious nod. 'May I introduce a novel concept in gastronomy created in honour of my host and Epicurus, the Epicurate's egg. An egg as you have never experienced, of many parts but, unlike the better known curate's egg, excellent in all of them.'

To the great surprise of all but Charles Pinker and Dr Hargreaves, who had concocted this dish together, this dish seemed to comprise of a hard-boiled duck egg sitting in a small nest. Charles Pinker had mentioned George's truffle-and-Worcestershire-sauce-injected quail eggs to his guest who had taken the concept to a new level. After much experimentation and wasted eggs, Dr Hargreaves had perfected a technique to inject different regions of a parboiled egg with different flavours prior to completing the boiling process. The parboiling had proved to be an important step in limiting the mixing together of the flavours and colours while still allowing them to spread within one region of the egg.

Each guest began to shell their eggs and was met by an impressive marbled egg, each one differently coloured. As they tasted what was once the white of the egg they experienced a range of wholly unexpected flavours such as fennel, caraway and rhubarb all selected to confuse the palate. Most surprising was that identification of these flavours was bizarrely inaccurate for such a range of distinguished palates.

'Good God,' said Dr Ottwater in surprise when he came to

the yolk. 'How on earth did you get eggs with green yolks?'

'Look at mine, this one's red,' said Mary Frances, equally amazed.

Each yolk turned out to be of a different colour too. When it came to the taste of this part of the egg, opinions were wildly divided, from spinach to definite hints of raspberry to suggestions that the egg was starting to go off. Dr Hargreaves could not have been more pleased with the result of his experiment as he explained the gastronomic principles.

'Your eggs are in fact all identical in terms of the mixture of flavours, the only difference is in the choice of food dye. Our eyes can pull flavours in the direction expected from a colour. Fennel with a green dye might taste like fennel, but with red fruity.' Looking around the table at disbelieving faces he pulled a large handful of eye masks from his jacket pocket. 'Put these on and try again.'

Blindfolded, they tasted their eggs for a second time. On this occasion a consistent pattern of flavours started to emerge with George Le Strang completely changing his original thoughts on the flavours and eventually identifying all three flavours accurately.

Next, came the turn of Credo Ottwater.

'First let me say that I am honoured to be in such distinguished company. Dr Hargreaves has given us all a wonderful demonstration of the influence of colour on our perceptions but I would humbly suggest that is no more than sleight of hand compared to the power of smell. To clean your palates and bring your understanding of flavour to a new level I present two sorbets. One has taste but no smell, the second contains elements that can only be smelled but is, in terms of taste, invisible to your tongue.'

Plates were brought bearing the two small balls of sorbet each with a small numbered flag. True to his word the first was clearly a lemon sorbet, but stark with no length of flavour: sweet and sour combining to give the impression of a lemon flavour without any depth or texture. The second, as promised, seemed initially tasteless in the mouth until the heat of the tongue began to release the volatile oils Dr Ottwater had meticulously extracted from lemon skin by selective distillation. An intense lemon taste built up over time and lingered long after the ice in the mouth had melted. When everyone had tasted the two sorbets, Dr Ottwater proposed the final experiment.

'Now mix the two together and taste them.'

The effect was electrifying. The harsh short-lived taste of one locked together with the ethereal disembodied smell of the other to create a complete three-dimensional experience of lemon. As spontaneous applause broke out around the table, Ottwater rose to take a bow.

The main course, devised by Mary Frances, was introduced simply as 'a whimsical dish'. With the removal of the silver cloches a heady and aromatic scent enveloped the diners. Around the meat centrepiece the plate was filled with a syrupy thyme and rosemary port reduction. Within this were nine small black balls, some looking like entire black truffles, others rather smoother. Mary Frances took a slice of meat smothered it in the sauce and after perching one of the small black objects on top, popped it in her mouth. She closed her eyes not through affectation, but through the powerful gustatory reflex that comes into play when experiencing the most exquisite of tastes. She had discussed the details of how this dish was to be cooked with the chef but he had exceeded her highest hopes. When her eyes opened the entire table was watching her with their knives and forks raised.

'Well guys, don't just sit there gawping at me. Taste it.' She sat back and, corralling a drop of sauce that had attempted to escape her mouth with her finger, enjoyed the spectacle of watching the others take their first mouthful. This was a remarkable dish and one that evolved with each mouthful. Most of the diners successfully picked out a black truffle first only to find the next mouthful tasting of black olive or prune, each pulling the sauce in a different gustatory direction. The meat had been gently cooked for almost eight hours at a low heat and changed in texture and taste with each slice. Not a single diner successfully managed to identify the cut of meat but all agreed that the way it combined with the sauce was nothing short of magnificent.

Mary Frances had also brought a wine that had been carefully decanted before the meal and which received almost as many accolades as the dish it accompanied. George Le Strang had declared it proof of the prowess of French viticulture and identified it as a Château Haut-Brion but, with a show of humility, declared himself uncertain of the year. When the course was over, knives and forks were laid to rest on the plates with the same sense of loss one has when a train containing a loved one pulls out of a station. Then came the moment when the exact nature of the dish and the wine were to be revealed by Mary Frances.

She asked Gerard to bring one of the empty bottles to the table. It bore a simple label with a wood-cut design bearing the name Heitz Cellar, a product of the new and self-confident Californian wine industry.

'One of our better Californian wines. Not Château Haut-Brion, Professor,' Mary Frances said to George Le Strang, 'but certainly its equal.'

George laughed politely. '*Très amusant*, Madame. But what wine did we really drink, because it was certainly French not American?'

'This was the very bottle I gave Gerard to decant earlier today. Isn't that right Gerard?'

Gerard looked panic-stricken at being addressed directly from the table and looked to Augustus for guidance who simply nodded supportively and Gerard followed suit.

'Rubbish, I've never drunk an American wine in my life,' said George, grabbing the bottle and taking a long sniff from the bottle.

'You have in fact been drinking American wine all your life, George,' said Dr Liddell. 'After Phylloxera destroyed the European vineyards last century, most of the vines were grafted on American root stock.'

George glared at his guest for this treasonable interjection. Taken aback, Dr Liddell took a tactical retreat.

'Though of course, Phylloxera was originally an American disease which is why the American vines could resist it in the first place.'

'Aha,' said George triumphantly. 'The American cavalry coming to our rescue only after shooting at us first.'

'I love French wines as much as you, Professor,' said Mary Frances in a conciliatory tone, 'but I am certain that one day a Californian wine will exceed the best from France.'

'I shall be long dead and selling fur coats in hell by the time that happens dear lady,'[15] replied George in language far more restrained than might have been the case if a lady had not been present.

'Well wherever it comes from it is jolly good,' said Charles, draining the last drops from his glass. George touched the base of his own glass only to push it a few inches further away.

When it came to the dish itself, a series of wildly inaccurate guesses as to the nature of the meat had filled the room with peals of her laughter. She finally relented on revealing the source of her whimsical title for the dish and source of the meat.

'Gentlemen, let me put you out of your misery. This dish was an unusual combination of two cuts of meat, one inside the other. Slow baked veal cheek stuffed with ox tongue. A rather tasty culinary pun: tongue in cheek.'

The first to rise to his feet was Charles Pinker. He looked toward Mary Frances, gave a small bow and then started

---

15 George Le Strang lived to see the day that this prediction came true. In 1976 an English wine merchant by the name of Spurrier arranged a blind tasting of the best of Californian and French wines in an event that has come to be known as the Judgement of Paris. A panel of distinguished French wine experts rated an American wine the best. The French suspected foul play, but nothing was proven.

clapping. Soon, almost the entire room was on its feet with the notably gracious inclusion of George and the understandable exception of Mary Frances herself. Mary Frances glowed in the admiration of her fellow diners. Sadly the vice-chancellor also remained in his seat, firmly opposed to the idea of lauding offal over a decent cut of English beef.

The appearance on the sideboard of several bottles of Sauterne and an army of scouts clearing the table heralded the vice-chancellor's own contribution to the dinner. Despite initial protestations he had eventually relented and provided a recipe. This involved the vice-chancellor contacting his former nanny, now approaching the age of ninety and living in a home in Torquay, for her recipe for bread and butter pudding. After some consternation it was confirmed that this dish, while by no means original, had not previously been presented to the shadow faculty and so was technically permissible under rule four of the constitution. The vice-chancellor's dessert, made with real Bird's custard powder, had been the highlight of his gastronomically impoverished childhood. When the recipe had been delivered to the chef, Monsieur Roger, Augustus was immediately consulted. This was the first dish that the chef had ever refused to cook despite some significant reservations over some of the menu suggestions from earlier years. Augustus had managed to placate the chef but had to grant him certain latitude to 'do what you can to improve it'.

After a growing frustration with the continental frippery of earlier courses, the vice-chancellor felt a growing sense of excitement as the door opened and the scouts appeared bearing plates. When everyone was served, Augustus leaned across to whisper in the vice-chancellor's ear.

'It is customary for the guest to introduce their dish.'

'Gentlemen, dear Lady,' the vice-chancellor said, rising to his feet. 'May I present some proper English cooking. For all the fancy talk around this table I rather think you have missed the point. Food should simply be tasty and wholesome, just as this dish is.'

With that, he sat down to silence and picked up his spoon. The taste was exactly as he remembered and transported him to a gentler, safer place. More objectively it could be described as a mostly textureless glutinous starch of a vibrant synthetic colour with the occasional raisin for variety, finished off with a lake of more Bird's custard. The vice-chancellor enjoyed the murmurs of surprised approval from around the table, though some of the comments did catch him by surprise.

'Really extraordinary.'

'The amaretto in the brioche really works with the vanilla in the *crème anglaise.*'

'Oh, and the dark chocolate instead of raisins is masterful.'

Looking across at the plates of his two neighbours he realised they were eating a different dessert.

'What exactly is that?' he demanded of Augustus.

'This is our chef's variation on the theme suggested by your recipe.'

'Rather like Rachmaninov's Rhapsody On A Theme Of Paganini,' said Charles Pinker who was in on the charade.

'Would you like to try some?' Augustus asked.

'Certainly not.'

'Oh you must,' said Mary Frances, leaning forward to catch the vice-chancellor's eye. 'It is truly divine.'

Unbidden, Gerard delivered a plate of this variation on a theme of an English nanny to the vice-chancellor. Monsieur Roger's version was a door that led to a new gastronomic world: a world that after a single spoonful the vice-chancellor thought was best left unexplored.

Dr Oliver Liddell had waited patiently for his turn, which he introduced with a historically accurate but rather long discourse on the sad demise of the final savoury course from the English dining tradition. He also felt obliged to discuss the loss from the dining table of certain English fish such as perch, pike and eel. It was the latter he had selected for this particular dish, smoked eel with a spicy persimmon chutney.

'We have also prepared an interesting international

comparison of cured meats,' said George Le Strang after thanking his guest. 'Including Bresaola and Parma ham from Italy, several types of Spanish ham including Pata Negra and two English hams: one from York and another which has... ' he paused for a moment before continuing, '... been produced locally.'

Arthur's wish had finally been granted. He now appeared on the plates being distributed around the table, camouflaged with the other meats and the smoked eel.

Total secrecy had been maintained by the shadow faculty with all the meats being delivered to the kitchen with no mention of their provenance. So apart from Augustus, George, Charles, Theodore and Hamish, the other diners had no idea they were participating in a grand gastronomic experiment, conceived by the man who was looking down at them from his portrait on the panelled wall of the dining room. The shadow faculty members all picked at the eel and other meats discreetly, watching to see who first tasted the small roulade of sliced meat placed at the 12 o'clock position on each plate.

Mary Frances, sensing the lack of conversation around the table, decided this was a good time to tackle the vice-chancellor on the future of gastronomy within the university.

'Vice-chancellor, I was just wondering, do you have any real intention of meeting the conditions of Professor Plantagenet's legacy?'

'I was of a mind to consider it, but I must say that all the nonsense I have heard around this table tonight has made me wonder. After all it is just food.'

With that he picked up the rolled-up slice of Arthur onto his fork. All the members of the shadow faculty watched intently for his reaction but frustratingly he merely waved his fork around in the air as he continued to talk.

'As hard as it is to turn one's back on a legacy of this magnitude, I feel the cost to Oxford's reputation of creating a faculty of gastron... of what is no more than a pretentious version of home economics, might be too high. There are plenty of girls' boarding schools around to teach about cooking and if you want continental cooking then you should go to the continent.'

Then he placed the entire piece of dried meat into his mouth. After chewing for a few moments he opened his mouth to pass judgement on this morsel only to find that no sound emerged. More alarming was the realisation moments later that no air could enter his lungs either. He pushed his chair back noisily as he rose to his feet in panic. Mary Frances, who had been about to launch a vocal counterattack in defence of both gastronomy and girls' schools, suddenly changed tack.

'Oh my, God. Augustus, he's choking,' said Mary Frances. 'You're a doctor aren't you? Do something.'

That the vice-chancellor was choking was already amply clear to everyone in the room and in light of Mary Frances' words they all looked to Augustus to save him. The delay in Dr Bloom's response, which was long enough for the vice-chancellor's colour to turn from suffused pink to an alarmingly dusky shade of puce, was motivated in part by Augustus' profound dislike for the man but also by the practical deficiencies in his medical training. With a determined pull on his jacket from Mary Frances, Augustus finally stood up. Bending over he peered in the vice-chancellor's mouth for any visible obstruction while his patient grabbed frantically at his arms. Seeing nothing he hit him ineffectually on the back. Only then did he recall a more appropriate response, the Heimlich manoeuvre, though he had never actually performed it. Placing his arms around the base of the vice-chancellor's ribcage he locked his fists together and gave a firm upward jerk. The small piece of his dear departed friend that had been stuck in the vice-chancellor's gullet flew through the air and landed on the tablecloth. With a deft flick of his fork, Charles Pinker deflected it towards the fireplace where it remained. With a rasping intake of air, the vice-chancellor collapsed back onto his chair.

'Well that was a close thing. Would a brandy help?' said

Augustus to break the silence.

A nod was sufficient response for Gerard who within a few moments slid a large glass of Cognac in front of the vice-chancellor. As it was clear the vice-chancellor was a man of little culinary refinement, Gerard felt that the Cognac used in the kitchens would suffice. He always kept a bottle handy as he was occasionally called on to flambé at the tableside.

During the commotion that followed, one of the more inquisitive and daring members of the shadow faculty of gastronomic science picked a small piece of Arthur from his plate and chewed gently, unobserved by his fellow diners. Afterwards he took a long draught of wine and murmured his opinion mostly to himself, but aware that one other interested party might be listening as well.

'Chewy and slightly stringy with a certain sweetness. More like Bresaola than ham, but veering towards Biltong at the edges. Strange hint of beer in there too. Interesting but sadly not a patch on Pata Negra.'

*

Within the wine cellars, in the chamber directly beneath the chapel, there now sat two old chairs side by side. In one of the chairs, illuminated by a sputtering candle, was a man in the garb of an eighteenth-century cleric. He was sipping a glass of wine while stroking a small Mallard duck that sat peacefully on its lap with its head under its wing. He looked up and, peering into the gloom past the racks of wine, tried to identify the source of an unusual sound. It was that of wood hitting the stone floor with a slow but rhythmical meter. The sound came closer until the form of Arthur Plantagenet came into view. He was still learning to master the art of walking with a wooden leg and it was with great relief that he slumped into the second chair.

'Chewy, huh! Imagine comparing me to a piece of Biltong,' muttered Arthur. 'Mind you, if I could have properly choked that ingrate Ridgeway it would have been worthwhile.'

'And have him down here for the rest of eternity, I think

not,' said Hieronymus Bloch, enjoying his first proper conversation in over two hundred years.

'Hadn't thought of that. Talking of eternity, why am I still here? I don't understand why I haven't passed over yet.'

'My mind has been much vexed by such questions since 1752. Worry not, your time will come as I am sure will mine. Take a glass of port with me and later perhaps I can entertain you with some Bach. I've recently been practising his *Fantasia in C minor*.'

The Reverend poured Arthur a glass of 1896 Dow port. Arthur, still distressed by the descriptions of the taste and texture of his leg from his former colleague, passed no comment. For a few minutes the two men sat and sipped in comfortable silence.

'So what did you discover in your grand experiment?' asked the Reverend Bloch.

Arthur lifted his glass and absent-mindedly sampled the aroma of the finest port ever created. The words formed in his mind and then hung suspended on his lips like the last drop from a bottle until finally he spoke.

'For all our superiority, humans cannot compare for flavour with a mere pig or humble crustacean. So morals apart, one shouldn't eat people on the grounds of sheer good taste.'

Epilogue

The final paragraph of Arthur Plantagenet's will was never read out on that memorable February day in 1970 in the offices of Cragsworth, Cawl and Barringer. The following day, Mr Barringer personally delivered the full text of Arthur's will to all the members of the shadow faculty of gastronomic science. Despite their obligations as executors it was some time before any of them happened to read it to the end. When Augustus Bloom came upon the document in his old age, this is what he read:

> *As my final legacy to gastronomy I require that the executors of my will record and publish details of this great experiment. Most importantly this publication should reveal the details of how my leg was prepared from a culinary perspective and, most importantly, the verdict in relation to the question of the gastronomic attributes of humans.*

The weight of this obligation forced Dr Bloom, against his better judgement, to share his knowledge of these events with the author. Though it has taken many years for this story finally to be told, in the publication of this book the last demands of Arthur Plantagenet are finally fulfilled. In his many years of pondering why his spirit had failed to pass over, Arthur himself had forgotten this final facet of his legacy. With the publication of this book, Arthur's spirit has at last found peace. He entered the cellars on the night of that fateful dinner in the summer of 1970 but has now left the precincts of St Jerome's College and fully passed over to the place he had briefly glimpsed during his brush with death in the closing days of the year 1969. We can all but wish to pass on with the confidence that Arthur Plantagenet had in the hereafter at the time of his death.

At the express instructions of the late Dr Bloom, this manuscript was not sent for publication until after the death of the last member of the shadow faculty of gastronomic science. Dr Bloom himself was survived for several years by Charles Pinker who passed away at the age of 82, sadly robbed of his faculties and memories by dementia but at last finding complete absolution in amnesia. He had, to the surprise of many, converted to Roman Catholicism on his retirement, citing his personal beliefs on transubstantiation. To his closest confidents within the shadow faculty of gastronomic science, this came as no surprise at all.

It is the express hope of the author that the shadow faculty of gastronomic science, regrouped in the hereafter, can now continue their culinary endeavours in peace and in the knowledge that this book will have made a small contribution to furthering the cause of gastronomy. Sadly Oxford University have yet to create a Faculty of Gastronomic Science, but a small private university of gastronomic sciences was founded in northern Italy in 2003. This is a small but momentous movement towards the goal first set out by the man who inspired this group of Oxford men in their grand gastronomic adventures and to whom this book is dedicated, namely Jean Anthelme Brillat-Savarin.

Appendix

A Brief History of the Shadow Faculty of Gastronomic Science

The history of the shadow faculty of gastronomic science begins at Christmas in 1964 with George Le Strang, Professor of Modern History, who was justifiably proud at having procured a truffled turkey that he generously donated for the last high table dinner of term. An act all the more magnanimous as this wasn't any ordinary truffled turkey but the finest Perigordian truffled turkey obtained through the contacts of Le Strang's aristocratic French uncle. As anyone interested in the science of gastronomy knows, one can't present a truffled turkey with a gathering of true gentlemen without the name of Jean Anthelme Brillat-Savarin entering the conversation.

This illustrious Frenchman wrote a slim tome entitled *La Physiologie du Goût* or *The Physiology of Taste*. Brillat-Savarin was spurred on in his literary endeavours by the belief that gastronomy deserved to be considered a science worthy of academic attention rather than merely a skilled kitchen craft. His book took Paris by storm when it was published anonymously at Christmas 1825, though sadly he lived barely a few weeks past its publication. After a period of intense speculation, Brillat-Savarin was identified as the author and for a while his star shone brightly over Paris and indeed across

Europe until the book quite unfairly faded from dinner table conversation.

Under the cover of darkness on that historic night, Friday 4th December 1964, a group of Oxford dons made a first step towards Brillat-Savarin's dream of elevating gastronomy to the level of a true science. Mellowed by the fine turkey and spurred on by lengthy and erudite discussions of the great man and gastronomy in general, the shadow faculty of gastronomic science was born in a truffle-scented and wine-soaked haze. Though if it hadn't been for the conscientious Reader in Criminal Law, Dr Theodore Flanagan, the new faculty might not have survived the amnesiac splendour of the after-dinner absinthe that was Professor Le Strang's other contribution to dinner that night.

As no-one had a definite memory of who actually suggested founding the faculty of gastronomic science, the credit is generally given to Theodore Flanagan as he had the presence of mind to draft a constitution for the faculty. He formally inaugurated the faculty with the help of the only suitable writing surface, a fine linen napkin that had been starched into a reasonable facsimile of parchment. The assembled founding members then enthusiastically signed Flanagan's constitution and celebrated with a particularly fine 1919 Baron de Saint-Feux Armagnac, in scenes that the collected dons fancifully likened to the signing of the Treaty of Versailles at the end of the Great War.

While the new faculty members slept off the excesses of the previous night, Gerard the mute senior parlour steward worked to clear away the evidence of the night's celebrations. On finding a napkin adorned with the beautiful copperplate script of Dr Flanagan, Gerard knew this was a document of some importance. The napkin arrived in Dr Flanagan's pigeonhole neatly tied in ribbon, freshly ironed but thankfully unlaundered. At breakfast, Flanagan took great delight in reading his magnificent document and just faintly recalling his involvement in the founding of Oxford's newest if unofficial faculty. He lost no time in spreading the word to the other founding members as they surfaced over the course of the day.

Only later did it sink in that Flanagan's elegantly brief constitution allowed no mechanism of electing new members. The choice of the words 'immutable rules' that had pleased Flanagan so much the previous night now seemed less appealing. In that turn of phrase he had firmly closed the door on correcting his minor oversight in relation to new members. So the founding members became the only possible members of the shadow faculty of gastronomic science. Poor Flanagan, needless to say, suffered mightily for his lack of legal foresight. Whereas an historian can be comfortably proud of knowing almost nothing outside his own period, Flanagan's protestations about the differences between criminal and contract law fell on deaf ears. Despite his two doctorates and esteemed academic reputation, poor Flanagan had to endure years of increasingly obscure jokes at his expense.

Over the next few years the faculty blossomed and expanded the horizons of gastronomic science in this small part of the world, but the path towards Brillat-Savarin's goal was not without obstacles. Unfortunate accidents and natural causes accounted for the loss of two members of the faculty under rule six. Dr Stanley Lovell, an enthusiastic young fellow and St Jerome's College's first experiment with a non-Oxbridge trained northerner, died during a demonstration of the extreme voltages creatable with a Van de Graaff generator. Although this demonstration had been done many times before and should have borne no risk, an inherited weakness of the heart was blamed for his early departure. Although tragic in its own way, this was not in reality a great loss to the faculty. Having been present on the inaugural night, he had signed up for the faculty with appropriate wine-fuelled enthusiasm, even though he had never heard of Jean Anthelme Brillat-Savarin before.

The second loss was more keenly felt. Gordon Maxwell, as a Lecturer in Modern Languages, had the major advantage of being able to read and enjoy the full nuances of Brillat-Savarin's text in its original tongue – French. Unplanned as it was, Maxwell passed away in a manner he would have surely approved of – in his rooms with a pot of tea, a plate of Madeleine cakes and the last volume of Proust's mammoth *La Recherche Du Temps Perdu* on his motionless chest with his thumb marking his place at the last page. While admiring the fact he had died in such a fitting manner for an Oxford don, at his memorial service in the college chapel the chaplain had spoken for all the faculty members, when he expressed the sincere hope that Maxwell managed to complete that last page before expiring.

Conrad Petersen, Professor of Biochemistry, was lost to the faculty but not this world, through rule four. His guest at the second ever dinner had inexplicably changed his plans at the last minute and by extraordinary bad luck produced a fine brace of chilled skylarks with pickled walnut stuffing that he had prepared himself in great secrecy hoping for great acclaim. Compliments were duly paid, but as skylark had graced the table at a previous dinner, Petersen knew the consequences. A stickler for rules, he was insistent that as rule four had been breached by his guest he must leave the faculty. Appropriate protestations were made but as Petersen was a rather humourless character they acceded to his decision with gentlemanly reluctance and inner relief.

The apparently harsh rules four and five that had banished Petersen were later to seem highly prescient when a Japanese guest of Augustus Bloom tragically died after a slip up in the preparation of his own recipe for Fugu. This Eastern delicacy prepared from puffer fish has the sole disadvantage that most of its internal organs, notably the liver and ovaries, are spectacularly poisonous. Indeed the whole fish is mildly poisonous but therein lies its unique appeal. Eating the flesh gives just enough of the poison, tetrodotoxin, to leave the tongue tingling and mildly paralysed. Even a trace of the liver is enough to paralyse everything including breathing, though the victim remains fully conscious, with the usually unavoidable consequence of death. Rules four and five ensured that no other members or guests of the faculty could be lost due to a puffer fish. The combination of these tragic events and Flanagan's constitution led to the shadow faculty of gastronomic science in its latter years being referred to as the 'Declining Dining Society'.

Post Scriptum

If you have read this far in the belief that these events were real or at least in the belief that this is a fictional story based on real events, then this work of fiction has achieved one of its goals. For the sake of any sensitive souls alive or dead, or indeed any institution, please be reassured that these events are entirely fictional. Despite what was claimed in the epilogue, direct or allusory references to real people and places are solely a literary device to add authenticity. No offence is intended and I hope none is taken.

With the exception of Arthur Plantagenet's leg, all other gastronomic matters discussed by the characters in this book are intended to be factual. Jean Anthelme Brillat-Savarin did indeed write the famous tome usually referred in English as *The Physiology of Taste*, most wonderfully translated by Mary Frances Kennedy Fisher. This master of modern culinary prose never, to my knowledge, visited Oxford, but from reading her writings and letters I suspect she may have enjoyed it as much as her fictional alter ego. I would recommend her writing without hesitation to all of you who have had the interest to read this book to the very end.

On Gastronomy and the
Origins of this book

This novel is set in Oxford in 1969. Both the time and the place have great relevance. This was an important year for mankind as the 21st of July marked the start of humanity's exploration of another planet when Neil Armstrong took his first step on the moon. It is also important as on Friday the 14th March that same year, the distinguished professor of physics at Oxford, Nicholas Kurti gave a lecture titled 'The Physicist in the Kitchen' at the Royal Institution in London. Professor Kurti was a low temperature physicist who was a fellow of Brasenose College, Oxford. During World War II he had contributed to the Manhattan project by devising a method of purifying uranium-235. At Oxford, he discovered a technique for cooling objects to within a millionth of a degree of absolute zero. As well as these achievements, he was an enthusiastic and experimental cook. During his lecture, Professor Kurti cooked a chartreuse soufflé while providing a live read-out of the temperature inside. Keeping up the link between gastronomy and space exploration he said: 'I think it is a sad reflection on our civilization that while we can and do measure the temperature in the atmosphere of Venus we do not know what goes on inside our soufflés.'

In this historic lecture, which was shown on television later that year, Professor Kurti created a reverse baked Alaska (a frozen Florida as he called it) that was cold on the outside and hot on the inside, a feat achieved with a newfangled machine called a microwave oven. Huge and fluffy meringues were created with the aid of a device that created a low-pressure vacuum. He also demonstrated the impact of injecting pineapple juice as a tenderiser to pork. Sadly it seemed to remove almost all texture from the meat once cooked and the famous chef Michel Roux, who had been called in to pass judgment, could only find one good thing to say about the professor's roast pork: 'but the crackling is superb'. Young as I was in 1969, I have clear memories of seeing both the moon landing and the professor's pineapple juice injected pork on television. Both events clearly made an impression on me as I have now written one book on space (*Journey by Starlight*) and this one on gastronomy.

In creating the eccentric collection of fictional gastronomes that feature in this book I have certainly drawn inspiration from Professor Kurti, but he has had a far greater influence on the development of what we eat than he could ever have imagined back in 1969. While manned exploration of our solar system stalled after the Apollo missions, progress in culinary matters has continued apace. Professor Kurti has certainly contributed to that process and can reasonably be claimed to have given birth to the movement that has become known as molecular gastronomy. Many years after his lecture at the Royal Institution, he teamed up with Hervé This, a French chemist who had been scientifically testing many of the precepts of traditional French cooking. In 1992 they organised a workshop in Erice, Sicily on 'Science and Gastronomy' that brought together scientists and professional chefs. This meeting fully set in motion a new approach to cuisine that was initially called 'Physical and Molecular Gastronomy', but later simplified to just 'Molecular

Gastronomy'. The rest of the world came to hear about this movement from the rise to international fame of chefs such as Ferran Adrià and Heston Blumenthal. Despite following the spirit of Nicholas Kurti's early endeavours, some of the leading proponents have tried to distance themselves from the term, 'Molecular Gastronomy', arguing that it makes the creative process of cooking sound overly complicated and elitist. Whatever name is given to our newfound love of experimental cuisine it has certainly transformed our attitudes to food.

In many ways I too feel that the term molecular gastronomy fails to accurately capture the spirit of Professor Kurti's, or indeed the Shadow Faculty of Gastronomic Science's, approach to food, which is one of enthusiastic experimentation with the primary purpose of entertainment and enjoyment. The philosopher Jeremy Bentham, an historical figure who features in this book, captures one part of this approach in his 'principle of greatest happiness'. The other historical figure who inspired this book and gave birth to the modern concept of gastronomy was, of course, Jean Anthelme Brillat-Savarin. His rather curiously titled *Physiology of Taste* (to give it its short title) is a wonderful read. It is a strange but delightful combination of autobiography, philosophical musings, anecdotes, aphorisms and above all enthusiasm. Many of his aphorisms are now widely quoted and indeed Professor Kurti opened his lecture with one of Brillat-Savarin's best known sayings: 'the discovery of a new dish does more for human happiness than the discovery of a new star'. It seems that in differing by only one letter, astronomy and gastronomy are forever going to be intertwined.

The *Physiology of Taste* is also full of other wonderful details. One portion of this book that rarely gets quoted, meditation XXII, addresses the cures of obesity. Brillat-Savarin acknowledges the usual advice that 'anyone who wishes to reduce his weight should eat moderately, sleep but little, and exercise as much as possible[16].' But he then shows his keen insight into human psychology by explaining why us weak humans can never maintain such a regime. His solution is to avoid 'everything that is starchy or floury'. He also recommended total avoidance of beer. My favourite tip, which I still find myself following in restaurants, is eating only the crust of the bread, more of the flavour and less of the carbohydrates. So it seems a rarely acknowledged fact that Brillat-Savarin beat Robert Atkins to the low-carb diet by 150 years. Brillat-Savarin also claimed other benefits from following his regime that might still be appealing today – 'soon as you begin you will find yourself fresher, prettier, and better in every respect'. Admittedly some of his other pronouncements might have less resonance today. He roundly claimed that 'every thin woman wants to grow plump', an aspiration that may have had more relevance in the days when consumption was rife.

Some aspects of molecular gastronomy, for the want of a better term, hark back to the era that was my character Arthur Plantagenet's area of expertise – ancient Rome. Banquets two thousand years ago are described featuring giant eggs or a roast pig that is opened to release live birds. Many of the exotic creations of Heston Blumenthal would not look out of place in such a Roman banquet. For all their attachment to exotic food such as the tongue of the nightingale and fried dormice, some aspects of Roman cuisine are less likely to catch on today. Despite liking anchovy paste on toast, I find it hard to imagine that garum, the Roman sauce that Arthur recreates from rotting mackerel intestines, is terribly palatable. As described in this book, Rome also provided one of humanity's earliest examples of the consequences of excessive exploitation of the natural environment by

---

16 This and the following quotations are, naturally enough, from M.F.K. Fisher's 1949 translation of *The Physiology of Taste.*

harvesting the herb Silphium into extinction. One can only hope that its popularity was to mask the taste of garum, in which case the loss would not be too severe.

As well as taking examples from the ancient Roman cookbook *De re coquinaria,* the dishes presented at the various dinners of the Shadow Faculty have a variety of origins. Some are taken from the pages of historical figures such as Brillat-Savarin or Auguste Escoffier and these sources are noted wherever possible. Others pay homage to important events in gastronomy, some of general relevance and a few from personal experience. The chartreuse soufflé served at the second dinner of the Shadow Faculty is a nod to Professor Kurti's 1969 lecture though it combines chartreuse with chocolate, which for those of you who have not yet tried it, is a match made in heaven. The full heritage of this dish also draws on my own time at Oxford University (many years after 1969). Back then a young chef called Raymond Blanc, before he became internationally famous, had a small restaurant in a nondescript row of modern shops in an area just north of Oxford called Summertown. His signature dessert at the time was, if my memory is to be trusted, a Grand Marnier soufflé that was presented to the table and then the liqueur was added through a small funnel. I'm sure the members of the Shadow Faculty would have been impressed as I was when I first tasted this wonderful creation.

Nicholas Kurti was a great enthusiast of using a syringe to inject food before cooking or eating. For example he also demonstrated injecting rum into mince pies. Injecting an emulsion of truffle oil and Worcestershire sauce into quail's eggs is my own extension of this technique, the result of an entertaining Friday evening of personal experimentation. These eggs are well worth trying, as are the martini oysters. I have experimented with many of the other new dishes and cocktails invented for this story but many are more conceptual and rather hard to find at a local supermarket or even delicatessen, so I have yet to taste beaver tail. I did suggest trying Fugu when we visited Japan a few years ago but, as with the Japanese ambassador in this story, this plan was sensibly vetoed by my wife Jean. Needless to say, Arthur's own preparation is entirely an exercise of literary imagination!

Leabharlanna Poibli Chathair Baile Átha Cliath

Dublin City Public Libraries

Leabharlanna Poibli Chathair Baile Átha Cliath
Dublin City Public Libraries

Come and visit us at

www.legendpress.co.uk

Follow us

@legend_press

Follow Ian

@IanFlitcroft